11/9

Ben Lovejoy

Published by Airbook Publishing

AIRBOOK PUBLISHING

www.airbookpublishing.com

Copyright © Ben Lovejoy 2015

Ben Lovejoy asserted the moral right to
be identified as the author of this work.

First published in Great Britain 2015
by Airbook Publishing.

Fourth edition.

A catalogue record for this book
is available from the British Library.

ISBN 978-0-9931922-0-3

This novel is a work of fiction. The characters and events in it
exist only in the imaginations of its author and readers.

The author specifically notes that he flies regularly as a
passenger on fly-by-wire airliners, and does so very happily.
Please refer to the afterword once you have read the novel (not
before, as it contains spoilers).

Acknowledgements

I would like to offer my grateful thanks to those friends who read an early draft of the novel and took the time and trouble to offer detailed feedback on the technical aspects.

Adrian Elkin, for insights into a number of aircraft systems, including the ACARS satellite datacoms system and Airbus flight-decks.

Andy Simpson and John Highet, for checking the flight-deck procedures and more.

Neil Ronketti, Simon Crouch and Mike Cater for invaluable advice on software testing and change control systems.

Simon Bradley, for feedback on military procedures and language (even if I did leave sitrep in).

Tim Dedopulos, for invaluable advice on navigating the publishing world.

Dave Langridge, Mark Lyons, Martin Stoll, Katrina Lowe and Brian Mansur for proof-reading and feedback, and Briar Kit Esme for a valuable suggestion on the back cover blurb.

My fellow members of the Write Together group who made the writing process a rather less solitary one than is generally the case.

Finally, a huge thank-you to everyone who chose to back the project on Kickstarter.

As has often been observed, a technothriller is the art of the plausible rather than the possible, and a number of liberties have been taken with facts for dramatic purposes. These liberties, and any factual errors, are mine rather than those of any of the people who kindly assisted with research.

A note on dates

This novel uses US date notations. The novel's title of 11/9 thus refers to 9th November.

In general, however, dates are spelled out in full.

The moment had arrived: in a little over two minutes, around half a million people would die.

Julian Fox was sitting in his car in the queue to board a ferry to Calais because in two minutes' time, air travel would cease to be an option. It would likely be months, perhaps years, before airliners would resume flying. Those that were left.

He connected his laptop to the wifi hotspot created by a smartphone. In the boot of the car was a second laptop, and in his pocket two further smartphones, each on a different network: nothing was being left to chance.

Fox typed from memory the IP address of an encrypted web-server hosted on a PC sitting alone in a serviced office they'd rented close to London's Heathrow Airport. When connected, the secure webpage prompted him with four input fields, labelled with nothing more illuminating than the numbers one to four, and a Submit button.

The first two fields required a username and complex password. Fox entered both from memory. The third field required a code generated by Google Authenticator using a QR code he'd destroyed immediately after use. The final one needed him to enter digits from the current date and time in GMT. He entered each in turn and clicked Submit.

The screen refreshed. The word Ready appeared, and below it a button: Activate. It felt almost too mundane that the final step, the activation of the devices, would be triggered by something as ordinary as clicking a button on a webpage in the browser of a perfectly standard laptop.

When Fox clicked that button, the software on the PC in the office would use its built-in SIM card to make six automated telephone calls in sequence: London, New York, Tokyo, Jo'burg, Sao Paolo, Sydney. When each call connected, it would play a recorded message containing a 16-digit code.

Agents in each of those cities would enter that code into a laptop connected to a powerful ACARS (Aircraft Communications Addressing and Reporting System) satellite data transmitter. Between them, those six transmitters could reach almost every commercial airliner in the skies. Once the final digit was entered, the transmitter would broadcast two short data-sequences on an aviation frequency reserved for engineering datastreams. The data was transmitted to low Earth orbit comms satellites and from there relayed to all aircraft within range: several thousand miles.

The datastream was part of an advanced diagnostic system fitted to all Airbus airliners to allow engineers to remotely interrogate various systems on board an aircraft in mid-flight to obtain real-time performance data.

The commands that could be transmitted to the aircraft were intended to be passive: requesting data, not affecting the aircraft in any way. But there were two exceptions unknown to Airbus. Codes #0x12AE and #0x12AF. Listed in the Airbus remote diagnostic manual as unused codes, the combination of the two in fact triggered a small subroutine in the fly-by-wire systems used on board the aircraft.

With the fly-by-wire systems used on modern airliners, pilots do not directly control throttles and control-surfaces the way they used to on older aircraft. When a pilot operates a flight control, an electronic signal is sent to the flight control computers telling them what the pilot has done. It is then the computers which activate the actual aircraft controls.

Codes #0x12AE and #0x12AF triggered 23 lines of code hidden amidst the millions of lines of code in the fly-by-wire systems. Code inserted twelve days previously by one of his team.

The innocuous-looking code was disguised as a sub-routine to optimise fuel-flow rates in the cruise. Its real effect was to instruct the engine-control computer to cut the fuel supply completely to all engines, then disable further throttle input. Zero fuel supply, zero engine thrust. On receipt of this code, the airliner would be instantly transformed from a fully-functional airliner into a 260-tonne glider. No matter what the flight crews tried, nothing could restart the engines.

Every airliner fitted with the remote diagnostic system had its own unique serial number. To send the code to a particular aircraft, engineers prefaced the code with the 12-digit serial number of the aircraft for which it was intended. The laptops contained the serial number of every Airbus airliner ever made, and would – when triggered – transmit the two codes to each one of them in turn.

The list of electronic serial numbers ran to 2497 aircraft. Around half of them would be on the ground, and the code would either have no effect or would merely cause a taxiing aircraft to come to an unexpected halt. For the 1300 aircraft in the air, however, the effect would be rather more dramatic.

Transmitting the code to all 2497 aircraft on the list would take around two minutes. Two minutes to cut the fuel supply to 1300 flights with a combined passenger and crew load of around 325,000 people.

A few airliners might succeed in gliding to a runway, but the vast majority of them would crash. Some in oceans or into largely uninhabited land. Many would crash onto towns and cities, where the death toll on the ground would add to those on board the planes. They had estimated that around half a million people would die. This operation would make 9/11 look like amateur hour.

Fox checked his watch again: 10:59 and 17 seconds. At precisely 11:00, he would activate.

* * *

Two thousand miles away, and 37,000 feet up, was a Skyways Airbus A340-600 heading from Shanghai to London Heathrow. It was a 15-hour flight, requiring two flight crews on board, the first handling the take-off and bulk of the cruise while the second crew slept in their crew beds before waking to take over for the last few hours of the cruise and the landing.

Captain Richard Williams had taken over the command twenty minutes ago. He'd been with Skyways since the start. A junior First Officer at BA, he'd been ready for a change, and felt that he would be promoted into the left-hand seat faster at a smaller and more dynamic airline. Six years later, and with more than 15,000 flying hours behind him, he'd made it. It had been hard to feel too much satisfaction in that of late, but it wasn't the time to think about that now.

He brought his attention back to the flight-deck, scanning the screens and instruments in front of him. There was little to do at this stage in the flight: the aircraft was on auto-pilot, following a pre-programmed course. It could find its way to Heathrow without any further input from Captain Williams or his First Officer, Mark Thompson.

A Category III Autoland system meant that the aircraft could actually touch-down at Heathrow under autopilot control. This system would have no opportunity to do its job today.

* * *

Fox sat and watched the seconds. 10:59:24. He waited. 10:59:31. He waited still. 10:59:44. Almost time. 10:59:53. He moved his finger onto the trackpad of the laptop. 10:59:57. He glided the pointer to the Activate button. 11:00:00. He clicked the trackpad button.

The screen display changed to Mission activated. The automated phone calls were now being made. Each of the agents in turn would be entering the codes. The laptops would be activating the transmissions. He watched the screen, which was auto-refreshing every few seconds.

The display updated: *London transmissions complete*. Almost involuntarily, he glanced up into the sky. Another refresh: *New York transmissions complete*. A few more seconds. *Tokyo transmissions complete*. Then in turn: Jo'burg, Sao Paolo, Sydney.

That was it. Killing half a million people was, with the right planning and preparation, that simple. He waited for the final confirmation message to appear on the screen.

* * *

Captain Williams always enjoyed landing his aircraft. After hours of being nothing more than an overpaid computer operator, monitoring the screens to make sure the computers were doing their jobs properly, the landing was when he became a pilot again.

He never ceased to marvel at how 200 tonnes of metal and carbon composites could feel so light and responsive, almost nimble in its handling. With his co-pilot handling the radio and secondary controls, Williams could concentrate on simply guiding the plane down onto Heathrow's runway 09R.

It was a task he'd done thousands of times before, yet it never lost its appeal. When flying, especially on the approach, he almost felt at one with the aircraft, as if its wings and control surfaces were extensions of his own body. There was a freedom and thrill in it that he could never explain to someone who had not experienced it for themselves.

The aircraft was equipped with all kinds of technology to assist pilots with the approach and landing – or even do it all for them. But Williams didn't need any of that. He was doing what pilots most love to do: performing a visual approach. Real flying.

His first officer was reading through the pre-landing checklist. Though they'd both made thousands of landings, nothing in civil aviation was left to chance: there was a checklist to complete for every phase of the flight.

"Speed 180, flaps 2," read out Thompson.

Williams double-checked that the air-speed was at 180, and moved the flaps lever to position 2. "Flaps 2."

Williams returned his attention to the runway, making a barely-perceptible adjustment to the right.

"Speed 170, flaps 3," said Thompson.

Williams eased the nose up a touch, repeated the airspeed check and eased the flaps lever to position 3. "Flaps 3."

"Skyways 251, Heathrow approach, continue descent, you are third in line behind an Asian Airways 747. Winds 25 at 280." Thompson acknowledged: "Heathrow Approach, Skyways 251 copy third behind Asian Airways 747, winds 25 at 280."

Williams already had the Asia Airways Jumbo-jet in sight. With 25-knot winds at 280 degrees, they were landing almost directly into the wind: perfect conditions.

"Speed 160, gear down," read out Thompson, reaching forward to pull the large landing-gear lever to the down position. Williams could feel the aircraft slow from the increased drag as the landing-gear created turbulent air beneath the aircraft.

"Three greens," reported his First Officer. Williams glanced at the panel to confirm that three green lights were glowing, indicating that all three sets of wheels were down and locked. "Three greens," he confirmed.

"Flaps full."

Williams moved the flaps lever to its final position.

"Full flap," he confirmed.

"Elevator trim."

"Trim ok," confirmed Williams.

"Parking brake off." Williams glanced at the lever position and confirmed.

"Speed 150 and pre-landing checklist complete," said Thompson, replacing the spiral-bound booklet into its pocket.

Through the cockpit window, Williams could see the aircraft two ahead of them touch down. While he concentrated on the runway, Thompson monitored the airspeed and glideslope on the screen in front of him.

"500 feet" announced the automated voice of the cockpit callout system.

Williams checked his screen to ensure everything was in normal range; it was. The A340 continued its descent towards the ground.

BWAAAAAAAAAAAAAAAAAAAAAAAAA!

"Land ASAP! Fuel! Land ASAP! Fuel!"

The sudden klaxon and fuel warning at less than 500 feet startled both pilots. Everything had been completely normal up until that point, and they hadn't eaten into their fuel reserves at all. To get a fuel warning didn't make any sense.

BWAAAAAAAAAAAAAAA-

Thompson reached forward and hit the Master Warn/Caution button on the ECM screen in front of him to cancel the klaxon.

Standard emergency procedures called for Williams to continue flying the aircraft while his first officer handled the trouble-shooting, but also called on him, as Captain, to make the decisions. The immediate decision was whether to proceed with the landing or do a go-around.

If he continued with the landing, and the fuel problem caused them to lose thrust, they might not make the runway. Heathrow was slap-bang in the middle of a densely-populated area of West London. Crash-landing short of the runway could put them down in an industrial estate, perhaps even Hatton Cross tube station. It was unlikely there would be any survivors.

If he aborted the landing and applied full thrust to go-around, they would require a great deal more fuel that they might not have. The result could be the same, only the location of the crash changed. But if they could climb quickly, they might gain sufficient altitude to be able to glide onto the runway if they subsequently lost thrust.

"It's a fuel-pump failure," said Thompson. "Engaging alternate."

Williams battled momentarily between the two competing instincts of a pilot in an emergency situation: to get the aircraft onto the ground pronto, and to climb. In an emergency, altitude = time and time = options.

But with now less than 400 feet to go, and thrust still being provided by all four engines, he judged that proceeding with the landing was the safer option.

"Landing!" he called out, letting Thompson know his intentions.

* * *

Fox watched the screen and waited. And then the message he'd been waiting for appeared. Two minutes and 23 seconds after he had clicked the button, the final confirmation appeared on his screen:

Simulation successful.

* * *

"Fuel pressure normal," reported Thompson.

"Acknowledged," replied Williams as he eased the aircraft down to a normal landing. Both pilots gave a sigh of relief as the plane touched down. There had been no time even to alert Air Traffic Control, so nobody on the ground would even know that anything had been wrong. This fact would, he knew, soon change: the emergency may have lasted only a few seconds – the paperwork to report it would take several hours, and the engineering investigation might take days.

* * *

1st December (11 months and 5 days earlier)

Sarah Green had been a Risk Analyst (Aviation) in the Dept of Homeland Security for two years. The job title sounded so scientific, she reflected, yet its reality was about 5% research and 95% guesswork. Her job, and that of twenty others in the aviation team, was to attempt to think like a terrorist, predict what they might attempt to do, evaluate the likelihood of them succeeding and make recommendations for steps that could be taken to reduce the risk. Having done that, it was the job of others to take those recommendations forward, assign priorities and persuade the politicians to approve actions.

There was a Red Flag system in place for threats she felt were particularly acute or urgent. Risks newly introduced by changes in policy or procedure. Risks that were once small but had now increased in likelihood for any one of a hundred reasons, from the development of a new technology to the opening of a new airline route. She'd used the Red Flag system once in the five years she'd been there: mostly, she wrote reports, passed them to her boss and that was the last she heard of it. She was rarely told whether her recommendations had been acted on.

She had some appreciation of the political realities. There were logistical constraints. Some risks couldn't be mitigated without massive disruption to commercial aviation. If the risk was deemed low, it was unlikely that such disruption could be justified.

There were financial constraints. Some of the systems she'd recommended would cost millions, and the aviation industry was not in the best of financial health. While 'safety first' was the motto of the civil aviation business, risks still had to be balanced against costs. The reason airport security confiscates key-ring pen-knives from passengers and then allows them to walk 20 metres past security into the Duty Free shop to buy a large glass bottle full of flammable liquid is financial.

There were civil liberties issues too. Many steps taken to protect passengers would be at the expense of the freedoms of some or all of them. Those were matters that needed to be delicately balanced. She understood that.

When her recommendations were acted on, she would probably never know about it if they prevented an attack. Some of the safeguards meant that terrorists would find a particular type of attack too difficult, so wouldn't even make the attempt. If an attempt was made, and detected as a result of one of the measures she'd proposed, it was by no means certain that she'd be told about it. Homeland Security operated in a compartmented 'need to know' manner: they probably didn't consider that a pat on the back, and a simple thanks for a job well done, counted as a 'need.'

It was hard at first. Her previous role had been as a commercial risk analyst for an airline. The risks she was attempting to mitigate there were financial ones. They included steps to guard against hijackings, back in the day when the motivation for them was ransom payments, but mostly she was just trying to stop the airline losing money. Here she was trying to stop them losing lives.

She'd had this glamorous image of herself as some kind of lone crusader, her piercing insights the only thing that stood between the safety of the American public and the terrorists doing their best to kill them. In her more whimsical moments, she'd fantasised about one day finding herself in the Oval Office after her recommendations foiled a deadly attack, being thanked by the President on behalf of a grateful nation.

The reality was decidedly less exciting. She was one of 30 or 40 mid-level staff who sat in a large, open-plan office surrounded by the tools of their trade, the most numerous of which were thick, ring-bound Operations & Procedures Manuals full of arcane details about everything from refueling processes to the steps airlines took to ensure that the number of meals on board an aircraft matched the final number of passengers checked-in and physically present at the airport.

All of them had to be read, and all of them had to be thought about, because you never knew where a weakness might be found. Procedures for tallying meal numbers might sound irrelevant and uninteresting, but hidden within them might be the perfect opportunity for a terrorist group to poison everyone on board, including the flight crew.

Green didn't mind detail, and wasn't deterred by the mundane. A tall, somewhat gangly-looking brunette whose child-like fascination with anything and everything kept her looking much younger than her 42 years, she had an endless curiosity about how things worked, how they might fail and what could be done to make them more efficient and more reliable. Spotting a security flaw in a set of Standard Operating Procedures was, to her, what scoring a goal was to a soccer player.

She did miss the feedback from her old job, though. When she made recommendations there, the impact on the bottom line was visible, neatly revealed in spreadsheets and summarised at monthly meetings. Here, she submitted reports and went home at the end of each day with no real idea whether her work had made a difference.

She set the thought aside and walked over to the flow-chart that ran almost the entire length of the 70 foot wall that divided the office space from the corridor alongside it. The flow-chart outlined every aspect of the design, production and operation of an airliner. Reference numbers covered the chart: these indicated the operations manual or other document describing that aspect of the flow in detail.

When they'd first set up the team, each member had been assigned a particular section of the flow-chart, and spent their time investigating those aspects. Assignments were made on the basis of specialist knowledge in each area. But time and experience had taught them that such a linear approach didn't make the best of the team: sometimes an expert would know too much, and wouldn't be able to think outside of the box – which was exactly what a terrorist needed to do if they were to find a loophole in a procedure.

So now they operated on a more free-flowing basis. Any of them could pick any area of the flow-chart to study. They had an online system which logged who was working, or had worked, on each area of the flowchart. That didn't mean someone else couldn't work on the same aspect – sometimes two independent approaches would reveal things that one person might have missed – but it enabled them to see what was being covered and what was as yet untouched.

Green had spent the last few months looking in detail at Despatch procedures: the things that happened at the gate to prepare an aircraft for departure. She was now ready for something new. She walked the 70 feet from the far-left of the chart, Aircraft Design, to the far-right, Disembarkation. Nothing grabbed her attention. She glanced at her watch: 12:35. She'd grab some lunch and return to the flow-chart then.

* * *

4th December

Istan Air Flight 1951 was on its final approach into Amsterdam's Schiphol airport. It was 11:41pm and a foul night, the runway lights barely visible through the cockpit windscreen. The crew were tired: the flight from Istanbul hadn't been a long one, but they'd been battling storms the whole way, with constant adjustments to course and altitude to avoid the worst weather.

The Airbus A320-100 was lifting and dropping 30 or 40 feet at a time as the turbulence battered them.

"Istan Air one niner fife one, Schiphol Approach, cleared runway one eight left, winds forty gusting fifty at zero one fife changeable, windsheer warning in effect."

"Schiphol, Istan Air one niner fife one, cleared land one eight left, winds forty at zero one fife changeable, copy windsheer warning."

The winds were strong, but the greater problem was that the direction was shifting as the storm passed over the airport – and the windsheer warning. Windsheer occurs when two blocks of air moving in different directions collide, and one airflow is pushed beneath the other, dropping rapidly, while the other is forced upwards, climbing quickly. Any aircraft caught in the windsheer can be pushed strongly and rapidly either upwards or, more worryingly, down towards the ground.

The auto-pilot was designed to cope with a wide range of conditions, but this was beyond its capabilities. This one would have to be a manual landing, and Captain Berker had taken control.

With fly-by-wire systems, the pilot may be flying the plane manually, but automated systems are still monitoring control inputs to ensure that the aircraft remains within the 'flight envelope': that the pilot is not asking the aircraft to do something it cannot do. For example, if the pilot attempts such a steep and slow turn that the aircraft would fall from the sky, the software will limit the angle of bank to the maximum that can be safely achieved. The aircraft is effectively being flown under automated supervision.

Stephanie York, in seat 2A, was a veteran traveller and unfazed by the turbulence. Regional

Sales Manager (EMEA) for a company making networking equipment for the telecoms industry, she was four countries into a whirlwind five-country trip that had immediately followed her honeymoon. Her husband, Danny, was a software engineer in the same firm, writing software for switches and routers. They'd met two years ago, at a company team-building event. The whole concept of love at first sight had always struck her as a bizarre one, until that moment. Less than a month later, they'd moved in together. They had now been married for 23 days.

She'd spent the last 45 minutes of the flight with her laptop opened but no work on the screen: she was looking at her wedding photos, before reluctantly closing it when the landing announcement was made. Her last visit of the trip was to Amsterdam, and as she'd be stuck there for the weekend, Danny was flying out to meet her. By the time she landed, he should already be at the hotel waiting for her.

She heard the double-bong sound that she knew was the pilots telling the crew that they were about to land. They always seemed to ignore the "Cabin crew, seats for landing" announcement, still fussing around the cabin clearing litter and opening curtains, but the two cabin attendants at the front of the Business Class cabin were now strapped into their seats. She smiled at the fact that they were even more blasé about the roller-coaster ride they were experiencing than their frequent flyers: they were both chattering away to each other. She turned to look out of the window, though in the dark and rain there was little to see.

The cockpit callout system gave them radio altimeter alerts at 500 feet, 200 feet, 100 feet and then 50, 40, 30, 20, 10 and 5 feet. With a normal landing, the last batch of these would be only about a second apart, as the aircraft eased down onto the runway. But this was not a normal landing: if anything, the turbulence had grown worse as they'd got closer to the ground.

The "Fifty" announcement was followed by a lengthy silence as a strong updraft pushed the aircraft upwards and Captain Berker responded by reducing thrust. He couldn't spare any attention to look at the altimeter – he was relying now on the audio callouts – but he could see visually even through the rain-hammered windscreen that the aircraft had climbed slightly as it crossed the piano markings of the runway threshold.

"Fifty" again. Another long pause. "Forty." Another pause. "Thirty."

Every aircraft type has a specific point on the runway at which it touches down. The larger the aircraft, the further down the runway the touch-down point. The A320-100 was a relatively small airliner and main-gear touch-down was specified at 107 metres from the threshold. The runway lights were blurred through the rain-streaked windscreen, but Berker could just make out the lights for their normal touchdown point flash by beneath them.

Schiphol's 18L runway is a long one: touching down even a significant distance beyond the normal landing point would not pose a problem. They had plenty of braking distance available to them.

"Forty." They had climbed again. Berker was winding the throttle up and down in a vain attempt to keep up with the rapidly-shifting winds.

"Thirty." There was still plenty of time to abort the landing and go around if required, but Captain Berker didn't think it would be necessary. He hoped not: flying in this kind of weather, he just wanted the aircraft on the ground as soon as possible and to get to the hotel for a well-earned drink.

"Twenty." They were only a few seconds from touch-down now: it was going to be fine. Berker would wait until the main gear was ten feet above the runway before cutting the throttle completely to allow the aircraft to settle onto the runway as he increased the flare to cushion the last few feet. Until that point, it provided sufficient forward thrust to maintain what should have been a three-degree glideslope.

Stephanie York had seen the runway edge-lights flashing past, and was a sufficiently experienced flyer to tell that the aircraft was taking longer than usual to land, but she guessed things were a little tricky given the weather. She wasn't concerned.

The callout system still hadn't announced ten feet, and Captain Berker saw his First Officer glance over at him. The unspoken question was whether they should be executing a go-around. Berker shook his head slightly: they still had plenty of runway ahead of them.

"Ten, retard." Thank god. He pulled the throttle levers back to zero, and in about a second they would be safely down on the runway. It was about two seconds before the "Five" announcement, and then another couple of seconds before the thump of the main gear touching-down. They were on the ground.

Berker lowered the nose-wheel onto the runway centre-line. He felt rather than saw the slight sideways motion as the aircraft skidded slightly to the right: they were aquaplaning! Although an airliner is a very heavy chunk of metal, its weight just after landing is offset by the remaining lift from the wings even with speed-brakes deployed. Berker applied left rudder to correct the skid.

York hadn't felt the slight twist in the orientation of the aircraft to the right, but the two cabin attendants facing her from their jump-seats had: both stopped talking and looked up.

All three, and every other passenger on the airliner, felt the violent skew to the left.

The aircraft was now facing about 15 degrees to the left. The automated safety systems that monitored the pilot's actions were programmed with a huge number of scenarios. Even something as rare as loss of directional control while aqua-planing was a scenario that had been considered and included in the system. Beyond a few degrees of yaw, the reverse thrust of the engines made regaining directional control difficult. The correct procedure was for the pilot to reduce reverse-thrust, re-align the aircraft with the runway heading and then re-apply full reverse-thrust.

Berker, who knew he was rapidly running out of runway, did not do this: instead, he fought for control while still maintaining full reverse-thrust. The automated systems kicked-in: the aircraft's deviation from the runway heading was beyond acceptable limits, and was in danger of running off the edge of the runway. It throttled-back to provide greater directional control, and automatically applied right rudder.

Berker felt the reduction in braking immediately, and heard the engines spooling back. He wasn't sure what was happening, but he could see the end of the runway lights ahead of through the rain. Swearing, he pushed the throttle levers forward again.

The aircraft twisted to the left once more. Again Berker applied full right rudder and stood on the brakes. He felt vibration as the left main-gear hit the rumble-strip at the edge of the runway, but he had things under control. He straightened-up, and then pulled back on the throttles once more to re-engage full reverse-thrust.

With full reverse thrust and maximum braking applied, the tyres were battling for grip on the rain-soaked runway surface. The aircraft was slowing, but had already passed the point at which they would normally have turned off the runway, and was still travelling way too fast. The far end of the runway was approaching rapidly and he could see they weren't going to be stopped in time.

"Hold on!" called Berker, as he prepared to attempt the turn onto the taxiway at the far end of the runway while the aircraft was still decelerating. He'd done it once before, on a simulator: simulated engine failure after landing, and he'd had to manhandle the aircraft in a screeching turn at the runway's end. He'd made it, but that was a simulator and a dry runway: this was the real thing and a very wet one.

He didn't make it this time. The nose-wheel skidded and the aircraft continued its path off the end of the runway. The nose-gear collapsed as it hit the runway lights in the grass, and the flight-deck was suddenly skimming the grass towards the fence and ditch beyond. Both engines were scraping along the grass, sparks flying. The airliner slammed through the fence and into the ditch beyond.

* * *

Danny York had arrived a couple of hours earlier. He'd checked-in at the hotel, then dashed back out through the foul weather to meet her flight. Her business trips were too frequent to do the meet-and-greet thing usually, but on a weekend away, especially one so soon after the honeymoon, it felt like the romantic thing to do.

He looked up at the Arrivals board and read down: 'THY 1951. Scheduled arr. 00:55. Expected arr. 00:55'. Excellent, it was still on time, and would be landing any minute now.

He'd never been very lucky with women. He was short – 5'6" – and had started balding in his early 30s. His natural shyness meant he rarely worked up the courage to ask anyone out, and also meant he didn't socialise enough to provide much opportunity for someone to approach him. At 37, he'd still been unhappily single.

Stephanie had been a dream come true. It had been one of those stupid team-building things that HR departments seem to feel are a good idea and which everyone else tolerates in return for a day out of the office. It was a treasure-hunt conducted around London in a series of hired black cabs. The teams had been deliberately mixed so that there was only one person from any department in each team. Stephanie had greeted him with a warm smile and an introduction. He'd always been rather suspicious of Sales & Marketing, seeing them as the people with the fake smiles and over-priced suits, but Stephanie struck him as entirely genuine. They'd struck up a conversation while taking their cab driver's advice that the pet cemetery could be found in Hyde Park, and he'd been astonished when a twenty-minute drive seemed more like two.

They'd gone for a drink the next night, followed by dinner, and he was utterly hooked. Much to his amazement, Stephanie was too.

He caught himself grinning at the memory, and felt slightly embarrassed that people would be looking at him. Nobody was, of course.

He'd booked a canal cruise dinner online for the following evening as a surprise for her. He hoped the weather would have improved by then! He knew Stephanie had been to Amsterdam quite a few times before, but he'd guessed a canal cruise wasn't the sort of thing you usually did on your own on a business trip. He still felt like a beginner at being in a relationship, and tried hard to do all the right things.

He looked up again at the board: 'THY 1951. DELAYED.'

That was odd, he thought: it had been showing on-time until a few minutes ago. How could they not have known about a delay until now?

The Schiphol Airport Fire & Rescue team spent most of their working lives training, preparing and practicing for something that almost never happens: a major crash within the airport perimeter. A great deal of their training was for the worst-case scenario: an airliner crashing and catching fire.

The mock aircraft they set alight each day was intended to represent each of the different aircraft types they might have to face. It had 'engines' beneath each wing-stub, and an additional 'engine' in the tail. There was a short upper-deck section to represent a 747 Jumbo or A380 double-decker.

A complex network of fuel-lines and burners allowed them to create fires in any or all of the engines, and in the fuselage section, of any desired intensity. They had constant drills in which they would be briefed on different scenarios then have to extinguish the fires and enter the aircraft for mock rescues.

Everything was timed, logged and videoed. There were tough time targets for every step of the operation. Time from siren sounding to rescue vehicles rolling: 12 seconds. Time from vehicles rolling to first vehicle on scene at the furthest part of the airport: three minutes. The videos were reviewed and any error, however minor, and any delay, however brief, was analysed and steps taken to ensure it would not happen again. It was an uncompromising business because in a fire on an airliner, seconds equate to lives.

Actual incidents were not everyday affairs, but not uncommon. Once a week on average the siren would sound and they would go tearing out to one of the runways. Almost all of their callouts, though, were precautionary. An aircraft with an engine out. A bird-strike. A warning light indicating a possible fault. Any one of these things had the potential to end in disaster, so all of them were treated as full-scale emergencies.

But the vast majority of them passed without incident. They would position their vehicles on taxiways adjacent to the runway, then set off in pursuit as the aircraft decelerated to a halt. They would carry out a visual inspection of the exterior to ensure that there were no signs of fire, then follow it back to the stand as a precaution. Then they would drive back to their base.

It was a strange profession. Most of them would spend their entire careers without ever experiencing the thing they practiced every day: dealing with a full-scale crash with an aircraft on fire. That would not be the case for the people on this shift.

Airports have to protect against a thousand different risks, some major, some minor. A lesson learned by early airports was drivers on perimeter roads can't resist looking at aircraft as they take-off and land, resulting in rear-end shunts as drivers fail to keep their eyes on the roads. This was addressed by various kinds of shielding. Some airports opted for solid panels on fences, others for grass embankments – the latter having the added benefit of reducing noise pollution. Schiphol had embankments created by digging ditches just outside the fences.

The front end of The A320-100 dropped into the ditch and slammed into the embankment at around 90mph. The effect was devastating. The initial impact was to the nose of the aircraft immediately in front of the flight-deck. The windscreens shattered a few milliseconds before the entire flight-deck was crushed by the momentum of 180 tonnes of aircraft pushing it into the earth. Both pilots died instantly, their bodies pulverised. The crumpling of the fuselage continued as it absorbed the energy of the crash like a giant car crumple-zone.

The front hold split open, and the floor of the business class section of the passenger cabin hit the ground. The effect was catastrophic. The floor was forced up towards the ceiling, and rows 1 to 5 of the aircraft simply ceased to exist. The seats were crushed into a mangled and unrecognisable mass of metal, foam and leather. The overhead lockers shattered into hundreds of pieces. Stephanie York, along with two of the cabin crew and ten of her fellow passengers, died instantly. Their bodies were ripped apart. The area that had been occupied by eleven passengers, two cabin crew and two flight crew was transformed into nothing more than a debris field.

The right-hand engine hit a concrete transmitter box embedded in the grass beyond the runway and was ripped off the wing. The fuel lines from the avgas tanks in the wing were severed and burst into flame. 710 gallons of jet fuel spilled from the wing, fuelling a massive fireball.

Further back in the cabin, the devastation continued, but didn't completely crush the passengers. Most of those in rows 6-8 were too badly injured to exit the aircraft without assistance. The sound of someone screaming competed with the roar from the fire.

The three cabin crew at the rear of the aircraft got the rear doors open. The slides inflated, but the rear slide was immediately obscured by thick black smoke. One of the crew pressed the button to play the automated evacuation announcement, but the PA system was at the front of the aircraft and had already been destroyed, and it was doubtful anyone would have heard it anyway over the screams and fire. Most of the passengers towards the rear of the aircraft were in shock, and the evacuation was slow.

There were two emergency exits in the centre of the aircraft but no crew seats next to them. The passengers in those seats had been briefed by the cabin crew before take-off, and agreed to take responsibility for opening them when instructed, but no instruction came. One of them eventually opened the left-hand door and exited. It was clear to the passengers on the right that opening that door wasn't an option.

The sirens sounded and the rescue team were all on board the rescue vehicles within 11 seconds, a second under the target. As the vehicles rolled, they pulled on their flameproof coveralls and jackets, and donned the breathing apparatus that would protect them from the toxic smoke of an aircraft fire.

"Rescue one, Schiphol Ground, crash location behind threshold of runway three six right. Fire reported, I say again, fire reported."

Chief Fire Officer Swager, in the lead tender, picked up the handheld mic."Schiphol Ground, Rescue one, copy threshold runway three six right, fire."

The location of the crash, at least, was good news: it was one of the closer locations and they would be there in around 45 seconds.

"Schiphol Ground, Rescue One, any details of extent or location of fire?""Rescue One, Schiphol Ground, negative."

It made little difference. Eye-witness reports were often unreliable, and a lot could change even in the 30 seconds remaining before they reached the scene.

As the fire vehicles arrived, the lead vehicle immediately switched on the over-cab nozzle to fire foam at the right-hand wing. The other crews jumped out and immediately began directing evacuating passengers away from the wreckage. It was obvious, though, that it was too late for many.

It had been ten minutes, and the Arrivals board was still displaying DELAYED. Danny York looked around for someone to ask about the delay. As he did so, he could see several airport staff in hi-viz jackets and clipboards making their way through the crowd of waiting people, speaking to each in turn. He approached one of them.

"Excuse me," he said. "Do you know anything about the delay to Flight 1951 from Istanbul?"

The young woman inclined her head towards him: "Are you meeting someone on the flight, sir?"

"My wife. Do you know what the problem is?"

"What's your wife's name, sir?"

Stephanie York, why?"

Can I take your name, sir?"

"Danny York. What's going on?"

The woman wrote down both names. "Please come with me, sir."

Danny stared at her. "Look, what's all this about? Is everything ok?"

"Please, sir, just come with me and someone will explain."

"Explain what? What's happened?"

"Sir, please, if you'll just follow me."

York did so, with a growing feeling of dread. Why couldn't she just tell him what was going on? They didn't just approach people awaiting an arrival unless it was something serious. He glanced back up at the Arrivals board: still showing DELAYED.

The woman led him to a set of doors marked AUTHORISED ACCESS ONLY. She tapped a code into a keypad beside the door and pushed it open, walked though and held it open for him.

Afraid to ask any more questions, he followed silently as she led him down a long corridor, through another set of doors and into a large, comfortable-looking lounge. Inside he could see about a dozen other people, some standing, some sitting. Several of them were crying, and he came to an abrupt halt as he saw it.

"Oh no. Please no."

The woman out looked across to an older woman in a dark trouser suit who came over to them. The blonde introduced them. "This is Danny York, here to meet his wife Stephanie York. Mr York, this is Esther Post, Senior Liaison Officer at Schiphol Airport."The older woman put an arm on his back and gently led him to a seat.

"Mr York, I'm afraid there's been an incident."

"An incident?" he repeated, dumbly.

"We don't have many details yet, but Flight 1951 overshot the runway on landing. The airport fire and rescue teams have responded, but we don't have much information at the moment."

"Fire and rescue? There's a fire?"

"We don't know, sir – that's just the name of the team. We're still waiting for further information. We'll let you know as soon as we have any news. Can we get you anything? Water? Coffee?"

"No. No, thank you. Nothing."

"I'll be back once I have any news."

She gave a small, tight smile – the kind intended to say I want you to know I sympathise and care, but I know it's not a time for smiling – and eased herself out of the seat, leaving him there alone.

He looked around the lounge. It was huge. He wondered what it was used for normally. They surely couldn't reserve this much space in an airport for the few occasions when-

He couldn't bring himself to complete the thought.

Overshot the runway? What did that mean? That could mean anything: something minor, ending up on the grass, everyone ok ... or completely missing the runway and crashing beyond the airport. Except the woman – he had forgotten her name already – had told him the airport rescue team had responded, so that had to mean the plane was within the airport perimeter, surely? So it couldn't be that serious? But then would they bring him, and the others, in here for some minor bump onto the grass? Why the hell didn't they know what was going on? Surely all it took was a quick radio call for someone to let them know the situation?

Maybe someone else here knew more. He stood up and walked over to a grey-haired couple standing arm-in-arm.

"Excuse me," he said, unsure of what he was going to say next. "Do you know anything? I mean, have you heard anything? They don't seem to know anything."

The man, smartly-dressed in his 60s, just shook his head. "No, we are waiting." York stood there, not sure of whether to nod and walk away, say something else or just stand there. He muttered "Thank you" and walked back to his seat.

Her mobile! He could call her! He pulled the phone from his pocket and hit the speed-dial. 'Please answer,' he pleaded. 'Please be ok. You have to be ok.'

"Hello!" came her chirpy voice.

"Stephanie! Thank go-"

"This is Stephanie York. I'm sorry I can't take your call at present, but leave a message at the tone and I'll get back to you just as soon as I can."

Voicemail.

After the tone, he just stood there, the phone to his ear. "Um." No, that was stupid, what message could he leave, for chrissakes?

It didn't mean anything, he told himself. You always switch your phone off before a flight, and didn't switch it back on again until back in the terminal, so probably she was just waiting to be bussed back. Yes, that would be it, of course.

Maybe he should send her a text, letting her know he knew about the incident and was waiting for her. She didn't know he was at the airport and might just jump straight into a cab.

Or would someone tell her he was here? Looking around again, the reality of the situation hit home. This wasn't a trivial event. They didn't do all this for a minor delay that would have her hopping into a cab at any moment. Whatever had happened, they would bring the passengers here first. That was the reason for this room.

This was crazy. How long had it been? They had to know something by now! He looked around for- What was she called? Esther? There she was, talking to someone else – another husband or father or brother or friend or .... He walked over to her. He waited a polite distance away. Strange how we English maintain our well-trained politeness even in the most extreme circumstances, he thought. It was a re-run of her interaction with him: the arm around the back, leading him to a seat, sitting with him, the short conversation. He supposed that with dozens or

31

even hundreds of people meeting passengers from the aircraft, it must become a routine.

He waited until she stood up again, and yes, the same brief, tight smile.

"Excuse me."

She turned and held out her hand, touched his arm. She said nothing.

"Look, you must know something by now. Please. You have to know what's happening."

"I'm sorry, Mr- Mr York, isn't it?" He nodded, impatiently; right now, he didn't give a damn whether or not she remembered his name, he just wanted to know what the hell was happening.

Ms Post squeezed his arm a little, another part of the training manual, he supposed. "We really don't have any further details yet, but I can promise you that everything possible is being done. The rescue teams are among the best in the world. As soon as they have time to get an update to us, we'll let you know, I promise."

Another woman in hi-viz entered the lounge with two more people in tow, and Post excused herself.

The rescue teams had the fire out now. The good news was that they'd extinguished it before it had reached the fuselage. Passengers were still coming down the slides on the left-hand side of the aircraft. Ambulances were arriving, and passengers being guided towards them to be checked out. Looking at the crushed front of the fuselage, he could hear screams of pain and calls for help, but they couldn't go in until all the able-bodied passengers had finished evacuating.

The vehicles were fitted with powerful roof-mounted floodlights, and they had positioned them to light the scene. They got the ladders and cutting gear ready on both sides of the aircraft: once they were able to enter, they'd be able to enter on both sides, at least at the rear of the aircraft: the foam-blanketed right wing would be too slippery and obstructed to make that safe.

Swager saw the cabin crew come down the slide from the left wing. He ran over.

"What's the situation in there?"

The woman was clearly struggling to remain calm and professional, but managed to give a succinct summary: "Most of the passengers are out. The rear section is clear. There are people trapped forward of the centre doors – row 7 forward. There are two crew in there too. The floor and roof-" She broke off.

"That's ok, thanks, you did good."

Swager turned to his team. "Lang, ladders centre left and rear left. Cutting gear and extraction kit in the centre. Radio a report as soon as you're in. Meijer, take a team and see if you can gain access through the exterior of the front of the fuselage. Peters, set up a triage area and let the paramedics know we expect multiple majors."

Swager turned back to the cabin attendant: "What's the TOB?"

Total On Board told them how many people, passengers and crew, they had to account for. The cabin crew manager announced the number at the start of the flight, and all crew were expected to memorise it for just this eventuality. The cabin attendant who'd given the report looked blank. "I- It was a busy flight, I can't remem-"

Her colleague cut in: "126. It was 126. Seven are crew."

"Ok, Peters, TOB 126 – make sure the paramedics get names and counts." He turned back to the cabin attendants. "Do you have the pax list?" Each aircraft had a list of the names of all the passengers and their assigned seat numbers. In the worst case, that could form the primary form of identification.

"No, it was at the front." She stared at the debris field where the front of the aircraft had been. Almost nothing was recognisable. Metal, plastic, papers, the

33

assorted contents of bags ... but nothing larger than a suitcase. Just debris.

"Oh god, Alida and Karin!" The two cabin attendants looked at each other for a moment, then embraced.

"Dames en heren, uw aandacht alstublieft .Ladies and gentlemen, your attention please."

York looked up as the PA announcement was made. The first announcement was in Dutch and he waited tensely for the English version.

"The first passengers are on their way to the terminal now. As soon as we have confirmed information on each passenger, we will announce your name. If we have not taken your name yet, please make yourself known to one of the staff here, and give them your name and the name of the passenger or passengers you are meeting. When you hear your name announced, please approach one of the staff. It is likely to take some time before we have confirmed information for all the passengers, so please be patient – everyone is working as fast as possible, but you can appreciate that we do not want any mistakes. Thank you."

York looked around. The first passengers on their way? Did that mean everyone was ok? It sounded like good news, but surely they would have reassured us if they knew everyone was ok? That 'confirmed information' phrase and the reference to not wanting any mistakes frightened him.

He could see mixed reactions in the faces around him. Some seemed to have taken comfort from the announcement, and there were some smiles and nodding, some relieved-looking conversations. Others continued to look worried.

The lead rescue crew had secured a ladder onto the leading edge of the left wing, leaving the trailing edge with the escape slide clear. The first crew in, in full breathing apparatus, had radioed that there was no smoke inside, so the following crews had removed their BA systems to permit easier movement in the cramped environment of a small airliner.

The crews took in portable cutting gear and tarpaulins to protect casualties from shards of metal as they cut them free.

"Rescue One Leader from Lang. Sitrep." Screams and cries could be heard in the background; Swager couldn't be distracted by that: there was work to be done.

"Lang, Rescue One, go ahead."

"Rows 9 and back clear. Row 8, one pax with suspected broken leg, will evacuate. Rows 6 & 7, multiple trapped pax, initial estimate all majors and fatals. There's nothing left forward of row 6. Further information to follow. Sitrep ends."

"Ten-four, Lang. Do you want medics on-board now?"

"Negative, in about two minutes: we'll evacuate the broken leg first to give us more room to work. Two medics once we've done that."

"Received." Swager called out: "Peters!"

"Sir."

"Two medics in two minutes."

"Got it."

Meijer returned, his team following with their gear.

"Access through the fuselage isn't an option, sir: we'd be cutting blind. We can see some body parts, but there's no way to gain access from the exterior until the team inside can guide us.

"Ok, Lang is evacuating one minor now – get two of your team ready to receive, you and the rest in through the rear to assist with multiple trapped.""Sir."

The passenger with the broken leg had been strapped to a stretcher, inflatable splints in place, and was being passed out onto the wing. Ropes were fastened front and rear, and the crew lowered the stretcher down to the ground. Usually this would be done very slowly and carefully, but they knew they had more serious cases in there and needed to get medics in fast. They worked quickly and apologised to the casualty for the jerks.

Overhead, the sound of helicopters filled the air as two air ambulances and a police helicopter arrived. The two air ambulances circled and landed, the police helicopter remained overhead, adding its powerful searchlight until additional lighting vehicles arrived.

The team inside could now concentrate on the trapped passengers. Peters had delivered the two medics, one doctor, one paramedic, to the rear ladders and they ran down the sloping aisle to the centre doors. The scene that greeted them was horrific: a wedge-shaped mass of metal, casualties and – undoubtedly – bodies.

The scene was lit only by head-torches from the helmets of the rescue personnel, the harsh mix of light and shadows adding to the screams to make the whole thing feel like a scene from a budget horror film.

Lang called forward the doctor, a diminutive woman called Loes De Vries. "You're the smallest person here. I need you to get as far forward as you can and give us a casualty report. Don't try to treat anyone yet, just in and out so we know what we're dealing with."

De Vries swallowed. As a doctor specialising in on-scene stabilisation, she'd attended countless horrific accidents. She'd served two years on an air ambulance, and had seen it all: motorway pile-ups, collapsed buildings, motorcycle smashes ... she was a professional, and there was little that could faze her. But this: crawling into a space filled with the sound of a screaming woman when she couldn't even yet see the casualties; this would be a tough one.

Lang handed her a harness: "Put this on, so we can get a rope on you and pull you back if needed." A keen rock-climber in her spare time (funny how so many trauma medics engaged in adrenaline sports, she thought), she was familiar with them and quickly slipped it on and buckled it around her waist. Behind her, Lang clipped a rope to the rear attachment point.

She knelt down, and eased onto her stomach. She had a dry-wipe board with pen clipped to the top and attached with a coiled plastic cord. She shoved this ahead of her, to be sure she could reach it when she was in the confined space ahead. Behind her, two of the rescue team were setting up small floodlights on tripods.

De Vries slid carefully forward into the small space in the aisle, twisted seats to each side of her. She shuffled forwards and was now alongside the seats in row 7. A woman to her left was the one doing the screaming. The ones who were screaming were low-priority – you knew they were breathing and conscious – it was the silent ones who needed the most urgent attention. Her job right now was triage.

Triage, performed here in its literal sense, had three categories: those who would survive, with or without immediate medical care; those who would most likely die, with or without immediate medical care; and those for whom immediate medical care would make the difference between life and death. Those were the priority.

She turned her head towards the screaming woman so she could try to assess her condition. Seat 7C was empty: the screaming woman was in seat 7B. Her head and face looked fine aside from small cuts. Her legs were bent toward her, but at a natural angle. The woman was holding her left shoulder. Query fractured collar-bone, query broken or dislocated shoulder. She made a note on her board.

But her professionalism couldn't over-ride her humanity: she reached out a hand to the woman. "We're here. We're going to get you out as quickly as possible." With nationalities unknown, and most

37

Dutch people speaking good English, it was standard procedure to default to English.

The passenger in 7A, a man in his 30s, had responded to her voice. He was clutching his left leg and grimacing. He told her he thought his leg was broken but he didn't think he was trapped.

"Ok, thanks," responded De Vries. On her board, she wrote '7A: Ok'.

She turned to the right. The man in 7D was unconscious, his head forward against what was left of the seat-back in front of him. De Vries leaned in to take his carotid pulse. It was strong and regular. She gently adjusted his head position to tilt it up slightly to keep his airway open, and noted '7D: Unc/ok'.

The man in 7E was in his 50s, and actually managed a smile. "A few cuts and bruises, but I'll live," he said, in a crisp British accent. She'd spent a year in England, and knew it was a common colloquialism there, and he probably be quite horrified if he realised what he'd just said: he would live, but there were undoubtedly those here who wouldn't. "My right foot is caught beneath the seat in front of me," he added, "but I think it won't take too much to free it."

"Thank you," replied De Vries. Most people instinctively felt panic when trapped, so a casualty who was calm about it was always a great help. '7E: Ok/Tr'.The space ahead of her was extremely tight. The roof and floor were only about two feet apart. Seat 6D to her right had twisted toward the aisle, and bags from the smashed overhead lockers had fallen to the floor, filling most of the space. She knew she'd have to pull one or more of the bags out to get through. To save time, she really wanted to temporarily put the bags in the empty space of seat 7C, but she knew the woman in 7B would freak out if she did. She'd have to pull them out completely.

De Vries reached forward and grabbed a small roller-bag. It was wet and sticky. She grabbed hold with both hands, and called back to Lang:

"Can you guys pull me back? I need to get a bag out of the way."

"Will do – are you ready?"

"Go ahead."

She was slowly dragged back: it wasn't comfortable, but it was quicker than trying to wiggle back while holding a bag. Once back into the larger area alongside row 6, she saw a large pair of hands reach in and grab the bag, lifting it easily over her head. She crawled forward once more.

She had to clear two more bags in the same fashion before she could get access to row 6. The floor was soaked with blood, and was uneven where it had crumpled and buckled. There was even less space than she'd thought.

She turned her head to the left. Despite all her training, she almost screamed: a squashed and headless torso greeted her. There was no sign of the head. She fought the urge to vomit. She could see nothing beyond the body, and called out:

"Hello – medic – anyone in there?"

There was no response, but there could be an unconscious casualty. She braced herself, and with a silent apology to the corpse tried to pull the torso aside so she could see past it. The left arm was severed at the elbow. She pulled herself forward slightly and peered into the small gap she'd opened up. What she saw was not recognisable as people: just a mass of bloody body parts and mangled metal. There was no-one alive there. She eased back and looked right. The space there was slightly larger, but only just. The crumpled aisle seat was empty aside from debris. In the passenger seat was a dark-skinned woman in her 20s. The left side of her face was smashed in, her skull was split open, her right eye was open and brains were visible.

'Just one row apart,' she thought. In row 7, relatively minor injuries; in row 6, carnage. It was often the way with major incidents: death and minor cuts just a metre apart. A police officer she met at one stabbing scene commented on the difference between assault and murder being two centimetres. Sheer, blind luck.

Rule 1 of on-site trauma response was 'Never assume death'. The black humour common to emergency services had come up with a bunch of sick exceptions. One of them, "... unless the head and torso are at least 15 metres apart", wasn't something she'd be repeating for a while. She reached forward to take a pulse from the woman with the smashed face and skull. As expected, nothing.

In 6A was a girl of maybe 6 or 7. She was unconscious, blood was running profusely from a scalp wound and she had an open fracture of her right arm, also bleeding. She managed to reach past the woman she presumed was her mother and take a pulse. Weak and thready, but present. This was her priority.

Ahead of row 6, the floor and ceiling met: there was nothing left beyond that."I'm coming out, I need two large dressing packs," she called. She shuffled back quickly. The paramedic had the dressing packs ready. She ripped off the board and handed it to him in exchange.

"One critical in 6A, the rest of row 6 is dead. Row 7 is all on there. Come in behind me with a collar and start with 7D. Lang, we need to get an unconscious casualty out first."

Both men acknowledged, and she crawled back in.

York looked yet again at the clock on the wall of the lounge: 02:14. Exactly one minute since the last time he looked at it. There were nine of them left in the lounge: all the rest had been called over and taken elsewhere. For good or bad news, he didn't know.

He made yet another call to Stephanie's mobile, maybe the 30th one since he'd been in this room. Stupid, he knew, but anything was better than just this endless waiting. Voicemail again.

He looked up to see a figure standing alongside him: it was Inge Post.

"Mr York, would you come with me, please."

"Just tell me. Please just tell me."

"Please, Mr York, there is a room just through here." She gestured, but he just sat there. A room. He'd seen enough hospital dramas to know what it meant when they took you somewhere private before telling you the news. No. This wasn't happening and he wouldn't go. If he didn't go, then they couldn't tell him anything terrible, and so nothing terrible could happen. He was staying right here until Stephanie walked in through the door. He just shook his head.

Esther Post sat next to him and took his hands in hers. "Please, Mr York. I need you to come with me, please? Just a few metres away."

"No. I know what you're going to tell me if I go with you, and it's not true. You've made a mistake and I'm staying right here until it gets sorted out, ok?"

"We don't have definitive news, Danny. I just need to update you. Please, follow me."

'No definite news?' he thought. He stood up, and followed as she led him through a door into a small office.

"Please," she said, "have a seat."

They both sat and she picked up a piece of paper. "You have to understand," she explained, "it's still quite a chaotic scene out there. So far we have four categories: passengers confirmed as unhurt, passengers who are receiving medical attention, passengers known to have been killed-"

"Some of them were killed?" he asked, almost whispering the words. He'd known, really, by this stage, that it was a major incident. He'd been terrified by the possibilities. But this was the first time it had actually been said, the first time anyone had spoken those words.

"Tragically, yes. There is a fourth category, of passengers not yet accounted for. Your wife is on that list at the moment."

"What does that actually mean? Unaccounted for?"

"We try to get names from everyone, everyone on the buses back to the terminal, everyone taken to hospital, everyone still on the plane. But it is still only two hours since the incident." York wished they would stop calling it an 'incident': people were dead, for god's sake, this was a plane crash. Why couldn't they call it what it was?

Post continued: "It's possible some passengers were taken back to the terminal early on without it being recorded. It's also dark out there and we can't be sure that there are no passengers who didn't get out and wander off in shock. We have people checking the area around the incident site."

York looked at her directly: "Do you know the identities of all the people who died?"

Post put the paper down. "No," she said simply.

"Why not? They must have boarding passes on them, passports – you must be able to tell who they are. Even seat numbers: you must have records of who was in each seat."

"Some people put their passports and boarding passes into bags in the overhead locker. And sometimes people change seats after boarding. We have to have positive identifications."

York was torn. He didn't want to do anything to make the terrible possibility any more real, but he couldn't stay here not knowing. It had to be done. "Ok," he said with a courage he didn't feel, "you have some bodies." He managed to say the words without emotion. "You have only a few of us waiting. Show us the bodies. At least, the ones who are the right sex and age. I have to know."

Esther Post looked away briefly, then looked back at the desperate man in front of her. Airports trained their staff for all eventualities. There were processes and procedures. There were rules and guidelines. There were manuals and checklists. But there was nothing to state at what point, and to what degree, you told a worried relative the truth: that was a matter for judgement. She decided to tell Danny York the unvarnished truth, couched in the gentlest phrasing she could muster.

"Danny, some identifications have been made, but sometimes visual identification isn't possible. And there is a part of the aircraft where identification of the victims may require prolonged examination."

"Prolonged examination? What does that mean?"

Again, Post reflected on how much wasn't covered by the manuals. "Danny," she said, gently, "there is a section of the aircraft in which survival would unfortunately not have been possible."

"Which section?"

"The front."

"You know the seat numbers, the rows, I mean?"

"Yes."

"Which seats?""Rows 1 to 5."

Danny York felt his throat constrict as he tried to ask the question. "And my wife? You know her seat number?"

Post replied carefully: " We know her assigned seat number. We have no way of knowing whether she moved to a different seat during the flight."

"Her assigned seat: what was it?"

Post took his hands again. That wasn't in the procedures manual, and the men who wrote it – it was always men who wrote these things – would probably disapprove, but they weren't here in this room with the husband of a woman who was almost certainly dead,

"Please understand, people do change seats, it is quite common, so we mustn't jump to any conclusions."

"Her assigned seat," repeated York, his chest tight.

Post looked down at the sheet of paper again. Her memory needed no refreshing, but she needed a moment before answering. "2A."

Danny York stared at her for a moment, then grabbed the piece of paper. Seat assignments were confidential, and listed on that sheet were the names and seat numbers of other passengers also presumed dead. She should under no circumstances allow York or anyone else unauthorised to see it. She did nothing to stop him.

Our own names, and those of people we love, leap up off the page. York, Stephanie: 2A

Fifteen printed characters. Just that. Her name. Her assigned seat. Nothing else. York didn't know what he expected. Something. Something that could tell him more. Something that could tell him she was ok.

"You're sure?" he asked. "I mean, airlines make mistakes all the time, right? You double-book the same seats. Get names mixed-up. Put luggage on the wrong plane. Someone types in 2A when they meant 20A. Just a simple error. Those things happen all the time, right?"

"As I say, Danny, nothing is known for certain yet. What I can tell you is that the names of those unaccounted for, and the names of the people whose assigned seats were in the section of the aircraft concerned, match. Everyone behind row 5 has been accounted for."

"No. You're telling me she's dead. She's not dead. She can't be dead."

"We don't know anything for certain at this stage. Nothing further will be known before morning. We have a hotel room for you here at the airport. I promise you someone will come to your room if we learn anything more tonight, but we don't think that will happen." She handed him a business card. "You can call this number, day or night, and there will always be someone there with the very latest information. Why don't you go to your room, try to get some sleep?"

"Sleep?" exclaimed York. "You think I'm going to sleep?"

"We have a doctor who can give you something to help you sleep. There is no sense in staying here through the night, nothing more will be known."

"No. I'm going to wait out there." He gestured back to the door to the lounge.

"Danny, you can if you wish. Nobody will make you leave. I will stay there with you all night if you wish me to. But at this stage, we are suggesting that everyone would be more comfortable in a hotel room. I promise you, someone will come straight to your room to wake you if there is any news, and you can come back here in the morning, whenever you wish. Just call the number on the card and someone will come to your room to escort you back here."

Danny was about to resist, and then wondered what the hell difference it would make. "The hotel is close?"

"It's right here within the airport complex, just a few minutes' walk."

"Ok."

"Do you have your luggage with you?"

"No, it's at my hotel in the centre of town."

"Do you have the hotel details with you? I will arrange for someone to collect your things and bring them to you."

York reached into his pocket and handed over the hotel key in its paper slip.

"Thank you, it will take about an hour. Your things will be brought to your room. I have someone waiting to take you there now."

"Ok."

The extraction of the last survivor took a further seven hours. The night-shift should have gone off-duty at 6am, but all of them had volunteered to carry on, working alongside the day-shift. It was a slow and frustrating process, hampered by the cramped conditions and the difficulty in cutting through the wreckage of the seats and fuselage while protecting the casualties from the cutting discs.

They had also done their best to protect the bodies and body-parts as much as possible. If the medics declared that a casualty needed to be out, now, they'd cut through severed legs if they needed to, but when casualties were stable they tried to respect the dead and preserve evidence for the air accident investigation team and the coroner.

Now it was done. The air accident investigators had arrived at daylight, and they would want to take photographs and measurements before the gruesome task of he further cutting work required to remove the bodies and body parts.

York had refused a sedative and spent the night alternately pacing the room, calling Stephanie's mobile and sitting on the bed staring at the wall. His luggage, delivered at 3am, remained unopened on the floor. Random memories of Stephanie had been running through his mind.

Several times, he'd picked up the bedside phone and started to dial the number on the card, ready to ask them to take him back to the lounge, and each time he'd dropped the handset back onto the cradle. What would be the point?

The knock on the door came at 7.10am. He rushed to it, praying that it would be Stephanie standing there. He'd take her into his arms and hug her so tightly, and never let go.

It wasn't Stephanie. It was a smartly-dressed woman in her early 20s.

"Mr York? My name is Mariane Schaak. Could I take you to meet with Esther Post?"

York stood there, not wanting to ask the question, but knowing that he had to.

"What is the news?"

"There is nothing definite, but Ms Post would like to meet with you to let you know the current situation."

Nothing definite. There was hope. Perhaps they would tell him that Stephanie was believed to have been taken to a hospital with minor injuries but they weren't sure which one. Perhaps she was right now sitting up wondering where he was? She would have called him, but her mobile was lost in the crash, and she didn't know his number – she was famous for relying entirely on the contact list in her Blackberry, she never knew the phone numbers of any of her family or friends. Yes, that would be it, she couldn't call him or anyone else to get his number. The hospital wasn't sure-

"Mr York?" The young woman broke into his elaborately-constructed scene.

"Sorry, yes, I'll come with you." He pulled the door shut behind him.

As they walked into the terminal building, he was astonished to see that it seemed to be operating normally. It was full of people. The departure boards were full of flights, albeit most of them showing delays. How could an airport just carry on when they had a crashed plane out there? How could they be so callous? And all these people, here to catch their flights, didn't they know about the crash? It must surely have been on the news? He wanted to shout and scream at them. Instead, he walked silently through the terminal.

The staff member led the way though a secured door and down a maze of corridors. He was shown into a large office, where he found Esther Post waiting for him. She got up from the desk, and showed him to a small black leather sofa on the right-hand side of the office. She looked tired.

Post had also volunteered to remain on duty. There had been a lot for her small team to do: liaising with the rescue teams, coordinating passenger lists and casualty lists, obtaining next of kin details for the known dead and arranging for local police to contact them – and above all, checking, re-checking and checking again that they were as certain as could be of the identities of those known to have been killed, and those believed to have been.

There were four known dead passengers, all from row 6. That left two pilots, two cabin crew and 13 passengers officially unaccounted for.

Officially they might still be listed as 'unaccounted for', but there was now little doubt remaining. Both pilots would have been on the flight-deck for the landing, and the two cabin crew at the front of the aircraft would have been strapped into their jump-seats. They were professionals, and would have been where they were supposed to be.

They'd received the passenger manifest from the airline, and that showed 13 passengers allocated to the seats in the section completely destroyed by the crash. Gate records confirmed that all 13 definitely boarded. And they had accounted for all but those 13 passengers. It would require detailed forensics to provide the final, definitive proof, but nobody on the rescue or investigation team was in any doubt: those 13 passengers and four crew were dead.

"Can I get you anything?" she asked, as soon as York was seated next to her. "Coffee, tea, juice, water?"

She knew he wouldn't want anything, he'd just want to know what news she had: it was simply a delaying tactic, to put off the moment when she'd have to have the same conversation she'd already had with two family members this morning.

"No, thank you," he replied. The politeness was instinctive: even in the most stressful of situations, the English maintain their social veneer.

"Let me bring you up to date on the situation," said Post, in a professional tone. She was trying to be a human being as well as a professional, but the previous conversations that morning had left her feeling as emotionally drained as she was mentally exhausted; now she was retreating into formality.

"The rescue crews worked through the night. The trapped passengers have been freed. Four passengers are confirmed dead, and we believe we know their identities. Fifteen people, four crew and eleven passengers, remain unaccounted for. I am very sorry to say that we are now as certain as we can be that all fifteen are dead. Stephanie York is one of those. I'm sorry, Mr York." She couldn't bring herself to use his first name; she needed the professional distance right now.

"No," said York. "Look, I'll visit the hospitals. Tell me which ones, and I'll go and check the survivors. There are probably unconscious passengers, right? And Stephanie never knows phone numbers without her Blackberry, she's probably been frantically trying to get a message to me."

"I'm sorry, Mr York: we know the identities of all those currently in hospital, as well as all those who were unhurt."

"But she's still missing, yes? You said she was unaccounted for. That doesn't mean she's dead. She can't be dead. We just got married, you see? She's got to be ok."

"I'm sorry, Mr York. There really is very little doubt."

It would be a further 48 hours before the official listings were changed from 'unaccounted for' to 'dead'.

* * *

Sarah Green returned from her lunch-break and went and stood in front of the flow-chart. She positioned herself at the far left, in front of 'Aircraft design'. She would, she decided, simply walk along the chart until something caught her eye.

Aircraft design ... Aircraft construction ... Aircraft testing ... Aircraft delivery ... Airline acceptance-testing ... First opera-

Hmmm. Aircraft construction. Once an aircraft was finished, tested and handed over to the airline, it became subject to all the security procedures involved in a post-9/11 airport. Someone getting a device on board an airliner at an airport had been identified as one of the key risks in the immediate post-9/11 panic, and a huge amount of effort had been put into making it, if not impossible, then very, very difficult.

But what if a manufacturer employee, or contractor, or anyone else who had access to the factory, managed to get something on board during construction?

Something with a very long-term timer, perhaps, or a device that could be activated remotely at a later date?

It would require a battery that would last some time, but if you had uninterrupted access to an aircraft while it was still being built, you had a hell of a lot more places you could hide it than after it was operational. With the right access, there would literally be no part of the aircraft that couldn't be used to hide it.

Given that delivery might be weeks or months later, it would require a very long-term timer – something that could be programmed for a date as well as a time, but that was trivial these days, even a mobile phone alarm could do the job.

Battery-life would be an issue, but then the package could be a lot bigger if it would be in the airframe itself rather than in the very limited hiding places available once an aircraft interior is fully fitted and the airliner is operational. In fact, given enough expertise, someone might even be able to wire it into the aircraft circuitry so that it drew its power from the aircraft itself.

Yes, that would be an interesting area to think about. She returned to her desk, logged into the task-management system and assigned herself to Aircraft Construction. She felt happy about having chosen an interesting area to investigate. She had

no idea that she had missed the biggest threat by
just one item on the flowchart.

* * *

2nd February

Air accident investigators face two directly
conflicting pressures. They are by nature and by
training cautious people. They take a slow, careful
and methodical approach to their work. They like
facts, and dislike assumptions. They know that no
crash is ever down to a single cause: there is so
much redundancy built into both systems and flight
crew procedures that almost no single failure can
lead to disaster. Backup systems, checklists, critical
actions that have to be performed by one pilot and
confirmed by the other ... there is always a chain of
events involved, often beginning with something
seemingly quite innocuous. They are thus reluctant
to voice anything approaching a conclusion until all
the facts are known.

But they also operate in a world in which
everyone wants instant facts. Whenever a plane
crashes, the media has one question: how could this
be allowed to happen? The press wants immediate
answers, and it wants simple ones. They have no
interest in the fact that answers are often complex,
and reaching them can take months, sometimes
years, of painstaking work. The longer the period
the official answer is 'We don't yet know', the more
strident the tone of the editorials and the greater
the demands for answers.

Airlines, too, want fast answers. If an aircraft
model is grounded pending the outcome of a crash
investigation, the costs soon run into the millions. If
a model is allowed to continue to fly, but passengers
are nervous, that too can have dire financial
consequences.

The same is true for the aircraft manufacturer.
Doubts as to the safety of a particular model can

affect sales. Even if a fault in the aircraft is found to be responsible, it is better to know that earlier rather than later, so that modifications can be made and the risk of a recurrence reduced.

Investigators are well-briefed on the dangers of rushing their work. In the early days of crash investigations, it was not unusual for an investigation to be led off-track, or even reach the wrong conclusions entirely, because of an assumption made at an early stage. The temptation to jump to conclusions was particularly strong when all of the initial facts – physical evidence, eye-witness reports and cockpit voice recordings – all pointed in a single direction. But experience had shown that things are not always what they appear. There could be a dozen different facts pointing in one direction, but it can take only a single piece of evidence to show the flaw in the 'obvious' conclusion.

Faced with the incompatible needs of a thorough investigation and rapid answers, investigation teams throughout the world have tended to adopt the same, unsatisfactory solution: interim reports.

The first interim report is typically issued a month or two after the crash, summarising what is known at that point, and making precautionary recommendations based on the current understanding of what may have happened. It's an approach investigators take reluctantly, but they accept it as the price for being left alone to get on with the longer task of the full investigation and analysis.

The interim report was 12,568 words long. But just two of those words made the headlines: 'pilot error'.

The body copy, and the voiceovers on the TV, included the two paragraphs intended to summarise the key finding:

The main precipitating factor in the accident was the failure of Captain Berker to execute a go-around when the aircraft was still forty feet above the runway at the planned touchdown point. Captain Berker continued to press ahead with the landing despite an unstable approach, resulting in a substantial overshoot of the touch-down target. Standing water on the runway resulted in greatly reduced deceleration, with braking performance further reduced by a severe skid and subsequent reduction in reverse thrust while directional control was re-established.

The key recommendation is for guidance to be issued to aircrews emphasising the importance of promptly executing GA procedures when required. There is a positive requirement for the Pilot In Command to be confident at all stages of the approach that a safe landing within limits can be achieved, and to execute a GA if such confidence is lost at any point.

Most reports did not get as far as the third paragraph, partly because a headline requires a single cause, and partly because the technical nature of the recommendation would have required too much explanation for readable copy or a short TV piece.

A secondary recommendation is for the manufacturer to review the safety envelope override programming to determine whether the sub-routine responsible for cancellation of reverse thrust during a skid maintains the optimum balance between retardation and directional control.

For the media and the public, the mystery was solved. It wasn't the best news in the world – everyone likes to think they can trust the Captain to get them safely to their destination – but it was the most reassuring of the possible conclusions. One man made a mistake. The aircraft is safe. The systems are safe. The procedures are safe. One rogue pilot failed to obey the rules, and he paid with his life. Story ends.

Posts by airline pilots on the civil aviation forums tended to adopt a more cynical line. PPRuNe, the Professional Pilot's Rumour Network, was one of the more vocal. Its members, most of them airline pilots, were well aware that 'pilot error' is by far the most common finding in any air accident investigation. Pilots know better than anyone about the chain of events required to cause a crash, and that in a major crash, the pilots are rarely around to defend themselves. They had a grim saying for that: the pilot is always first on the scene of a crash.

The cynics took the view that it was in almost everyone's financial interests to focus on the element of human error. If it's the aircraft at fault, there are hundreds of millions of pounds and thousands of jobs at stake. If it's the pilot, the airline takes a bit of a hit in the short-term, but then everything gets back to normal. The family and friends of the pilot may be devastated by the findings, but their feelings cannot compete with the money at stake.

The attention of the pilots on the PPruNe forum focused on the software. If the autoland software had sacrificed directional control for maximum deceleration, the aircraft would have run off the side of the runway, but would it have hit the ditch? Or would maintaining full reverse thrust have brought it to a halt before it ran out of airfield?

What modelling work had been done on the relative risks of loss of directional control versus loss of braking effort? Did the code that detected a skid also take into account that a slippery landing surface would result in greatly extended braking distances? Was the software responding only to the aircraft dynamics, or was it also taking a read of the remaining runway distance and prioritising directional stability versus bringing the aircraft to a halt?

The debate was fiercely fought on both sides. There were those who maintained that the system was fighting a losing battle and that the outcome would have been the same, or worse, had it not kicked-in. And there were those who felt that that automated protective systems had been taken a step too far and shouldn't actively over-ride the pilot's commands except in the most clear-cut of cases, like flying into the ground.

No consensus was reached, but the debate – which ran to 34 pages – certainly gave anyone reading it pause for thought.

York had been inconsolable. The first two weeks, he'd done almost nothing but sit at home reliving the horror of it, crying uncontrollably, unable to think of anything else.

York's colleagues at work were sympathetic to his loss. His manager had told him to take all the time off he wanted, but York had reached the point where he couldn't stand it any more. He needed to lose himself in something, and he felt work was all he had left. He was, though, discovering something else.

The psychiatrist Kübler-Ross suggested that people go through five stages of grief: denial, anger, bargaining, depression and acceptance; York was moving into the anger stage.

Since meeting her, Stephanie had been his life. Now she was gone, and somebody was to blame.

He started reading everything he could find on the crash. When the interim report blamed the Captain, he quickly found the dead pilot an unsatisfactory target for his anger: the man was gone, and York had no way of judging whether or not the conclusion was fair. He didn't know anything about flying a plane.

But he did know software, and that third paragraph had caught his attention:

A secondary recommendation is for the manufacturer to review the safety envelope override programming to determine whether the sub-routine responsible for cancellation of reverse thrust during a skid maintains the optimum balance between retardation and directional control.

He'd had a vague awareness of fly-by-wire systems being used on both Airbus and Boeing airliners, the kind of passing interest anyone of a technical bent would take, but now he made it his mission to learn as much as he could about it.

He'd known that automated systems could fly and land the plane, but hadn't realised that the systems could take over even when the plane was being flown manually. The idea that software could actually override pilot input shocked him. As much as he knew the value of software, he also knew its limitations and weaknesses.

The products he worked on were 'mission-critical': failure of a switch or router could cause an entire section of a telecoms network to fall over. They worked to a standard known as five-nines: 99.999% reliability.

A typical piece of network software had over a hundred thousand of lines of code, more complex examples might have half a million lines. There were always bugs. Errors. Omissions. Permutations that hadn't been considered.

They had test analysts, whose job was to work out ways to test the software, and test engineers, who performed the actual testing. The tests involved hooking up the kit to test harnesses to simulate inputs and measure outputs. Every time a bug was found, they'd review the code, work out the reason for it, correct it and send it back to testing.

Testing was very thorough. But even so, bugs did make it through. Most of them were minor, resulting in less than optimal performance but without any major consequences. Those would be corrected through a routine firmware update.

But occasionally, a major bug would make it through. A rare combination of variables that hadn't been anticipated. An unusual sequence of events. A problem elsewhere that in turn caused one of their switches to fail. With the sums of money at stake in networking solutions, they worked very, very hard to detect and fix bugs before the equipment was released to customers, but they didn't always succeed. One of the products he maintained was on firmware version 10.2, and there would still be further bugs, yet to be discovered.

Airline software was a whole other level. There wasn't just money at stake, but lives. Real live people. People like Stephanie. Could a software bug have killed her?

His googling took him to the PPRuNe thread on the crash. He saw that airline pilots worried about it too. These were the people who knew, and even they were concerned that a bug in the programming could have caused, or at least worsened, the crash.

He posted some questions on the forum, using a pseudonym not because he had anything to hide but because he couldn't bear to talk about Stephanie. He posted the questions as an interested bystander, a software engineer who happened to have taken an interest in the subject.

He started asking about other examples of fly-by-wire software overriding pilots. There was no shortage of examples. Were there other crashes caused by automated systems? It was, he was told, disputed territory. There had been cases of crashes where the pilots said one thing and the report said another.

The best-known of these was the crash of Air France flight 296, a newly-delivered Airbus A320 scheduled to do a low-altitude fly-past at a French air-show. The plan had been for a low and slow pass over the runway at an altitude of 100 feet. The aircraft instead made a pass at 30 feet, and failed to clear the trees at the end of the runway. The report concluded it was pilot error, flying below the planned height; the pilot maintained that he'd set the auto-pilot to maintain a radio altimeter height of 100 feet throughout the pass, and it had indicated that it was doing so. His co-pilot, perhaps fearing for his career, maintained a public silence on the matter.

York spent more and more time reading about the issue, and thinking about it. How could lives be trusted to software that might at any second decide that it knew better than an experienced airline pilot? The first rule of any software-based decision system was that it was only as good as the data it had available to it. Automated trading systems had been the holy grail of the financial services industry for a time. The theory was that if you programmed a computer system with all of the trading principles, the strategies, the tactics, the what-ifs, and then plugged it into live data-feeds, it would do a better job than any human trader. It would react in milliseconds rather than seconds or minutes. It would be immune to doubt or emotion. It would be entirely rational.

And that was precisely why such systems failed. Trading was not an entirely rational process. A bull market or a bear market doesn't just reflect objective facts about the economy, or the strengths & weaknesses of a particular stock, it also reflected investor confidence. Herd instinct. Feelings. Intuitions. Emotion. The automated trading software had none of that data.

He'd done a lot of reading on air-disasters and near-disasters. The common thread to many of the near-disasters was that the pilots had taken an unorthodox approach. Air Canada 143 – better known as the Gimli Glider – had been a spectacular example. When a series of errors led to the Boeing 767 running out of fuel in mid-flight, the Captain looked in the emergency checklists for the 'both engines out' procedure to find that there was no such checklist. An experienced glider pilot, he applied glider techniques to maximise the distance they could fly. Unable to reach any airport, they ended up landing at a former Air Force base that was now a motorsports complex. No automated system could have come up with the solution, and quite possibly wouldn't even have permitted the Captain to attempt it, instead it would most likely have made a doomed attempt to reach a current airport.

"It's crazy," he said to Pete Bright, one of the software engineers at work. "The pilot had selected full reverse-thrust, and the software overrode him. The plane ran out of runway and that's why it crashed. Nobody seems to know if the software even had a data feed for the remaining runway distance."

To Bright, it was becoming a familiar refrain. He felt for York, they all did. But he also felt that it was becoming an obsession, that it wasn't healthy.

York continued: "How can a bunch of guys like us, sitting in a comfortable air-conditioned office like this, decide that we, that our software, can know better than the Captain landing a 200-tonne airliner, in a storm, at night, what action to take? It's absolutely nuts."

Bright was reluctant to argue the point, but he had learned that York would not accept silence as a response. "It does sound it when you put it that way, but the manufacturers have a massive amount of data on the performance characteristics of the plane. They know better than the pilot what it can and can't do. All they're trying to do is make sure the plane keeps flying, and pilots don't demand the impossible."

"But sometimes pilots have done the impossible," insisted York. "The Gimli Glider. You can't glide an unpowered 767 the distance that guy did, the aircraft performance data says so. And you can't safely land an airliner on an active racetrack without killing anyone, but that pilot did."

Bright felt trapped. He knew that York expected a response, needed a response, but didn't want to get into an academic debate with him: he knew that what was a theoretical issue for him couldn't get any more personal for York.

"You may be right. But isn't also possible that those cases are the exceptions? That in most cases, the software actually protects pilots from their own mistakes? I mean," he added quickly, "I know it's of no comfort to you if this was an exception to the rule, but ..." He tailed off.

"Automated protection is fine, makes sense, but it has to be failsafe. Ultimately, it has to accept that in extreme circumstances, the Captain knows what he's doing." York paused and looked directly at Bright. "You understand, don't you, that I can't just shrug this off, sit back and let the same thing happen to someone else?"

"What can you do?"

"I don't know. Something."

The something started out harmlessly enough. He wrote letters, lots of letters. Letters to MPs, letters to newspapers, letters to airlines, letters to Airbus. He got back polite replies telling him his concerns had been noted, or that his letter had been forwarded to someone else who would in turn send a polite reply. Both Istan Air and Airbus sent replies clearly written by lawyers, expressing sympathy in the cold, corporate way that only lawyers can, and explaining that as the investigation was continuing and that legal proceedings might follow, they were unable to comment further at this time.

Something more effective had to be done.

* * *

Jen Williams had no intention of attending the stupid school meeting with her parents. Her father spent half his life away from home, was away at the times that mattered.

The time she'd got caught up with that stupid cow Ella and her mates, and they'd got caught shoplifting. She was 12 years old, and the whole thing had scared her half to death. The store detective, the manager, the police. Right then she'd just wanted him to put his arms around her and tell her everything was ok. But he wasn't there, of course, he was halfway round the world in Hong Kong. Her Duke of Edinburgh weekend in Snowdonia. The other fathers had been there, to see them off from the start and welcome them back at the end; he'd been in LA. The sports days. The swimming championships. The school orchestra concerts. Her 13th birthday. And all the small stuff

– the times she'd wanted help with her maths homework. If any father could help with that, it was hers, but usually he wasn't there.

But when he wanted to side with the head in giving her a lecture on how she was throwing away her future, oh yes, he was available for that.

They kept saying they were concerned for her future when it clearly wasn't true. None of them were. They were making a lot of fuss about pieces of paper and university and careers when her generation was inheriting a planet headed for disaster, and none of her parents' generation were doing anything about it. Or, rather, her father was: making things much, much worse. Aviation was already the fastest-growing source of CO_2 emissions in the UK, and by 2050 things would be four times worse. If air travel were allowed to keep growing at its current rate, it would wipe out all the other emissions savings that were supposed to be achieved in the same period.

The planet was close to an irreversible tipping-point: the ice-caps, glaciers and permafrost were melting; temperatures were rising and whole swathes of the Earth would be turned into desert. Flooding from rising sea-levels, droughts from increased temperatures, famine from lost arable land and a meat industry that consumed eight kilos of grain to produce one kilo of meat.

And it wasn't just the human species who would suffer the effects: within 50 years, a third of all animal species could face extinction.

You didn't need a geography or biology A-level to understand the threat, you just needed to visit the websites of the environmental groups. All the facts and figures were there.

She wasn't going to sit back and watch it happen. The government wasn't going to do anything: they'd already excluded international aviation from the 2050 emissions targets. If the politicians wouldn't act, her generation would.

Action On Aviation, AOA, was her opportunity to do her bit. One thing her father had given her was a good understanding of how the aviation industry worked. A couple of years ago, before she'd known the true facts, she'd even been considering following her father into the industry. God, she'd been naive then. In the post-9/11 days, he couldn't get her onto the flight deck during a flight, but he'd done everything else. Let her fly Skyways's simulator at Gatwick during a family day, taken her round the hangars, given her flying lessons in the light aircraft he owned as part of a small syndicate of fellow pilots. Jesus, didn't that just say it all: they flew big planes for a living, and flew small ones for fun.

It embarrassed her now. She'd been so enthusiastic, so keen to learn. Her father loved talking about it and she'd loved learning about it. She could so easily have ended up working in the industry that was doing more than any other to choke the planet. Instead, she was a virtual walking encyclopaedia on a subject she'd grown to despise.

Her introduction to environmental groups had been a revelation to her. She'd never realised just how bad things were, how much the politicians and big business were covering up the true scale of the threat. Even mainstream scientists, she'd learned, were downplaying the facts. Most of them were in the pay of governments. The climate change deniers claimed that scientists were exaggerating the dangers when the truth was they weren't going far enough. They issued cautious reports talking about indications and trends and possibilities and complex systems and the effects of solar radiation and natural warming & cooling cycles when they should have been shouting from the rooftops that we were killing our home.

She made up for her earlier naivety by throwing herself whole-heartedly into the cause. She'd delivered leaflets. Written letters. Visited MPs. Helped with the website. Gone on protests. Her father had gone ballistic when she'd joined the group that had cut through the fences at Heathrow and occupied the main runway for 15 minutes before they were removed and arrested by police. He'd really lost it, telling her that if she didn't care about screwing up her own future with a criminal record, with possible terrorist charges, she should at least care about his. How did it look, he'd shouted, when the daughter of a captain of a major airline got arrested for bringing the world's busiest airport to a halt for fifteen minutes?

She'd told him she didn't care how things looked, she cared about how things were. Why didn't he care about that? Why didn't he care about the planet?

When she'd first joined AOA, she'd thought about keeping quiet about her father's job, afraid they would see her as the enemy. But she knew it would only be a matter of days before she'd find herself complaining about her father being part of the problem, so decided instead to be up-front about it.

Julian Fox, the founder of AOA, had welcomed her enthusiastically when he learned of her background. "Information is power," he'd told her. "The more we understand about how the industry works, the greater our ability to defeat it. You can make a huge difference here."

He was a total inspiration. His family had serious money, and he could easily have spent his life jetting around the world, sitting on beaches and sipping champagne. Instead, he'd decided to do something meaningful with his life, devote his time and seemingly boundless energy to a cause that meant more than any other.

"Nothing else matters," he'd told her. "I've done the charity bit, helped build schools in Africa and orphanages in India and raised money for cancer research and campaigned for anti-poverty groups all of that stuff. But I came to realise that none of that is worth a damn if we've so fucked-up the planet that entire populations get wiped out by drought and famine and disease and war. Some studies show we've got less than ten years before we reach the tipping-point, then it's over. No way back. We're screwed."

"And what are our glorious politicians doing about it? Talking! Flying in private jets to exotic locations to eat expensive meals and drink expensive wines and talk. The Earth Summit in Rio. The Kyoto Protocol. The Johannesburg Declaration. All just political talking-shops. They come out, all smiles for the cameras, waving bits of paper with fine-sounding rhetoric and empty promises and meaningless targets that wouldn't solve the problem if they were increased tenfold."

Not only had Julian created AOA, paying the bills himself, supplemented only by a few sporadic donations from supporters, he refused even to be credited. His name didn't appear in any of the publicity materials, and he nominated a deputy as the contact person for the organisation: he was so modest about the whole thing.

Jen had been thrilled to be taken so seriously by this man who was so enthusiastic, so committed to making a difference. To have him sitting down and listening to her tell him everything she knew about the airline business, hanging on her every word, was just incredible.

Julian was 28, but it really didn't feel like he was so much older. He dressed like her friends did. He was 6'2", had long, wavy blond hair and the most amazing deep blue eyes. When he made eye-contact, you felt like you were the only person in his world.

"It's down to people like us," he'd told her. "You and I. So few people your age take the time to get involved. Sure, they might join a facebook group or go on an occasional tame demo, but they don't have the commitment you do."

"I know," she said, "they care more about celebrity magazines and TV shows than their own futures. It's pathetic."

Fox smiled at her, that slightly crooked smile where the edges of his left lips curled down a touch. "Don't worry about them. They'll understand one day, and appreciate what you've done for them. Come on, we've done enough for one day – let's grab some beer from the fridge."

* * *

Fox read one of York's letters in the Guardian. York was campaigning for legal restrictions on fly-by-wire systems, blaming automated systems for a crash in Amsterdam earlier that year. Fox couldn't care less about a plane crash: one less plane in the air was all to the good as far as he was concerned. But he thoroughly approved of scare stories. Scare stories made people think twice about flying. Maybe there was some mileage in this fly-by-wire business.

He'd toyed with the idea of setting up a dummy organisation, claiming to be fighting for tougher aviation safety standards. Its real purpose would be to create FUD: Fear, Uncertainty and Doubt. It was one of the strongest weapons in the armoury of environmental campaigners.

The movers & shakers in the green movement understood well that talk of the destruction of the planet was just convenient language, a way of getting through to people who would otherwise not give a stuff about the sustainability of their lifestyle. Mindless drones who cocooned themselves in artificial worlds of temperature-controlled boxes and whose meaningless lives were mostly devoted to the acquisition of consumer goods. Bigger TVs, newer cars, fancier gadgets ... Juvenal was right, only in today's modern world bread and circuses had been replaced by 4x4s and reality TV shows.

You couldn't point out the futility of the consumer society, or the absurdity of living a life so utterly removed from the reality of nature, or the gross irresponsibility of pursuing a lifestyle that could be open only to the privileged few in developed countries in this generation, selfishly consuming resources on a scale that amounted to robbery from future generations. There was not even the slightest possibility of persuading a society used to air-conditioning and privately-owned vehicles and meat in every meal and heat, light & power available at the flick of a switch that it was time to return to a simpler life. A life that respected the natural world. A life in which people got up with the sun and went to bed with the sun. A life in which people grew their own food and lived in harmony with the land.

No, the only way to reach them was to scare them out of their comfortable, complacent little substitutes for lives. You had to create visions of the apocalypse before you could reach them.

But even this was wearing thin. People had been hearing it for so long. It had started in the 70s, when people were told we had only 20 years' oil remaining. In the meantime, the oil industry had discovered new fields and developed new extraction techniques. Rising prices meant that oil reserves that were once uneconomic to tap were now profitable. The result? We have about 40 years' supply remaining today.

Global warming, too, was proving less convincing. It's hard to persuade people to take serious predictions of 15-20C rises when the reality was a rise of 0.7C in the last 100 years, and a trend suggesting 1.4C in the next 100.

The threat had to be made very much more real, and very much more immediate. He was working on that.

But in the meantime, a few new scare stories wouldn't hurt. Perhaps this fly-by-wire business would prove the hook on which to hang his dummy safety campaign. It wouldn't take much: a website, a few press releases, a PR agency, some photos of the wreckage of ... what was it? Istan Air Flight 1951.

This guy York clearly wanted publicity – maybe he could be recruited as the front-man for it? Fox would put up the cash, that was no problem. A week to create the legal organisation, website and a few staff. Then a letter to Danny York c/o the Guardian.

"Where the hell were you last night?" demanded Richard Williams, rising from his chair at the kitchen table as his daughter Jen walked through the door shortly before 10am on Saturday morning. Jen was well beyond the normal teenage rebellious phase. Bunking off school, coming home drunk, staying out overnight, piercings, tattoos and alternating between swearing and refusing to talk at all. Mostly the latter where he was concerned: she declared herself a committed environmentalist and appeared to view commercial aviation as one rung below drug-dealing. He'd worked hard to become an airline captain, and to have a daughter who was ashamed rather than proud stung more than he would generally admit.

His wife Emma had little more luck lately at getting through to Jen. They'd had another meeting with her school head to discuss her absenteeism, only Jen had failed to turn up for it.

"Well?" repeated Richard, "where were you?"

"Out," replied Jen.

"Richard ..." said Emma.

"Out where?" continued Richard, holding out a placating hand to his wife. "You were supposed to be at the meeting with us and the head of your school, to discuss the fact that you rarely bother to turn up there these days, or had you forgotten that?"

"I hadn't forgotten."

"So, you just decided to make fools of your mother and I, did you?"

"No, you manage that all by yourselves."

"Right! That's it!" he shouted. "Go to your room, and don't come out of it until you're ready to apologise."

"What, you think I'm like seven? You can't send me to my room like I'm some stupid kid. I'm fifteen years old, daddy dear, and I'll be sixteen in a couple of months. I'll officially be an adult then, and then you won't have to have any more stupid meetings at the school because I won't be there any more."

"You think you're leaving school at sixteen?" he exclaimed. "No way. No fucking way."

"Richard," said Emma, "sit down, please. Shouting and swearing isn't helping."

"What is going to help with her?" He sat down.

"Talking, and listening."

"Mum," said Jen, "I appreciate what you're trying to do, but there really isn't any point in this. It's my life, my decision and I'll do what I like. Neither of you can stop that, so why not just accept it and we can stop having these pointless arguments?"

"Jen, darling, I know that right now you feel that school is all a waste of time, believe me, I felt the same thing at times when I was your age."

"Oh mum, you're not going to give me all that 'when I was your age' crap again, are you?"

"You will not speak to your mother like that!" shouted Richard. "Apologise, right now!"

Jen looked at her father, and for a couple of seconds it looked like she was going to refuse, then she shrugged. "Fine. Whatever. I'm sorry. There, can I go now? I'm only here to get changed and pick up a few things."

"No you bloody well can't go. You're going to sit down, and we're going to talk about this like a family."

"You can talk all you like, dad, you're not going to change my mind, so why waste the time?"

"Have you had any breakfast yet, Jen?" asked Emma.

"I'm not hungry."

"Listen, why don't you go upstairs, have a shower, get changed and I'll make some breakfast and we'll talk. Just talk. We're not going to force you to do anything–"

Richard Williams looked like he was about to say something, then slumped back in his chair.

"– we just want to understand your viewpoint, and we'd like you to understand ours. That's not much to ask, is it?" Her tone was gentle, but Jen recognised the steel beneath.

"But that's it, mum: it's not a 'viewpoint', it's my life and I get to decide how I live it. You can have all the 'viewpoints' you like. I have plenty of 'viewpoints' about dad's career, but it doesn't stop him carrying on with it, does it?"

"Ok, well, I'm invoking executive privilege here. For two more months, your life is not entirely your own, and while your father and I want to respect your choices–"

Richard's face suggested less than wholehearted support for this statement.

"– we are going to have a proper, civilised–" Emma gave Richard a meaningful look, before continuing: "– conversation about the reasons for those choices and the likely implications of them on your future happiness. There is going to be no shouting, no swearing, no insults and no sulking. You want to be treated like an adult, then you can behave like one."

"Does that apply to dad too?" asked Jen.

Emma raised a hand before Richard could respond: "It applies to all of us. Clear? Now, you've got 20 minutes before breakfast is ready. Go."

When Jen had disappeared upstairs, Richard smiled at his wife.

"What?" she asked.

"I'm just remembering why I married you," he said.

"Good. I hope you can also remember a little further back, to when you were a teenager. You were a teenager once, I take it? I mean, you weren't actually born fifty years old?"

Richard grinned, and squeezed her bum: "Need some evidence?"

Emma removed his hand, but gently. "I need you to remember how utterly pointless it is to try to force a teenager to do something against their will, especially a teenage girl."

"But what if we can't persuade her? She's bright, she'll probably pass enough GCSEs if she gets her act together soon, and she can make up any others while she does her A-levels, but if she's determined to walk out, what do we do about it?"

"We take it one day at a time. Come on, you can help me make breakfast, and you are not going to give your daughter an excuse to start another one of her rants by eating bacon in front of her: for this breakfast, we are all going to be vegetarians."

* * *

It had taken Fox less than a week to set up Safety in Our Skies (SOS). A maildrop address and telephone answering service – actual offices could come later if they proved necessary. A suitable pseudonym for its ostensible chairman until he could recruit York into the role (David King had a suitable ring to it, he thought). A logo and letterhead. A small website. And a few bits & pieces to bring 'Mr King' into existence: a business card and a pay-as-you-go mobile phone among them. He'd used aliases before and had the routine down now.

In these post-9/11 days, there was a huge focus on airline safety. It was trivial to google for half a dozen threats the fake group could be campaigning on and create a webpage for each of them.

Four or five paragraphs on each was enough: another lesson learned in the Green movement. Go into too much detail, and you gave people facts they could check. Not that any of them lied, of course, but there were always different estimates, different interpretations, and they naturally chose the ones that would best make their case. No, it was better to keep it general. Talk about the dangers in broad terms, sprinkling in a few vague figures here and there, always careful to use phrasing that was hard to challenge. 'It has been estimated', 'some scientists believe', that kind of thing. And if estimates for a particular event ranged from 10 years to 400 years, then you of course used 'in as little as ten years from now'.

For the fly-by-wire page, he'd googled Flight 1951. He found the interim report, and then hit on the same forum thread that York had found. That was perfect, because it was pilots doing the talking. Sure, most of them pooh-poohed the concerns, thought it was safe, but there were enough juicy comments on there to create a good scare story.

The beauty of scare stories involving technology and big corporations was that it was fashionable to be a skeptic. People not only had a general mistrust of what big business said, they actively wanted to disbelieve them, find holes in their statements, prove how savvy and intelligent they were by not falling for the PR guff. The irony, of course, was that it made it easy to make them believe any reasonable-sounding counter-view. Propaganda was so much easier when the target audience was already a willing accomplice in it.

The homepage led with the fly-by-wire campaign, complete with a photo of the wreckage of Flight 1951. He wrote a press release on the subject, calling for a detailed government investigation into the safety of fly-by-wire systems, and drawing attention to that neglected paragraph three in the executive summary, explaining what that secondary recommendation meant in layman's terms:

The interim report on the crash expressed concern that when the Captain was using full reverse thrust to stop the plane as quickly as possible, the on-board computers actually cancelled this. It is quite possible that had Captain Berker been allowed to remain in control of his plane, he would have brought it safely to a stop. Airbus has been asked to look at the suspect computer code, but in the meantime other airliners with the same computers are still in use.

Most of the media considered it old news. They'd already told their readers it was pilot error, and weren't inclined to give coverage to an old crash story resurrected by some campaign group they'd never heard of. Crackpots trying to get their conspiracy stories in the news were a dime a dozen.

But one or two took a different view. A good scare story, especially one concerning the safety of airliners, was always good for selling a few papers. It got a few column inches here and there. It was enough for now. It was the human interest angle that would give it legs for the media: the distraught husband of a woman whose life was tragically cut short because a computer thought it knew better than the captain of the aircraft. A man so determined to ensure that the same fate didn't befall someone else that he was making it his personal mission to alert the world to the dangers. They might still view it as a conspiracy theory, but it was one that tugged at the heartstrings. It would be covered.

He – or rather, the non-existent David King – was ready to contact York.

* * *

Danny York, sitting at his kitchen table with the cup of black coffee that was his usual breakfast these days, re-read the letter he'd received that morning:

Dear Mr York

First, may I extend my deep sympathies for your loss. I cannot begin to imagine the horror of what you have experienced.

You may or may not be aware of Safety in Our Skies (SOS). We're a small, grassroots campaign group which highlights dangers in the aviation industry and uses publicity and political lobbying to try to persuade the industry to address these risks.

We noted your letter in the Guardian on the subject of fly-by-wire systems, and share your concerns. Indeed, we have a webpage about just this issue: www.safetyinourskies.org/flybywire

It struck me that we may be able to work together to draw attention to the risks of these automated systems? Perhaps we could meet for lunch to discuss the matter?

Yours sincerely

David King

Founder, Safety in Our Skies

York hadn't heard of SOS, but was heartened to learn that someone was tackling the issue. He'd call Mr King from work and arrange that lunch.

For the meeting, Fox had swapped his usual ripped jeans and t-shirt for a Saville Row suit, Brooks Brothers shirt and tie for his appearance as David King. York had told him he worked close to Tower Hill, so 'King' had suggested The Butlers Wharf Chophouse as a smart but not stuffy restaurant close to Tower Bridge. The impression he wanted to give to York was of someone who had the resources to promote the issue, but wasn't ideally suited to the front-man role. He wanted to persuade York to be the spokesman.

York gave his name to the maitre-d, and was shown to 'King's table.

"Mr York? So glad you could make it."

"Please, call me Danny."

"David. I hope you didn't have any problems getting away from work?"

"No, my workload is quite manageable at the moment, everyone's being very understanding and encouraging me to ease myself back in gently."

"Good. What is it you do?"

'King' was just making polite conversation. He had no interest in what York did, or indeed in any other aspect of his life: he cared only about whether York's grief and one-man campaign could be

73

exploited to contribute to the cause."I'm a software engineer: I write embedded code for telecoms equipment."

'King' looked at him in surprise: "You didn't mention that in your letter to the Guardian. I would have thought it would have lent more weight to your argument, the fact that you're a professional in the field."

"I wanted to," replied York, "but I didn't want to risk embarrassing my employer. I'm fully aware that most people are going to think I'm just some grief-crazed obsessive, believe me, I've seen it in the eyes of my colleagues at work when I talk to them about it. And the company is being very kind, so I don't want them getting dragged into any controversy."

'King' saw his hopes of using York as a spokesperson fading. "Ah, so you'd be uncomfortable being in the limelight, so to speak?"

York hesitated. "I want to draw attention to this issue. I just don't want people to use my employer's name in connection with this. They've been understanding, but I think there are limits. If they felt it had become professionally embarrassing, well ..."

'King' decided to set aside the hurdle for the moment. He wanted to see whether York had what it took to communicate the issue in a way that would frighten the flying public.

"Why don't you talk me through the problem as you see it? I have people who advise me, of course, but I'm not an expert myself. How would you describe the issue to a lay person?"

"The bottom-line?" asked York.

"The bottom-line."

"A fly-by-wire aircraft doesn't have two pilots, it has three: the two human ones, and a computerised one that monitors everything they do. If the computer doesn't like what the human pilots are doing, it can override them, it can take over. A bunch of lines of computer code written by guys much like me, guys who have never flown an aircraft in their lives and wouldn't know how to, can take precedence over a decision made by the Captain of the aircraft. In the case of Flight 1951, the computer cancelled reverse thrust – in effect, switched off the brakes – and the result was the plane smashing through a fence and crashing into a ditch, killing 17 people. That's the bottom-line."

'King' was impressed. This was exactly the kind of 25-second soundbite that the TV stations need. It was succinct, easy to understand and frightening. He decided to probe some more.

"Ok, but you're just speculating about Flight 1951, right? You don't know what would have happened if the computer hadn't reduced the braking. Maybe the software was right, and failing to correct the skid might have resulted in an even worse crash with even more people killed."

"You're right: I don't know that. But my point is, it's by no means certain that the coders did either. Everything they do is guided by theoretical models of aircraft dynamics. In a real-life emergency, the Captain is the one with the full picture of what's happening, and the countless number of variables that go to make up that particular scenario. Should a piece of software, written in an office five or ten years before the emergency, be trusted more than the Captain to make the right decisions to save the aircraft?"

'King' pressed him: "Ok, so what's the solution? The Captain is trying to save the aircraft, the software is trying to do the same, if they come up with different solutions, either of which could be right, how do we decide which one takes priority?"

"Ultimately, you have to let the pilots fly the plane. By all means have warnings that kick in. Have default states. Have pre-programmed routines. Whatever help and assistance the automated systems can provide to the crew, that should be done. But when the Captain of the aircraft, someone with tens of thousands of flying hours on which to call, when the Captain decides on a course of action, the software should not be able to override them."

'King' nodded, a suitably sombre expression on his face, but inwardly he was smiling. This was perfect! York had it all: the technical understanding, the ability to articulate it in a way that would get the message across to Joe Public and the moral authority that came from being the grieving husband of one of the victims of a crash that might have been caused by the fly-by-wire system.

'King' paused, and thought for a few moments. He made a decision. A relatively expensive one, but money had never been an issue for him, and this would offer extremely good value for money. He didn't, at that time, realise just how good.

"Danny," he said, "how strongly do you feel about this?"

"What do you mean?" replied Danny. "My wife of 23 days was killed in this crash – how strongly do you think I feel about it?"

"Forgive me," said 'King', "I phrased my question clumsily. What I mean is this. Suppose you didn't have to worry about what your employer thought. Suppose you were free to draw attention to your software expertise, so that the public could see that you know what you're talking about. Would you then be willing to do so?"

York nodded. "You mean once I receive 'compensation' from the airline?" He almost spat the word – it was an insulting one. As if mere money could in any way compensate for what he had lost. "Yes, I suppose then I could take a year or two out. If I wasn't currently working for anyone, then what I said wouldn't reflect on an employer. Provided I could make my case, which I think is a reasonable one, I don't think it would harm my future employment prospects. Unless it was with an aircraft manufacturer, of course!" He managed a small smile at that.

'King' smiled in return. "You wouldn't necessarily need to wait for the compensation," he said. "We're a small organisation, as I say, but we do have one or two generous benefactors." He saw no reason to mention that he was the only benefactor for an 'organisation' that had existed for a little over a week. "Suppose I talked to them, and they were willing to cover your salary for a year or two – plus whatever benefits you currently have, of course, we wouldn't want you to lose out financially – so that you could campaign on this full-time for a while. Would that have any interest for you, do you think?"

York's head was spinning. When he'd received the letter, he hadn't known what to expect, but certainly not this!

'King' interrupted his thoughts. "I'm sorry," he said, pleasantly. "That rather came out of the blue, didn't it?"

"Just a little!"

"Well, there's really no need to make a decision today. Let's enjoy lunch, you can mull it over for a few days and let me know. How's that? Now, let's turn our attentions to the rather more pressing matter of the menus! Would you like some wine?"

* * *

Most of the work done by Sarah Green and her colleagues in the Risk Analysis division was so-called Desk Research: working from paper documents and online searches. Government roles weren't the most glamorous or best-paying in the world, but there were some advantages: whatever document they wanted, be it a technical manual for an aircraft, screening processes at an airport, flight rosters, evacuation procedures ... when it was the Department of Homeland Security doing the asking, they got it.

Aircraft manufacturers, airports and airlines all provided total cooperation. Usually willingly – they all shared a common commitment to making commercial aviation as safe as it could possibly be – but Homeland Security had the powers to subpoena anything and everything it considered relevant should the need arise.

There were occasions, however, when desk research wasn't enough, when you needed first-hand experience of something, to see for yourself. This was one of those occasions: Green needed to see airliners under construction to get a real sense of how things worked and where the risks might lay. She went to see her boss.

The government had worked hard to learn the lessons of 9/11. One of them had been that in the various security services, the left hand too often didn't know what the right hand was doing. There were too many areas with no clear lines of responsibility, and two many layers of management, meaning that concerns expressed lower down got filtered through too many levels. The guys at the top would not even be aware of many of the concerns that had been raised.

That was the reason for forming the Department of Homeland Security. A single organisation with a clear remit and reporting lines kept as flat as practical. Usually, with twenty analysts in the Aviation section of Risk Analysis, there would be a Director of Risk Analysis (Aviation). Here, there wasn't: she reported directly to Thomas Wilkinson, Divisional Head, Risk Analysis.

Wilkinson was ex-FBI. Thorough, careful, cautious but not overly endowed with imagination. Looking older than his 58 years, he'd been a civil servant all his life, in law enforcement for most of it. An administrator for the past 18 years, he had a reputation for running a tight ship, managing budgets well and keeping his bosses happy with clear, crisp reporting. He liked to do things by the book, though Green felt his main interest these days was counting down the days 'til he was eligible for retirement on full pension in two years time.

It was an unfair characterisation. Wilkinson was no less committed to his work than Green, he'd simply been doing it for longer and had a better understanding of how things worked in government. Sure, he wasn't going to do anything dumb so close to retirement, but he would do his job, and do it well.

"I need to visit Boeing's factory in Everett," she told him.

"What for?" he asked.

Green explained that she was focusing on the aircraft construction phase, and needed to get a feel for things.

"Ok, get me a one-page memo by close of play today summarising the case and the costs, and I'll let you have a decision by the end of the week."

It was the sort of response Green had come to expect. No less frustrating for that, but generally he signed things off; he just seemed to feel that nothing was real unless it was provided in memo or report form.

* * *

Back at the loft apartment he liked to think had an 'of the people' feel, despite it's price-tag of well over a million, Fox took off his suit and with it his David King identity.

It had been a very successful lunch, he thought. He was sure York was going to accept his offer, and he could see him being an effective weapon in the propaganda war. Of course, his style and manner was a little pedantic, he needed a little more stridency in the message, but 'King' would get him some media training.

He was feeling optimistic.

* * *

Thomas Wilkinson returned his attention to the memo he'd received that morning.

To: Thomas Wilkinson, Divisional Head, Risk Analysis

From: Matt Hampton, Director, Department of Homeland Security

Subject: Resource Prioritisation Program

Reference: DOHS/BD/RPP004

Further to recent budgetary discussions, I'm pleased to say that it has been confirmed that the Department of Homeland Security will see its budget rise in line with inflation in the next fiscal year.

The Resource Prioritisation Program formed an important element in budgetary negotiations, and it is essential that we deliver on its promises. This means ensuring that resource allocation keeps pace with the different phases of our work.

As you know, we have been extremely pleased with the valuable work carried out by the Risk Analysis division, and feel that an excellent job has been done in identifying risk areas which are now being targeted by preventative measures. The view going forward is that your work is best supported by ensuring that adequate resources are applied to those measures. It has therefore been determined, in line with our previous budgetary discussions, that we will need to action a reduction of 10% in your division's spend in the coming fiscal year. I am confident that under your excellent management this can be achieved without any impact on the vital work done by your team.

Please have your outline proposals ready to present at the next meeting of the Divisional Heads on the 23rd. Thank you for your continued support.

Matt

The memo was a typical piece of government-speak: bad news disguised as good. The role of the Department of Homeland Security was growing all the time, with more and more objectives thrown at it. Hampton's claim to be 'pleased' that their budget was not being increased was a bare-faced lie: they needed a 15% increase and, knowing they weren't going to get it, had asked for ten. Instead, they'd got zilch, a cost-of-living increase.

The worst news was confirmation of what he'd argued so strongly against in all the budget meetings they'd had over the last few months: less money for risk analysis. Risk analysis was one of those unglamorous backroom divisions that was mostly felt to have done its job. But all the guff about having done a great job, and most of the risks now being understood, was all so much horseshit. The reality was that terrorists were always seeking new ways to attack, and every loophole closed simply meant they would look elsewhere. The role of Risk Analysis was to keep one or two steps ahead of the terrorists. To out-think them. To spend less money on that was so short-sighted, it was bordering on the criminally negligent.

It was all the more frustrating when he knew that 'preventative measures' was code for 'visible measures': things the public could see. There was a degree of complacency in some quarters, senior people who felt like they had most of the bases covered already and that the priority now was public reassurance. A lot of the money was being spent on putting uniformed personnel in airports, and ever more expensive screening technology against marginal risks, rather than on the fundamentals of figuring out what terrorists were likely to try next and how they could be stopped.

But Wilkinson had worked for the government for a long time. He knew how things worked, and he knew enough to recognise when a battle was lost. Up to a point, a divisional head stepping up to the plate for his team was respected, even admired. There was, though, a line you didn't cross – and that memo represented an unmistakable drawing of the line.

He wasn't obsessed with his pension, but he couldn't afford to ignore it either. It would be calculated based on a percentage of his average salary over the last three years of service, which meant three years of a Divisional Head's salary provided he remained in post. He wasn't going to be stupid about it.

He sighed and pulled up his divisional budget spreadsheets to figure out where the 10% cuts were going to come from.

* * *

Fox fired-up his laptop and downloaded his mail and quickly skimmed down the list of headers. He had several email accounts, each of which appeared in their own folders. In the SOS account under his David King identity, there was a message from York thanking him for lunch and saying he'd be in touch once he'd had time to think things over. He clicked onto his AOA account.

There was an email from one of his volunteers, but the subject-line looked suspiciously like spam. That was the trouble with having lots of teenagers involved: security wasn't their strong-point, so it wasn't unusual for them to have their email accounts compromised. It was another reason he kept things on an entirely 'need to know' basis. Compartmentalised. Protected.

He clicked on the email to be sure it was spam, and his virus-checker popped up: Virus detected – message quarantined. He hit the delete button and moved onto the next email. It was from a friend who was organising a demo in support of striking tube workers the following week. It was small beer, some stupid demo, but it all helped, and you never knew when you might need a favour, so he cultivated a reputation for always being there, always being willing to do his bit. He hit reply and started typing a response, confirmi–

Wait a minute. A virus. He knew of a few attempts at cyber attacks in the various green and anti-capitalist groups he'd been involved in, most of them aimed at banks and big business, but it was all very amateurish and he wasn't aware of any major successes.

But bugs in the fly-by-wire systems ... what if they could introduce one? What if they could get something into the systems that would wait for a certain date and then, next time they tried to fire-up the engines, nothing. All those airliners sat at their airports going nowhere! All those overweight businessmen and self-important celebrities and middle-class families jetting off to their holidays in Tuscany, all stranded on the tarmac. Wouldn't that be something?

It wouldn't be easy. It would need a sophisticated approach, not like the naive 'email a virus to a bank employee' or 'send someone an infected CD masquerading as evidence of an employee guilty of fraud' efforts he'd seen so far. It had been one of the weaknesses of the radical edge of the progressive movement: most of those involved were low-level grunts who were good for throwing things at windows but not much else. The minority who had brains, the ones who were capable of conceiving and executing meaningful attacks on the system, had positioned themselves solidly outside it. They had almost nobody on the inside, nobody who was in a position to orchestrate a meaningful attack from within.

Fox knew nothing about the detail of fly-by-wire systems, but it was obvious that it would be a major undertaking. It wasn't a job for some punk kid who thought he was god's gift to hacking. No, this would need a real software expert.

A real software expert. He had one of those! Or he thought he almost certainly did: within a few weeks, York could be on the payroll!

Of course, he was a 'useful idiot', someone who just wanted to fix one small thing and then carry on as usual, not someone who shared Fox's vision of a world without all the crap that was part and parcel of an energy-centric, materialistic culture. York wasn't a revolutionary, and wasn't out to defeat aviation in the way Fox was. There was no way he could be talked into this kind of operation.

But maybe with some misdirection ... ? After all, what better way to demonstrate the vulnerabilities of fly-by-wire systems than by using them to disable an aircraft? If York could be persuaded that this would be a small-scale but high-profile demo ... stranding a few airliners at the threshold of the runways, just before take-off, at some of the world's busiest airports: Heathrow, JFK, O'Hare, Schiphol, Charles de Gaulle ...

If there were some way of fooling York into thinking it would be just a few aircraft involved, while the reality would be grounding as many as possible, perhaps he could be brought on board?

Were there other technical ways to disrupt commercial aviation, he wondered? Cutting through chain-link fences and invading runways or climbing onto the tops of airliners was all very well for getting TV coverage and generating a few why-oh-why headlines in the *Daily Mail*, but the police response was always swift. They rarely disrupted things for long. If the green movement was ever to make a real impact, to change things for good, it needed to be much more sophisticated in its methods.

York had joked about being unable to work in aviation if he took on this public role – did that mean it was a possibility at present? Fox didn't know enough about software development to know how transferable the skills might be from telecoms to aviation. He should find a way to ask.

* * *

Jen Williams had sat impatiently through the pointless family breakfast summit a week ago, but she and her father alike knew when her mother meant business, so both of them had been on their best behaviour. No shouting, no swearing.

They both claimed to understand, both reckoned they'd been through the same thing when they were teens, but that was just so much crap. When they'd grown up, they had the whole world in front of them.

What kind of future was her parent's generation leaving her? They'd totally screwed the planet, and it was up to her generation to sort out the mess.

Even her friends, so many of them didn't give a fuck. Some of them were oblivious, others too cynical to do anything about it. She didn't blame the cynical ones so much. They were faced with such a huge task that it was easier to pretend that nothing could be done and just take what they could until the whole precarious system breathed its last. It took guts to face up to what had to be done, the changes that were needed.

Her mother tried to get her to agree not to bunk off school for the remaining two months of the term, and work hard to get the best grades she could. She wasn't willing to promise – unlike her father, when she promised something, she meant it. But she'd said she'd be better, and she meant that. She didn't see the point, but she understood it upset her mum, and she really wasn't trying to do that, she was just trying to do the stuff that mattered more.

Her mother had reluctantly accepted her vague commitment. Her father clearly wasn't happy, but from the top of the stairs she'd overheard him being warned to keep his cool and take it one step at a time. She'd enjoyed that.

At least there were some people who understood. People like Julian. It had been a while since he'd quizzed her on everything she knew about how the airline business worked. Since then, he was still just as friendly, but he seemed to have less time for her. She got the impression he had his inner circle, then the rest. She really wanted to be part of that inner circle, and whatever it took to prove her commitment, she was willing to do.

* * *

Wilkinson reviewed Green's memo, summarising the case for her planned visit to the Boeing factory near Seattle. He wasn't convinced it was necessary.

They had production manuals from both Boeing and Airbus. Photos and video footage of the production lines. She had only to pick up the phone to speak to a production manager to answer any questions she might have.

Wilkinson was more self-aware than people have him credit for. He had a good understanding of his strengths and weaknesses. He knew he was intelligent, dedicated, diligent. He knew he had a talent for connecting the dots. But he also knew that an investigation needed more than one type of personality. There were those who were good at following a chain of logic, and those who were good at taking a leap in the dark. Some worked well with just the facts of a case, others needed to get a feel for things. Like revisiting the scene of a murder some time afterwards. He'd never seen the point in that. He was happy visiting the murder scene at the time, then referring to photos and maps and diagrams. Others seemed to get some kind of insight from standing there afterwards, looking around. It made no sense to him, but he'd seen it work.

So as an administrator, he'd developed a guiding principle over the years. Provided people followed procedures, and were within guidelines, he was generally happy to let people work the way they wanted to work.

Of course, there had to be limits. You couldn't let people fly off all over the world on a whim, or spend vast amounts of time pursuing something which gave every indication of being a blind alley. So he'd formulated an unofficial policy for it: every member of his team got one indulgence, one opportunity to do something they felt was important, even when he disagreed. If they proved him wrong, and got results from it, then the counter was reset and they were eligible for another indulgence another time. If it achieved nothing, then that was their one shot: their future requests had to be things that made sense to him.

Green hadn't yet used up her first indulgence, so this could be it. He signed-off her request.

* * *

Green smiled wryly as she glanced down at her Economy boarding pass as she joined the back of one of the lengthy queues for Security. In her former role as a relatively senior manager in an airline, she'd been eligible for 'space available' upgrades when flying on business. In other words, if there was a spare seat available in First Class, she'd be upgraded. It wasn't automatic: airline employees were lowest priority, so if there was a frequent flyer with lots of miles flying in Economy, they'd be ahead of her in the upgrade queue. But she'd been upgraded more times than not.

Things were rather different as a government employee. Almost everyone flew Economy, and generally on the cheapest-available ticket. If that meant an indirect flight with a three-hour layover somewhere, then that was what they got.

But Green didn't mind. In her previous job, she'd been trying to save the airline money; here she was trying to save lives. She always felt a little pompous when she thought about it in those terms, but all the same it did give her a quiet satisfaction. There was only so long you could spend a third of your life doing something that you didn't feel really made a meaningful difference in the world. Whenever she flew anywhere, she was for a time transported back into her previous life. The contrast with how she felt now pleased her.

One thing hadn't changed, though: she never got to relax on the journeys! She always spent most of her time looking for holes in the security, flaws in the systems, weaknesses in how procedures were carried out.

As she looked across the zig-zagging queues, she saw them start the shoe-checks. This was when passengers were asked to remove their shoes and place them on the conveyer-belt to be x-rayed. The current security level called for 25% of passengers to be asked to remove their shoes for screening on a random basis. She glanced at her watch to see how long they did it for: they were supposed to keep it unpredictable.

Some time later, when she was close to the front of the queue, they stopped the shoe-checks. She looked at her watch again. Exactly 15 minutes. That was poor: doing a straight 15 minutes in an hour made it easy for a terrorist to size up the length of the queue and judge when the shoe x-rays would end. There were always one or two people in the queue who would stop and repack bags and let people past them. That was supposed to be noticed by the security staff, and flag them up for extra screening, but when there were masses of people jammed into the queues, it could easily pass unnoticed. She made a note on her phone to send an email about it.

Green spent so much time trying to think like a terrorist, paying close attention to the security procedures, that she always half-expected to get pulled aside on the basis of looking suspicious. Her Dept of Homeland Security ID should act as sufficient explanation, but she hadn't yet come to anyone's attention.

It wasn't part of her role to test security procedures, there were staff whose job was to fly from place to place doing just that. They would try different methods of circumventing the various special checks in place: laptops, shoes, liquids – and the ones that passengers didn't know about. Some of them would carry dummy weapons concealed in their hand-baggage. There were plenty of tests.

All the same, she couldn't resist a small check of her own. She took out her laptop, placed it in a tray and then placed her jacket on top of it. She was pleased to see the security woman notice, and ask her to place her jacket in a separate tray.

She was again alert at the gate, ensuring that the airline staff were checking photo-IDs properly; they were. Again, there were personnel who would arrive at the gate with a photo of someone else to see whether it was detected.

Opening the overhead locker to place her bag inside, she first checked to see whether there was any hole, any crack, in the plastic that would allow something to be slipped in out of sight. It was fine.

* * *

York had been thinking of little else but King's offer. It was such a big step, taking time out from his career, not knowing whether there would be a job waiting for him when he got back, and perhaps putting his future employment prospects at risk. King seemed to know what he was talking about when it came to the media, so he could end up with a very public reputation as a crackpot conspiracy theorist.

But without Stephanie, he had no life. He'd had no life before her, and only been half-aware of the fact: now he knew it. So, really, what did he have to lose? It was too late for him, and too late for Stephanie, but if he could save just one person from going through what he was going through, it had to be worth it.

He took King's card out of his wallet and picked up his phone.

* * *

Fox was at an AOA meeting discussing the idea of getting a flash-mob to occupy a terminal at Heathrow Airport. It was so much easier now to get a large number of people together, thanks to email networks, websites and social networking sites. They'd once organised a protest outside Shell's AGM at a couple of day's notice simply by creating a Facebook group. Over a thousand people had shown up.

That was the future of protests. Instead of an unimpressive straggle of people stretched out along the few miles of a demo route, you aimed to pack as many people as possible into a small area for a brief period of time. A thousand people in one place for half an hour made a much more impressive spectacle for the TV cameras than some ropey old march.

The plan at Heathrow was simple. A thousand or so people enter Terminal 1 posing as holidaymakers. They'd join the queues at check-in desks, making them enormously long. When they get to the front of the queue, they simply walk back and join the end of it again. The more committed types, who didn't mind being arrested for obstruction, would take it a stage further and go to the check-in desk, pretend to be searching their pockets for tickets and passports, or simply standing there refusing to move out of the way. Every time the police arrested one of them, a new protestor would take their place.

They could cause thousands, perhaps even tens of thousands, of people to miss their flights, or force the airlines to delay flights, with all the knock-on effects that would have. And, of course, Fox would quietly tip off a few friendly media contacts so that there would be TV cameras there to capture the chaos.

Flash-mobs were notoriously difficult to counter. The typical strategy was to alert people a few days in advance that something would be happening at a particular time and day, and a very rough location. They'd be asked to check a particular website address a few hours ahead for the exact location. Usually, the first the authorities knew about it was when the mob showed-up. Even if the police infiltrated an email list, they wouldn't know the location of the protest until 2-3 hours ahead, making it very difficult for them to put sufficient resources in place to tackle it. And in this particular case, protestors would be asked to take bags with them so they'd be indistinguishable from real passengers.

Fox felt a vibration in his left pocket. It was David King's phone. He ignored it: he couldn't answer the phone in the name of King while he was in front of AOA people. He let it ring out and go to voicemail. But right now, only one person had that number: Danny York.

Fox smiled inwardly. Experience had taught him that when you make someone an offer and they phone you, it's usually to accept. If they were refusing, they typically did so by email, whether fearing that they might be talked out of it, or simply wanting an opportunity to explain the reasons in their own words. The phone vibrated again to indicate a text, almost certainly a voicemail notification. Things were looking good.

He had to wait half an hour before he could bring the meeting to a close and excuse himself while the AOA activists hit the computers to start recruiting the protestors. He used the excuse of needing a cigarette to walk outside and down the street a little to check his voicemail. He didn't notice Jen following him out of the building and following some distance behind.

Jen was happy. She'd been able to contribute quite a lot to the meeting. It had been her suggestion that they target Terminal 1, because it was mostly short-haul flights to European destinations. These were the flights with least justification, where people should be taking trains instead, especially now that Eurostar connections made it so easy. More importantly, she'd been able explain that short-haul flights had the tightest turn-around times. Most aircraft on short-haul routes made four flights a day, for example London – Paris – London – Paris. Turnaround time – the time between a plane arriving at a gate and departing again – was typically in the order of 45 minutes. If passengers weren't at the gate on time, the aircraft might be forced to fly empty, or nearly so, in order to allow the return flight to depart on time. Delay the first flight of the day, and you delayed four flights. Delay the first flight long enough, and you could force a cancellation of at least one of the legs.

Julian had been pleased with her input. He'd originally planned to hit Terminal 3, which was all long-haul flights, and she'd really impressed him with her argument about being able to cause much greater disruption on short-haul routes. "That's brilliant, Jen," he'd told her. "Fantastic to have you on the team."

She'd never smoked, and in truth felt a little superior to those who did. A couple of friends had started smoking about a year ago because they thought it was cool; she just thought it was a waste of money even before you thought of what it was doing to your lungs.

She forgave Julian. He was such an amazing man, he had to have some faults! But when he'd told them he was heading out for a smoke, she decided a bit of teasing about it was a good way to flirt.

She'd intended to sneak up behind him with a "Hey!". It would give them a chance to chat alone. She wasn't dumb, she knew he was much older, even if he didn't seem it to her, and he wasn't going to be interested in her in that way. But she enjoyed the attention and approval he gave her, and a little recreational flirting couldn't hurt. She'd waited 20 seconds, then followed him out.

But before she could sneak up on him, he'd taken out his phone. She didn't want to interrupt, so held back. She was about 30 feet away, so couldn't tell that he was just listening to his voicemail. She just saw him end the call, and was about to rush up to him when he immediately dialled a second call.

He was obviously busy, so she decided to leave him a jokey voicemail about it. She selected his number from her phone's address book and pressed SEND. She could see he was on the phone, and expected it to go straight to voicemail. Instead, it rang. Then she heard the ringing tone of his phone from his pocket. How odd!

She hit END to cancel the call, and walked back inside. Why would he have two phones, she wondered?

'King' had picked up York's voicemail saying that he'd decided to accept the offer, and could they meet to discuss the details? Perfect. He called him back right away.

"Danny," said 'King', "I was so pleased to get your message. I'm absolutely delighted you've decided to accept."

"It was too good an opportunity to pass up, David. Do you really have the funding in place to make this possible?"

"It's all arranged," he assured York. "Either one year or two, whichever you like. And with six month's compensation whenever you decide to leave, so that you have time to get re-established afterwards."

"Well, that's fantastic!" replied York. "It's very generous. I really appreciate what you're doing, and please thank the donors for me."

"I'll do that, I know they'd be as delighted as I am that you've chosen to accept. Now, when are you free to meet?"

"As soon as possible," said York. "Maybe after work in the next day or two?"

"Let's have dinner tomorrow," replied 'King'. "I'll get a contract of employment drawn-up. How soon can you start?"

"Well, technically I'm on three month's notice, but I'm sure they'll be amenable to less. I'd already discussed the possibility of a sabbatical with my boss, and as I guess this will be a temporary post, I can just tell him I'd like to go ahead with that. Let me have an informal word tomorrow and then I can let you know."

"Perfect," said 'King', "you can let me know over dinner. I'll make a reservation and email you the details if that's ok?"

"Sure," said York.

"Excellent. Then I'll look forward to meeting you tomorrow. And welcome aboard!"

Fox hung-up, then checked the Missed Call display on his own phone to see who had called him. Hmm, that was strange: it was Jen. Why would she call him when he'd just left a meeting with her, and she knew he'd be back in a few minutes? He walked back inside to find out.

* * *

"We call that the Everett Stare," laughed Ron Turner, Production Chief at the Boeing Assembly Plant at Everett. "Everyone who stands where you're standing, and looks out at that sight for the first time, has exactly the same expression."

Green chuckled. She was standing on a walkway inside in the world's largest building. She'd been around airliners for most of her working life, and when she'd had occasion to visit an aircraft in its hangar the size of the building had never failed to impress her. But to stand inside a building and look down on three 787 Dreamliners, knowing that behind the partition to her left were another three, was something else entirely. The building also housed 4,000 office staff. The scale of it was hard to comprehend, even standing there inside it.

"Do you ever reach the stage where you're immune to it?" asked Green.

"Well, we grizzled old-timers like to pretend we are, but secretly I'm not above a bit of standing and staring when no-one's looking."

"Grizzled old-timer, indeed: you're younger than me!:

"You can't be a day over 25," smiled Turner.

"Better not let your wife hear you flattering the ladies."

"No, better not, I guess. And do I need to look out for a jealous husband?"

"Boyfriend. The term feels a little silly at my age, but I can't bring myself to use 'partner' or, far worse, 'significant other'. It's been a while since he's been jealous, though."

Her tone suggested to Turner that he shouldn't pry.

"Well, I guess I'd better start you on the grand tour."

They took an elevator down to ground level, bringing them to the rear of one of the three 787s. If anything, the size of the building looked even larger standing underneath, looking up at the ceiling way above the tail-fin. Turner gestured for Green to walk up the steps leading into the rear door of the first of the three 787s.

"We're all very proud of these," he said, when they reached the gantry at the top. "Composite body, 20% lighter than conventional aircraft alloys. As you know, lighter means better fuel consumption."

Green nodded; she was familiar with the economics.

Turner showed her inside, then continued: "The composites also mean a more airtight construction, enabling us to maintain a higher cabin pressure. That means passengers and crew alike get less dehydrated and arrive feeling less tired."

Green smiled: Turner was clearly used to visiting airline execs, and was slipping automatically into a sales pitch. She decided she'd better steer the conversation back on track.

"How many people have access to each aircraft during construction?" she asked.

"I'd need to check the numbers, but a lot. There are literally hundreds of different jobs going on here during final assembly."

"So how does security work around here? I mean, we just walked onto an aircraft without anybody checking who I am."

Green laughed. "Believe me, if you didn't have that pass round your neck, you'd have been approached half a dozen times before you got this far. The letter and colour-coding tell people where you are and aren't allowed to go – and there are very few visitors with that particular coding. Even with the pass, you need to be accompanied at all times by a full-time employee with the appropriate access. Security here is very tight."

"But suppose an employee who did have the appropriate access pass wanted to plant something on the aircraft. What's to stop them doing so?"

Turner called over to an employee who was bolting seats to the floor. "Hey Phil, can I borrow you for a second? Bring your work order, would you?"

The employee, in blue overalls, came over. "Help you with something, Mr Turner?"

"This is Ms Green: she's with Homeland Security. Just using you as an example," he said, seeing Phil look a little scared. "Show her your work order."

He handed over a clipboard. "Here," said Turner, "this sheet specifies exactly what Phil here is doing this shift. It specifies what time his shift starts, what time it ends, which aircraft he's working on, which areas of that aircraft he is working in, and exactly what he's doing. If he were on any other aircraft, or anywhere other than–" Turner turned the clipboard toward him to check. "–the rear cabin, questions would be asked. This section here shows which supervisor will sign-off on his work when he's done." Turner handed back the clipboard. "Sorry to disturb you, Phil, we'll let you get back to work."

Green persisted: "Ok, but say an employee was working on say the wiring that runs under the floors. They'd have legitimate access, planting something would only take a few seconds."

"Which would be immediately spotted when their supervisor checked the work."

"But suppose they shoved it under some wires?"

Turner smiled. "Ms Green, you probably know lots of stuff about airliners but it's clear you've never seen one being constructed."

"What do you mean?"

Turner flicked through the paperwork on the much thicker clipboard he carried. "Give me a minute here." He flicked through some more. "Ah, here we go. Next aircraft along. Follow me."

Turner led Green off the aircraft and then up the front steps of the next one in line. Halfway up the aisle, a woman in green overalls was kneeling on the floor with several of the floor panels off to one side. "Lynne Foster, this is Sarah Green, Homeland Security. She's worried about what happens if someone wants to hide something under the wiring there." Green was grinning, and Foster did the same.

"What's the joke?" asked Green.

Turner reached into a pouch on his belt and pulled out a pair of latex gloves. "Here, put these on and I'll show you."

Green put on the gloves.

"Now, kneel down here. Got your cellphone on you?"

"You know I don't, they took it off me at Security."

"Oh, that's right," he grinned. "Well, let's see." He flicked through his paperwork again until he found a memo concerning planned roster changes. He handed it to her. "You tear and fold this until you have the smallest possible device you could imagine being any threat."

Green considered the matter for a moment, then tore off a quarter of the sheet and folded it until it was about the size of a box of matches.

"Ok, Lynne, give me a hand lifting out the wiring harness, would you?"

The two of them lifted a section of the bundled wiring until it was a few inches above the duct it had been sitting in. "Ok, now put your 'device' in the ducting," invited Turner.

Green put it in the bottom of the ducting. "Squash it down tight," said Turner. She did so.

"Done," she said. Ron and Foster between them replaced the wiring harness on top of it. "Go ahead," said Turner, "push it down tightly." Green did so. There was no visible bump in the wiring.

"Hidden good?" he asked?

"Yes," she said.

Ron Turner gestured to the wiring technician, and they positioned one of the pieces of floor panel over the duct.

"See these clips?" he asked Green.

"Sure," she said.

"They just snap into those slots there. No tools needed, you only need tools to open them. Go ahead and snap the panel in place."

Green pressed down on it. It wouldn't snap into place. The floor panel was rigid, it didn't flex, so she couldn't even get part of it to snap into place. She gave up and sat back. Turner and Foster lifted the panel off, lifted up the wiring and Green retrieved her piece of paper.

"Thanks, Lynne," said Turner as they stood up and started walking down the cabin. "In aircraft design, nothing is heavier or larger than it needs to be. There's not a millimetre of wasted space. Almost every component on a modern airliner is custom-made. The bolts are aircraft grade alloy, for the optimum balance of strength and lightness. If a plastic part is strong enough, like those clips, they are made of plastic, because it's lighter. Every wiring duct is exactly the size it needs to be, and not even a fraction bigger."

Turner waved an arm at the plastic panelling at one side of the cabin. "You ask the average passenger what's behind those panels, and they probably think it's mostly empty space. The reality is it's solid insulation with wiring and air-conditioning ducts. No empty space at all." Turner's arm swept the cabin. "Fuselage, floors, ceilings, galleys, you name it, it's all the same. If there's a space somewhere, it's because something fits inside it, and is an exact fit. There are vanishingly few places you could hide anything that didn't belong there, and the inspections would spot them."

"So you're saying it's impossible to fit even a small device anywhere on an aircraft as large as this? That's hard to believe."

"There were instances of tools being left on board back in the pre-9/11 days. Things are very different now. I don't say it's impossible, but believe me, it wouldn't be easy, and the chances of doing so without it being spotted afterwards? Slim. Damned slim. C'mon, I'll show you the flight-deck, then the avionics bay and the holds. If you really want to, we can scare you up some overalls to crawl inside the fuel-tanks in the wings."

* * *

Wilkinson had been working on the budget spreadsheets for over three hours. While the media loved to give the impression of bloated government spending, most of the waste tended to be in large-scale mistakes. Entire IT projects that came in five times over budget and still didn't do the job they were supposed to do. Aircraft and other defence kit specced to fight the last war, rather than meet future needs. There were plenty of examples, but those obscured the fact that there were plenty of teams of people working efficiently on budgets far smaller than was the case in the typical commercial environment.

He'd so far found savings candidates for around 0.8%. Sure, he'd find more of them as he kept beavering away, but even if those survived closer scrutiny, there was no way he was going to get close to 10%. The only way to do that was to cut back on their most expensive commodity: staff. And those kind of savings weren't going to be achieved by reducing the number of cleaners or junior assistants. No, the only way to do it would be to lose two or three analysts.

* * *

"Hey, Jen," said Fox , walking back into the kitchenette where she was getting some coffee. "Looking for me?"

"Looking for you?" she asked.

Fox held up his phone. "You called me."

"Oh," said Jen, "yes." She felt embarrassed. The moment had passed. It was like one of those silly joking asides you made that someone didn't hear and asked you to repeat, or worse, explain. Many things might have been mildly amusing as a spontaneous comment, but didn't really survive repetition or explanation. Telling Julian she'd just intended to sneak up on him would sound way too lame.

At that moment, someone else walked in. She felt even less like explaining it in front on an audience.

"Oh, it was nothing."

Julian smiled. "What sort of nothing?"

"Oh, I thought you said that you were going to the corner shop for cigarettes, and I wanted to ask you to get me some mints. Then I realised you'd said you were just going out to smoke a cigarette." It sounded unconvincing even to her.

"Oh, I see." Julian smiled again. "No problem."

Jen took her coffee and excused herself before she made an even bigger fool of herself. Fox watched her go, a thoughtful expression on his face.

* * *

Green declined the offer to crawl inside a fuel-tank: she was happy to accept Turner's description and his promise to send her plans and photos.

Between the six aircraft in the plant, she felt like she'd inspected almost every inch. Cabins, flight-decks, avionics bays, holds. Wiring ducts, air-conditioning pipes, galley ovens, wardrobes, insulation materials, even poked around inside the landing gear wheel wells.

Turner seemed to imagine that her job was done, that he'd demonstrated the impossibility of the bad guys interfering with one of his planes. He didn't appreciate that her job was only just beginning. She wasn't going to accept Turner's assurances, she was going to examine the plans, study the photos and try to think like a terrorist. If she felt it justified, they might even try to get one or more covert agents a job in the plant to conduct some some practical tests of just how good security really was.

It wasn't that she suspected Turner of misleading her in any way, quite the reverse. But she knew the personality type. People like Turner were careful and methodical. They understood the way things were designed, knew the way things were meant to happen, and worked with people who were good at doing exactly what they were supposed to do. Such people didn't always think about what might possibly happen instead. That was her skill, her job.

'Trust but verify' was a commonly-cited motto in the security services. Supposedly first coined by someone in the USSR during the cold-war days, it had been adopted by President Reagan and done the rounds since then. She trusted Turner, but would verify for herself what might be possible with imagination and determination.

She'd asked Turner for some time to simply stand there silently inside one of the six aircraft – cabin, flight-deck and hold – to simply soak it in. Her main reason for being there at all was to get a feel for things, to spot the things that wouldn't be obvious from the countless pieces of paper that she would study over the coming months.

"You said the plant also houses 4,000 office staff," she asked Turner on their way out. "What do they all do?"

"Oh, a huge number of functions," he replied. "You can probably imagine the amount of paperwork involved in designing and building a new airliner. Well, actually, you can't. But if we stacked up all the pieces of paper into a 787-shaped block, the paper 787 would be way, way bigger than the real thing."

Green was thinking about the one step she'd skipped past on the flowchart: aircraft design. Maybe she could get a bit of a feel for that while she was there.

"Are the aircraft designers based here?" she asked.

"Some of them. Again, there's a whole host of design teams. What most people think of as the aircraft design, the fuselage and wings, is only one part of it. There are engine designers – they don't work for us, they're General Electric or Rolls-Royce, but some of them are based here. The interior designers. The flight-deck designers. The software designers."

"Software?" asked Green. "I knew Airbus aircraft were all fly-by-wire, but I thought you guys had a conventional design."

"The triple-seven and 787 are also fly-by-wire. But even before those, there were always a few dozen computers on board any modern airliner. There are autopilot computers, navigation computers, engine-management computers ... plus a bunch of things on the cabin side for things like in-flight entertainment and passenger Internet access."

"I see," replied Green. A thought occurred to her. "Say, the passenger computer systems, those are completely separate from the flight-deck computers, right?"

"Physically and virtually," replied Turner. "It's one of the things we have to satisfy the FAA about. I told you we don't have many empty spaces on an airliner, but that's one exception: we have to show the FAA there's an air-gap between the flight and non-flight computer systems, as well as software firewalls."

"Why do you need a firewall between them if they are physically separate systems?"

"Everything is networked. They all draw their power through the same systems, and some of the passenger systems, like the moving map, takes a data-feed from the flight navigation computer, so we have firewalls to ensure that stuff like that is all one-way data traffic."

"I see," said Green. "Could we take a wander through the offices of some of the designers? Not the interior, just some of the flight-critical ones, like airframe, engine and software."

Turner hesitated. "I guess," he said, "but I'm not sure what you'd learn. It's just a bunch of guys working away on PCs. Some pretty high-end PCs, admittedly, but it's not like standing inside an aircraft, you're really not going to see anything you couldn't see watching a bunch of people doing accounts or something."

"You're probably right, but humour me? As I say, this trip is all about getting a feel for things, and you'd be surprised what trivial things can spark a thought sometimes."

"Ok," replied Turner, "we just need to call back into Security to get you a different pass for that, and I'll make a few calls to see who's free to welcome visitors."

"I appreciate it."

* * *

Fox returned to his apartment, walked over to the desk and filing cabinets that formed the home-office corner of his apartment and unlocked the filing cabinet drawer for Safety in Our Skies.

So far, SOS had very little physical existence. An accommodation address. The computer server hosting the website, sitting in a data-centre in the Docklands. And the contents of this filing cabinet drawer. Now that York was on board, that would have to change: they'd need a small serviced office somewhere, and perhaps one or two administrative staff to make it seem more substantial.

The filing cabinet was in his apartment rather than at the AOA offices because Fox was a careful man. There were several keys to security, and compartmentalisation was one of them. Nothing where it didn't belong. Another was minimising the paper trail. He pulled out the slim file of papers he'd accumulated while researching material for the SOS website, ready to shred the ones he no longer needed.

He fed several papers into the cross-cut shredder next to his desk. He picked up the report on the crash of Flight 1951, the one used to reel York in. He reached towards the shredder with it.

And stopped.

Slowly, he pulled the hand containing the report back toward him. He placed it on his desk. He sat and stared at it.

His earlier idea had been to introduce some rogue code into the fly-by-wire system to ground aircraft, ideally all on the same day. It would be massively disruptive, and hugely embarrassing for Airbus, but they'd investigate, find the bug, fix it and everything would soon be back to normal.

And here he was looking at a crash which might have been caused by the fly-by-wire system. What if they did that instead? Instead of causing the planes to fail on the ground, have them fail in the air. Cause them to crash. That would foul things up for a hell of a lot longer than a few days.

Was he capable of that? How many people would die?

He logged-on to his PC and googled to see how many airliners were in the sky at any one time. Airlines liked to work their aircraft hard: the leasing costs were huge, so the more hours in a day they spent in the air, the lower the effective costs. He was shocked to see that around 2,700 airliners were in the air at any one time.

Christ, the aviation problem was much worse than he'd ever imagined! He realised that this was the main shock he felt: that the scale of the problem was so great, not the idea of killing so many people.

How many of those 2,700 were Airbus airliners, he wondered? Some googling on market share suggested that it was close to a 50/50 split between Boeing and Airbus. So call it 1300 Airbus airliners in the air at any given moment.

Thirteen hundred airliners. One thousand three hundred. Some more googling on passenger numbers. Average loading across long-haul and short-haul flights came out at around 250 passengers. Thirteen hundred Airbus airliners times 250 passengers each. Three hundred and twenty-five thousand passengers.

And it wouldn't end there. If those 1300 airliners dropped from the skies, some of them would come down on towns and cities. How many deaths on the ground? Christ, the total death-toll could reach half a million people. Could he really kill half a million people?

The idea was unthinkable.

But how many would die if we didn't radically change our lifestyle? Billions. Literally billions.

He thought again of those 1300 flights in the air at any one time. And those were just the planes in the air at any given hour of the day or night. Worldwide, there were 27,000 airline flights a day. Just airline flights. With private jets, cargo planes and smaller private planes, the total almost doubled. 27,000 airline flights today. 27,000 yesterday. 27,000 tomorrow. And tomorrow, and tomorrow, and tomorrow. It was utter madness.

One act, one unthinkable act, would change all that. Thirteen hundred plane crashes in one day? Look at 9/11. Four planes lost, and passenger numbers down for two years. What would be the result of one thousand three hundred plane crashes in one day? The aviation industry would never recover! It would take years just to replace the planes themselves, not to mention the pilots. And who in the hell would want to fly after that? After half a million people were killed in a single day! Nobody. All those self-important business people catching their flights, no amount of salary or bonus was going to induce them to fly again after that. The airline industry would be history.

He really could kill the airline industry! The thought of it was intoxicating. Imagine it. Just imagine it!

Half a million deaths would be regrettable, of course. But set against the billions that would be saved? It was a price worth paying.

It would be an incredible amount of work. Probably years in the planning. And there was no way York would be part of it. Not knowingly, anyway. But this was too big an idea to let go. There had to be a way to make it happen. There had to be.

* * *

Turner led Green through into Software Development. Green was surprised to see 40 or 50 people working in a huge open-plan area, with individual offices visible on both sides.

"Wow," said Green, "how many people work on software?"

"About 120 here, and hundreds of others in sub-contractors around the world."

"All of them working on the 787?"

"No," said Turner. "As you probably know, an airliner can have a working life measured in decades, and when we sell a particular model we guarantee to support it for a fixed lifetime, typically around 30 years."

"Sure," said Green, familiar with this from her airline days. "You guarantee to make spare parts, sort out any design issues that take time to emerge, offer servicing & repairs to airlines too small to do their own work and so on."

"Right, and that includes software updates. Sheena Blake's team here, for example, is working on an update to the 767 fault-logging system. Once that's complete and tested, it'll get shipped out to all our 767 customers for installation."

"How often do you update the software in an airliner?"

"Anything urgent would be done asap, but that's unlikely with a model as old as the 767 – anything major would have come to light by now. Routine updates are issued on a quarterly basis."

"How do the airlines install the updates? I don't recall seeing a DVD slot on any of the flight-decks," she laughed.

Turner smiled. "Nothing quite so newfangled as that. It's done via floppy disk!"

"You're kidding me?"

"Nope. Everyone thinks that airliners are very hi-tech complex things, and that therefore we have the very latest technology, but actually the reverse is true. The latest technology is by definition not tried-and-trusted. In the aviation industry, safety is all, and that requires reliability. Reliability means older technology, and once we have a solution that works and works well, we don't like to mess with it,"

"Makes sense," said Green. "What does this update do?"

"There are different levels of faults that can occur in the various systems. There are flight-critical ones, things the pilots need to know right away. A fuel-leak would be a particularly dramatic example. Those trigger the Master Caution system, so that the flight-crew gets an unmistakeable audible and visual warning. There are lesser faults that are not flight-critical, but the pilots may want to know about. Those throw up a warning light but aren't hooked into the Master Caution alerts. Then there are really minor things, that shouldn't distract the pilots, but still need to be fixed. Those just get logged. Some of them, category three faults, throw up an alert during the shutdown process, so that the flight-crew can let the ground engineers know about it right away, others are what we called Stored Fault Conditions. Those are things so trivial they can wait for the next routine maintenance, so only show up when the engineers plug in their diagnostic kit during servicing."

Green nodded.

"Sometimes the priority accorded to an alert will change. For example, one of the Stored Fault Conditions was the air-conditioning system going slightly out of range. Normally not a big deal, so it could wait for routine servicing, but we've had several instances of one particular component going from a minor fault state to complete failure within the course of a few flights, so we've upgraded it to category three, so now it gives an alert at shutdown."

"Ok," said Green, "and that's all this update does?"

"Oh no," said Blake. "There are always tweaks, even at this stage of a model's life, so there are always a number of small changes. There are seven in this one, all minor, so all will go out in the next quarterly update."

"And the airlines install them straight away?"

"There are different standards for different levels of update. If it's all Stored Fault stuff, they can leave it until the next service. There are tighter deadlines for categories two and three, while category one stuff has to be installed within 48 hours. An update is always classified by the highest category update. For example, if an update contains one category one fix and five category two fixes, the update all gets classified as category one."

"Thanks," said Green. "Interesting stuff."

* * *

2nd March

Danny York was feeling good for the first time since that awful night. He was finally in a position to try to get the issue in the public eye so that it would be properly investigated.

York didn't know much about how these things worked, but he imagined some stark warnings in press releases, a concerned media running stories, the regulatory authorities ordering a full-scale investigation into the whole safety of the fly-by-wire concept and finally major revisions so such a crash could never happen again.

His boss had been great, though York suspected this might have been down to the fact that he hadn't exactly been the most productive member of the team since Stephanie's death. He'd been told that he should take the rest of the week to do handovers, then he could take the rest of his three months' notice as 'gardening leave'. That had left him free to take up the SOS post from Monday, and 'King' was delighted when he'd shared the news over dinner.

"That's brilliant news, Danny! And perfect timing: we're just about to move into slightly larger offices."

"Will you be moved by Monday?" asked York.

"Yes, it's just serviced offices, so moving is a very simple affair."

"Great! So, um, where do I start? You'll appreciate this whole campaigning business is very new to me."

"We'll sit down on Monday and create a plan of action," said 'King'. "But essentially the first task is to combine our respective researches and write some hard-hitting press releases based on specific risk scenarios. We've got a good email database for both the general and aviation press, and we'll pick a few of them to wine & dine, see if we can sweet-talk them into a decent amount of coverage."

"I guess that will be mostly the aviation press?" asked York.

"Actually," replied 'King', "they're probably the toughest nuts to crack. They can be a bit too close to things to necessarily see the bigger picture. No, the tabloid press is likely to be our greatest ally: they love a good sensationalist story."

York frowned. "You know the publicity business, of course," he said, "but I'd hope we could interest the serious press. Surely we need some sober reporting if we're going to get the FAA and CAA to take the matter seriously?"

'King' realised he was going to have to tread carefully. "We want both, of course, but we mustn't lose sight of the fact that the regulatory authorities mostly do what the politicians demand of them, and politicians do whatever they think matters to the public. A Daily Mail headline is worth a hundred dusty old reports." He smiled and half-shrugged in a placating gesture: "It's not the way it should be, I agree, but ultimately we have to do what works."

"I suppose you're right. I just don't want us doing things in a distasteful manner."

'King' patted his arm. "Don't worry, I give you my word that we won't issue a single press release without your explicit approval."

York felt relieved, feeling confident that 'King' would be true to his word. He was correct in this, but would have been confused and concerned had he known the reason.

'King' walked into the serviced offices on the 21st floor of an office block close to Victoria Station a little after 8am on Monday morning. He'd had a busy week.

The offices had been the easy bit: the company he'd approached was a huge one, with a few dozen locations across London and a promise of 'sign today, move in tomorrow.' He'd chosen the location as somewhere central and respectable, but not too ostentatious.

Staffing had proven more tricky. He'd needed a couple of people to lend an air of plausibility to the organisation, but the last thing he wanted was anyone who would actually achieve anything. The game-plan had changed.

He could have used some of the people from his network, but the new goal was too big to risk involving anyone who might give away anything to York. He had to bring in people who knew nothing of who he was or what his plans were.

He'd opted for a geek to run the website, create a forum and do some web-searches, and an office administrator. There were no shortages of candidates, and he'd chosen carefully. Gary Andrews was an unkempt Goth of 23. His social skills were on a par with his interview technique: 'King' had asked him how he liked to spend his spare time, and had been treated to an enthusiastic description of the joys of the online game World of Warcraft. Jade Robins was 19 and had been through three office admin jobs in the past twelve months. When asked about this, she admitted that she'd lost her last job for spending too much time on Facebook, but explained that she'd had little to do and didn't think they'd mind so long as she got her work done. 'King' had told her she needn't worry here, as that was his attitude entirely. He'd made sure both were aware the organisation didn't believe in monitoring staff Internet usage. He felt certain neither of them would have trouble filling their days, and were unlikely to come volunteering for extra work when they found their workload light.

While most organisations these days opted for open-plan offices, 'King' had told the serviced office company that he was old-fashioned about these things and preferred individual offices. A corner office for himself, a large office for York, both window offices with impressive views over the West End, and two smaller offices without windows on the other side of the corridor for Andrews and Robins. That way he could work privately, and there was limited opportunity for the others to chat and get too curious about what the organisation was or wasn't doing.

York arrived at 8.30am; he was keen. He was carrying a thick file of papers, and an external hard drive.

"I've brought in my various research materials," explained York.

"Excellent," replied 'King'. "There's a laptop on your desk, so why don't you get settled-in, copy your files across, sort out your paper files and we can meet in my office at 10am to plan our strategy for the next few weeks."

"Sounds good."

"If you'd like tea or coffee, there's a kitchen area just down the corridor to the left."

"Great," he said, "see you at ten."

York walked into his office, dropped the papers on his desk and put the USB hard drive next to his laptop. He looked around the office, then walked over to stand at the window, looking out over London. It was quite a view.

Before he'd met King, if someone had suggested to him that might take on a role in a campaign group for a time, he would have envisaged it as a sacrifice. Maybe a quarter of his salary. A tatty desk in some pokey little office in Hackney. A dilapidated old desktop PC probably still running Windows XP and OpenOffice.

He'd gladly have done it, if it gave him the opportunity to play his part in preventing another tragedy like the one that killed Stephanie, but there was no sacrifice here. He'd swapped his cubicle in an open-plan basement office for his own spacious office with a fantastic view. His laptop was a brand-new high-spec one. The office decor was clean, modern, attractive. And he was on the same salary as before, with three months' gardening leave cash in the bank.

He shrugged off the momentary feeling of guilt at the pleasure he felt, then sat down at his desk to get settled-in.

"Here's how I see things," said 'King' as they sat in his office for their strategy meeting. "As I mentioned over dinner, nothing will change without the public caring about it, and to make people care, we have to frighten them a little. It's not how we'd like to do things, but believe me, it's a lesson we've learned the hard way in the campaigning game. Ultimately it's all PR and marketing, and for safety issues fear is what we're selling."

"Have you been involved in campaigning for a long time?" asked York, realising he knew little of King's background.

"A while," said 'King', briefly. "Actually, I started out in marketing, but soon found I needed to be doing something more meaningful, so decided to put the skills to better use. Now, what I think we need is to have an initial series of say three press releases, all addressing the fly-by-wire issue, but coming at it from different angles."

"Ok."

"For maximum impact, I suggest we lead with the Flight 1951 crash. I know that's going to be hard for you, but it's an actual crash with deaths. So far the public has been fed a story of pilot error. They haven't heard much if anything about the role of fly-by-wire systems. We need to see if we can correct that. 'Flight 1951: the untold story', that kind of thing."

"Don't worry about it being hard for me," said York, "this is why I'm here. But do you really think we can get the media to pick up on it again at this stage? They seemed to very quickly treat it as old news once the interim report was published."

"It won't be easy, but I've got a few friendly journalists I can talk to." 'King' paused, and gave York a direct look. "It would help a lot if you're willing to tell your own story. A plane crash is dramatic when it happens, but afterwards is just a piece of old news. A widowed husband, struggling to cope after the crash, that's a human interest story that makes it fresh news. Do you think you'd be willing? It would be a few paragraphs of quote, just talking from the heart, letting people know why this matters."

York hesitated only for a moment. "It's not the sort of thing that comes naturally to me, talking about my feelings, and I'm not sure I could do it in an interview, but in a press release, yes. You're right that it's why the issue matters."

"Excellent. So that's our first press release. Do you have thoughts about other angles?"

"Well," replied York, "another might be the fact that even pilots have expressed concerns about it. I downloaded a lengthy thread about it on a professional pilot's forum, but I don't know whether any of them would go public. Do you have any contacts among flight crews?"

"It's the next thing on my agenda," said 'King'. "I'm going to be commissioning some market research which I think should assist."

"Market research?" asked York, puzzled.

'King' smiled. "Yes, everyone thinks of clipboards and questions about soap powders, but market research is also used to explore industry views. We'll find a company to organise some focus groups and one-to-one interviews with pilots and airline engineers. At the very least, we'll get some anonymous quotes, but hopefully we'll also find one or two willing to go on the record."

"Sounds very well thought-through."

"I have a certain amount of experience," said 'King'. "Now, any thoughts on a third angle?"

"Well, it's related, but there's been at least one other crash where fly-by-wire was implicated, at least by some, and a number of incidents. But if we're citing pilot concerns, I guess that will include those."

"Don't worry about that," said 'King', "that's just a question of the right slant. The second release focuses on the fact that pilots are worried, and the third goes into chapter and verse on the French crash and anything else we can find. Gary can help out with further web-searches." York had been introduced to both Gary and Jade earlier.

"Alright. So, how does this work? I've never written a press release in my life!"

"You draft them and then I'll review them. Once Gary gets in and sets up the email, I'll send you a how-to guide and a couple of examples, but it's pretty straightforward for a logical-thinking chap like you. A good press release mimics the structure of a news story. It's a pyramid structure: the headline and opening paragraph summarise the whole story, then each successive paragraph goes into increasing detail. The idea is that an editor can cut it off at any point, and you'll always have told the whole story, you only ever lose some detail. You'll see what I mean when I send you the examples."

"Ok," said York. "What else do we need to cover?"

"I think that's all we need discuss for now. The main thing is to review your research, make sure we've got our facts straight, and then get those releases written. We ideally want to put out one a week, so we keep the momentum going."

York was surprised. He hadn't known quite what to expect from the meeting, but certainly something more than a 10-minute discussion. But everything King said made sense, so maybe that really was all they needed to cover for the moment.

"Fine," he said, "I'll get some tea and then set to work!"

"Just let me know if there's anything else you need, and do call on Gary for any web-searching help you need – I want you focused on communication, you can delegate any of the grunt-work."

While York returned to his office, 'King' turned to his laptop and went to google, typing in 'market research aviation'. He selected UK results, and quickly found a market research agency specialising in the aviation sector. The call he was about to make was a perfectly innocent one: to commission the market research he'd described to York. He had a different objective in mind, but the research would be exactly as he'd described it.

"My name is David King," he said, when the call was answered. "Could I speak to someone about commissioning some focus groups or depth interviews, please?"

He waited to be connected.

"Mr King? I'm Wendy Baker, I understand you're looking for some qualitative research?"

"That's right. I head a campaign group called Safety in Our Skies, and we're interested in getting some expert views on flight-deck automation."

"That sounds fine," she said. "Is it airline pilots we're after?"

"Pilots and engineers. They need to work on Airbus aircraft, as we have a particular interest in fly-by-wire systems."

"Ok, are there any additional screening criteria?"

"The engineers need to work on the fly-by-wire systems. We need to get an understanding of exactly how those systems are controlled, how faults are identified and fixed, that sort of thing."

"And the pilots?"

"I'd like you to find ones who have misgivings about the amount of automation on modern airliners, especially in the area of fly-by-wire. I've done some forum searches, and most of them seem to prefer flying by hand to letting the autopilot do it, but if possible I'd like those who think there may be dangers in going too far down the automation route."

"We'll see what we can do," said Baker. "These are obviously quite hard-to-reach respondents, with shift work, travel and so forth, so we'd suggest depth interviews rather than focus groups if that is ok?"

"I'm happy to take your advice on that, but it's likely that we'll have some follow-up questions, so if we go the depth interview route it would be helpful if you could feed the transcripts through to me as the interviews are completed so that I can let you know what else we need to know."

"Fine, if I can just take some details, I can put some ballpark costs together for you and we can then discuss things in more detail if you'd like to proceed."

'King' gave her his SOS number and email address. He smiled to himself; Marx wrote that capitalism contained within it the seeds of its own destruction, and here he was using part of aviation's marketing arm to help bring about the destruction of a very large portion of the industry.

It took York a couple of days to draft the press release. Part of that time had been debating with himself the tone the release should take. King had advised him to be definite in the main body of the release, saving any hedging for the more detailed 'Information for editors' section which would explain the background. York still felt a little uncomfortable with the approach, but he understood the thinking and had decided in the end to go along with it.

THE CRASH OF FLIGHT 1951: THE UNTOLD STORY

The crash of Istan Air Flight 1951 at Amsterdam's Schiphol Airport on 21st March blamed on 'pilot error' was partly the fault of on-board computers still fitted to thousands of similar airliners, according to the official report.

Although the crash investigators found that pilot error was the primary cause, they also found that the Captain of the aircraft was fighting with the automated fly-by-wire systems as he battled to bring the stricken airliner to a halt. On-board computers were found to have cancelled the reverse-thrust Captain Berker was using to slow the aircraft. The result was the Airbus A320-100 plunging into a ditch, killing 17 people.

So-called fly-by-wire aircraft do not allow pilots to control the plane directly. Instead, they effectively use controls to tell the on-board computers what it is they want to do, with the computers making the final decision – including overriding the Captain in some circumstances.

Campaign group Safety in Our Skies (SOS) today calls on the government to carry out a full public enquiry into the safety of fly-by-wire airliners before there are more crashes and an even higher death-toll.

Danny York, who lost his wife of just 23 days in the crash, said:

"My wife Stephanie died because a computer thought it knew better than the Captain of the aircraft how best to avert disaster. This crash has had a devastating effect on my life, and the lives of Stephanie's family and friends. No-one who has not experienced it for themselves can possibly understand the pain of having a wife cruelly taken away. We must act before other lives are lost."

The 'Information for editors' section ran to three pages. It explained how fly-by-wire systems work, and went into greater detail about the exact circumstances leading up to the crash. It included the relevant excerpts from the interim report into the crash, and links to photos of the crash available from PA and Reuters. York had been careful to keep this section calm and factual, even a little dry, to assuage the slight guilt he felt over the rather bold phrasing of the main text.

King's office door was open, and he looked up as he saw York standing there, printout in hand.

"You've written it?" asked King.

"Yes."

"Fantastic! Let's take a look, shall we?"

York handed it over and sat in one of King's visitor seats. King held the release in both hands as he read it. He nodded enthusiastically as he read the headline and opening paragraph. He nodded again as he read the rest of the first page.

"Great. This is really good, Danny, exactly what we need to get the media to take the issue seriously."

He skim-read the 'Information for editors' section. "Fantastic. I don't think we need change a single word of it."

"Really?" asked York. He'd fully expected to have to do battle over the somewhat academic wording of the supporting text.

"It's the perfect balance. You have the strong appeal in the main story, then all the facts and figures in the background. Really, I'm going to send it out just as it is."

"That's great," said York, still a little surprised. "When will we send it?"

"No time like the present. Email it over to me and I'll email it out to our media distribution list right now. Send a copy to Gary too, so he can add it to the website. Tell him we'll need a Press Releases section, and he should put it in there as a PDF."

"Ok! I'll do that right away."

York returned to his office, emailed it to both men and then went to see Gary to explain about the PR section they wanted to add to the website.

King opened the email with the attached press release. With a small smile of satisfaction, he clicked the Delete button. The press release wasn't going anywhere.

* * *

In the Action on Aviation offices, Jen Williams was looking forward to the Heathrow protest. It was a way of hitting out not only at the aviation industry, but also at her father. She intended to make sure she was visible on TV, and if he was concerned that someone in his stupid airline would recognise her and cause him embarrassment, then tough.

She was still feeling pleased that she'd been able to impress Fox with her suggestion to hit short-haul flights, and had been thinking hard about other suggestions she could make. She'd come up with what she felt was a fantastic addition to the plan.

"What if we bought cheap tickets for a handful of the protestors? That way, we could get them through Security and into the departure lounge. While the rest of us are causing chaos at check-in, they put bags down at various locations and walk off: in the main departure lounge, in toilets, shops, at gates ... we could create multiple bomb-scares!"

"Yeah," said Fox, "could do." He sounded distracted.

"We might even get the terminal evacuated," she enthused. "Imagine that, the whole of Terminal 1 evacuated!"

"It might work," said Fox, "but they're going to know all those bags have been through Security, so I'm guessing they'll take a quick look at the contents, take away the bags and that will be the end of it. Unless we gave the bags suspicious-looking contents, but then that would be detected at Security anyway. Let's just stick to the plan."

Jen felt bitterly disappointed. She'd been excited at the idea, and had felt sure Julian would be enthusiastic. Why wasn't he?

He hadn't been around much in the last week, and when he was, he seemed distracted. Was it a girl, she wondered? Was he seeing someone?

Jen's heart was racing. This is dumb, she told herself. What did it matter whether he was seeing someone? It wasn't like he was going to be interested in her, even if she was 16 in two months. Following him? What the hell was she thinking. Apart from anything else, last time she'd just followed him into the street it had ended in an embarrassing conversation – what was she going to say to him if he caught her following him home from the meeting?

He headed down into the tube station, and she fought to keep him in sight without getting too close. By the time she reached platform level, she'd lost sight of him. Most of London's tube network was old, predating the modern metro style of escalators down onto a central platform with tracks on either side. Instead, the escalator ended in an enclosed central area, with brick archways leading onto separate platforms for each direction.

She looked through each archway. He wasn't in sight. The only way to see which way he'd gone was to walk through the archway. If he was standing close to it, he'd see her. She shrugged; she'd act like she was just catching the tube.

She tried the northbound platform first. She tried to look casual as she glanced to her right. No sign of him. She could hear the train approaching on the opposite platform. Adopting a bored expression, she looked round to her left. Nothing – he had to be on the other side.

As the tube train rushed into the opposite platform, she hurried over. She looked left: there he was! Three or four carriages down. As the tube doors opened and he got on, she ran down the platform to get into carriage next to his. If she stood at the end of the carriage, she should be able to spot him through the windows in the carriage-end doors.

She positioned herself by the end door and again affected the bored look of the commuter as she glanced through. The carriage was moderately crowded, with a number of passengers standing, and she couldn't spot him. She adjusted her position to take a look from a different angle. There! She could just see the top of his head, over the head of a slight shorter passenger in between them. Without his distinctive blond mane, she didn't think she would have been able to identify him.

The tube stopped at several stations before the man in front of him got off, and she got a clear view. It wasn't him! The hair she'd been looking at instead belonged to a woman in her 40s! Damn! She looked around the carriage, hoping he hadn't got off at one of the intervening stations.

There! There he was, just getting off and turning away, down the platform of Victoria station towards the exit. The doors were starting to close. She lunged for the door, getting her left arm and part of her shoulder in the closing gap. The woman to her left tutted loudly, but a man behind her reached over and helped her push open the door. She smiled her thanks, then hurried down the platform. She didn't want any more mistakes, so closed up on him.

Fortunately the crowds at Victoria made it easy to get close while still being able to use the mass of people as camouflage. She followed him up to street level, then dropped back as the crowds thinned. She saw him walk into a tall office-block. She gave him a few seconds, then followed in through the doors. He touched a pass to the electronic barriers and walked through, disappearing round a corner to the elevators. Now what?

She got her mobile out. Teenagers might know little about following someone, but they did know how to buy a little time when you didn't want someone approaching and talking to you. She walked as far to the left as she could. She couldn't see him, but could see two of the elevators and a woman waiting. Pretending to make a phone call, she waited.

An elevator arrived and the woman got in, followed by Julian. She ducked back as he turned to face the closing doors. She watched the numbers on the display. The elevator stopped at the 2nd floor. She kept watching. It stopped again on the 16th floor, then again on the 21st. Then she saw the numbers count down as it returned to the ground floor.

Still feigning a phone call, she looked around for the panel that would tell her which companies were on which floor. She spotted the aluminium board behind reception. The 2nd floor was blank. The 16th floor was a firm of lawyers – she recognised the LLC suffix. The 21st floor was something called Regus. She made a mental note of the names of the company, then turned and left.

Turning to face the elevator doors as he pressed the button for the 21st floor, Fox glanced back at reception. He spotted a young woman in reception jump back as he did do. He only caught the briefest glimpse, but he thought he recognised her. He quickly punched the button for the 2nd floor as the doors closed.

Alighting on the 2nd floor, he hurried across to the stairwell and ran down the stairs to the ground floor. He looked out at reception just in time to see her exit through the door: it was Jen Williams.

Watching her walk away, Fox slowly turned back to the elevators. As he headed up to the SOS offices on the 21st floor, he swore. He'd been an idiot, trusting her! Her father was an airline pilot, for chrissakes, and he'd fallen for her line that she just wanted to use that info to help oppose the aviation industry. Clearly that wasn't the case: she was just trying to learn what she could.

A mole in AOA was one thing, but now she'd connected him to these offices. That could blow the whole plan.

He regretted the decision he needed to make. He had liked her, when he'd thought she was genuine. But this was too big a security hole. It needed firm action. He had a phone call to make.

Jen hadn't been any wiser after she'd googled Regus: it was a company providing serviced offices. Whatever it was, it was clear it was a business meeting rather than a liaison, so she'd put it from her mind.

She'd given herself a good talking-to on her way home. Whether or not Julian was involved, chasing him – literally as well as metaphorically – was ridiculous: if he'd been interested in her, he'd have made it clear by now. But the lecture hadn't entirely succeeded: there were times when he did seem to pay particular attention to her. Take today. The Heathrow protest was being planned in strict secrecy, with just a handful of AOA activists in the know, and he'd picked her as one of them.

She knew part of it was her knowledge of the aviation industry, such as it was, but he could have quizzed her in a general way. Instead, she was one of just five people who had been invited to all three of the planning meetings, and today, in the final one, they were going to be told the date and time.

"Hey Jen," smiled Julian as she walked into the meeting room. "Ready for the big day?"

"Absolutely!"

"Great. You've just got time to grab some coffee, we're going to start in a couple of minutes."

"Can I get you one?" she asked.

"I'm good," he said, with a smile, indicating the mug in his hand.

"Oh, yes, sorry! I'll just get one for myself."

Idiot! She cringed as she walked to the kitchen. She quickly made a coffee and walked back into the meeting room, picking a seat well away from Julian and telling herself her main priority in this meeting was not to do anything else to make herself look dumb. Sitting still and keeping her mouth closed seemed like the best plan.

Julian stood up, closed the door and then returned to his seat. He looked around the table and smiled.

"Wednesday," he said. "An email has just gone out letting people know that there will be a flash-mob protest on Wednesday morning, and they should be ready to leave home at 8am, checking their email then for the location." He grinned. "Ideally, we'd want the protest to start at 6am to catch the first flights out, but I didn't think we'd manage to get many activists out of bed quite so early!"

They laughed, but they all knew it was an issue. There were times when the most effective time for a protest was first thing in the morning. There was a hard-core of supporters who'd happily stay up all night if needed, but when you needed hundreds of people, well, you had to work with what you had.

"The email will explain the plan, ask them to bring one or more bags and tell them to get to Terminal 1 at 10am. We always have to assume the authorities have managed to infiltrate the list, so by 8am they'll know the plan, but that leaves them very little time to prepare – and the beauty of this one, is they won't be able to tell the protestors from the passengers."

They all smiled at that.

"Mostly the protest will take care of itself, but I do have a couple of extra things planned. Jen had a good idea the other day, and I'm afraid I was rather distracted and a bit dismissive of it at the time."

Jen was startled.

"My apologies, Jen. Her idea was to abandon some bags in other parts of the airport to create some bomb-scares. Her initial thought was to buy some cheap tickets to get people through Security into the Terminal 1 departures lounge, but I think we'll successfully bring Terminal 1 to a halt anyway. So, the bomb-scares will be in other terminals. Three of you will find a crowded place in a terminal, put your bag down and then walk away. Nigel, you do Terminal 3, Jan Terminal 4 and Helen Terminal 5."

"What about Terminal 2?" asked Jan.

"That's closed for renovations. When you've dropped your bag, give it ten minutes to see whether a member of the public reports it. If not, just mention to a cop that you saw an unattended bag and point them towards it."

"Do we want to coordinate times for that?" asked Helen.

"Yes, let's go for 10.30am, so everything's happening at once. So go straight to your respective terminals at 10am, identify a suitable place – ideally you want somewhere temporarily crowded, so you can drop the bag unnoticed but it will be spotted when the crowd thins out, anywhere with a big travel group is good for that – then drop the bag at 10.30 and report it if necessary at 10.40."

"What about me?" asked Jen, feeling pleased that he'd taken up her idea but a bit annoyed that he didn't seem to be involving her in the plan.

"I have a special role in mind for you, Jen. Are you willing to risk arrest? Not for anything major, just breach of the peace or some other nonsense like that."

"Yes," said Jen, immediately. Willing? Daddy have to come and fetch his daughter from a Police station? She'd love that.

"Cool. We're going to be creating chaos in the terminals, I want you to add the icing on the cake: disrupt the Heathrow Express."

The Heathrow Express was the fast rail link between Heathrow and central London. It was the quickest and most expensive way to get to & from the airport. The protestors would be taking the slower and cheaper Piccadilly Line tube, or a bus.

"Sure," said Jen, "what's the plan for that?"

"I'll assign a small group of people to you. Your job is to stand on the platform, close to where the train emerges from the tunnel, and you'll all frantically wave it down as if there's an emergency. The driver will hit the brakes, get out and come back to investigate. Meantime, you and your team cross to the opposite platform and do the same thing to the train going the other way. It will probably be some time before they are satisfied that nothing is wrong, at which point, once the trains start running again, you do the same thing to the next train in. Just keep at it as long as possible. Game?"

"Definitely," she said.

"Perfect. You'll start on Platform 1 of Heathrow Central at 10am. Are you bringing friends with you?"

"One, my best friend, Alison."

"Ok," said Fox, "I'll assign about a dozen more protestors to your team, so the driver sees multiple people flagging them down and it looks convincing.

We want to make sure the drivers see you – do you have something very bright you can wear?"

"I've got a yellow coat – would that do?"

"That will be perfect," he replied, smiling.

Fox waited until he was back in his apartment before he made the call.

"Yes?" said the brisk voice at the other end of the line.

"No need for names on the phone," said Fox. "You did a little job for me last year, on Waterloo Bridge."

"I remember."

"I have a similar assignment for you. This one needs to look like an accident, but that should be straightforward. The target will, rather helpfully, be positioned on the edge of a railway platform as a train emerges from the tunnel."

The person on the other end of the line chuckled. "I won't ask how you've arranged that."

"No," said Fox. "Are you ready for the details?"

"Go ahead."

"Wednesday morning, 10am. Platform 1 of the Heathrow Express at Heathrow Terminals 1 2 3. There will be a small group of people who are going to stand close to the tunnel exit to flag down the train. One of them is a young woman with black-and-pink hair who will be wearing a yellow coat. She needs to end up under the wheels of the train."

"Making it look like an accident costs extra," said the voice. "Twelve grand in all. As before, half in advance."

"That's fine," said Fox. "I can drop the money in the same place. Tomorrow night, 1am?"

"Ok."

"Pleasure to do business with you."

"I aim to please."

* * *

On Wednesday morning, Jen was excited. She'd been to several protests before, but never one that she'd helped to plan, and where she would be playing such an important part. She quickly showered and dressed.

"You're up early for a change," said her mother.

"I'm meeting up with Alison in the school library – we're comparing notes on our history assignments before we hand them in. I, uh, missed a few classes, so want to check some facts."

Emma Williams gave her daughter a strained smile. "Well, it's progress of a sort."

"Yeah," said Jen, keen to escape before she had to make up any details. "See you later."

She grabbed her bag and leather jacket and dashed out of the house. She was halfway to the tube station before she realised she was supposed to be wearing her yellow coat.

Did it really matter? The driver was going to have a dozen people waving him down, and if she went back now she risked being questioned by her mum on the fictitious history assignment. Her mother might also wonder why she'd come back to swap her leather jacket for a coat she hardly ever wore these days.

And Alison seemed to wear that cream jacket of hers all the time. That would be good enough, surely? So long as the driver clearly spotted them.

But she had promised Julian, and she wanted him to be pleased with her role in the protest, so she swore and turned round to get her coat.

Jen had met Alison in the ticket office of their local tube station, and they'd caught the Piccadilly Line out to Heathrow Terminals 123. She wasn't supposed to tell anyone the plan until they got there, but Alison was one of her best mates. She'd been good so far, she hadn't even told her where the protest was going to be, but now, on the day, she could finally show-off about being so central to things.

"Listen," she said as they reached the platform, "the main protest will be in the airport, but you and I, and a few others, are playing a special role."

"We are? How do you know?"

"Because I helped plan things. I was at all the meetings."

"You and your 'boyfriend', you mean?"

Jen wished she'd never mentioned Julian to Alison. She hadn't said anything about her feelings for him, but Alison knew her too well. "Don't," she said.

"Ok, ok, so what are we doing?"

Jen filled her in on the plan, before adding: "We might get arrested, just for obstruction or something, are you cool with that?"

"Hell yeah."

The two laughed, as the tube pulled in and they got on board.

* * *

"DS Phipps," said the detective, as he picked up the phone.

"It's Darren."

"About time I heard from you," said Phipps. "You've been slacking lately – what have you got for me?"

"A protest – a big one – at Heathrow."

"Ok, when."

"10am."

"Today?"

"Yes."

"Why the hell have you left it until now to tell me?" Phipps looked at the clock on the wall opposite. "That's in less than two hours!"

"The email only went out at 8-o'clock, Mr Phipps! We were told a few days ago that there would be a protest this morning, but no details as to where, and you weren't very impressed last time I told you something was happening but I couldn't tell you where."

Phipps grabbed a pen. "Ok, 10am at Heathrow, where?"

"The email just said to go to the Terminal 1 check-in area."

"And then what?"

"That's all they've told us – you know how these things work, Mr Phipps."

"Yeah, maybe."

"So fifty quid, Mr Phipps?"

"It's scarcely worth it, for what you've told me."

"You know where and when!"

"Yeah, and with about 90 minutes to prepare for it by the time I get through to the right people at Heathrow."

"It's going to be big, I know that much."

"Ok, Darren, fifty pounds if the info is good and if it's a significant protest. Call me this afternoon."

* * *

"Julian, it's Jen. I'm just by the entrance to the Heathrow Express."

"That's great, Jen. You're wearing the yellow coat?"

"I forgot it when I left ho-"

"Fuck it, Jen, I told you to wear it!"

"Hey, it's ok! I remembered and went back for it, ok?" Why was he getting so wound-up about a stupid coat?

"Ok, good. Sorry, Jen, I didn't mean to blow up at you, it's just I've got a lot to organise this morning, and I want everything going exactly to plan."

"It's ok," she said, sulkily.

"Look, I mean it, I'm sorry. Forgive me? I'll buy you lunch later."

"Sure," she said, brightening.

"Ok, you wait there and I'll send you about a dozen people – I'll tell them to look out for that yellow coat."

"Alright."

"Wait until about quarter to before you go down to the platform, we don't want you looking conspicuous by hanging around too long down there. Then wait until exactly 10am, and flag down the first train to approach platform 1, ok?"

"Sure, I know what I'm doing."

"I know you're going to do a great job."

"Thanks." Jen hadn't quite forgiven him for getting angry with her, but she was looking forward to lunch. She'd just need to dump Alison before then.

The small group of protestors assigned to the Heathrow Express operation had arrived as a group, looked around then approached Jen and Alison.

"Jen?" asked one.

"That's me. Have you been told what you're doing?"

"Waving down trains, he said."

"That's it. We'll hang around here until quarter to ten, then we'll go down onto Platform 1. We'll gradually wander towards the end of the tunnel where the trains emerge, then we're doing the first one to arrive after 10am. But just wait for my lead, and just join in when you see me waving, ok?"

"Sounds simple enough."

"It is, but just remember to ham it up – we want to make the driver panic and slam on his brakes. If some passengers on the train fall over, all the better, just adds to the chaos."

At 9.45am, Jen said "Let's go" and she and Alison led the group down the long escalator to the ticket machine area between the two platforms. There were no barriers, so they wouldn't need tickets to get onto the platform.

Jen turned to the group. "There's no reason we can't be a group of travellers, so we can all stand together. Just try to look bored or tired, and don't go near the platform edge until I move – we don't want to do anything to look out of the ordinary."

The rest of them nodded.

"I need to see which way the trains are coming in, then we'll slowly wander up to that end of the platform, ok?"

"Sure," said one.

"Ok, let's go."

The group moved onto the platform. They didn't have long to wait, as a train arrived almost immediately, and they started moving up the platform to the end from which the train had arrived. Jen figured they wanted to be about 30 or 40 feet in from the tunnel to be sure the driver saw them.

As the group gathered around her, Jen looked up at the indicator display. It was 09:51, and the train indicator was showing Here for the train already in the platform and 14 minutes for the next one. That would be 10:05. That, then, would be their target train.

A couple of minutes later, the train in the platform pulled out, and they were ready. The next train to emerge from the tunnel would be the one.

The group chatted intermittently as they waited. Jen kept glancing at the indicator board, thinking that 14 minutes had never felt so long.

Eventually, the indicator counted down to two minutes.

"I've always wanted to be an actress," laughed Alison, "do you think I could put this on my CV? Hysterical woman on Heathrow Express platform."

"Alison!" said Jen, trying to keep her voice low. "For god's sake!" She looked around to see if anyone was within earshot, but the only person close to them was a young guy in a leather jacket and a skinhead haircut. He had earphones in and wasn't looking in their direction.

"Ok, ok," said Alison, "but come on, it's not like this is a bank job. It's just a bit of a laugh, really."

Jen reached out to Alison's shoulder, turning her friend to face her. "This is serious, Alison. I know you think it's just a laugh, but we're trying to do something important here. If you don't think it matters, then go, but don't risk blowing it, ok?"

"Hey, there's no need to get shirty with me. Just because you're one of the important organisers –" Her sarcastic tone was clear. "–doesn't mean we all have to take it deathly seriously, you know. Some of us are just in this for the craic."

"This is not some childish game," said Jen. "If you can't act like a grown-up, then just piss off."

"For fuck's sake, Jen, you used to be fun! What's got into you lately?"

Jen looked up at the indicator. 1 minute. "I don't have time for this now, so just shut it."

"You can shut it," retorted Alison. "I'm off."

She started walking away from the group, but paused as she felt the air movement from the approaching train. She wanted to at least see the fun, and sod it, she'd join in and then talk to Jen about it later. The girl really needed to lighten-up.

She turned and saw the headlight in the tunnel as the train approached. Jen started waving madly, and the others joined in. Alison was about fifteen or twenty feet away but figured she could join in from there.

Suddenly, a figure behind Jen rushed forward and pushed her! Jen screamed and tried to grab hold of someone to prevent her fall. She succeeded in snatching someone's arm and keeping both feet on the platform, but she was leaning out over the edge as the train rushed into the station.

For Alison, it felt like time stood still for a moment. Her friend's upper body was leaning out over the track and the cab of the train was just there seemingly motionless for a moment. Then everything started moving again.

There was a sickening thump as the front of the train struck Jen, sending her flying back diagonally down the platform, her head hitting the floor. There was a screeching of brakes and screaming from the protest group and from other passengers who witnessed the sight of Jen being struck. Alison saw Jen flying towards her and then hitting a seat at the back of the platform. She could hear someone screaming over and over again "Jen! Jen!" before realising that it was her own voice.

A klaxon sounded, and people in hi-viz jackets came running up the platform: two policemen and two or three Heathrow Express staff. Alison ran to Jen and knelt down beside her, her fingers reaching out towards Jen's face but somehow not quite touching. Jen was motionless and her eyes were closed. Blood was pouring from her head onto the white stone tiles of the platform floor. Her right arm was twisted back at the shoulder into an impossible angle.

"Jen! Jen! Please! Jen!"

"Get an ambulance!" someone shouted.

The klaxon was still sounding, and there was a mass of people shouting and screaming. Suddenly Alison felt someone pulling at her shoulders, from behind, trying to pull her away from Jen. "Leave me alone!" she screamed, and the hands left her.

One of the police knelt opposite her and took Jen's pulse. "She's alive!" he called. "We need a paramedic down here, now."

Blood started leaking from Jen's nose. Alison started crying. "Jen! Please! No! Jen!"

Someone arrived with a first-aid kit and started trying to stem the blood. As they did so, Jen's eyes flickered half-open. Alison touched her cheek. "Jen! Can you hear me? It's Alison."

Jen's mouth opened, as if speaking, but Alison couldn't hear anything. She bent down to put her ear next to Jen's mouth. "Julian," she said. Her eyes closed again, and she slumped back.

"I've lost the pulse!" shouted the policeman. "Where the hell are those paramedics." He tore open Jen's coat, looked at the blood soaking through her blouse and started chest compressions. Alison didn't know first-aid and just knelt there, helplessly, crying.

Two paramedics, a man and a woman, arrived. The man took over CPR from the policeman, while the woman opened up a defibrillator. She tore open the blouse, and Alison was shocked to see that the whole right-hand side of her chest was just a bloody crushed mess.

The paramedic fixed the pads onto the left side of Jen's chest. The policeman put his hand on Alison's shoulder and eased her gently back; this time, she allowed it.

"Clear!" shouted the female paramedic.

Alison saw Jen's body jerk as the charge was applied.

"Charging. Clear!"

Jen's body jerked again.

"Charging. Clear!"

Again.

A 50-year-old man in a yellow vest arrived at a run, the lettering BASICS DOCTOR on the front.

The paramedics repeated the defibrillation process a dozen more times. The doctor halted her, and felt with his hands around the chest, then around underneath her, his hands running up Jen's back. He withdrew his blood-soaked hands, looked at the paramedic and shook his head. He looked at his watch.

The paramedic nodded, and started peeling off the defibrillator pads.

"What are you doing?" shouted Alison, reaching forward to grab the paramedic's arm. "Why are you stopping? Do something!"

The policeman pulled her gently away. The paramedic looked her in the eyes. "I'm sorry," she said.

"Time of death, 10:19am," said the doctor.

* * *

"I know this is difficult for you, Alison, but I just need you to tell me again exactly what you saw." Alison and other witnesses had been taken to Heathrow Police Station, and she was now sat with a female detective, DS Amanda Lowe, in a room with soft furnishings. It didn't look like the inside of a police station, she thought.

"Alison?" repeated DS Lowe. "I need you to tell me again what you saw, as the train arrived."

"I've told you!" she said. "He pushed her! This man deliberately pushed Jen!"

"What exactly did he do? How did he push her?" Her voice was soft, but the questions to Alison felt like physical blows.

"He just stepped forwards quickly, reached out with both hands and shoved her in the back."

"Where was he before he stepped forward?"

"I don't know!" cried Alison. "I hadn't seen him before then, he was just suddenly there, pushing Jen in front of the train!"

"Have you ever seen this man before?" asked DS Lowe.

"I don't know, I only saw him for a moment, and then I saw Jen falling and then being hit and-" She broke off, sobbing.

"I understand how hard this is," said Lowe.

"No, you don't," said Alison, through her tears. "You don't. You can't. We'd just had an argument, it was stupid, I wanted to-" She broke off again.

"We want to catch this man, Alison. This man you say killed your friend."

"Say? What do you mean, 'say'? Don't you believe me?"

"I believe you think it was deliberate," said Lowe. "It's important that we find him and talk to him. Anything you can tell me about what he looked like, what he was wearing, will help. Let's start with his age: how old do you think he was?"

"I don't know, maybe 25, 30, but it was all so fast."

"I know. Ok, so 25 or 30. How tall was he?"

"I don't know."

"He came up behind Jen – was he taller or shorter than her?"

"Taller. He was quite tall."

"Ok. What sort of complexion?"

"Complexion?"

"Was he white? Black? Asian?"

"White. A skinhead."

"Ok, totally shaved head? Bald?"

"Yes. Yes, I think so."

"Can you tell me what he was wearing?"

"Something dark. A jacket. Maybe a black leather jacket."

"Ok, could you see any scars? Tattoos?"

"I don't know. I don't think so. I just don't know," said Alison, starting to sob again.

"Ok, Alison, we're going to ask a police artist to talk to you, see if we can get a drawing of the man, he's on his way here now, ok?"

"Ok."

"Is there anything else you can tell us, anything else you saw or heard? Even the smallest thing might help."

"No. No, I don't think so. I mean, she asked for Julian, but she had a bit of a crush on him."

DS Lowe was suddenly alert. "She spoke to you? I thought she was unconscious the whole time?"

"She was conscious for just a moment. She just said his name, that was all."

"Is Julian her boyfriend?"

"No! He was the organiser of the protest. She fancied him."

"Protest? You were involved in that?" asked the detective.

"Sort of. Not the main one, we were just trying to disrupt the Heathrow Express. We were just going to flag the driver down, as if–"

"It's ok, Alison. So there was a group of you on the platform, as part of the protest?"

"Yes, about ten of us."

"And this Julian, he was the organiser. Was he on the platform?"

"No, he was in the terminal, I think. Jen phoned him when we got there and he sent the others down to us."

"Ok, so Jen was in charge of your group?"

Alison hesitated.

"It's ok," said Lowe. "I'm not concerned about the protest, I just want to find out what happened to Jen."

"Ok," said Alison, "yes, Jen was in charge of that bit."

"What was the name of the organisation they belonged to?"

"They call themselves Action On Aviation," said Alison.

"Ok." The detective made some notes. "And the man who pushed Jen, he wasn't part of your group?"

"No. At least, I don't think so. I didn't see him arrive with the others."

"And this Julian – do you know him?"

"No," said Alison, "I've never met him, but Jen talked about him a lot."

"Do you know his surname?"

"Fox."

Lowe made another note.

"Ok, Alison, I'll need to ask you some more questions later, after the artist has seen you. Can you tell us the names of her parents?"

"Oh god, Emma!"

"Emma is her mother?" The detective was deliberately using the present tense; she knew how hard it was to hear the past tense so soon.

"Yes."

"And her father's name?"

"Richard."

"Ok, and can you tell me her address?"

"Yes, it's 23 Wilmington Drive, Hampstead."

"Alright, Alison, that's all we need for now. I'm going to leave you with a WPC, and then we'll get the artist to come and talk to you."

DS Lowe walked through into the Custody Suite and spoke with the Custody Sergeant.

"Steve, can you tell me whether we have a Julian Fox in custody, from the protest?"

"Doesn't ring a bell," replied the Sergeant, "but let me double-check." He entered Fox's name on the computer system. "No, no-one who's given that name, anyway."

"Ok, thanks." DS Lowe walked back upstairs to her office. "Ahmad, I need you to find someone for me, and bring him in as a witness. His name is Julian Fox, and we believe he was the organiser of this morning's mess. The organisation is called Action On Aviation."

"Ok, Sarge. And if he doesn't want to cooperate?"

"Point out to him that there are at least a dozen things we could arrest him for, including several offences under anti-terrorism legislation. I'd prefer that he came in as a witness, but if nicking him is the only way to get him here, then do it. I want to talk to him, and I want to do it today."

DC Ahmad Singh picked up his jacket: "On my way."

Fox hadn't proven difficult to find: he was at the AOA offices being interviewed by a journalist from the London Evening Standard. He had immediately agreed to accompany Singh back to Heathrow Police Station. DC Singh had shown him into an interview room, and gone to fetch DS Lowe.

"Mr Fox, the law requires me to caution you, but please understand that I am not involved in the investigations into the protest itself. My only interest is in understanding how Jennifer Williams came to die. You can have a lawyer present if you wish, but as I say, I'm not interested in the protest – there are other officers dealing with that."

"I understand," said Fox, "and a lawyer won't be necessary. I was shocked to hear about the tragic accident, and want to do anything I can to help."

"Ok, then please have a seat," said Lowe. "We record witness statements as a matter of routine, I assume you have no objection?"

"None at all," replied Fox, easily.

DS Lowe started the tape recording and waited for the beep to end after the synthesised voice gave the date and time.

"Interview between myself, DS Amanda Lowe, and Mr Julian Fox regarding the unexplained death of Jennifer Williams. Present is myself and DC Ahmad Singh. Mr Fox, you do not have to say anything but you may harm your defence if you do not mention now anything which you later rely on in court. Anything you do say may be given in evidence. Mr Fox has been advised of his right to have a solicitor present and has declined such representation."

"I would also like it on record that I have voluntarily attended this interview and have been advised that I am here simply as a potential witness in regard to Jen's movements," said Fox.

DS Lowe nodded. "Mr Fox, we understand from another witness that Jennifer was leading a splinter protest in the Heathrow Express station, is that correct?"

"Yes," said Fox.

"Please can you describe the form that protest was to take?"

"She had simply been asked to cause disruption to the rail service," said Fox, choosing his words carefully.

"Disrupt the service in what way?" asked Lowe, making notes in a slim black notebook.

"Cause delays, ideally have the service be suspended in some way."

"What was the plan to do that?" asked Lowe.

Fox shrugged. "There wasn't really a specific plan for it, she was just asked to find a way to cause hold-ups: holding doors open, reporting suspect bags, waving down drivers, that sort of thing."

"I see." Lowe flicked back a few pages in her notebook. "According to the others in her group, they had been instructed to flag down a train."

"I guess that was how Jen decided to kick things off," said Fox.

"The other protestors who were with her, how were they selected?" asked Lowe.

"Fairly randomly," said Fox, "she just asked for about a dozen people to be sent over to her, so I just pointed at a few people and asked them to go to the entrance to the station and look for the girl in the yellow coat."

"Ok. So how did Jen come to take a leading role in the protest? She was rather young for such a role, wasn't she?"

"Well," said Fox, "I wouldn't really say it was a leading role. She was keen to get involved, and her father is a pilot, so she had a bit of knowledge about the aviation industry, so she was able to make a few suggestions. Ironically, it was because I thought things might get a bit rough in the main protest, and didn't want someone of her age getting hurt, so I thought it would be better to have her playing a minor role in something out of the way. Unfortunately, well ..."

"Yes. Did you know any of the others in her group?"

"No, they were just whoever was around. Oh, I believe she had a friend with her."

"Alison."

"I didn't really pay attention to the name, but it could have been, yes."

"But she arrived with a friend this morning?"

"Well, I didn't see her this morning, but I seem to remember she said something about a friend coming with her."

"You didn't see her this morning?" asked Lowe.

"No, she just phoned me when she was at the station, and I sent some people over to her."

Lowe ran her finger back up her notes. "You said earlier that you told them to look for a girl in a yellow coat – how did you know how she was dressed if you didn't see her that morning?"

"She told me," said Fox, "on the phone. I asked her what she was wearing so I could describe her to the group."

"Ok." Lowe passed a copy of the drawing across the table. "Do you recognise this man?"

Fox picked up the drawing, looked at it for a moment then handed it back. "No."

"Could he have been one of the group you sent over to her?" asked Lowe.

"Possibly, I wasn't really paying much attention to them, to be honest, it was just a random group of people."

Lowe turned the drawing round again to face Fox: "But you don't recognise him? You haven't seen him before?"

"No."

Lowe spent the rest of the interview going into the background of AOA and Jen's involvement with it. Fox had said she was just one of a group of the volunteers who came and went at AOA. Lowe ended the interview feeling that she was no further forward.

* * *

Richard Williams had been on a rest day in San Francisco when the call came in. It was shortly before 3am local time.

"Hello?" he asked, sleepily. All flight crews learned to switch off their mobiles when they went to sleep: spending half their lives in different time-zones made it all too easy for someone to call you in what was the middle of your night. It was the hotel phone that had rung, and only two people had that number: the airline ops people, and Emma.

"Richard ..." He heard the sound of Emma sobbing.

"Emma? What is it?" He sat up in bed, instantly coming awake.

"It's Jen."

"What's happened?"

"I– She–" More sobbing.

"Emma! What's happened? Please, speak to me!"

"Oh Richard!"

"Emma, please, what's happened? What's happened to Jen?"

"There's been a terrible accident."

"An accident? What sort of accident? Is she ok?"

"No," said Emma, simply.

"How bad is it?"

"Richard ... she ..." Her voice trailed off.

"No," he said.

"She was at a protest at Heathrow. Some anti-aviation thing, you know her. There was a train. She was on the platform. It's not clear how it happened, but she was hit. Richard, the train hit her! She's dead! Jen's dead!"

"I'm coming home. Do you have a friend with you?"

"I'm still at the police station, Sue and Ian are here."

"I'll call ops now and get on the first flight out of here. I'll call you as soon as I know which one. I'm on my way, Emma."

The flight home as a passenger had felt like the longest journey he'd ever made. When he'd eventually got there, he and Emma had collapsed into each other's arms and cried and cried.

He had a million questions. He'd had time to go over and over them in his head on the flight home, but he was conscious that some of them couldn't be asked. Like what the hell was Jen doing at Heathrow, at an anti-aviation protest of all things, when she should have been at school. But he knew that Emma had no more control over Jen that he did. Had, he corrected himself. That didn't feel real yet.

Through tears and silences, Emma gradually managed to tell him the story. Including Alison's incredible claim that Jen was deliberately pushed. He had to speak to the police, and then he had to speak with Alison.

* * *

It had been two days since the worst day in Alison's life. For some reason, she couldn't picture the moment of impact now. She remembered the moment before it, when time seemed to be frozen, and she remembered everything afterwards, but not the impact. Only the sound of it – that terrible sound.

She barely remembered the questions she'd been asked by the police, or the description she'd given to the artist. The drawing he'd done had looked something like him, she thought, but she could remember so little.

She remembered the stupid argument she'd had with Jen. Walking off on her like that. Maybe if that hadn't happened, she'd have seen something, been able to do something.

She remembered the blood and Jen's arm and chest and the heart machine and the doctor shaking his head and–

And she remembered Emma arriving at the police station after being taken to the hospital to identify Jen's body. She remembered that look on her face. She would never forget that look.

"What happened, Alison? What happened?" Emma had asked.

She would have given anything to be able to tell her that it was a horrible accident. It wouldn't help much, she knew, but the knowledge that someone, for some reason none of them knew, had deliberately killed her ...

"I don't know," she had sobbed. "Someone just pushed her. I don't know, I don't know."

Her own parents had arrived shortly afterwards. Richard was away in San Francisco, so her parents had insisted Emma stay in the spare room until he arrived the following evening.

Nobody had questioned her further that night, they could all see she was distraught and exhausted in equal measure. She hadn't slept at all that night, and the questions had begun in the morning. All the same questions the police had asked, and she still had no better answers. The whole thing made no sense.

And now Richard was here, asking the same questions again.

"Why would anyone push her?"

"I don't know! I know it doesn't make sense, but I know what I saw. I turned, and was facing her, looking right at her, when the man just ran out and pushed her!"

"Alison," he said, trying to keep his voice calm, "I spoke with the police and they say no-one else saw this man. All everyone else saw was her jumping and waving and then her losing her balance."

"I saw him. I'm telling you, I saw him push her."

"But why? Why would anyone push her?"

"I keep telling you, I keep telling everyone, I don't know! I know it sounds crazy, but it's what I saw."

Richard was trying desperately to think clearly. He hadn't slept for more than 24 hours.

"Did it look targeted, like he was pushing Jen specifically, or was he just pushing the group randomly?"

"I don't know."

"Do you know anyone who would want to hurt her?"

"Jen? No! Of course not."

"Who knew she was going to be there?"

"No-one. She was very secretive, she wouldn't even tell me where we were going until I got the email with everyone else."

"Ok. I've arranged to meet the investigating officer at Heathrow Police Station later that day, so we'll see where they are with it"

"Mr Williams? I'm DS Amanda Lowe. Please, follow me."

She led the way through into an interview room. "Once again, Mr Williams, I'm so sorry for your loss. You tend to get hardened to a lot of things in this job, but the death of a schoolgirl, that's something we all feel."

"Thank you," he said. He didn't know whether it was sincere, and didn't much care, he just wanted answers. "What more can you tell me, since we spoke?"

"Very little else at this stage, I'm afraid. We've interviewed everyone who came forward at the time, and none of them saw anyone push her. We've examined the CCTV footage, but the platform was crowded and all the video footage shows is the moment when Jennifer emerges from the crowd. We are still in the process of reviewing CCTV footage before and after the tragedy."

DS Lowe continued: "We called in the Rail Accident Investigation Branch to carry out a detailed examination of the train and track, and we are conducting forensic tests on the clothing to see whether there is anything of assistance there. We have witness appeal signs in the station, on the trains at Paddington station. We've had a few more people come forward from that, but none of them added anything new. We've circulated the drawing, and so far nobody has come forward to say that they recognise him."

"Will the drawing be in the papers? On the TV?"

DS Lowe hesitated. "The problem, Mr Williams, is that we have no evidence of a crime here. We have a group of protestors jumping around at the edge of a platform. We have one of them apparently falling into the path of the train. All the witnesses bar one say that she fell. Nobody else even saw any sign of the man Alison described. I'm not saying it won't happen, but that kind of nationwide appeal can only be done where we have good reason to suspect someone. At the moment, we don't."

"I spoke with Alison this morning, she seems pretty clear about what she saw."

"Alison has had an enormously traumatic experience. She's witnessed her best friend die. Did she tell you about the argument they'd had?"

Williams nodded: "Yes, she did. She told me that's the only reason she saw it so clearly, because she'd walked away and then turned around."

"She is enormously upset, and also feeling a huge amount of guilt. The last exchange she had with her best friend before she died was an argument. Sometimes in that kind of situation, people look for something to distract them from that guilt. Someone else, someone who was really guilty, perhaps."

"So you think she imagined it?" asked Williams, accusingly.

"She probably saw something. There were 14 of them, all standing close together. They were jumping and waving. It was a very confused situation. It may well have looked to her like someone pushed Jen."

"But you don't think they did?"

"I'm keeping an open mind, Mr Williams. As you are probably aware, there have been tragic cases over the years where a mentally unstable person pushes a complete stranger in front of a train – there was a case on the tube last year. It does happen, and it may have happened here. We are certainly doing everything we can to see if we can find the person Alison thought she saw, but it's a pretty vague description, and nobody else saw him, so it may prove difficult to get the drawing circulated nationally."

Williams was about to object when she held up a hand and continued: "But there are other avenues for us to explore. I have an entire team of people going through all of the CCTV footage throughout the station and in each of the airport terminals to see whether we can spot anyone matching the description of the man Alison described. If we can, then we can hopefully trace his movements through the terminal and find out where he came from or where he went to. If we can connect him to a particular flight, or find footage of him passing through Passport Control, then the time-stamps should enable us to identify him. In the meantime, if this man does exist and was involved in your daughter's death, he most likely lives in London. And anyone who saw him is most likely either from London, or a visitor to the UK who will take the Heathrow Express again when they return home. The posters are at Paddington, on the trains and at Heathrow."

Williams had to admit the argument made sense – at least, for now. "Ok," he said, "but if you don't track him down from that, I'll want to speak to whoever needs to authorise a nationwide appeal."

"Of course." Lowe shuffled some papers to give her a moment before she asked the next question she had to ask. "Mr Williams, I know this is a terrible time, but you understand there are some questions we have to ask ..."

Williams looked at her blankly.

"Was your daughter experiencing any difficulties in her life? At home? At school? With friends?"

"What do you mean?"

"As I say, Mr Williams, these are just routine questions we have to ask."

Williams shrugged. "She had some issues with school attendance, but I don't see what relevance that has."

"Do you have any reason to think Jen may have been upset or depressed about anything?"

For a moment, Williams didn't understand, then he snapped at her: "Suicide? You think my daughter killed herself?" He was outraged at the suggestion.

"I'm sorry, Mr Williams, we just have to consider all the possibilities in a case like this."

"No! My daughter did not kill herself. For god's sake, she was at a protest, in the centre of things. I didn't approve of it, for obvious reasons, but it was something she cared about, in however misguided a fashion. No, DS Lowe, Jen did not commit suicide, and don't you dare even raise that suggestion with my wife, am I clear?"

"I'm sorry, Mr Williams, it's just a question we have to ask. When we begin an investigation like this, we have to start with a completely open mind. Then we seek to eliminate things. Everything we can eliminate takes us one step closer to understanding what did happen. Suicide is one of the things we have to eliminate."

"Well, it's now asked and answered. So what's the next step in the investigation?"

"I'm afraid it's mostly now wait-and-see. We've interviewed all the people we know to have been there at the time, as well as the organiser of the overall protest. We really have very little to go on until someone else comes forward with any further information."

"So you're doing nothing?" demanded Williams.

"Mr Williams, you have to understand that a great deal of police work involves asking the public for help, and then waiting for the one call that will provide a clue. When that call comes in, that points us in a new direction and we pursue the leads from that. It can be a slow and frustrating process at times, and I do understand that you want immediate answers, but typically the answers aren't immediate."

"I understand that, but so far you seem to know nothing about the circumstances of her death."

"Again, Mr Williams, it's a process of elimination. From everyone we have interviewed, I am fairly satisfied that this man, if he exists, was not part of the group assigned to the protest on the platform. It was a fairly small group, and none of those involved recognised him."

Lowe didn't want to add that they had also been able to pull out the CCTV footage of the group assembling at the entrance and travelling down the escalator: for family members, there was something particularly cruel about video footage of the last few minutes of someone's life. At that moment, the person had been alive, and there's a feeling that you could somehow warn them, or stop them, or freeze time at that moment. Sometimes, media coverage of video footage of the last moments of someone's life is essential to an investigation, but the police avoid it wherever possible.

She continued: "We have accounted for the movements of all staff. We have taken photographs of all of those arrested in connection with the protest, and are reviewing CCTV footage of the main protest to see whether anyone matching his description is among them. There's a lot more work to be done, Mr Williams, and I'll keep you fully informed in the coming days."

* * *

6th May

The days had turned into weeks, and finally into months. The promised updates from DS Lowe had grown less frequent, with Richard Williams feeling helpless and frustrated. He wanted to understand everything about how his daughter came to die, and more than two months later he understood almost nothing.

The police had concluded their investigation, and declared it an accident. All the evidence pointed in that direction, they said. They had reviewed all of the CCTV video footage from the arrival of the first flight at just after 6am until the end of the day, and reviewed the photos taken of passengers at Immigration. With such a vague description, there were literally hundreds of potential matches. DS Lowe said that all had been painstakingly tracked through the CCTV system, and only two of them were in the Heathrow Express station at the time of the incident. One could be seen on the opposite platform, waiting for the local Heathrow Connect service at the time of the impact, and the other was seen boarding the previous train. Nobody had responded to the appeals for information on the man, nobody else had seen him.

The inquest into Jen's death had taken just one day to reach a finding of Death by Misadventure. It was officially an accidental death.

Both he and Emma desperately wanted to believe it. Neither of them would ever get a satisfactory answer to the 'why' question, he knew, but they at least wanted to be able to move on from the 'how'.

But it was Alison: two months later, she remained absolutely adamant that Jen had been pushed. He admitted to himself that what DS Lowe had said about guilt made some sense, but Alison could just as easily have imagined that one of the other protestors had accidentally knocked Jen; that would surely relieve the guilt every bit as effectively?

What did you do when the police investigation was done, the inquest verdict was in and the media had lost interest? Hire their own investigator? A private detective was, to him, something out of a 50s crime novel. He supposed they really existed, for divorce investigations if nothing else, but this? When god knows how many police and airport security personnel had drawn a blank, what could a private detective possibly achieve?

He didn't know, but did know that he had to explore every possible avenue. He picked up the phone.

"DS Lowe, it's Richard Williams."

"Mr Williams, how are you and Emma coping?"

"Not very well, to be honest. Listen, I know that you're satisfied that it was an accident, and everything you've said makes sense, but Alison still insists Jen was pushed, and neither of us feels able to move on until we have got some kind of definitive answer."

"I'm sorry, Mr Williams, I do understand what you're saying, but I really do think this was just a horrible, senseless, tragic accident. We've exhausted every lead, and now that the case has been closed, there's really nothing else we can do."

"I know," said Williams, "and I appreciate everything you've done. Look, this is probably going to sound silly however I phrase it, so I'm just going to come right out and ask. We want to hire someone to continue the investigation, just to satisfy ourselves that no stone has been left unturned. It's no reflection on your investigation, it's just something we have to do for our peace of mind."

"Mr Williams ..." began DS Lowe.

"Please. You're not going to talk me out of it. But I wouldn't know where to start looking for someone who could handle this sort of thing. I was wondering whether you could suggest someone, an ex-copper, perhaps?"

"Mr Williams, I do know how hard this is for you, but there have been literally thousands of police hours spent on this investigation, all of it based on a single vague description by a single witness. There is nothing a private investigator could do that we haven't already done."

"You may be right." Williams paused. "One of the things that has been especially hard about this is we've had to face the fact that there are a lot of things about Jen's life that we didn't know about. We need to understand as much as we can. Perhaps we will find someone with a reason to want to harm her, perhaps we'll just finally satisfy ourselves that there is nothing left to know. Either way, we have to do this, ok?"

There was silence on the line for several seconds, then: "Ok. I'll ask around here, see if I can come up with a recommendation for you."

"Thank you. I appreciate that."

Lowe had called back later that day with a name and number, though urging him once more to accept that it was an accident. Williams had thanked her for the advice, then made the call right away.

He hadn't known what to expect from a private detective agency. He'd watched too many bad movies, probably: the image he had was a weary-looking retiree in a smoke-filled office in a dilapidated old building in a run-down part of the city. He hadn't expected a modern office in the West End, all frosted glass walls and stainless steel. The offices looked more like an ad agency than a detective agency.

"Mr Williams?" asked a smiling man in his early fifties. "I'm Stephen Adams. Please, come through."

Williams followed him through into a small but well-lit meeting room.

"It's good of you to see me at such short notice," said Williams. "And please, call me Richard."

"My pleasure, Richard. Can I get you anything, a tea, coffee, water?"

"I'm fine, thanks."

Adams opened a large notebook. "Ok, then, let's get right down to business. I took the liberty of speaking with DS Lowe after your call, and in fairness to you, Richard, it does sound to me like the police investigation was a very thorough one. They reviewed all the CCTV footage, something we couldn't do without a whole slew of Freedom of Information requests which may or may not succeed. We could spend a great deal of your money revisiting everything they've done, but I honestly don't think it would achieve anything. If I were betting on this, I'd say it was an accident, pure and simple. Even if someone did push her, and it looks exceedingly unlikely given that the one suspect wasn't seen either before or afterwards, then it was almost certainly a random attack rather than anything targeted."

"I appreciate your honesty, Mr Adams."

"Stephen, please."

"I appreciate your honesty, Stephen, and can see why you come recommended. The one area where I think the police investigation was less thorough than it could have been was in regard to whether anyone had any reason to harm Jen."

Adams gave Williams a direct look. "Do you have any reason to suppose that to be the case?"

Williams shook his head. "No, but as I explained to DS Lowe, it had been a bit of a difficult time with Jen. The teenage phase when we think-". He corrected himself, with obvious effort: "thought she was still a child while she thought of herself as an adult. So there may be aspects of her life we didn't know about."

"Most parents of teens would say the same thing. The usual rows and things aside, though, would you say your memories of Jen are mostly happy ones?"

"Yes," said Williams, without hesitation. "Usual rows and things aside."

Adams put down his pen. "Then I'm going to ask you a question, Richard, and I'd like you to go away and think carefully about it before you answer, ok?"

Williams swallowed. "Ok."

"Let's suppose you are right, and there are aspects of your daughter's life you knew nothing about. And let's say that we are able to find out about those things. There may be things you would really rather not know. Perhaps drugs. Perhaps other things. I'm not saying there will be, but we never know what we're going to find until we start looking. And without blowing my own trumpet here, I'm good at what I do. So if there were things going on with your daughter, I'll probably discover them."

Williams nodded.

Adams continued: "So my question for you, the one I'd like you consider very carefully before you say yes or no, is this: are you absolutely sure that you want to know anything more than you know now? Are you certain that it wouldn't be better just to accept that this was an accident and move on? And when you consider that question, I'd like you to think about whether the same is true of your wife. Would she want to know whatever we might learn about your daughter's life? Because I'm a professional, Richard: if you pay me to investigate something, I'll investigate to the very best of my abilities, and whatever I find, I'll tell you, I won't hold anything back."

Williams turned the question over in his mind. The fact that Adams had asked it further impressed him: the man clearly didn't need business at any cost, and was obviously a man of integrity. He also seemed to be a sharp cookie: the question about whether Emma would also want to know was a particularly good one. And it wasn't like he could make that call later, decide how much he wanted to share with her: they had never had secrets from each other, and he knew that if they went ahead with this, it would be a joint voyage of discovery.

Adams added: "You don't have to answer today. If you do decide to go ahead, I'll in any case need to meet with both of you to learn as much as I can about Jen's life. So why don't you go home, sleep on it, maybe talk it over with your wife, then let me know tomorrow."

Williams shook his head. "No. We have to do this. If we learn things we don't like, then we'll have to learn to live with it. But we can't go on not knowing."

Adams nodded. "Ok. Then let's arrange a time to meet with both of you."

* * *

"I can't understand it," said York. It's been three months now, we've put out six press releases, you've spoken with your contacts, and yet not a single piece of coverage that we've been able to spot – not even a paragraph buried on page 20 somewhere!"

"I know," said 'King'. "It's extremely disappointing. The problem is that the media isn't taking it seriously. I've spoken to my friendly journalists about it, and they've all told me the same thing: it's old news, the investigators blamed it on pilot error and there have been no reports since of any problems with fly-by-wire, so they're satisfied that the report was correct. It's not a story to them."

"It's just so frustrating! I felt sure some of those releases would get at least some journalists to sit up and take notice, but nothing. What do we have to do to get the media to pay attention?"

'King' paused. "You know," he said, "I've been involved in campaigning for some years now. I've always tried to take a gentle approach, try to reason with people, but sometimes – as we're finding here – that doesn't work. Sometimes it takes something a little more ... disruptive ..."

"You mean a protest? Like that Heathrow one?"

"We're in a bit of a Catch-22 there," said 'King'. "We couldn't pull off that kind of protest because there isn't the public awareness, and there isn't the public awareness because there isn't the media attention."

"So what do we do? Damnit, there has to be some way of getting through!"

"Danny," said 'King', softly. "I've been giving this a lot of thought, and I think there may be a way of making this headline news, but I've hesitated to mention it to you."

"Why?"

"Because I'm not sure how far you'd be willing to push things, and I don't want to suggest anything that might be uncomfortable for you. Some campaign methods are a little, well, unorthodox."

"Unorthodox?" asked York.

"Yes. How would you feel about something which caused widespread disruption? Let's say all Airbus planes unable to take-off on a particular day?"

York was taken aback at the idea. "How on earth would we do that?"

"Let's say we could, would you be comfortable with that?"

"Well, yes, so long as we could be sure that nobody would get hurt. This is about saving lives, so I wouldn't want to risk anything that might put people in danger."

"No, this would be disruptive, but there would be no danger to anyone," said 'King'. Which was entirely true of what he was describing to York, of course.

"Ok. It would certainly draw attention to the issue, I just can't conceive of any way we could pull it off."

"But if we could, you would be comfortable with that?"

"Nobody gets hurt?" pressed York.

"Nobody gets hurt," reassured 'King'.

"Then, yes, I'd be comfortable with it. But how could we possibly do that?"

"Again," said 'King', "I don't want to put you in an awkward position by suggesting anything that wouldn't be acceptable to you, so let me ask you a few more questions, ok?"

"Ok," said York, feeling puzzled. How could they ground all Airbus aircraft?

"You'll appreciate that we couldn't pull off something like this without a certain amount of subterfuge, of course."

"I would suppose," replied York, dryly. While he had no idea how such a thing might be done, he didn't imagine it was going to be by saying 'Excuse me, Mr & Mrs Airline, would you mind awfully if we switched off all your aircraft?'.

"And if you were to play a very direct role in a deception, would that be acceptable?"

"I believe in personal responsibility," said York. "If I'm going to be a party to something, then I should be willing to play my part, so yes."

"Do you think you could maintain a fiction over a period of time? Even with people you worked closely with?"

York considered the question. It was the age-old question of whether the end justified the means. He disliked lies, but if the end were to save others like Stephanie, and the means was misleading people he worked with for a time, then yes.

"Yes," he said.

"Are you sure?" asked 'King'.

"I'm sure," said York, "but I still can't believe it could be done. Who would possibly be in a position to ground every Airbus airliner in the world?"

"You," said 'King', simply.

"Me?" York was bemused.

"The way it could be done, and the way we'd give the world a very visible demonstration of the dangers of allowing software to take too much control, is to use the software to ground the aircraft. You could write that code."

York was stunned. The concept was incredible, and his mind was racing. He could see, in principle, that it would be possible, if you had the right access, some sequence of activities in the pre-flight checklist, perhaps, to trigger some code to shut down the engines ... but there were so many practical barriers, he barely knew where to begin explaining them to King.

"I don't think you appreciate just how many safeguards there are," he said. "Sorry, I don't mean to be patronising, but this is my field. First of all, for aircraft to fail to start-up, there are only a certain number of systems that could bring about that result. I don't know enough about aircraft to tell you exactly how many, but off the top of my head it would be things like engine start-up circuitry, fuel-flow control, that kind of thing."

"I'm listening,' said 'King', carefully adopting a neutral expression but secretly delighted: if York was thinking seriously about how to do it, he was in!

"Second, software development is modular," explained York. "Any one developer would be working only on one small section of the code, and in a carefully-controlled environment – and I think we can be confident that this would apply to Airbus! – a given developer would not have access to other modules. Not to change them, anyway."

'King' nodded.

"Third, software developers work in teams. Any code written by one person would be checked by another, so anything dodgy should be spotted. Fourth," said York, running through the process in his mind, "once the developers are happy with it, the code is passed to the test engineers. Their job is to make sure it does what it's supposed to do. They will run it through a vast array of automated tests to make sure that it works under all possible conditions."

"Anything else?" asked 'King'. He didn't know much about software, but he did know people. The first stage in getting anyone to address a tough challenge was to define the problem: map out all the barriers they'd have to overcome. You didn't try to minimise the problems, on the contrary, you encouraged them to voice them all.

"Anything else?" asked York. "You mean, that's not enough?"

"What else?" repeated 'King'.

"Well, let's see ... there's the lead-time: the time between getting the code approved and it being put into operation. In telecoms, speed to market is second only to reliability, but an airliner? They must write that code years before the first aircraft is handed over to an airline. We can't wait that long."

"What else?" asked King.

"The small matter of the fact that I've been a vocal critic of fly-by-wire systems might prove a bit of a hindrance at the interview, don't you think?"

"Well, there our lack of success at PR acts in our favour: with no media coverage, it's unlikely anyone would even know about it. We can remove your details from the website. So far as your last boss is concerned, you took a sabbatical. So, any other issues?"

York laughed. "You mean, apart from figuring out which module could do the job and getting access to the right software module and fooling anyone else who examined the code and getting it through testing and making something happen this decade? No, I think that's pretty much all we'd have to do."

"Ok," said 'King'. "So, five challenges."

"Challenges?" asked York. "You sound like one of those awful gung-ho management types, 'there are no problems, only challenges'!"

"Still," said 'King, "humour me. In principle, what would someone need to do to overcome each of the issues?"

"Christ," said York, "I have no idea. I'd need to sit down and think about it."

"Then I guess you have your new assignment," said 'King'.

King hadn't fully appreciated the power of his approach. Software developers are essentially professional problem-solvers. They are never happier when faced with a tough challenge of a kind they haven't faced before.

York walked slowly back to his office, and reached for a blank sheet of paper. Despite spending his life working on computer systems, when he needed to think through something new from scratch, he tended to start with pen and paper.

He picked up a pen and wrote at the top of the sheet:

Objective:

Ground an airliner prior to take-off.

Method:

Disguised code in the fly-by-wire software.

He pushed the piece of paper to one side, and picked up five new sheets. At the top of the first, he wrote:

Problem 1:

Few code modules could ground an aircraft

Initial thoughts on possible solutions:

1. Engine start-up routines

2. Fuel

3. Lock on brakes

4. Fail a critical part of the pre-flight checklist so pilots abort flight

York put that sheet to one side and started on the next:

Problem 2:

Getting to work on one of the few relevant modules

Initial thoughts on possible solutions:

Only two thoughts occurred to him immediately:

1. A CV featuring specialist experience in one of the key areas

2. Befriend the project manager and express a preference for a particular area

Neither struck him as particularly viable approaches in his case. He didn't have any aviation experience. That in itself shouldn't matter much:

telecoms was a 'five nines' environment, so he had experience writing extremely robust software. But he couldn't convincingly claim specific experience in any aspect of aviation software, let alone enough to get him assigned to a specific module.

Befriending the project manager was easy enough when you've been somewhere a while. There'd been quite a few occasions in his career when he'd wanted to work on a particular product line, and usually he'd been able to arrange it. But he'd be going in cold to a company where he knew nobody and nobody knew him.

Well, he thought, it wasn't like he was going to come up with the answers today. He put that sheet in the 'Problems' pile and started on the next sheet.

Problem 3:

Passing peer review

Initial thoughts on possible solutions:

1. Obscurity

It was the only approach that occurred to him at the moment. Most code modules were long and complex. If what he wanted to achieve could be done in a few lines of code, that code could be hidden in a large block of code doing something legitimate. Make the legitimate thing rather uninteresting, and the chances were that it wouldn't be spotted.

It was, though, a potential weakness. Software geeks weren't like normal people. They could develop obscure interests, and your particular module might become one of them. Again, though, he recognised that he couldn't expect to come up with solid answers at this stage, just initial thoughts. He added that sheet to the pile. Next:

Problem 4:

Passing testing

He smiled at that one. In demanding environments, testing was ruthless. You had to be sure that the module would do what it was supposed to do under any and all circumstances. You hooked up equipment which simulated every possible variable in the input data, and other equipment which measured each of the output data, to ensure that every single scenario produced the correct result.

Someone who didn't work in software would probably see this as the greatest challenge, but that was the reason for his smile. It wasn't. The key wording was testing to ensure the module produced the correct result. In other words, that it always did what it was supposed to. So long as it actually did what it was supposed to, it would pass testing. Testing would not generally reveal that it also did something else.

In their case, too, they wanted to ground all the affected aircraft on a particular day, so the trigger would most likely be something that checked the date. On any date except the target one, nothing untoward would happen. Testing should not be an issue.

With no aviation experience, York had no idea just how wrong he was about that.

Initial thoughts on possible solutions:

1. Not an issue – ensure the module works, and use a date trigger

York added that sheet, and started on the last piece of paper:

Problem 5:

Time-lag between coding and commercial flights containing that code

Well, there was an obvious solution, but it was a tricky one: you wanted to get your code into one of the updates rather than the original code. While it might be years between initial coding and commercial flights, software updates would be done within days in the case of a critical bug down to maybe quarterly for trivial improvements. Either way, perhaps three months to wait in the worst-case.

Initial thoughts on possible solutions:

1. Software update

What made it tricky was getting assigned to updating software he hadn't written in the first place. It wasn't that it was unusual, it happened all the time. People came and went, and you would often have to maintain someone else's code. But you then had to express a desire to work in a particular area, and have the original coder have moved on. That seemed to be pushing coincidence somewhat.

There was a lot of thinking to be done.

* * *

Stephen Adams also had a lot of work in front of him. You always started with the basics: the subject's daily routines. What did they do? Where did they go? Who did they see?

Generally, that was led by surveillance, but of course that wasn't possible in this case: you had to piece things together retrospectively, and that was a lot tougher.

Alison was straightforward: she was eager to help, so he could approach her openly. He could safely assume she was an innocent party because she was the only one crying 'murder' when everyone else was saying 'accident'. You don't carry a double-bluff that far. He'd ask Williams to talk to her, arrange a meeting.

But you couldn't do the same with other people. The problem in these cases was that you didn't know who were the good guys and who were the bad guys, assuming there were any bad guys. So you had to take an indirect approach.

It had simply been called subterfuge when he started out; these days, the new guys, they called it 'social engineering'. Either way, it was the same job. You arranged to bump into people. You adopted identities as appropriate. If a particular identity was needed, and it required someone younger, or older, or female, or whatever was called for, you used someone else in the team.

He had spent 90 minutes sitting down with both parents getting them to tell him everything they knew about their daughter's life in the last 6-12 months. Who her friends were. Where she hung out. Her hobbies. Organisations she was involved with. Anything and everything that would tell him who he needed to talk to and the places he needed to visit.

Investigations also focused on the 'classic trinity': means, motive and opportunity. Who had the ability to commit the crime? In this case, anyone with two arms. Who had a reason to kill her? That was the one that would likely take the time here. Who had the chance to do so? That one might prove easy or difficult: it depended on how many people knew where she would be that morning, or could have followed her there.

But motive would be the tricky one. In questioning her parents about Jen's life, he had concentrated mostly on the last few weeks and days because whatever provoked a murder was likely to have been very recent. With the exception of unhappily-married couples, where resentment built up slowly over years, murderers didn't tend to spend months or years plotting the crime. The typical time interval between triggering event and killing was measured in the range of seconds to days.

There were only three common motives for murder: an argument that got out of hand, sex and money.

An argument. That was immediate, and he was already sure he could rule it out. It would have been witnessed, and the police would have found out about it right away.

Sex. Maybe she'd broken up with a boyfriend. Maybe she was in a relationship and slept with someone else. Possible but unlikely: crimes of passion also tend to be immediate, especially when those involved were young. The idea of someone roughly her age planning to murder her sometime after learning the news wasn't a particularly credible one.

An older lover was a possibility that couldn't be discounted, however. Perhaps Jen was threatening to reveal the relationship. If the lover was an adult, the fear of the relationship being exposed would be a powerful motivator. Sleeping with a 15-year-old girl was a serious matter at the best of times, add in a marriage or a career ... Had Jen been sleeping with one of her teachers? If she had threatened to make the relationship public, that would certainly provide sufficient motive for silencing her.

Money. Mostly that was immediate too. A robbery or burglary gone wrong, neither of which applied here. Occasionally it was something planned, a spouse wanting to collect on a life insurance policy or a relative after an inheritance, but this was a 15-year-old girl. If it was about money, that suggested drugs. If she was involved in drug-dealing, there were about twenty dozen ways she could end up dead; that was one of the possibilities he was alluding to when he warned Williams they might learn things they wished they hadn't.

It was possible it was none of the three, but those covered the most likely possibilities.

* * *

"So," smiled 'King' as they met in his office the following morning, "how did you get on with your assignment?"

York waggled his hand in a 'so-so' gesture. His single sheet of paper per problem had grown to three or four sheets each. He spread out the first set on the desk.

"Problem one. I can think of a few different approaches we could take to ground the aircraft, and that's without knowing anything more about them than I've learned in my research since the crash. With some more specific searches, I can doubtless find others. In truth, there are so many inter-related systems and checklist requirements, identifying potential routes is probably fairly trivial."

"So problem one is solved?" asked 'King'.

York laughed. "Hardly! But solveable, yes, I'm sure of it."

"Ok, problem two?"

"How do I get myself assigned to one of the relevant modules? The more time I spent considering problem one, the easier this one looked. An airliner doesn't go anywhere without a checklist of 30 or 40 things being completed." York pushed forward a checklist. "This is for an Airbus A330/A340 – there are 36 items on the list."

"Where did you get that?" asked 'King'.

"You'd be amazed what you can download from the net," replied York. "I even found flight and operations manuals for several aircraft. But this ... promise not to laugh?"

"Go on."

"Microsoft Flight Simulator."

"A game?" asked 'King'.

"A pretty realistic one, that a lot of people take very seriously. There are geeks out there who've constructed complete dummy flight-decks, using multiple monitors and realistic controls. The procedures are well-researched and very much true to life."

"Well, perhaps," said 'King', the skepticism in his voice apparent, "but you can't rely on a game!"

"Rely on it, no," said York. "The reality will be more complex, but it's unlikely the game just made stuff up, it's far more likely that it simplifies things by leaving stuff out. So in addition to the 36 things shown here, there are probably another dozen or two in real life. I just used this because it was easy to find, and it was enough to persuade me that the problem is soluble. I'm sure more thorough searches will get us the real checklists, probably some commercial pilot's training school will have them online somewhere."

"So problem two is also solvable."

"I believe so, yes."

"Problem three."

"Getting the dodgy code through peer review."

"Peer review?" asked 'King'.

"Whenever you write or amend some code, one of your colleagues will check it. Any code that does something it isn't supposed to has to be sufficiently well-disguised that it won't be picked up by peer-review. One approach is obscurity – you do it in such a roundabout way that it isn't obvious what the code does, but that's very risky."

"Why so?"

"Coders aren't like normal people." He smiled. "We get a positive kick out of finding new and more efficient ways to do something. If we spot code we can't understand, our first instinct is to dive right in and unravel it."

"So what's the solution?" asked 'King'.

"The easiest way is to imitate some library code. To avoid reinventing the wheel, quite a lot of software uses standard blocks of code to do standard things. For example, if you need to run a timer, you won't write that bit of the software yourself, you'll just import a timer routine from the code library. If a reviewer sees what appears to be library code, they'll skip over that."

"Ok," said 'King', " so that's problem three solveable too."

"Potentially," said York, "yes."

"Problem four?"

" Testing. When the reviewer is happy, they'll pass it through to the test engineers, who will throw it through every conceivable scenario – usually a mix of manual and automated testing – to try to make it fail. The good news there is that testing is primarily designed to ensure that the module does what it's supposed to. So long as it does, the testing probably won't pick up on the fact that it also does something else."

'King' smiled. "Sounds good. And problem five?"

York frowned. "Problem five is the tricky one. It's no good me working on original code for a new aircraft because the time-lag between writing the code and the aircraft entering commercial operation is measured in years. And it's also an unpredictable time – a few production problems can greatly delay the launch of a new airliner. More than one has been released two or three years later than planned. So any date-activated code couldn't be relied on."

"So what's the solution?"

"The solution is to work on a software update. I'll need to check the situation in the aviation industry, but typically those are issued at least quarterly, and often more frequently. The big problem is that I'll need to be working on an update to an airliner in current service, and be working on a mission-critical part of it. Expressing an interest in working on a particular aspect of the software wouldn't be an issue in the case of a brand new system. Project managers are used to geeks and their interests, and will accommodate them when they can. But there will be someone whose job it is to look after the updates to each aspect of the software. We'd need to wait until one of those left the company and then I'd need to express an interest in taking over. That could potentially take years."

'King' looked thoughtful. "Perhaps we wouldn't need to wait."

"What do you mean?" asked York.

"You could identify someone we need to leave, and we then just have to arrange for them to receive a better job offer elsewhere."

"Just like that?" laughed York.

"It would take some arranging, of course. Perhaps a bribe to a head-hunter, perhaps a favour from a friend. Anyway, that can be my problem as & when. You tell me who, and I'll figure out a way to make it happen."

'King' had a simpler solution in mind, of course.

* * *

Green pressed 'Send' to send to Wilkinson her report on risks in the production stage. Despite Turner's assurances, she'd identified 23 risk areas she felt needed greater safeguards.

She was a methodical person, so tackled one thing at a time, but what she'd learned during her Boeing factory visits about the enormous role that software played in an airliner's operation had been nagging at her, and she was keen to start work on that. She hadn't appreciated just how much software there was in even an older airliner, and a fly-by-wire model must have masses more. She logged-in to the task management system and changed her assignment from Aircraft Construction to Aircraft Design.

She really needed to learn a lot more about how that worked, especially on fly-by-wire aircraft. She started googling. Two hours later, she had some appreciation of how much she didn't know. She looked up the agency's liaison at Airbus, and checked the time. Noon in Washington, so 6pm in Paris – probably too late for a non-urgent call. She entered his email address, and typed a brief email explaining her role and her desire to learn more about the controls and checks on software installed in aircraft, and requesting copies of the relevant documentation.

The reply was waiting for her in the morning. She'd expected a whole ream of attachments, so was surprised to find there was only one. She read the email.

Thank you for your email concerning the controls & checks on software. You'll appreciate that the procedures governing this are both comprehensive and complex, and that the number of 'relevant documents' is very substantial.

I'm attaching an index of documents in the first instance. If you would be kind enough to advise which of these will be of assistance, I can arrange for these to be placed on a secure FTP server for you. If it would be helpful to have an initial telephone conversation to help you identify the most relevant documents, our Director of Software Development, Gunther Frison would be pleased to hear from you.

Green opened the index PDF. There were pages and pages of it! She looked for a document count: 1168 documents. Many of them were memos, but a substantial number were procedures manuals, flowcharts and checklists. Her experience of such things told her that many of the flowcharts would refer to other documents. The task was a massive one. She would definitely need that call.

It was 9.30am, so 3.30pm in Toulouse. She made the call. The name looked German, but as she was calling France she started in the tiny bit of French she remembered from school.

"Bonjour, Monsieur Frison. Parlez-vous Anglais?"

"But of course. And it is really Herr Frison."

"Ah, I thought that might be the case. My name is Sarah Green from Homeland Security in Washington, I understand you've kindly agreed to help steer me in the right direction in regard to the security procedures for software installed on your aircraft."

"With pleasure. I imagine you found the index a little daunting!"

"Well, I'm used to dealing with lots of documents, but yes, I'm hoping you can help me narrow things down a little."

"I shall do my best to assist, Ms Green. Perhaps you could outline the focus of your interest?"

"I'm looking at the scope for terrorists to inject code into any of the aircraft systems in order to cause a crash," explained Green. "I'm sure you have a great many procedures designed to safeguard the code, so really I'm looking to examine those."

"You suspect we haven't thought them through properly, Ms Green?"

"I assure you that no criticism is intended, Herr Frison. I recently visited Boeing to look at the construction process and this morning submitted my report on recommendations for additional safeguards. We have made similar recommendations in dozens of different aspects of aviation procedures; from pilot vetting to baggage-scanning. This is merely another area we'd like to examine."

"Many of the documents are updates and amendments. I can e-mail you a list of the major policy documents, which should give you a good starting point."

"Thanks, that will be helpful."

The email with the attachments arrived less than an hour later. It was, as promised, a much more manageable number: 32. This was, Green reflected, one of the trickier parts to her job – knowing just how much material you needed in order to do it properly. Too many documents, and you might miss seeing the wood for the trees; too few, and you might not have the document you needed to spot the fatal flaw in a process. Well, she shrugged, this wasn't an exact science. She opened the first document, the catchily-titled *Software Design Methodology for Airbus Firmware: A Management Framework*.

* * *

Adams knew that you got the most from interviews when the interviewee felt comfortable. It was why he preferred to conduct interviews in their own homes most of the time, as he'd done with Richard and Emma Williams. But a teenager didn't necessarily feel most relaxed at home, especially when they might need to discuss things they wouldn't want their parents to know. He'd suggested to Alison they take a walk along London's South Bank after she finished school.

They met at Waterloo and walked past the Royal Festival Hall and along the river toward Tower Bridge.

"You understand," asked Adams, "that everything I ask you, is designed to help me find out who killed Jen."

"You believe me?" Alison, sounding surprised.

"I don't believe or disbelieve anything at this stage," replied Adams. It was the truth: while he considered it most likely that Jen's death was an accident, you couldn't go into any investigation with preconceptions. You had to be capable of adopting a mindset where you understood that your initial theories and prejudices were just that, and that you knew nothing at all until you'd been able to prove or disprove it. If you couldn't do that, you were in the wrong line of business. Sure, sometimes your initial theories got confirmed by the evidence, but it was the times when you were proven wrong that made for the most interesting cases.

"Ok," replied Alison.

Adams continued: "My job is to understand what happened, and I can only do that if I have all the facts. That means I need you to be 100% truthful with me." He smiled at her. "You ever watch courtroom dramas?"

Alison gave a puzzled nod. "Sure, sometimes."

"You remember when people go into the witness box, they swear to tell the truth, the whole truth and nothing but the truth?"

Alison nodded again.

"The whole truth. That part is important. It means you don't just answer my direct questions, you tell me absolutely everything that might be relevant. I was in the police for twenty years. I've seen it all, heard it all and I'm not here to judge either one of you, just to find out what happened to her. If either or both of you were involved in anything illegal, the police aren't going to hear about it from me. If you hold back on anything, even if it doesn't seem relevant to you, that might be the one piece of info I need to figure things out. So you tell me everything, Ok?"

"I understand," said Alison.

Adams started with the same questions he'd asked her parents. Mostly he got the same answers, but unsurprisingly Alison knew more about the people Jen hung out with.

"So no boyfriend?" he asked.

"Not in the last few weeks. She was seeing this guy Clem for a while, but she wasn't that into him and she wasn't into all the stuff he wanted to do."

"Like what?"

Alison gave him a patronising look: "You don't need to know that."

"Maybe. But we'll assume not for now. So how did they break up?"

"He started seeing this other girl, he didn't really make a secret of it, Jen dumped him."

"How did Clem take that?"

"He didn't seem bothered. He's still with the other girl."

"Did Clem see Jen, or call her, after they broke up?"

"I don't think so."

"Ok. What if she'd be involved with someone secretly. Say, a married man. Would she have told you about that?"

"Yes."

"You're sure," persisted Adams.

"We told each other stuff."

"What if the man she was seeing swore her to secrecy?"

"It doesn't count. You tell your BFF everything, especially guy stuff."

"Was there any teacher she was especially close to?" asked Adams.

"You mean, was she doing a teacher? No."

"Would you have disapproved if she had been?"

"Not particularly."

"Anyone who had a crush on her?"

"Not that I know of. Lots of boys fancied her, but crush, no."

"Did she have a crush on anyone?"

"Not really."

"Not really?" queried Adams.

"Well, she had a bit of a thing for Julian Fox, the AOA guy. But no serious intent."

"So there was nothing going on between the two?"

"No."

Adams nodded. He didn't yet consider it an established fact – it was possible that Jen had been seeing someone and had been persuaded to keep it absolutely secret – but he considered it low likelihood.

"Was she involved in anything illegal? Remember, I'm not here to judge her, but it could be very important if she was."

"Not unless you count under-age drinking or smoking a little pot. Oh, and a bit of shop-lifting years ago."

"The pot – she just smoked it? Did she ever sell any of it, even a little, even occasionally?"

"No."

"Where did she buy it?"

"There's a guy at school. You tell him what you want and he gets it."

"Did she owe him money?"

"No, he didn't do credit," said Alison, sarcastically.

"Did she owe money to anyone?"

"No."

"And you don't know anyone who would want to hurt her?" asked Adams.

"No. I mean, someone obviously did, but I don't know who."

"Alright, let's move on to the day itself. How many people knew where she was going to be that morning?"

"Nobody. She wouldn't even tell me where we were going until that day – I learned about it from the email, the same as everyone else."

"I thought you said she told you everything?" challenged Adams.

"She did, but she was very serious about the AOA thing. A bit too serious, if you ask me, but it mattered to her. She told me it was a protest and that she'd fill me in after I got the email in the morning."

"So if she wouldn't tell you, she probably didn't tell anyone else?"

"Definitely not."

"So absolutely nobody knew where she was going to be that morning."

"No. Well, her AOA 'committee' or whatever, I suppose."

Adams nodded. "Could anyone have followed you? From her home to Heathrow?"

Alison considered it for a moment, then nodded. "It was rush-hour, the tube was very crowded, so yeah, if someone could have kept us in sight, we wouldn't have noticed them. We were chatting all the way there anyway."

Adams made a few notes in his notebook. "Ok, thanks. I may have more questions later, but that gives me enough to go on for now."

* * *

Wilkinson finished reviewing Green's report on the risk factors at the construction stage. It was good, solid work, and he would be endorsing all of her recommendations, but he wasn't convinced that she had learned anything from the visit that couldn't have been learned from telephone calls, documents and photos alone. His instinct that the visit was unnecessary was vindicated.

He looked again at her email request for a visit to Airbus. There was no way. She'd had her free shot at Boeing, and the costs of a visit to Europe would simply be too high. He picked up the phone.

"Sarah Green."

"It's Thomas. I have to turn down your request."

"Sir, I think this could be important. It's a critical area, and the Boeing visit showed me just how much easier it is to spot potential flaws when you've seen the operation for yourself."

"They're all critical areas, Sarah, and you did as good a job on Gate Security, which you did without any visits, as you did on Aircraft Construction, which you did with a visit."

"That's different, Sir: I worked in the aviation industry for more than a decade, I know about that kind of stuff. This is different. I don't have the same kind of background knowledge in this area."

"You know how this works, Sarah: we encourage analysts to work both within and outside their area of expertise. Those with the expertise are most likely to spot security holes, but sometimes they know too much and it needs an outside pair of eyes to spot things. The whole point of you working on something outside your own area is that you don't know too much about it."

"Yet you let me make the Boeing visit," challenged Green.

Wilkinson was losing patience; he had a lot of work to do. "Yes, I did, and this time I'm not. If you feel more comfortable working inside your sphere of experience, I have nobody working on Staff Vetting. We could certainly use your expertise there."

Green had to admit he had a point. She'd completely revamped her own airline's approach to vetting after uncovering some gaping holes. The only reason she hadn't chosen that area here was that she'd spent so much time working on it before, she hadn't been able to face the thought of doing more work on it. But it had now been a while now, so maybe her time would be put to better use. "OK, Thomas, I'll give it some thought."

"I appreciate that, Sarah."

Green logged into the task management system. One of the key lessons leaned after 9/11 was the danger of being too compartmentalised: information that was common knowledge with one team might be wholly unknown to another. 'Need to know' was a valid principle in the right context, but it could introduce more dangers than it prevented when over-used. The task-management system was thus open to the whole team: any of the analysts could check any area to see who else was working, or had worked, on each element.

She checked Aircraft Design. Bill Stephenson had worked on it. She didn't know him well, but he came from an IT project management background and certainly gave every impression of being extremely competent. She decided to have a quick chat with him about her on-board software concerns, to see whether he'd addressed the area already. She looked to see what he was working on now: Air Traffic Control.

She looked across the open-plan office to see whether she could spot him at his desk. He was there, so she pushed back her chair and wandered over.

"Hey Bill."

"Sarah – how goes it? What are you working on?"

"That's what I came to see you about, actually – got time for a coffee?"

"Sure."

They walked between the desks to reach the kitchen area. She selected a latte and Bill got a black filter coffee.

"What's on your mind?" he asked.

Green filled him in on her visit to Boeing, and her concerns about on-board software. "I was about to select Aircraft Design as an out-of-expertise area to work on, but Thomas is keen for me to work on staff vetting – something I know all too much about – so I really just wanted to run it past you to see whether on-board software was an issue you'd covered already?"

Bill smiled. "It certainly is! I spent a lot of time reviewing the code development processes at both Boeing and Airbus, and both are extremely robust as you'd expect. There were a number of areas I felt could be reasonably tightened, though between ourselves I viewed most of them as the icing on the cake. The chances of getting rogue software onto an operational airliner are so low as to be statistically indistinguishable from impossible."

"Just for my own curiosity, could you give me the Idiot's Guide to stopping bad guys programming software to crash planes?" She phrased it carefully. While the agency ethos might be openness, and a mix of expertise and fresh eyes, she knew from painful experience that not everyone reacted well to the perception that anyone was questioning their competence – especially geeks.

"There are five main stages to it," he said. "First, it's rare that the entire code for any complete module is written by a single software engineer. Most of it is a team effort. Second, once a developer considers a module complete, it goes forward to peer review. Other developers examine the code, specifically looking for problems. Coders are detail guys: anything they can't make sense of, or doesn't look right, they'll home in on it."

Green smiled. She'd had experience of that particular character trait.

"Third," continued Stephenson, "software testing. Essentially a PC on which the software is running is plugged into special test kit that simulates whatever hardware it's designed to control. The test kit systematically generates every single possible combination of input signals, and checks that the output signals are correct for that scenario. Typically, tens of thousands of permutations are tested. Anything out of spec is logged and will be investigated and corrected. Fourth, coders can't add software modules to live systems themselves. Everything goes through a revision-control system, which ensures that only modules which have been reviewed, tested and approved are released. Finally, once the software is installed on a test aircraft, a further series of tests will be carried out to ensure that it operates within spec in the real environment. Only when it passes all those tests will it make it onto production aircraft."

"What sort of weaknesses did you find when you did your review?" asked Green.

"It was mostly minor stuff, to be honest. My biggest concern was the degree of interaction between different modules in the real environment. For example, take the ground proximity warning system. If an aircraft gets too close to the ground, a warning system kicks in, sounds a chime, lights a warning light and activates the cockpit callout system, which will give a 'Terrain' warning. That system, though, is deactivated if the systems know – or think – the plane is landing. So if the plane is on a glide slope, and the landing gear is down, then the GPWS won't be activated. There are huge numbers of those kind of interdependencies, and I wasn't satisfied that the testing systems were covering all of them."

"But now they do?"

Stephenson shrugged: "You know the system. We recommend, whether they do it ..."

"Right."

"But overall, you feel confident a terrorist couldn't make an attack in that way?"

"Nothing is impossible, but yes, it is vanishingly unlikely. Aside from anything else, it would be a massive amount of work – there are about a thousand easier ways to bring down a plane."

"Though software could bring down a whole bunch of them."

"Not really," said Stephenson, "aircraft manufacturers take a very cautious approach to unexplained crashes after a series of disasters in the early days of commercial aviation. These days, if there is even a hint of a system or component being to blame, they'll ground all aircraft of that model pending immediate replacement of the suspect part. It's incredibly rare that a fault – deliberate or not – would get the chance to cause a second crash."

Green nodded: she remembered a couple of examples of the chaos caused in her airline when a particular model was grounded while replacement parts were dispatched and fitted.

She thanked Stephenson for his time, and wandered slowly back to her desk, mulling it over in her mind. The outside perspective argument was still valid, of course, and it was possible she'd think of something that Stephenson had missed, but the software side was a very technical field and she felt that the odds were against it in this particular case.

Back at her desk, she moved herself from Aircraft Design to Staff Vetting.

* * *

Two weeks into the investigation, Adams suspected he might know more about Jen's daily life than her parents did. Alison had been open about the fact that Jen had bunked-off school two or three days a week, and he'd been able to piece together most of the ways that she'd spent that time. He was reasonably satisfied that Jen hadn't been involved in anything significantly illegal, and as yet had discovered no obvious candidates for enemies.

In terms of how Jen had spent her time, Action On Aviation had featured heavily. Alison had been able to tell him little – though she respected her friend's views, it wasn't something in which she had any great interest herself – but she did know that

Jen visited in the offices at least once or twice a week.

Like many such protest groups, AOA was informally organised, with little in the way of a paper trail. As far as he'd been able to ascertain, the organisation had no legal existence at all: no Limited company, no registered charity, no formal identity of any kind. The offices were rented in Fox's name, and he was the one who appeared to call the shots.

Adams had two objectives with AOA. First, to discover whether Jen had been sleeping with Julian Fox. Second, to find out whether anyone else within AOA might have had reason to harm Jen.

He needed to get someone on the inside to gain the confidence of a few people and start asking some discreet questions. He had a couple of people in the agency who had been hired partly for their detective skills, and partly because they looked a lot younger than they were. Claire Sorin was one of them. Aged 26, she could pass for a teenager with ease, and even a schoolgirl with a little preparatory work. For this role, she was going to be 17 and a committed environmentalist who'd recently moved into the area. Jen's death had been headline news, so it wouldn't be unreasonable to ask a few questions about her once she was in the door.

Claire Sorin was parked about 150 feet down the road from the AOA offices, her car facing away. This gave her a view of the front door through her wing-mirror without any likelihood of her being spotted.

This type of surveillance was the most boring part of the job, mused Sorin. You never knew whether you'd be there for five minutes or five hours. Take your eyes off the target for even 30 seconds, and the whole time would be wasted. The only saving grace was that she didn't have to wait for a specific person: any AOA volunteer close to her own fictional age of 17 would do.

Tonight, she was lucky: a group of three teenagers, two girls, one guy, emerged after only 40 minutes. If she was really lucky, they'd be heading to the nearest pub, on the opposite corner, that she'd scouted out earlier; she wasn't quite that fortunate: they were walking down the street, engaged in an animated conversation. Sorin was wearing an oversized smart coat, horn-rim glasses and a long brown wig over her short blonde hair. A mobile phone held to her ear completed the disguise: if they did happen to glance into her car as she passed, they'd see a businesswoman on the phone, her left arm blocking any clear view of her face.

Once the three had walked past, she slipped off the wig and glasses, and with a practised manoeuvre eased herself out of the coat. Within seconds, the medium-build brunette businesswoman in the car had been replaced by a scruffy, slim teenage blonde in a denim skirt and tatty leather jacket with a badge. She patted her side pocket to make sure she had her bag of pound coins, picked up a cheap-looking backpack, let herself quietly out of the car, locked it with the key to avoid any alarm blip and followed the teenagers at a distance.

Three streets later, the three walked into a different pub – probably their local. Sorin gave them five minutes before entering the pub. She headed to the bar, taking a bored-looking glance around as she did. By the time she reached the bar, she'd located both targets: the teenagers sat at a table to her right, and the Ladies in the far corner to her left. She headed into the Ladies, walked to the vending machine on the wall and spent £12 emptying it, shoving the contents into her backpack. This done, she returned to the bar, ordered a beer and took it over to the closest empty table to the toilets.

Now she had to hope for the best. If neither of the girls visited the bathroom, her plan B was to follow them out when they left and ask them for a light. Plan A was more reliable, though.

She was in luck: both girls got up and were headed in her direction. She quickly picked up her bag and headed into the Ladies ahead of them. When the two girls walked in, she was rattling the drawer of the tampon machine in frustration. She turned to them.

"Excuse me," she said, "this is really embarrassing, but the machine is out." She gestured to it. "Do either of you have a spare I could have?"

The smaller of the two girls, a redhead with pale green eyes, reached into her bag and produced one. "Here," she said.

"Thank you so much," said Sorin with a big smile. "Excuse me one minute, and then I'll get you a drink."

The redhead shook her head: "It's OK, we've all been there."

"No, really, I insist. Just give me a moment," she said, slipping into one of the cubicles.

Emerging a couple of minutes later, she washed her hands and waited for the two girls to appear. "I'm Claire," she said. It was something they generally did to avoid stupid mistakes: make up a surname, but use their own first name.

"Aggi," said the redhead.

"Paula," said her friend.

They walked back through the bar, and Claire was introduced to Carl. She insisted on getting a round of drinks for them all.

She let them lead the chat for ten minutes before explaining that she'd just moved up to London from Southampton and didn't really know anyone yet.

"What brought you to London?" asked Aggi.

"My boyfriend got a job with Greenpeace, so I moved up with him."

"Oh, right," said Aggi, "that's cool. We're all involved with Action On Aviation – have you heard of that?"

Sorin looked thoughtful for a moment. "Didn't you guys do that big protest at Heathrow a few months ago? I read about that horrible accident with the girl and the train."

Aggi nodded: "Yeah, that was bad."

"Did you know her?"

"A little, not well. But Julian was very complimentary about her."

"Julian?" asked Sorin.

"He runs AOA," explained Carl.

"Oh, OK. Such a shame about the girl, but I guess accidents happen sometimes."

"Yeah."

"So have you got other demos planned? It would be great to get involved in something locally."

"Come along on Saturday morning," said Paula. "We have an introduction for new people, supposed to start at 10am but it's a bit 'ish', if you know what I mean."

Claire laughed. "Yeah, most protest groups seem to be the same. Where do you meet, here?"

"No, we've got offices about half a mile from here. Got some paper? I'll give you the address."

The induction was indeed 10am-ish – past 11am, in fact. Claire was one of four newbies, and the 'induction' was given by a guy of about 20 who was a bit too full of his own self-importance. He explained rather pompously that they had to adopt a strict hierarchy for security reasons, and that new volunteers would need to do the donkey work for a while until they could prove themselves. He eventually handed over to Julian Fox, who was quite a contrast in style to the puffed-up teenager. Fox was charming, affable and thanked them profusely for caring enough to get involved.

Afterwards, Claire introduced herself.

"How did you learn about AOA?" asked Fox.

"I was kind of press-ganged into it by Aggi," laughed Claire. "I was in a pub, and she rescued me from an embarrassing situation. I bought her a drink, and when she found out my boyfriend was involved with Greenpeace, she dragged me along here."

"Not too reluctant a convert, I hope?"

Claire shook her head. "Not at all. The aviation industry is one of the biggest culprits. Oh, I know it's only responsible for 2% of CO_2 emissions, but it's the rate of growth and the fact that it's all totally unnecessary. You can't blame people for wanting to heat their homes, and it's not their fault that we have crap insulation standards, but there's no excuse at all for jetting off on holiday. It's just utterly selfish." She had briefed herself by visiting both the AOA and Greenpeace websites, as well as reading through a rather interminable thread on an environmentalist forum. The posts had all been so self-righteous, she'd wanted to reach through the screen and slap them, but you had to be a decent actress in this job, and she'd leaned her part well.

Fox nodded. "That's what we're all about. Have you been involved in protests before?"

"Small ones," said Claire, "but I was in Southampton before, so it was a bit of a trek to get to the big London ones. I would have made it for that big Heathrow one you had, though, if I'd known about it in time."

"There'll be others," said Fox.

"The death of that girl must have been a real shock," said Claire, watching Fox closely to see how he reacted to mention of Jen.

"It was," said Fox, frowning. "A terrible accident."

"Were you friends with her?"

Fox shrugged. "Not really friends, but she was a keen volunteer. Anyway, let's not dwell on such things. Neil will process your form and fix you up with something to do, and if you want to grab a drink in the meantime, I think the others have gone through to the kitchen."

Claire smiled. "Yes, I could use a coffee."

"Neil can have that effect on people sometimes," grinned Fox. "Anyway, welcome aboard."

* * *

Fox had known that getting York into Airbus was going to be the one area where he would need to exercise patience. There were crude methods he could have attempted – arranging for an existing coder to meet with an accident to create a vacancy, bribing someone to recruit York, that kind of thing – but he had rejected all of them. He didn't know the field, and had no contacts, so everything would have had to have been done from scratch. Too many new people, too many unknowns, too risky.

This didn't mean that he couldn't employ a more subtle proactive approach, however. Market research had once more served him well. He found another small agency, this time one specialising in the IT sector, and posed as an IT recruiter wanting to branch out into the aviation sector. What IT skill-sets were airlines looking for at present? What were the greatest recruitment challenges their IT departments were facing? And which recruitment agencies did they use at present? It was a small project, and it didn't require deep cover: a £100 off-the-shelf company and a website of a few pages did the trick.

The research agency carried out telephone depth interviews with IT project managers in Boeing, Airbus and a few smaller aircraft manufacturers, and came back with a list of the key skill-sets in demand. From there, they were able to create an infiltration strategy: get York intensive training in the skills he lacked, and revamp his CV to provide a profile that would put him in demand. Once that was done, York could make speculative approaches to one of the biggest recruitment agencies used by Airbus.

York was concerned that Airbus would be aware of his letters in the press criticising fly-by-wire systems, but those had been months ago, and had garnered little attention. Thanks to 'King', none of the press releases had gone anywhere. York's name was removed from the SOS website, and a Google search found nothing incriminating in the first three pages; it was unlikely that anyone would search deeper unless they had good reason to. Fox simply suggested that York use the formal Daniel E. York as his name to minimise the likelihood of the name ringing any bells.

* * *

"So how did Fox react when you mentioned Jen's death?" asked Adams, as Claire Sorin reported back to him.

"He was difficult to read," she replied. "He moved the conversation on straight away, which I guess is understandable enough when you're trying to enrol a new recruit, but he seemed a bit too casual about it to me. I mean, perhaps he really is that cold, but that's not the impression I had of him generally."

"So you think maybe he and Jen were involved, and he was trying to downplay his feelings?"

"I'm not sure, but yes, I definitely got an odd feeling about it."

Adams nodded. "OK, I think we need to see what we can learn about Mr Fox." He reached into a drawer and held up a USB key. "Remember your training on our spyware software?"

Sorin made a wavy motion with her hand. "I think so. Self-installing, right?"

"Right. All you need do is find a time when his laptop is logged-in, insert the key into one of the USB ports and the software will automatically install. You get a small window saying Installing then about a minute later the window closes. Just unplug it, and you're done. After that, it'll capture everything he types, and take a screengrab every minute, emailing the log to us the first time the laptop is used each morning." Adams handed the key to her. "Remember, a minute can be a very long time when you're standing at the target's laptop and they could walk in at any moment, so choose your moment carefully. Don't take any chances: if you're not sure you'll have enough time, leave it until another time."

Sorin's next three visits proved abortive. The first time, there were just too many people there: there was no chance at all of getting into Fox's office without detection. The second, Fox was holding a meeting in his office, and didn't leave it until he left the building at the end of the evening. The third, Fox didn't show up at all.

She didn't want to arouse suspicion by being there too often, so had settled on twice a week. It was the end of the second week before she had her chance.

She was updating the membership database, and was hoping along the way to be able to take a copy of it: it might prove useful. She didn't have a direct view of Fox's office door, but the toilets were off the main open-plan area, so if Fox went to the loo, that would be her chance. Timing would be tight, she knew, but there were only two others in the office, so it was her best chance.

She and Adams had considered the possibility of some kind of ruse to get Fox out of the office for a few minutes, but had rejected the idea: anything out of the ordinary was likely to lead him to logout of his laptop, and they needed it logged-in to be able to install the spy software.

It was a little after 8.30pm when Fox emerged from his office and headed into the toilet. Sorin's heart was racing as she concentrated on casually picking up her coffee cup and walking towards the kitchen. Fox's office was right next door. Feigning a stretch, she took the opportunity to check on the two other volunteers: both were engrossed in what they were doing.

The moment she was out of sight of them, she quickened her pace and darted into Fox's office. She was in luck: Fox hadn't bothered to logout. She pushed the USB key into one of the ports on the side and watched as the messages appeared on the screen.

Installing device driver software. The PC was recognising the USB key as a drive and installing the drivers to allow it to be accessed. She knew it would take around ten seconds for the next message to appear, but it felt like an eternity. Finally, it appeared: Your device is ready to use. The auto-installation software would now run. It was only a couple more seconds before a tiny window opened at the bottom-left of the screen and the word Installing appeared.

Sorin glanced nervously towards the door. She knew she'd only been in there about 20 seconds, and she was praying Fox had been well brought-up: her training taught her that the average man spent slightly under two minutes in a public toilet if he washed and dried his hands afterwards, but only just over a minute if he didn't.

She had considered leaving his office and moving into the kitchen during the installation, just in case either of the other volunteers wandered by and saw her in the office, but had decided that was likely to increase the risk: by staying there, she could pull out the key and get the hell out the moment it was finished.

She strained to hear the sound of a toilet flush, but the toilets were too far away and through two closed doors. She could hear nothing.

She jumped at the sudden sound of a phone ringing! It was Fox's mobile, on his desk. Would he hear it from the toilets? And if so, would he come running out to answer it? The message on the screen still read Installing. Sorin froze for a moment. If she grabbed the key and dashed out of the office and into the kitchen, she'd be safe, but then there was no telling when she'd get her next opportunity. If she stayed, she might be caught, and then it would be over.

Operating more by instinct than thought, she left the USB key in place and dashed into the kitchen. Just as she got there, she heard the toilet door bang and the sound of footsteps running: Fox was dashing to his office to answer the call.

Sorin thought quickly. His attention would be on his phone for the few seconds it took him to reach it and answer it, and the installation window was designed to be as discreet as possible, so he probably wouldn't notice it at a casual glance. But once the call was complete, he would almost certainly return to working on his laptop and then he couldn't miss it.

She heard Fox pick up the call, and quickly came up with a plan. It was a desperate one, but the only one she had. She picked up the coffee jug from the perculator and quickly poured two mugs of coffee. She picked up the mugs and taking a moment to calm herself and adopt a casual expression, she walked to Fox's doorway. He looked up, and she motioned with one of the mugs, smiling at him. If he shook his head now, she had no plan B.

The moment seemed to last forever, but then he smiled and nodded. She walked over to his desk with the mugs. Just before she got there, she pretended to trip and both mugs went flying across his desk, spilling coffee everywhere. Fox leapt back, dropping his phone.

"Oh my god!" cried Sorin, "I'm so sorry!"

Fox spoke into his phone: "I'll call you straight back." He sounded irritated but not livid.

"Sorry!" repeated Sorin.

"Ok, don't worry about it," said Fox.

He bent down behind him to pick up the mugs off the floor. Sorin used the moment to grab the USB key and yank it from the socket. She'd had no time to look at the screen, so didn't know whether or not the software had installed.

"I'll get some kitchen towel," she said, running out to the kitchen. She put the USB key into her pocket, grabbed the kitchen roll and dashed back to mop up the coffee from the desk and wood floor. "I'm such a klutz! Are you ok? I didn't get any on you, did I?"

Fox checked his shirt. "No," he said, smiling. "No harm done."

Sorin finished mopping up the coffee and pick the mugs from the desk where Fox had put them. "Shall I get you another one – carefully?"

"It's ok," said Fox, "I think we won't risk it."

"I'm sorry, I'll leave you to get back to your call, and I'll get back to the membership database."

Sorin waited an hour before leaving, saying goodbye and repeating her apology for the coffee to Fox. As soon as she was back in her car, she called Stephen Adams to relay the story.

"So you didn't see whether or not the window had closed?" he asked.

"There wasn't time – I had about a second to grab the key before he stood up again and spotted it. What happens if it didn't finish installing?"

"Well, the good news is that the window would have disappeared as soon as you removed the key, the bad news is that if the installation was interrupted, not only will it not work, but a second automatic installation may fail. We can still do a manual installation, but that takes several minutes."

"So we just have to wait and see whether the emailed logs arrive?"

"Exactly. We won't have long to wait: the logs are sent the first time he logs-in to his laptop each morning."

"Christ, I hope it works, I don't think I could go through that again."

"We'll soon know."

Adams was smiling as he walked up to Claire Sorin's desk the following morning, carrying two cups of coffee. He grinned as he handed one to her: "It seemed appropriate."

"Does that grin mean it worked?" she asked, desperately hoping it did.

"Received the first set of files just after 8am," Adams confirmed. "I've only had a quick look through so far, but already discovered something very interesting."

Sorin knew from experience that Adams enjoyed his little moments of drama, and if she merely nodded, he'd just wait for her to ask. "What was interesting?"

"Our Mr Fox has an alias. Before leaving last night, he logged out of his main account and logged-in to a second one, accessing an email account in that name."

"What is the alias?"

"David King. There were no keystrokes after the login, and only one screengrab, of an Outlook account in that name, so it looks like he just did a quick email check and logged-out."

"So now we wait for more log files?" asked Sorin.

"We'll give it a few days," replied Adams, "but if we don't learn more within that time, we may have to take a rather more proactive approach."

* * *

Sarah Green had hit on a compromise: she'd work on staff vetting, but begin with vetting of software engineers in aircraft manufacturers.

Boeing and Airbus had sent her details of the recruitment criteria they applied, and the vetting procedures used. Most large employers in sensitive industries used the same four categories of vetting as government agencies:

1. Developed Vetting (DV)
2. Security Check (SC)
3. Counter Terrorist Check (CTC)
4. Baseline Personnel Security Standard (BPSS)

The two highest levels, DV and SC covered access to classified materials, and were typically only applied by governments. Airlines ran the BPSS for all staff, and CTC for staff in particularly sensitive positions – such as flight crews.

The BPPS was essentially just a very low-level paper-trail check. Identity documents were verified, and previous employers were contacted to ensure that the stated employment history was accurate. The CTC added more detailed employment checks (including verifying the identity of those providing the references), and a check against national security records. This involved a criminal record search, as well as a search against other national security records – for example, ensuring that the candidate was not on a No-Fly list.

Green was surprised and concerned that the standard vetting for software engineers working for aircraft manufacturers was only the BPSS. It would be entirely possible for someone on a No-Fly list to be writing software running on an airliner!

Green had used the Red Flag system exactly once in her time at Homeland Security: this allowed analysts to flag up a serious security flaw that required immediate action. That issue would be immediately escalated for senior review, and any necessary actions would typically be put in place in anything from 24 to 72 hours.

By its very nature, the Red Flag system had to be used extremely sparingly. It was intended to ensure that the most glaring security lapses received immediate attention, and over-use would render it useless. If every potentially serious flaw were red-flagged, the escalation system would be swamped and would grind to a halt. Given the attention it would generate, any analyst thought long and hard before deciding to press the button. Those new to the role were tempted to flag up all sorts of things, so initially had to get the approval of a more experienced analyst before red-flagging something. Experience gradually taught you that only the most extreme issues justified the procedure.

Green was senior enough to press the button on her own initiative, but decided to talk again with Bill Stephenson before making the final decision.

* * *

Claire Sorin was writing up a report on a marital infidelity case. They were rarely interesting, and usually rather seedy and sad, but they were the bread-and-butter work that paid the bills for detective agencies, so she didn't begrudge them.

When her phone rang, she looked down at the display to see it was Stephen. She wasn't looking forward to an update on the Williams case as she had a horrible feeling that the 'more proactive approach' Adams had mentioned was going to be no easier than installing the keylogger. Her suspicion was correct.

"Pop in, would you, Claire?"

"On my way."

Adams was sitting at the small meeting table in his office with a laptop and an external hard drive. Next to him was Jim Cater, one of her colleagues.

Adams smiled, and gestured for her to take the seat next to him.

"This is not looking like good news," observed Sorin, gesturing to the laptop and drive.

"Well," replied Adams, "there's good news and bad news."

"Uhuh."

"The good news is that there is definitely something odd going on with Fox. It may not be related to the Williams death, of course, but you know the form."

Sorin nodded: investigators didn't believe in coincidences. If one odd thing had happened, and another odd thing was discovered, the smart money was on the two being related.

"Fox checks the David King email account at least once a day. We haven't yet learned much, but he sent an email to Regus – the serviced office company – advising them that one of his offices wasn't needed any more. I've checked the lease on the AOA offices, and they are not owned by Regus. AOA doesn't appear to have offices elsewhere, so somewhere Fox is renting another set of offices under a false name."

"And the bad news?" asked Sorin.

"In three days, that's the only thing he's done under that login: the rest of it is just email checks. So we need to take the initiative here."

Sorin grimaced. She didn't know exactly what was coming next, but she knew she wasn't going to like it.

If Adams noticed her expression, he didn't react to it. He continued: "Which is where this comes in." He gestured to the external hard drive. "We need a complete copy of the documents stored on the David King account. Thanks to the keylogger, we have the login for that account, and the software on here is already configured. All you need do is login as King, then run this app." He moved the pointer to a file called accountxfer.exe.

"Copying the drive?" challenged Sorin. "Surely that will take hours?"

"We're not copying the whole drive, only the files associated with the David King login. As it's an alias, there are unlikely to be thousands of them, so the copy should only take 5-10 minutes."

"Impossible!" said Sorin. "The only time he left his laptop last time was to grab a coffee and go to the toilet. There's just no way."

"This is different. Last time, you had to get access to his laptop while he was logged-in. This time, you don't. We have both sets of login details-" Adams handed her a slip of paper with the username and password- "so even if his laptop is logged-out, you can login to the David King account to do the copy."

"That still means ten minutes of uninterrupted access to his laptop."

"That's where Jim comes in. Next time you go to the AOA offices, Jim will position himself nearby. If Fox is in his office and the place is quiet enough for you to get into his office unseen, you text Jim. He'll call Fox using a disposable phone and claim to be an aviation insider with some information that will enable him to cause even greater chaos at Heathrow than he did last time."

"And then?"

"Jim will claim to be in the pub where you met the AOA girls, and tell Fox he's going to wait there for exactly five minutes; if he's not there inside that time, he'll leave and never contact him again. That'll force him to rush out. When he gets there, Jim will call him again, directing him to a second pub another five minutes' walk, telling him to wait for him there. The idea Jim will put to him will be totally impractical, but even if Fox dismisses it instantly, it's a ten-minute walk each way, so that gives you twenty minutes, twice as long as you need."

"What could possibly go wrong ..." quoted Sorin, sarcastically.

"Jim will be watching him from close to the first pub. If he doesn't head on to the second pub, he'll call you straight away so you have about five minutes to unplug the drive, log out and return to your desk. No sweat."

Sorin nodded. After her scare last time, she knew she couldn't afford to do anything which would raise Fox's suspicions, but she had to admit the plan seemed like a sound one.

They spent the next few minutes discussing the plan in more detail, then agreed to try that evening. Sorin wasn't looking forward to it.

Sorin was in luck: although there were half a dozen people there when she'd arrived, by 9pm it was her, Julian, Neil and a Scandinavian girl she hadn't met before called Tij.

She texted Jim: Now.

Less than a minute later, she heard Fox's phone ring. She couldn't hear any of the conversation. There were two obvious ways this could go wrong, she thought: either Fox doesn't take the bait, or he takes his laptop with him. She caught herself half hoping for one of those outcomes, so that she wouldn't have to venture back into his office.

The thought was short-lived, as Fox hurried out of his office sans laptop. "Nipping out for half an hour," he called. "Ok," replied Neil.

Sorin waited a few minutes before grabbing her mug and standing up. "Can I get either of you a coffee?" she offered. Neil just shook his head. Tij smiled: "Sure, let me help you."

"No need," said Sorin, quickly. "You carry on."

Tij looked for a moment like she might insist on helping, then nodded, and handed over her mug: "Black, no sugar, please."

Sorin had the hard drive in her inside jacket pocket. Pretending to brush some fluff from her shoulder gave her an opportunity to check that both Neil and Tij were staying put. She darted into Fox's office and sat down at his desk. The laptop was at the login screen.

She logged-on as David King, then plugged in the drive. It seemed to take an eternity for Windows to recognise the drive and declare it ready for use. She opened the window and double-clicked accountxfer.exe. Like the keylogger, it was designed to be discreet, opening a tiny window with the single word Processing.

She stood up, left Fox's office and went to the kitchen to get the coffee. She glanced at her watch, and made a note to return in ten minutes. Walking back into the open-plan area, she handed Tij her coffee and returned to her own work.

She slid her phone out of her pocket and checked the signal strength, to reassure herself that she wouldn't miss a warning call. Four bars: it was fine.

Jim Cater watched Fox leave the offices, and followed him down the street. So far, so good. Fox was walking briskly but not hurriedly. At that pace, it was a five-minute walk to the pub, and Cater walked on the opposite side of the street, keeping his distance. Surveillance work was always much easier when you knew where the target was headed. Or, at least, thought that you did.

Sorin tried to concentrate on what she was doing, but couldn't do it. She watched the clock in the bottom-right corner of her screen. Was the PC clock showing the same time as her watch, she wondered? She checked her watch. It was. Eight minutes to go. She tried to force herself to relax.

Behind and to the left of her, Neil noticed her glancing at her watch.

For Sorin, time seemed to pass incredibly slowly. The digits of the clock on her PC screen seemed frozen. She knew it was irrational, but checked her watch again anyway. Still eight minutes.

Fox reached the pub, and looked around before entering. Cater waited thirty seconds, then took the phone from his pocket and called Fox again.

"Julian, please forgive my caution, but I needed to be sure you weren't being followed. Do you know the Red Square pub in Warrington Square?"

"I don't have time for cloak and dagger games," replied Fox. "If you want to speak to me, you can do so here."

"I will meet you there, I promise. My job is on the line here: I have to be careful."

"No," said Fox. "You chose the pub, you presumably watched me walk into it, and can see I'm alone. Now, do we talk here, or do I go back to work?"

Cater thought quickly. Fox seemed to mean it. He quickly checked his watch: if he could delay Fox by five minutes, Claire ought to have time to complete the copy.

"Okay," said Cater, "I will be there in two minutes."

"Make it one," said Fox, hanging up.

This kind of subterfuge work was a balancing act, reflected Cater. For major operations, you had contingency plan layered upon contingency plan. For something like this, which ought to be very simple and fast, you tended to wing it. Usually that worked long enough to get the job done, but not always.

His cover here was pretty thin. He had enough of a story that he could make himself appear a well-meaning but naive sympathiser with a totally impractical idea that Fox would quickly reject. It was only intended to last a couple of minutes, as Fox would be ten minutes from his office, but now he needed to spin it out for five minutes to be sure. Making Fox wait didn't look like an option.

He hurried down the road and into the pub.

Neil noticed Claire check her watch for the third time in a few minutes.

"Waiting for something?" he asked her.

Sorin looked up. "Sorry?" she said.

"You keep checking your watch."

"Oh!" She paused. "Yes." She paused again. "Supposed to be having a drink with a friend this evening. She was due to have phoned me half an hour ago, and when I tried to call her I just got her voicemail. Anyway, if she doesn't call soon, I'm going to forget the whole idea and go home."

Neil nodded. "You do right. I really hate unreliable people."

Tij nodded her agreement too. "It's just rude. Sometimes you can't help delays, but you should always phone."

Sorin was afraid she might be starting a lengthy conversation, when Neil returned to his work, and Sorin breathed a sigh of relief. This assignment was turning her into a nervous wreck. Neil seemed to have happily accepted her impromptu story, she thought – but she still had to get back into Fox's office and retrieve the drive. She looked again at the PC clock: four minutes.

The ring-tone of her phone startled her.

"Hello?" she said.

"It's Jim. He's on his way back. You've got less than five minutes."

"You're late," she said, "you were supposed to call me half an hour ago." She looked round at Neil, who gave her a thumbs-up.

"I'll hang-up so you can complete your side of the conversation, but be quick about it – he'll be there in about three or four minutes, maybe less if he is annoyed enough: people can walk quickly when they're pissed-off." Jim hung up.

"Ok," she said. "I'll be a few minutes finishing up here, then I'll meet you there." She hung up.

Sorin glanced at the PC clock again. Two minutes. She closed the file and logged-off. She slowly stood up, put on her jacket and made a show of checking around to see if she'd got everything. She reckoned by the time she got to Fox's laptop, it should be complete.

"Goodnight, Neil, Tij."

"Night, Claire."

"Seeya."

Sorin stood up and walked towards the exit. She employed the same fluff-brushing technique to check that neither of the others had got up, then darted quickly into Fox's office. Reaching the front of his desk, she was relieved to see that the transfer window was closed: it was complete.

She pulled out the drive, and stuffed it into her jacket pocket. She then hit CTRL-ALT-DEL and selected logoff.

Fox was feeling annoyed at the time-waster. You got them every now and then: people who thought they'd come up with some great plan, when it was obvious to anyone with any experience that it was hopelessly flawed. Still, he reflected, at least he'd given short shrift to the tour of London business the idiot had tried to send him on.

He walked back into the AOA offices, and shrugged off his jacket, heading for his own office. He bumped into Claire Sorin, just coming out of it.

"Oh!" said Claire. "Sorry! I seem to make a bit of a habit of clumsiness around you."

"What were you doing in my office?" he asked.

"I was just leaving, and walked in to say goodbye, before seeing you weren't there."

"Ok," said Fox. He glanced around his office. He was careful, and didn't leave sensitive documents sitting around. He walked round his desk and glanced at his screen: it was logged-off. He smiled. "Well," he said, "at least you didn't throw coffee at me this time!"

"No," smiled Sorin. "Anyway, I'd better go, I'm meeting a friend."

"Have a good evening," replied Fox.

* * *

Stephen Adams was puzzled. Analysis of the data within the David King directory of Fox's laptop had revealed relatively little, but there was an email from Regus, the serviced office company, regarding an office suite in Victoria. The account was in the name of Safety in Our Skies.

A credit reference check and Charity Commissioner search had found no registered company or charity in that name, but googling it turned up a very sparse website. It was a campaign group calling for improved safety standards in the aviation industry.

Adams couldn't understand why someone vehemently anti-aviation should be running an aviation safety group under a pseudonym.

The summary section in Martin Wingfield's report was equally intriguing:

"The directory is reminiscent of the drives seized in mid-level white-collar fraud cases. While the paucity of data is partly as a result of relatively brief and infrequent use of the login, much of it is due to deliberate and relatively advanced steps to protect against discovery of the data. Sent and Deleted email folders have been regularly emptied, as has the trashcan. The browser has been used in 'Private browsing' mode, meaning that there is no Internet history, cookies or cache. There are no bookmarks. These are the hallmarks of a user who is going to significant trouble to minimise the electronic trail left on the machine.

The good news is that there appears to be no encrypted data on the drive, nor any evidence of the use of secure deletion software. Forensic analysis of the drive is likely to recover a high proportion of deleted data. This would, however, require physical access to the original laptop drive for several hours in order to carry out a bit-level copy. The work required would also be relatively expensive – estimate attached."

Adams had glanced at the estimate and winced. While he was confident that Fox was up to no good, there was no evidence that he had anything to do with Jen's death, and Adams didn't feel justified in asking Richard Williams to fork out for the costs of a forensic analysis, leaving aside the ... extra-legal ... measures likely to be necessary to get physical access to the laptop for the required time.

He shook his head. So far, they had expended a great deal of time, effort and Richard Williams' money, and were no closer to solving the mystery of his daughter's death, assuming that there was any mystery to it.

They knew – or at least, strongly suspected – that Fox was involved in something dodgy, but had no real clue as to what that something might be, or whether it had any connection to Jen's death.

Personally, he still suspected the most likely possibility was the correct one: a tragic accident.

He had always aimed to be straight with clients. Detectives have a particular mindset. They hate mysteries, and always want to solve them. It was all too easy to get carried away in an investigation, to get so caught up in things that you ended up spending your clients' money on finding out everything there was to learn, irrespective of its relevance to the client's actual objectives. Adams tried hard not to do that.

He would report back to Williams that, while Fox was undoubtedly involved in something suspicious, there was nothing linking him to Jen's death, and he was unsure that further investigation was justified. It would then be for Williams to make the call on whether or not things went further.

* * *

Sarah Green picked up the phone and dialled the internal number.

"Bill Stephenson."

"Bill, it's Sarah again. Could I borrow you for a few minutes?"

"Sure – grab a coffee?" Green smiled: Bill liked his coffee, it seemed.

"I'll wander over to your desk now."

Green walked over to Stephenson's desk, and then the two of them walked slowly towards the kitchen area.

"What's up?" he asked.

"It's the staff vetting thing. I thought I'd combine my two concerns and start by looking at the vetting of the software developers."

Stephenson gave her a slightly skeptical look. "Ok," he said.

"Did you know they only have a BPSS check? There's no CTC check."

Stephenson raised an eyebrow. "I didn't, but I wouldn't lose much sleep over it, personally."

"Why not?" asked Green.

"For a terrorist group, it doesn't really stack up as a viable approach. First, the chances of pulling off an attack in that way are minimal, for all the reasons I mentioned before. Way too many checks and balances. And then you have to look at the difficulty of even attempting it. Avionics software is a highly specialised field. You can't just get any old software developer into that sort of work. It's what's known as 'five-nines' work: it must have 99.999% reliability. Only someone who comes from a five-nines environment could even get a foot in the door."

"So who could?" persisted Green.

Stephenson thought about it for a moment. "You'd have to have a background in one of a pretty small number of fields. Defence systems. Medical firmware. Bank trading systems. That kind of thing: environments where a system simply cannot be allowed to fall over or give false outputs."

"Defence work would presumably require CTC clearance?"

"For sure."

They reached the kitchen area and Stephenson got himself a large black coffee while Green opted for a skinny latte.

"But medical or banking?" she asked.

"Probably not," acknowledged Stephenson, "but don't underestimate how much experience you'd need to get into any of those fields. Then you'd need additional specialist skills for the avionics stuff. It's not like a terrorist group could just pick some guy up off the streets and get him a job at Airbus. You're talking literally years of experience in software engineering, probably a decade or more. Most terrorist groups are impatient: they want things they can do quickly. The few exceptions don't tend to think a decade ahead, especially for something that probably wouldn't work anyway."

"I was thinking about red-flagging this," said Green.

Stephenson shook his head. "It's not justified. The risk is tiny, and the chances of it even being attempted are as small."

Green thanked him for his time, and wandered back to her desk. She was still concerned, but Bill seemed convinced it was such a small risk, she wasn't sure she could red-flag it.

Stephenson felt annoyed that Green hadn't seemed to be listening to him. This was his field, and it was frankly insulting that Green was ignoring his expertise. He understood the 'outside eyes' principle. Sometimes a fresh look by someone who wasn't intimately involved in a particular field could uncover something the experts had missed. But this wasn't one of them. This was a risk he'd considered, assessed and categorised as too low to be worthy of serious consideration. If Green red-flagged it despite their conversations, it was effectively accusing him of incompetence: missing something so vital that it needed to be acted on immediately.

He finished his coffee, but didn't head back to his office: he went instead to see Wilkinson. He wanted to give him a heads-up about Green's frankly off-the-wall obsession, and warn him that he might be about to receive a completely inappropriate red-flag memo.

* * *

Sorin poked her head round Stephen Adam's office door with a questioning look.

"Sure, come in," he said.

"Please tell me the data transfer worked," she pleaded. "That whole thing became a complete nightmare – I never want to see those offices again in my life!"

Adams smiled. "Don't worry, we got it."

"And?"

"Martin has just done a preliminary scan so far. It would appear our Mr Fox is the cautious type: the only emails in his mail directory were recent ones. It appears he regularly deletes the contents of both his trash and sent-mail folders."

Sorin nodded: Martin was their IT guru. He was a freelancer who worked for a number of different agencies, including acting as a consultant to the Met's computer crimes division. He was very good, and very reliable.

"But we can get at deleted data, right?"

Adams nodded. "If it's justified. But we'll see where the live stuff takes us first."

"But I'm off the hook either way?" asked Sorin. "No more forays into Fox's office?"

"You are," laughed Adams. "The fieldwork is done, now it's up to the backroom boys."

* * *

Green had spent a further ten minutes mulling it over before opening up the Red Flag template.

A Red Flag memo had a fixed format. There were three headings, known as the Three Rs:

1. Risk

2. Reasoning

3. Required actions

It was not a requirement that the memo be a one-pager, but it was expected: Wilkinson frequently argued that anything important could be reduced to a single side of paper.

Considering whether or not to write the memo had probably taken her a total of an hour or so; actually writing it took less than five minutes.

She opened an email to Wilkinson, selected High Priority and typed RED FLAG: VETTING OF AIRCRAFT MANUFACTURER SOFTWARE DEVELOPERS into the subject line. She attached the memo and clicked Send. As per SOP, she picked up the phone to alert Wilkinson and make sure he saw it straight away.

"Thomas, it's Sarah. Just wanted to make sure you got the Red Flag memo?"

"One moment ... yes, I have it, thanks. I'll get back to you ASAP."

Wilkinson pressed the phone hook to end the call and immediately phoned Stephenson.

"It's Thomas. Sarah just sent the Red Flag memo. You're 100% sure this is below the threshold?"

"100% sure, sir. Way, way below."

"Ok, thanks."

The Department of Homeland Security was intended to be a flexible agency, able to respond quickly, and with its senior staff given a lot of autonomy, but it was still a government body with the attendant bureaucracy that entailed. Wilkinson was not authorised to kill a Red Flag memo on his own initiative: it had to be immediately passed on to his boss. He was, however, expected to either endorse it or not.

For a bureaucrat, the decision was an obvious one: CYA. 'Cover Your Ass' was Rule 1 in any large organisation. Nobody ever got fired for being too cautious. The safe and obvious course of action was to pass it upstairs with his endorsement.

But Wilkinson prided himself on not being a bureaucrat. He knew that the the whole point of graded responses was to ensure that resources were deployed where they would make most difference. If you red-flagged something that was in reality a tiny risk, you were diverting time, money and manpower away from more important activities. If he was just going to rubber-stamp everything that crossed his desk, his job became pointless. He had reached the position he had because he'd demonstrated sound judgement and an ability to appropriately prioritise.

Stephenson had made the same arguments to Wilkinson as he had earlier to Green, and Wilkinson had been persuaded.

He forwarded the memo to his boss with a one-line commentary: *Based on expert advice within the team, I am not endorsing Red Flag status at this time.*

* * *

Stephen Adams finished his succinct outline to Richard Williams as they sat at the small conference table in his office.

"So that's the position. I'm fairly sure Fox is involved in something shady, but there's not the slightest suggestion that he was involved with Jen or is in any way responsible for her death. All other leads were dead-ends. I can continue investigating Fox if you'd like me to, but it's going to be expensive, and my honest view at this point is that your daughter's death was exactly what the police investigation concluded: a tragic accident."

Williams sipped his now-lukewarm coffee silently. Adams waited patiently: there was nothing for him to add, no further information that would help Williams make his decision, and he was smart enough to know when it was time to keep quiet and let someone think.

Thirty seconds passed.

"Emma thought we should have dropped it before now," said Williams, finally. "She'd grown more and more skeptical about Alison's story – and to be fair, Alison hasn't exactly been increasing her credibility with her behaviour of late."

Adams didn't pry; he didn't need to know the specifics. "She's a teenager who's lost a friend at a time when she assumed everyone was immortal. She's bound to go off the rails somewhat."

Williams said nothing, but nodded. He sipped his coffee again, not noticing that it was almost cold.

"What's the total bill to date?"

Adams passed a single sheet of paper across the desk. "The full bill is itemised, but that's the bottom-line so far."

Williams picked it up, glanced at the number and didn't react.

"And if we continued?"

Adams was well-organised. He slid another piece of paper across. "That's just to access, copy and analyse the drive. After that, well, it depends where if anywhere it takes us."

Williams picked up the second sheet. Again, his face remained expressionless. He picked up his coffee cup again before noticing it was empty and putting it back on the table. Adams picked up the coffee pot and refilled it. Williams didn't seem to notice, instead abruptly standing up and walking to the window, staring out. Adams waited.

Williams stood there for several minutes, not moving, not speaking. Finally, he turned to face Adams. "Thank you," he said. "Thank you for all you've done, and for your integrity. You've done enough. It was an accident. If it weren't, you'd have found out by now. I'm satisfied. Let me take your bill now and I'll settle it as soon as I get home."

* * *

Red Flag issues were supposed to be implemented within 24 hours where practicable, and within 72 hours in all cases. It was now a week later, and Sarah Green popped into Wilkinson's office to check that the measures were in place.

"Not yet," said Wilkinson.

"But it's past the 72-hour deadline," she said.

"Sarah, not everything can be given top priority."

"Sure, I understand that, but surely that's the whole point of red-flagging: to make sure the critical issues are."

Wilkinson looked uncomfortable.

Sarah stared at him. "You didn't endorse the red flag, did you?"

"It's your job to recommend red-flagging where you feel it's merited, and it's my job to assess whether that is the appropriate action. We both did our jobs, Sarah."

"But the risks ..."

"I spoke with Stephenson. His view is that the chances of such an attack succeeding are minimal, and the degree of preparation and especially the timescale make it an utterly impractical avenue for a terrorist group."

"I spoke with him too," said Green, coldly, "and I understand his view. But what's the point of our whole outside-perspective approach if we're always going to defer to the specialist?"

"The outside-perspective approach is to ensure that an expert doesn't overlook something outside the box because they've spent too much time working inside it. Once an outside head has identified a risk, it's perfectly reasonable to allow an expert to assess and comment on it. The final decision is always made by non-specialists anyway."

"So we're just ignoring the risk."

"Of course not," said Wilkinson. "The steps you've recommended are not overly onerous, so although the risk is a small one, the steps you've suggested are proportionate. I've recommended their implementation, just not on a red-flag basis."

Green bit her tongue. She was frustrated. She was convinced Wilkinson was wrong about this, and concerned that bureaucracy might mean nothing happening for months. At the same time, she understood his perspective, and knew that an angry response was unlikely to get her very far. All she could realistically do now was wait the weeks or, more likely, months it would take them to act.

* * *

17th August

The strategy had taken three months, but had finally paid off: Daniel E. York had just been placed on 12-month contract in the avionics division of Airbus. He would initially be working on an engineering diagnostics module, enabling ground engineers to examine flight performance data to help airlines maximise the efficiency of the engines. The module gave read-only access, so wasn't something he could use to ground aircraft, but it was a huge step in the right direction.

Walking into the Airbus plant at Toulouse, France, for the first time was a confusingly emotional experience for York. This was the company he blamed for Stephanie's death, and he felt a slow, burning rage toward it. Despite the fact that the reason he was there was specifically to help publicise the issue, York couldn't quite shake off a feeling that he was somehow being disloyal to Stephanie. He was, after all, on the Airbus payroll. It was an irrational feeling, he knew, but the sensation was there all the same.

Battling against both emotions was the child-like awe that everyone felt the first time they experienced the sheer scale of the plant. Although Airbus aircraft were manufactured at fifteen different facilities across Europe, the final assembly process – when the separate fuselage sections were joined, the wings were mated to the fuselage and the tail, landing gear and engines were all installed – took place here. Outside the plant, presumably ready for flight-testing, were two A380 double-decker aircraft. He didn't want to be impressed at the sight, but couldn't help himself.

He'd also been impressed at the ultra-modern facilities in the software development section. Top-spec PCs, fingerprint logins, all the latest development tools, and what the team referred to as 'aircraft in a box': PCs programmed to simulate every aspect of the operation of each one of the company's fifteen airliner models. When York hooked up a laptop containing one of his software modules, he would be able to tell the simulator to behave like the Fuel Performance Monitor on an Airbus A330, and it would do exactly that, right down to the last detail.

York had initially been concerned that his schoolboy French would be a barrier, but Airbus had employees from all over the world working at HQ, and the official language of the complex was English. Socialising was the only thing done in French, and he didn't intend to do much of that.

Airbus had a week-long induction programme for new software engineers, starting with an overview of the company's operations and ending with detailed training in the specific processes and procedures used in software development. York paid very close attention to all of it.

Danny York felt like a character in a bad spy movie as he walked into the mobile phone store to buy a Pay As You Go handset. King was becoming increasingly security conscious, and had insisted that phone calls took place on unregistered cellphones. He chose something quickly, a cheap Nokia, then went to the till to pay.

"Your name and address, monsieur?" asked the assistant.

York had memorised a randomly-chosen local address, but now couldn't think of the postcode. For a moment, he froze, then quickly said, in ungrammatical French: "It is for my mother, I don't want her getting junk mail, leave it blank, please."

For a moment, he thought the assistant was going to insist, but he merely shrugged and said "45 Euros." York made the payment in cash, so that there was no way the phone could be linked to him.

"Is the phone ready for use right away?" asked York.

The assistant nodded. "Make any chargeable call to activate it. You must make at least one call every six months to keep it active."

York thanked him, took the bag and headed back to the serviced apartment Airbus had arranged for him until he had time to find his own place.

Back in the living-room, he checked the phone's battery: two bars. He plugged in the charger just in case. King had asked him not to store his name, so he stored it simply as 'K'. He entered the number and hit send.

"Hello?" asked King.

"It's Danny," he said. Another one of King's rules: first names only.

"Danny! Good to hear from you. How are you settling in there?"

"Well, I've completed the induction training and studied all of the software update procedures manuals in great detail. It's mostly bad news so far," said York.

"Tell me," said King.

"The procedures for controlling software releases are even more rigorous than I expected. First, there are effectively internal firewalls built into the systems, to ensure that a particular subsystem can't interfere with any other subsystem. What that means in plain English is that, in my case, any software I write will have access to the fuel performance system and the engineering data transmission system and nothing else. It would do me no good, for example, to come up with a way to tell the aircraft to lock on the brakes because my software can't talk to the brake system."

"That doesn't sound too bad," said King. "That would allow you to switch off the fuel supply, surely?"

"No," said York, "that's the second and third pieces of bad news. The second is that the system I'm working on has read-only access to the fuel-control systems. I can find out exactly what it's doing in real-time, but I can't change anything."

"And the third piece of bad news?"

"The testing regime is tighter than I expected. Not only is each module tested to ensure it does what it is supposed to, it then goes through a further bank of testing specifically designed to make sure that it doesn't have any unforeseen or unwanted effects. Most of that testing is automated so that it can test against every possible permutation of aircraft configurations and identify all possible side-effects of the software under all conditions. In essence, each software module is subjected to destruction-testing. Even if I could somehow get around the read-only restriction – and I have no idea how I might do that – if I hid some code to cut the fuel supply under certain conditions, it would be picked up in testing."

"But wasn't your idea to embed a hidden date in the code, so everything would be normal except on that date?"

"That was my plan, yes, but you have to understand that I have to disguise the date, so the testing system is simply going to see that there are three variables in there – it won't know they are day, month and year – and it's going to test with every possible combination of variables. If any combination causes the fuel to cut off, it's going to be picked-up."

"But the crash," objected 'King', "if the tests really covered every single permutation, they'd have identified the set of circumstances in play then.

"That's the difference between what the safeguards do protect and what they don't," explained York. "Effectively there should be no circumstances in which the various software modules can, in themselves, cause a crash. What they can do is decide they know better than the pilots. It was a combination of what the pilot was trying to do, and what the software was trying to do, that led to the crash."

King was silent for a moment. "Is there any good news?" he asked.

"Only that the coding I'm actually supposed to be doing is straightforward. I'm going to be able to do my job, so I guess I'm going to able to sit it out here until a suitable opportunity arises – assuming it does."

Another pause from King. Then: "Ok," he said, brusquely, "keep me informed."

* * *

Green had been right: it was more than three months later when she received the email letting her know her vetting recommendations had finally been accepted:

SUBJECT: VETTING OF AIRCRAFT MANUFACTURER SOFTWARE DEVELOPERS: STATUS UPDATE

Recommendation: Counter Terrorist Check to be added to vetting process for software developers working on aircraft software systems

Response: Recommendation accepted; employers advised

Detail:

1. New hires

Requirement for CTC check on all new hires added to vetting requirements with immediate effect. To prevent unnecessary delay in filling urgent vacancies, and to take account of backlogs in CTC reports, airline manufacturers may employ a new software developer for 30 days pending receipt of the CTC report. Procedures must be put in place to ensure that the CTC status of affected employees is verified once the 30-day grace period has elapsed.

2. Existing staff

Requirement for CTC check on all new hires added to vetting requirements with immediate effect. Given the numbers of employees working on software development, consideration must be given to the practicality of obtaining CTC reports on all employees within a short period of time without causing disruption to project timescales. A period of 90 days is therefore allowed for CTC reports to be obtained on all existing software developers. However, employers are advised that 90 days is a maximum rather than a target. Where practicable, reports are to be obtained well before expiry of the 90-day grace period. Procedures must be put in place to ensure that the CTC status of affected employees is verified once the 90-day grace period has elapsed.

3. CTC failures

In the event that any software development staff fail the CTC check, a report will be sent to the CTC team in the Dept of Homeland Security for referral to the appropriate national security agency (in the case of US employees, the FBI) for further investigation and disposition.

Green sighed: it was typical governmentalese. Start with the right words – immediate effect – then rob them of any meaning by adding caveats that meant action would actually take anything up to three months. She was under no illusions that the call for faster action 'where practicable' had any meaning: no action would be taken against companies provided they met the 90-day deadline.

Not only that, but the action standard was weak too. No 'immediate review of their code', no 'instant suspension from work on safety-critical systems', just a report to be forwarded for an investigation. The FBI was good, and if there was one thing 9/11 had achieved it was to improve coordination between the different security services, but it would still be outside of Homeland Security's direct control, so there was no way to know how long a CTC follow-up investigation might take.

She didn't know what else she could do. She'd pushed it as hard as she could, and perhaps Stephenson was right: given the timescales on which a terrorist group would need to plan, and the limited likelihood of success, maybe the timing of the preventative measures was good enough to do the job.

She shrugged. Two years working for a government body, and another ten before it for a large corporation, had taught her that not all battles could be won, and sometimes an unsatisfactory compromise was as good as it got. If you stressed too much about it, you'd just end up bitter and frustrated. Sometimes, she thought, you just have to do what you can do, and call it good.

* * *

York couldn't help but smile at the irony of the system he was working on. In the 1970s, large airliners had a flight crew of three: the Captain, the First Officer and the Flight Engineer. The Flight Engineer's job was to monitor the performance of the engines and other systems, and to tweak them as required during the flight.

Modern airliners were so reliable, and their systems so sophisticated, that they no longer required Flight Engineers. Most of the in-flight tweaking needed was done automatically by computer systems. Ground engineers could plug in laptops to examine stored performance data, and could then make tweaks to the on-board systems to maximise efficiency for future flights.

But automated systems could only do so much. In some areas, like optimising fuel efficiency, there was still no substitute for a human engineer examining real-time data during the flight. The efficiency gains to be had from this were very small, with a predicted fuel saving of between 0.4% and 0.7% – nothing like enough to justify even the weight of an on-board flight engineer. But in the highly price-sensitive airline industry, small savings multiplied by 18 flying hours a day across an entire airline fleet added up to significant lumps of cash. What modern airliners did was allow ground engineers to transmit codes to airliners in flight to request specific real-time performance data. They could then analyse that data on the ground. Effectively, Airbus had reinvented the Flight Engineer – except the modern version sat in a office at an airport and typically worked on dozens of aircraft during a single shift.

For safety reasons, ground engineers can't make adjustments to the systems of an aircraft during the flight, but the tweaks required can be logged and then uploaded to the aircraft via a floppy disk drive once it's back on the ground. The new parameters will then be used for future flights, and the fuel usage data compared to confirm the effectiveness of the changes.

York had been struggling for days to think of some way his current work could ground aircraft, and so far he'd made little headway.

His module had read-only access to the fuel-management system: it could find out what it was doing, in real-time, but it couldn't make any changes. Only the engineering software could do that.

The only good news was that ensuring the fuel supply could only be cut when the aircraft was on the ground proved trivial: among the performance data available to his system was the altitude and air-speed of the aircraft. Altitude couldn't be relied on, as it was measured above sea-level rather than above ground level except when low enough to switch to radio altimeter, but airspeed alone would be sufficient: so long as airspeed was at or below taxiing speed (around 25 knots), he could be sure the aircraft was on the ground and not already committed to a take-off.

In his weekly update call to 'King', York outlined the problem.

"Once a ground engineer has uploaded new parameters to the fuel-management system," he explained, "my module needs to verify that the new parameters are being used. I've explained to my team leader that my recommended approach would be to log the revised parameters as they were uploaded by the engineers, then store those for comparison against the values being used in-flight. That's given me a legitimate reason to obtain a copy of the software used to send new instructions to the fuel-management system."

"So you've got that code?" asked 'King'.

"Yes," confirmed York, "and now that I've seen how the instructions are passed to the fuel-management system, it would be relatively trivial to introduce an instruction to cut the fuel supply altogether. When the pilot applies thrust, a signal is sent to the FADEC, which is essentially an engine management system rather like the one that controls the fuel-injection in your car. If we reprogramme the FADEC software to ignore commands, it won't matter what the pilots or auto-pilot does, no fuel will go to the engines."

"That sounds fantastic!" exclaimed 'King'.

"In theory, yes, but we're a long way from a solution. While I've seen that code, I don't work on it, so have no ability to change it."

"I see," said 'King'.

"Then we still have the problem of software testing. However much I disguise an instruction to cut fuel supply, it's such a critical function that it's absolutely guaranteed to be discovered during testing."

"Any thoughts on how to overcome that?"

"Not yet. Maybe not ever. You have to remember this is a highly controlled environment. Much as I retain my concerns about letting software override pilots, I can't argue with the quality control measures I've seen here so far."

"Do you know who handles the updates for the engineering software?" asked 'King'.

"Well, I know his name, from the copy of the code I've received. Why do you ask?"

"Maybe you should make friends with him. Chatting with him may give you some ideas."

"Can't hurt, I guess," he said.

"Keep me updated."

* * *

Breakthroughs often happen in a very random fashion.

York had been devoting all his efforts to trying to figure out how on earth he would get suspicious code past peer review in a team which comprised smart people with great attention to detail, and then to how he would defeat the rigorous and largely automated testing processes specifically designed to prevent the kind of thing he was trying to do. After more than a week of battering his head against these two brick walls, he'd been no further forward.

Long and hard thought had got him nowhere. The answer had come to him thanks to his desire, in a country dominated by coffee, for a decent cup of tea.

The French didn't understand tea. The canteen had only one real tea, and that was supplied in the form of a cup of hot water covered by a saucer, with a no-name tea-bag placed on top. By the time you'd paid for it and walked to a table, or back to your desk, the water was lukewarm. Dunking the anonymous teabag into lukewarm water produced an insipid tea that was barely worthy of the name.

Standing in the canteen queue one lunchtime, he'd noticed one of his colleagues in front of him hand over a teabag to the canteen assistant. The assistant dropped it into a cup and – miracle of miracles – filled the cup with boiling water. Real tea!

"So that's how you get a proper cup of tea around here!" exclaimed York.

His colleague grinned. "Yes, there's a Carrefour that sells Twinings Earl Grey, so I keep a box in my desk. Took me a couple of days to train the canteen staff, but they now know how to keep the eccentric Englishman happy."

"Fantastic," said York, "I must get some and do the same." York held out his hand. "I'm Daniel York, by the way. Coder working on engineering diagnostics on the A340."

"Nigel Fatherington, sysadmin on the RCS." The two shook hands.

"Thanks for the tip," said York, "lukewarm water with a vague tea flavouring was driving me to distraction."

"Yes, I drink tea by the gallon, and I lasted about three days before hitting on this plan. If you want a few teabags to keep you going in the meantime, just drop by my desk – I'm in section A19."

"Ah, just round the corner from me, I'll do that, thanks! I'll replace them when I get mine."

He'd taken Fatherington up on his offer that afternoon, and the two of them had wandered over together to get some decent tea.

York had been back at his desk for about ten minutes when the idea hit him. The RCS! That was the solution!

The best part was the irony of it: the weakness he'd identified, the key to bypassing the vetting and testing processes, was exploiting a supposed strength of the security procedures – an extra layer of protection common to almost all major software operations. The RCS. He'd explained it to 'King' in an excited phone call that evening.

"The Revision Control System," York explained. "Whenever you update software, it's vital to keep track of what stage things are at, and to ensure that nothing is released to the client until it has passed testing. So the developer writes the code, one or more colleagues reviews the code, then it's tested. Once it has passed testing and is ready for release, it is copied onto a server called the Revision Control System, or RCS. From there, it goes to the client.

"With you so far," said 'King'.

"The RCS has access to everything due for release to the airlines. So, the engineering update coder writes his software, which is duly peer-reviewed and tested. His software module is of course perfectly innocent, so passes both stages and is copied to the RCS server. In the meantime, I write a revised version of his module. Once his code is on the RCS server, I replace it with mine. When the update goes to the airlines, it's my version, not his, that gets uploaded into the aircraft."

"And then your code will cut the fuel? What about all the built-in safeguards you mentioned?"

"When my code is triggered, the system will think it is in the hangar and in maintenance mode. I can then do whatever I like. So I instruct the fuel management system to cut the fuel flow. None of the safeguards will kick in because the plane thinks it's stationary."

"But if it's that easy to doctor the software, surely the RCS must be well secured?"

"In theory, yes," said York. "The RCS isn't part of the main computer network, it's totally isolated. You need to be physically sat at the right terminal in order to access it. Coders have no access at all: the RCS is run by sysadmins."

"So if you have no access ... ?" asked 'King'.

"Any of the sysadmins – which means anyone who uses the terminal while a sysadmin is logged-in – can add a new user. It's just a question of adding a username and password and swiping that user's finger across the fingerprint reader. Takes two minutes. All I need is for one of them to fail to lock their terminal when they go for lunch, or for a break, and I'm in. It shouldn't happen, but it does, all the time. I've seen it. They go for a coffee, nip to the loo, get a personal call on their mobile, and off they go. And I've just found an RCS sysadmin with a six-cups-a-day tea habit. "

"So you wait until he's on a tea-run, create a login and you'd then have access to the RCS anytime you wanted?"

"I'd need to find a time it was unattended, but yes: I'd then be able to login to the RCS and replace the code at my leisure. Once I've done the code-switch, I delete the password file associated with the login so there's no trace back to me."

"And the change wouldn't be detected after that?"

"I'm sure there are safeguards, but the only software that should be on the RCS is code that has already been reviewed, tested and proven, so the safeguards at that stage will most likely be against silly mistakes rather than a deliberate attack. File-size comparison is the most likely one: the system knows what the size of the correct version should be, and it checks that the one being released to the client is identical. The chances of there being two versions exactly the same size is exceedingly low, so that sort of check would do the job of making sure the right version is being copied. I'll do some reading-up on it, but I'm sure it won't be a problem."

'King' took a deep breath. "So you're saying this is solved? You really can do this: cut the fuel supply to all A340 aircraft?"

"All non-flying ones, yes. Thanks to my work, I know how to read the real-time performance data, so I'll build in a safeguard to ensure that the airspeed reading is either zero or less than 25 knots. That way, we know it isn't in the air and isn't at a critical stage in a take-off run: it's either stationary or taxiing."

'King' scribbled a quick note: Remove airspeed check. "Danny, you're a genius."

"There's one problem left."

"What's that?"

"How to trigger the code. My initial idea was to make it date-activated with a disguised date, but that would be picked up in automated testing. It would run through all possible values for those variables – and thus all possible dates – and then the routine would be activated and detected. I've got to find some other way to trigger it, something that wouldn't be picked in testing."

"Any ideas?"

"Not yet, but 90% of solution-finding is a decent understanding of the problem."

"Assuming you can do that, what sort of timescale are we talking about here? Days? Weeks? Months?"

"The next update is on 1st December, that's exactly six weeks from now. We'll want to do the code-swap on the RCS as late as possible, probably overnight the day before the update. That protects us both against accidental discovery, and a last-minute revision overwriting our code. That gives me five weeks six days to get everything ready. I'm confident I can do that."

"Excellent work, Danny. Keep in touch."

* * *

Fox was delighted with the progress York had made. He'd felt dejected by his previous update, but now everything seemed to be coming together. He did, however, face a few challenges.

First, once York had revised the software module, Fox needed to get hold of it, however briefly. Second, he needed a coder to remove the airspeed check from the code. Third, he needed York to unwittingly install the further-doctored version. The second challenge was the greatest.

He knew there was no way he could persuade any coder to knowingly doctor the code to cause over a thousand aircraft to crash. The green movement was a broad church. Within it, most were naive fools who imagined that catastrophic climate change could be averted by argument and PR, appreciating neither the strength of the forces they were fighting nor the apathy of the majority of the population who cared more about fast food and holidays in Tenerife than they did about the future of civilisation.

There was a minority who realised that more robust measures were needed, and who were willing to engage in direct action to actively hamper genocidal activities like aviation. But even amongst those who appreciated the need for violence as a mechanism for change, most would be squeamish when it came to doing things on a sufficiently large scale to bring about lasting change.

The chances of finding someone with the necessary skills and the courage to act on the scale required was effectively zero.

Mercenaries had their place. He'd developed some contacts over the years for use when necessary, like dealing with the Jen problem. But even hired killers could get squeamish when faced with the necessity to kill thousands in order to protect the planet. How on earth did one find a coder willing to do so?

He had one idea, but he had absolutely no idea how practical it might be. He had some research to do.

* * *

Gilbert Leclerq sighed when he received the email forwarded from the Dept of Homeland Security in Washington. It was requesting – actually, demanding – that they carry out additional reference and security checks on all software development employees.

It was one of a succession of 'requests' from the US government. Whilst all involved in the airline industry appreciated the different environment in which they were operating since 9/11, many of those who worked at Airbus felt considerable resentment that the American government could dictate to a French company (Leclerq, in common with many of his compatriots always thought of the company as French despite its pan-European nature) how it should run its business.

While the emails were always gently phrased, 'requesting' rather than requiring Airbus to comply, nobody was under any illusions: the USA represented the largest market in the world for airliners, and a single stroke of the FAA's pen could render unairworthy any aircraft whose manufacturer had failed to act on such 'requests'.

Part of the resentment was the feeling that the bureaucrats who drew up the rules had little or no understanding of the headaches they caused. It sounded innocuous enough, carry out additional vetting on one area of the business, but Leclerq doubted that the US Government had any appreciation of the number of software developers employed or contracted by the company. They were talking about literally hundreds of software developers at the Toulouse plant alone, with numbers running into thousands when you counted all the work sub-contracted to external suppliers. It was such a huge part of the business that the IT Director had half-jokingly described Airbus as a software house with a metalwork shed attached.

He could at least take comfort in the fact that his team would only be responsible for those directly employed at the plant. The government checks would not be his responsibility, and checking references was low-level grunt work that could be delegated to the most junior staff.

Leclerq tapped into the employee database to check the numbers, then sent an email asking one of his managers to assign a manageable number to each junior, together with a link to the procedures document on the Sharepoint system.

Alan Durand had been with Airbus for less than a month. A college graduate, he'd managed a one-month placement in the HR department in his final year of studies, and the HR manager had found him keen, hard-working and a quick study. He'd been offered a post as soon as he graduated, and was determined to progress through the ranks as quickly as he could.

The latest assignment he'd been given wasn't the most exciting, and he'd been told to fit it around his existing work as & when he could. The deadline was 90 days, but he was out to impress. His aim was to exceed his manager's expectations at every turn. He clicked the link and read through what was required. It was pretty basic, mostly verifying that the companies actually existed and then phoning the HR departments to confirm the job titles and employment dates. Looking at the number of employees he'd been assigned, he couldn't see any reason why he couldn't get the job done in nine days rather than ninety. He pulled up the first CV and decided there was no time like the present.

* * *

Figuring out how to ground the planes had been a pretty classic programming exercise, reflected York: the principle of how to achieve it had been surprisingly simple, but the devil, as usual, had been in the detail.

The principle was as basic as could be: fool the engineering update module into thinking the aircraft was sat in the hangar when it was in fact in operation, then modify the FADEC system to cut the fuel supply on receipt of the right instruction.

The practice was rather more challenging. Every time he thought he'd cracked it, and he started the laborious task of following the code through line-by-line, he'd hit a snag.

The big frustration was that he had test kit sitting just a few tens of metres away. He could hook up a laptop to the test equipment, and it would take a matter of moments to get it to simulate an A340 either sat at a gate or rolling along a taxiway. He could then check that the code worked and, if not, quickly identify the bug. Easy. Except for the small matter that he didn't dare risk testing his code. Every test run was logged, and all it took was for one of the project managers to notice that he was testing someone else's code and that would be that.

So he had to do it the old-fashioned way: make a coding change, then visually read through the code working out what would happen at each stage to ensure that it would do what it was told.

The main issue was that the engineering update system didn't rely on a single check to ensure that the aircraft was out of service, it instead read a whole range of inputs, every one of which had to be correct. His code modification needed, once triggered, to modify each of those values, any one of which changes could potentially have knock-on effects elsewhere in the code. It wasn't just a question of making sure that his modification would take effect when triggered, he also needed to ensure that nothing he did would cause anything to fail before it was triggered.

A single mistake might mean that the aircraft would refuse to throttle-up at all after the update was made. While that would cause a certain amount of chaos for the airlines, a bunch of aircraft in hangars refusing to start would generate limited media interest compared to all A340s on the ground failing at the same moment whilst full of passengers.

York also couldn't afford to fall behind on his own work: that would focus attention on him at a time when he needed to be as anonymous as possible. Working very long hours without explanation carried the same risk, so he compromised on spending two hours a day working on his 'personal' project, and working very intensively on his official work for the rest of each day.

It had taken three weeks, but finally he was certain he was there with the main code. On receipt of the correct trigger, the FADEC system would check that the aircraft speed was below 25 knots and, if so, cut the fuel supply. Until it was triggered, the aircraft would continue to function normally.

He was now ready for the final piece of the puzzle: how to allow them to trigger the code. He had exactly three weeks to do it before the next update went out. If he missed that deadline, it would be another three months before the next opportunity.

While Green had almost managed to persuade herself to let the matter rest, she'd made a few calls to the CTC unit at the FBI and arranged to be copied in on anomaly reports.

There were two stages to a CTC: the enhanced reference checks were carried out by the employers, while the national security checks were carried out by the government in the country of employment. The check was only complete once both elements were done, but an employee who failed either part of it would be flagged-up in an anomaly report.

Airbus, it seemed, was making an unexpectedly prompt start: she'd received an anomaly report that morning. She was shocked to find 14 names on the list already, spanning most of the alphabet from Brevet to York. She sought out Bill Stephenson to get his reactions.

"It's pretty surprising, don't you think? I mean, we're two weeks in: they can't have carried out the reference checks on more than a tiny proportion of their coders, and yet we've already got 14 of them who've failed enhanced reference checks."

In truth, Stephenson was as surprised as Green was, but he still felt slightly sore about the fact that she'd ignored his input in the first place, and wasn't happy that she was apparently proving him wrong. He was too professional to mislead her: if things really were as lax as the headline figure suggested, it needed to be addressed. At the same time, he wasn't going to give her the satisfaction of rolling over completely at such an early stage.

"Well," he replied, "you have to remember that software development is a pretty competitive field. It's not unheard of for coders to massage their CVs a little. Give themselves a little bump in experience, perhaps a slightly more generous job title. They know that employers generally only follow up references for the most recent employer, so if they wanted to exercise a little creativity on their CV, they'd likely to do so on earlier positions. It's not ideal, of course, but it doesn't make them terrorists."

"So you're still not concerned?"

Stephenson shook his head. "Not especially so, no. Remember that these checks are pretty binary affairs. Some junior clerk in a huge HR department checks a date on a CV then phones the company to get the dates from them. Any mismatch, and it's flagged as a fail. But look into the detail of it and most likely you'll find the guy was out of work for three months, didn't want the gap to show up so changed his leaving date from February to May. Or added a 'senior' to his job title. Or some HR bod transposed two digits and entered 4th June as 6th of April. Some of it perfectly innocent errors, some of it slightly naughty CV-massaging, but in all likelihood nothing to worry about from a security perspective."

Green nodded. "Makes sense. I'm just a bit surprised by the numbers."

"It does seem quite high at such an early stage, but perhaps they just have a very efficient HR department, or things are quiet and they put a lot of people on it to carry out hundreds of checks." Stephenson thought about it for a moment. "Are all those 14 in one country?"

"Yes, France."

"Well, look, 14 is a very manageable number – raise it with Thomas and see whether he can pull some strings to have the national security checks for those 14 expedited by the French government."

"Good thought," replied Green, "I'll do that."

Green returned to her desk to forward the file with names, dates of birth and nationalities to Wilkinson. Damn! Nationalities. They might all be working in France, but of the 14 names, 5 of them were of different nationalities. Two Americans, a Swede, a Finn and a Brit. The Americans should be easy: if Thomas would sign-off on it, they could easily arrange for those to be done within a day or two. But expediting the others would mean asking favours of the national security agencies of four different countries: France, Sweden, Finland and Britain.

She shrugged: she could only ask. She tapped out a quick email, and forwarded the document to Wilkinson.

Thomas Wilkinson was not in the best of moods. One of his most experienced analysts, Boyson, a guy who'd been in place since the initiative was started soon after 9/11, had handed in his notice first thing in the morning. And with the pressure to cut his budget by 10%, it made financial as well as human sense not to replace him. No redundancy payment, and one less person to let go.

The drawback was that Boyson wanted to leave as soon as possible – within a month, or even earlier if possible. Technically, the analyst was on three months' notice, and Wilkinson would be within his rights to require him to serve out the time, making for an easier transition. In practice, though, it never worked like that: if you pressured them to remain in post when they wanted to be elsewhere, you just got a disgruntled employee who did little work of any real worth. No, if someone wanted to leave quickly, you just had to suck it up and say yes.

When Green's email arrived, Wilkinson sighed. Analysts were tenacious people. In Myers-Briggs terms, they tended to be INTPs: logical, focused, critical. If something didn't fit, didn't seem right, they would worry it to death. It was a character trait vital to them doing their jobs: they wanted everything to be water-tight.

But, he reflected, it could also be a pain in the ass. They had little ability to accept that the world was less than perfect. They were very good at prioritising action within their particular area of study, but weren't good at seeing the wider picture outside it. Green was good at her job, but now she was trying to go above her pay-grade. She'd done her bit, now she needed to let other people do theirs.

He'd indulged her enough already. He composed a short reply thanking her for her suggestion, but that he was happy for the reviews to go through channels. He ended the email by asking politely what area she planned to tackle next: when you dropped a hint with an analyst, you had to set aside all thoughts of subtlety.

* * *

12th October

York almost laughed aloud when he finally hit on the solution: the method of triggering the code had been staring him in the face the whole time! ACARS!

His official project was working on a system that allowed engineers to obtain real-time data from aircraft in flight. The system used ACARS: the Aircraft Communications Addressing and Reporting System.

He'd imagined real-time data transfer with aircraft in flight would have been a relatively recent development, and had been surprised to learn that ACARS was actually introduced back in 1978. Based on the Telex format, it was originally used to enable airlines to receive automated reports on the flight status of all their aircraft.

The first generation of ACARS was extremely crude, reporting only four 'events', known as OOOI: Out of the gate, Off the ground, On the ground, and Into the gate. The systems used aircraft sensors like parking brake and switch sensors to detect each of the four flight phases, and to transmit a short data message back to the airline. The message comprised the flight phase, the time at which it occurred and a few other key pieces of data like fuel readings.

ACARS could also be used to transmit data from the ground to the aircraft, such as updated weather reports and suggested changes to flight plans.

Over the years, ACARS gradually increased in sophistication. Airlines could send short codes to an aircraft in order to interrogate the status of a whole range of systems, including speed, position, altitude and ETA. In this way, airlines could keep accurate track of exactly how all of their flights were performing against their timetables. Delays could be detected at an early stage, and steps taken to minimise the knock-on effects.

York was working on the latest development in ACARS: enabling engineers to monitor fuel performance data in real time. Fuel was the single biggest operating expense for airlines. More expensive than their aircraft leases, more expensive than their staff. The numbers were almost too large to comprehend: a large airline like BA, for example, spends almost five billion dollars a year on fuel, or over $13 million per day. A tiny percentage saving added up to hundreds of millions of dollars of savings, and every one of those saved dollars goes straight onto the bottom-line of the airline's profit-and-loss account.

Aircraft manufacturers thus did everything possible to maximise fuel savings to make their aircraft more attractive to airlines than their competitors' models. Making seats out of carbon-fibre rather than aluminium, for example, made the aircraft 5% lighter. Japanese Airlines had even gone as far as shortening the length of its cutlery to save weight.

Hence the system York was working on: allowing airline engineers to monitor the fuel performance of their aircraft in real-time during flights. Airbus aimed to make their aircraft as fuel-efficient as possible, but there were scores of variables: passenger loadings, routing altitudes, airline-specific cruising speeds, fuel margins carried (part of the weight any aircraft has to lift is the fuel it won't burn en-route: while there are legal minimum reserves, some airlines are more conservative than others). Airlines had asked for the ability to analyse the fuel performance of their own fleets in their own operating environments, enabling them to make tweaks to further boost fuel efficiency.

ACARS was the mechanism by which York's system worked. Every airliner fitted with an ACARS system had its own unique 12-digit code. Engineers would transmit the code of the aircraft whose performance they wanted to analyse, followed by a series of short hex codes which told the aircraft what data the engineers wanted to receive. For example, code 308891245127 followed by #0D26BB instructed the Airbus A340 assigned that unique identifier to report its basic flight data: originating airport code, destination airport code, heading, airspeed, groundspeed and altitude. Code #0D26BC told it to transmit engine performance data, which included throttle settings, engine RPMs, engine temperatures, fuel remaining, fuel burn-rate and estimated total fuel burn for the sector.

York could add a hex code to trigger the activation of his shutdown sub-routine.

It wasn't entirely straightforward: the on-board systems had internal firewalls in place to prevent systems that shouldn't be talking to each other from doing so. There was no way to send data from the engineering query system to any of the active flight systems. He could set the fuel-management system to shut-down fuel supply on receipt of a single byte of data, but the firewalls wouldn't allow that byte to be sent from the engineering query system.

But he could, he realised, do it in reverse: have the engineering update code check the value of a flag on the interrogation system once a minute. When the right code was received, the interrogation system would change a value from 0 to 1. When the engineering update system detected that change, that would activate the subroutines he had written to set all the relevant variables to the correct values for an aircraft sat in the hangar. At that point, none of the normal flight safety systems would kick in. He could tell the aircraft to do anything at all that would be safe in the hangar, and it would comply. A second code would then operate in the same manner to instruct the FADEC computers to set the fuel supply to zero. With the FADECs offline, it wouldn't matter what either the pilots or the auto-pilot did with the throttles: no fuel would be supplied to the engines and they would flame-out within seconds.

There were a great many different backup systems on board a modern airliner designed to cope with any failure that might cut off fuel supply. Backup fuel-pumps, cross-feed valves (to pump fuel from one wing tank to both engines), even gravity pumps to allow fuel to flow 'downhill' from the fuel-tanks to the engines hung beneath the wings in the event of a total loss of hydraulic or electrical power. Not one of them would operate because the aircraft would believe itself to be undergoing maintenance, so all of the backup systems would be offline. Not even the valves for the gravity pumps would operate. The pilots could try any manual recovery procedures they liked, bypass anything they liked, but none of it would restore fuel to the engines because none of it would be actioned.

"I've got it," he told 'King' that evening. "I know how we trigger the code on demand."

"Fantastic, how do we do it?"

York explained about ACARS.

"But how do we transmit the codes? Wouldn't that require access to all kinds of sophisticated airline equipment?"

"It's not as difficult as you might imagine. ACARS is in essence nothing more complicated than a laptop hooked up to a satellite phone, albeit one operating on different frequencies. The kit will fit into a couple of suitcase-sized packages, and cost a few thousand dollars. Signals are sent to a satellite and from there relayed to all aircraft within range."

"And what's the range?"

"Essentially it's line-of-sight to and from the satellites. To reach every aircraft in the world, we'd need six ACARS transmitters spaced around the world: London, New York, Tokyo and so on."

"And there's some kind of master code? Attention all aircraft kind of thing?"

"No, we have to send a signal to each aircraft in turn."

"Wouldn't that take hours? I was rather hoping we could hit every aircraft at the same time, for maximum media impact."

'King', of course, was not thinking of the news coverage, at least not directly: he didn't want airlines to have time to figure out what was happening and issue emergency landing instructions to their fleets.

"No, the instructions are just very short codes. A few bytes. Each transmission will be just an ID code for the aircraft, and two codes. I've done the calculations, and we're talking hundredths of a second per transmission. I can write a simple piece of software to send them to every Airbus in the world in just two minutes."

'King' was startled. "Two minutes? We can shut down every Airbus engine in the world within a two-minute timeframe?"

"Every Airbus on the ground, yes. We won't know which ones are on the ground and which in the air, of course, so that's why the code checks the speed of the aircraft. If it's below 25 knots, it's definitely not in the air or at a critical phase in a take-off or landing roll."

"Right," said 'King'. That particular check, he thought, would not be in place by the time the transmissions were made. "So that's it? It's solved? You really can make this happen?"

"Can you purchase the satellite comms stuff, if I send you links to the kit? The total outlay is likely to be $20-25,000."

"Sure, that won't be a problem."

"Then yes, we're there."

'King' was silent for a moment. He could scarcely believe that victory was within reach. Six transmitters. Two modified pieces of code. Two minutes of transmission time. That's all it would take to crash over a thousand airliners simultaneously. That's all it would take to kill half a million people. That's all it would take to effectively end the aviation industry overnight.

Nobody would want to fly. Aviation insurance companies would be unable to meet the claims. Airlines would go bust. Even if airlines could somehow figure out a way to pay for it all, neither airliners nor pilots could be replaced overnight. At the very least, it would be years before there was a civil aviation industry again. And who knows what might happen in the meantime? Public opinion was shifting all the time. Perhaps with a little more help, this could be it. No more jets burning what little remained of the Earth's dwindling oil reserves and pumping their pollution into the upper atmosphere. No more criminally wasteful use of energy to propel the unthinking masses from their boring little suburban boxes to some far-flung beach twice a year. No more-

"Are you still there?" asked York.

'King' was dragged out of his reverie. "Yes. Sorry. It's just a big moment, isn't it?"

York nodded, though there was no-one there to see it. "Yes," he replied. "Yes it is."

"How long will it take you to write the code?"

"A week should be safe. Writing the code will only take two or three hours – the time-consuming part is checking through the whole of both software modules to make sure I haven't missed anything, and that there's nothing else in the code that could block it. It may be a little quicker or slower, but we have just over a fortnight before the update: I can definitely get it done in that time."

"And we can trigger anytime from then?"

"It's a non-critical update, so airlines don't have to carry out the upgrade until the next maintenance cycle. Maintenance cycles are determined by flying hours rather than elapsed time, so there's no definite date by which the upgrade will have been done, but I've been making a few casual enquiries. Most airlines work their aircraft hard – they don't make any money when sat on the ground – and a small A-check is every 740 flying hours, so we can be pretty sure that almost all of them will have the upgrade installed by six weeks from release. Say seven weeks to be safe."

York thought for a moment. "Actually," he continued, "I'm being an idiot! There's no need for guesswork. I can add in a test code: one that does nothing to the aircraft except send back an OK message. I can then write a piece of software to count the number of OKs we get back. So let's plan for seven weeks, but we'll run the test first to be sure."

Seven weeks before the end of the airline industry, thought 'King'.

"Fantastic. Just fantastic, Danny. Let me know the moment it's done: I have a plan to extricate you from Airbus without risk of discovery once this is over, but one aspect of that needs to be put in place before the update, and I'll need a couple of days' notice to arrange things."

York felt relieved that King had been thinking about his future. He really couldn't take much more of this strain, and wanted to get the hell out as soon as he could once the update was done.

"There's just one other thing we need to solve," added York. "We'll need people in each of the six cities to activate the transmissions."

"We can't automate that? Fly there, setup the kit and then activate it remotely?"

"We could," replied York, "but I wouldn't want to rely on it. The most practical way to do this is to find hotel rooms with balconies on the appropriate side of the building for the satellite view needed. But hotel wifi connections aren't always the most robust, many of them logging out their users every 24 hours. And while the satellite kit is weatherproof, the laptops aren't, so we'd have to run the cable through the open balcony door. Hotel cleaners don't always respect Do not disturb notices, and all it would take is one careless one to disturb the cables, or a suspicious one to report the setup to a supervisor. No, automation leaves way too much to chance."

"So we need techies in five other cities around the world?" asked 'King', dismayed.

"Not techies, no. Setting up the kit isn't particularly technical, it's just a question of placing the satellite dish in a position where it has a view of the right area of the sky – something we can take care of ourselves by booking the right hotel rooms – and connecting a few cables. The pre-installed software will take care of aligning the motorised dishes. The process is pretty much identical to something caravan and motorhome owners with satellite TV systems do every time they park-up in a campsite. We didn't need technicians. But we do need 100% reliable people."

"Ok," said 'King', "then that's one for my to-do list."

* * *

Fox had been doing his research, and was now confident he could make the necessary change to the code himself.

Although C++ was a complex programming language, and there was no possibility of him actually writing any code from scratch, code already written was not entirely impenetrable if you knew what you were looking for.

In this case, the change needed to remove the airspeed safeguard was a trivial one: he didn't need to remove the airspeed check altogether, he just needed to change the number. He knew Fox was setting the check to 25 knots, so all he had to do was change a single value from 25 to a much higher number, say 750. Airliners typically cruise at up to 550-600 knots, so none would be travelling as fast as 750 knots.

Search for instances of the number 25 in the code, and hope he could make sufficient sense of the code to work out which of them was the airspeed check. Change the number to 750. It ought to be that simple.

The worst-case scenario was dozens of examples of lines of code with the number 25 in them, and him unable to work out which was the critical one. In which case, he would need to resort to plan B. But it was far, far safer if he was able to make the change without the involvement of any further outsiders.

Fox was correct that it was, in principle, that simple. But like all those who have learned a very little about a subject, he was in the dangerous position of not knowing what he didn't know.

* * *

York had also been correct: the code needed to remotely trigger the fuel shutdown was trivial and took very little time. It was, once again, the tedious line-by-line checking process that took the time. They were only going to get one shot at this – any failed attempt was going to lead to major alarm bells and, he was sure, closure of the RCS loophole. He had to be absolutely sure that nothing elsewhere in the code could interfere with his code.

But after his fifth walk-through, he was certain that he had missed nothing. There were six days to spare, and he could afford to spend a few more days checking a sixth, seventh and even eighth time, but really there was no point. They were ready. It was time to make the call to King.

* * *

'King' was at that moment making the most nerve-wracking decision of the whole scheme: selection of the transceiver operators.

He didn't have to concern himself with finding people comfortable with the true scale of the attack – that would be something they would learn only after the event. But he did need people who could be counted on not to go to pieces afterwards. With agents scattered on six continents, arranging for their disappearance wasn't a particularly practical proposition.

Nobody who had played a key role in killing half a million people was going to go running to the authorities, but it took a tough-minded person to keep completely quiet about what they'd done, not to confess to even their closest friend. Because that was all it would take: one drink too many, one unguarded moment.

He'd considered using professional hit-men as the actual agents, but rejected it as too risky. His only contact in that particular field was in London, and those guys were by definition mercenaries. If they got any hint in advance of the scale of what was being planned, they might easily decide there was greater profit in going to the authorities than carrying out the job.

There was one further complication to this particular plan: the five other agents were going to be in cities on the other side of the world, and the airline industry would cease to exist within minutes of them pressing the button. The only way for them to get home would be overland or by sea. He needed people who could drop out of sight for several weeks or more without arousing suspicion.

So: he needed people with a genuine commitment to the cause; who were tough-minded enough to cope with what they'd done; and who led sufficiently unconventional lives that disappearing for weeks would not attract undue attention.

It was a job description which pretty much specified Action On Aviation activists. AOA was also the only place he could recruit people he knew well enough to know who could and couldn't handle it.

The danger there was, so far, everything had been done through his David King alias; AOA people knew his real identity.

The idea made him extremely nervous. He was happy enough for his role to be revealed after his death – or, at least, after the world had realised the necessity of what had been done – but he did not have the temperament needed to be a martyr. Spending the rest of his life in a maximum security prison was not part of his plan.

But he could see no realistic alternative. He started drawing up a list of names, and planning the story he would tell them. He wanted to ensure they knew there would be casualties, though not the scale of them. If he couldn't tell them that much, there was no way they had the mental toughness needed to survive afterwards. Two names came to mind immediately. Those two, he could probably even tell the full story, though he wouldn't chance it. They would understand his caution. He could handle London himself. So he needed three more names.

* * *

Green knew that she wasn't top of Wilkinson's Christmas card list right now, and had decided that what she most needed now was some professional distance. In selecting a new area to study, she'd deliberately opted for one that she felt unlikely to reveal any significant new risks: ticket sales.

Her airline work meant that she was already very familiar with the safeguards in place to ensure that unusual transactions were flagged and appropriate checks made. For example, plane tickets purchased for cash, tickets made by one individual on behalf of an apparently unrelated passenger and one-way tickets were all given special codes, with details passed to border authorities in both departure and destination countries. More controversially, passengers of particular nationalities travelling to certain countries would also be given special security codes. Passengers flagged with these codes would find both themselves and their luggage tagged for additional checks.

The triggers for transactions viewed as suspicious had been arrived at by a combination of inputs from police and security services, and consultations with airlines around the world. The result had been a set of fifteen criteria, some of them obvious and well-known, such as cash transactions, others more subtle and kept as closely-guarded secrets.

Initially, airlines and travel agents would flag only those transactions falling into one of the fifteen categories. More recently, sales staff were given the authority to add a subjective code to any transactions which gave them any cause for concern, regardless of whether any of the objective flagging criteria had been met.

She doubted that there was anything new to bring to the party, so she could go through the motions and be confident that she wasn't going to end up feeling frustrated or at loggerheads with her boss.

But despite her best efforts, she couldn't quite bring herself to let go of the software issue. She was still receiving emails with details of CV anomalies detected by airlines, and the number of software developers flagged had grown to 105.

So she'd done what she'd learned to do over the years: compromise. While she got on quietly and efficiently with her new project, she decided to make a few enquiries about the CTC checks in her own time. She had no idea who to contact in the overseas countries, but could at least make a lunchtime call to the CTC unit in the FBI to check up on the two Americans.

Brown-bagging at her desk for lunch provided the perfect excuse. She quickly learned that the guy responsible for follow-ups on any employees who failed the CTC was one Dale Fisk. They transferred her call, and got his voicemail.

She hadn't been sure what reception she might get – despite the new era of openness, there was always the possibility that the FBI would think she was trying to tell them how to do their job. She made every attempt to sound light and friendly as she left a message explaining who she was and that as this was an area of particular interest to her, she'd appreciate being kept in the loop regarding the follow-ups.

Fisk returned her call within 15 minutes.

"Afternoon, Ma'am. Fisk here, from the CTC unit in the FBI. You left a message for me."

Green had had a number of dealings with the FBI in her time at Homeland Security, and never failed to be impressed at how polite agents always seemed to be. It was as if they put them through some kind of gentleman's finishing school as part of their training.

"Thanks for getting back to me so quickly," she said, "and I hope you don't mind the call."

"Not at all."

"I just have a particular interest in this risk, and I was wondering if you'd mind just keeping me up to speed with developments?"

"May I ask why, Ma'am?"

"Please, call me Sarah."

"Then may I ask why, Sarah?"

Despite the formality of the question, Green could hear the smile in his voice. She hesitated. It wasn't professional to discuss internal differences of opinion with people outside the team, but at the same time she wanted to make it very clear that she wasn't planning to interfere in any way. Time for another one of those compromises. Her life lately seemed to include rather a lot of those.

"I guess it's a case of professional pride. We don't generally get to find out whether our recommendations do any good, and in this case there has been some ... internal debate as to the necessity for this step. I'm just interested to see

245

whether I was right. Not a very noble motive, I know! But I promise I'm not wanting to interfere in any way, just satisfy my professional curiosity."

"Heh," replied Fisk, "your boss not quite sharing your view, eh?"

Green was startled. "Is it that obvious, or are you that good at your job?"

Fisk laughed. "I'd like to claim the latter, but in this case it was a pretty easy guess. Usually people only want to prove themselves right when they've been overruled."

"I guess so. Well, now you know my motives, I don't suppose you'd be willing to indulge me and let me know the state of play?"

"I always try to indulge a lady who asks nicely, Ma'am."

Green felt a little disappointed. She was used to men who seemed to find any female colleague an excuse to flirt, and she was somewhere between bemused and irritated at those who did so on the phone to someone they'd never even met. For all Fisk knew, she could be a 65-year-old grandmother. But it was an old and familiar tale; she dismissed it from her mind.

"The updates I've received show that we're up to 105 employees? It seems like a huge number."

"It's not a dramatic one in the context of the tens of thousands of software developers working on aviation software. We have benchmarks for this kind of thing, and the numbers are nothing unusual."

"Do you mind if I ask how the checks are going?"

"We've got a bit of a backlog at present. There are quite a few positions where CTC checks have been added to the requirements, and we haven't yet reached the new staffing levels needed, but we're getting there. Of the 17 Americans flagged up so far, we've completed 12 of them."

"And the results?" asked Green.

"You're on the losing side of the bet so far, I'm afraid. Mostly clerical errors, a bit of CV naughtiness – nothing we're concerned about, though some of them will be having some uncomfortable conversations with their employers – and one undisclosed bankruptcy. That was five years ago and she's got her finances back under control, so no worries there either."

"I won't complain about being proven wrong, if the trend continues. Do we have any info on the overseas checks?"

"We're keeping a watching brief. We've asked to be copied in on the findings, with varying responses. Some countries have agreed only to let us know when checks are complete, but not the results, promising only that the matter will be dealt with locally. Others have agreed to identify individuals who failed the CTC. Only Britain has agreed full disclosure."

"Nothing of interest there?"

"Nothing yet. Just an oddity. Guy by the name of York. Seems some of his experience was invented, but he'd been trained in all the relevant areas so that wasn't a particular issue."

"So what was the oddity."

"A change of name. Sort of, anyway. His employment records didn't initially check out because he used to be known as Danny York but is working for Airbus as Daniel E. York."

"Nothing too odd there, surely? A friend of mine did the same thing when he was going for a promotion. Decided that Andy lacked gravitas so restyled himself as Andrew. That was always his legal name anyway."

"Yes, and the same for Mr York: the name on his birth certificate is Daniel. But not Daniel E. Not the initial nor any middle name. Not on his birth certificate, passport or bank accounts. So far as the Brits have been able to tell, Danny York became Daniel E. York only when he started working for Airbus."

"Strange. But not really the stuff conspiracies are made of. Has anyone, you know, asked him about it?"

"Ah, that's not really the British style. They prefer to do things quietly, behind the scenes, so they're still investigating."

Green smiled. Her work hadn't brought her into direct contact with the British security services, but she'd heard a few stories.

"Well, it's a little intriguing, but not exactly a threat to national security, I think."

"I agree," said Fisk. "Look, I'd like to promise to keep you up to date, but things are a little crazy here, so could I ask you to take the initiative and give me a call anytime you want an update? I'm more than happy to keep you in the loop, just be easier if you prompted me."

"Sure," said Green, "and I appreciate your attitude. I was concerned you'd think I was treading on your toes."

"Not at all, Sarah, always happy to hear from you."

* * *

"We're ready," said York in his call to 'King'.

"The code is complete? Nothing else to do."

"It's complete."

"You're a genius."

"A tired one," commented York, wryly.

"I'm sure. Now listen, I've been giving some thought to how we protect you against discovery. If I understand correctly, you use the fake RCS login you created to upload the update, and delete it afterwards so there's no trace of your fingerprint in the system once the update is complete."

"That's right."

"But you're going to come under suspicion because yours is the code affected."

"My code, and the code of one other developer, yes. But I'll be able to show that the code I submitted was clean, and I've deliberately written the revised code in quite a different style to my own – I've used the kind of naive style one would expect of a beginner, so that it could have been almost anyone."

"Ok," said King. "From what you've said, though, they are going to work out how the code was switched – the use of the RCS."

"Oh yes, once they start investigating how the hell something so major could happen, it won't take them long to figure out that it was the RCS. That's why I'm going to make the switch late at night, when there's no-one around to spot me at the terminal."

"That's the bit that concerns me," said 'King'. "The risk might be low, but it's still there. I'd rather you weren't even in the building at the time the RCS is accessed. In fact, I'd like to ensure you have a watertight alibi, showing without any doubt that you were somewhere else at the time."

"That would be nice, but if I don't make the switch, who does? It's not terribly difficult, a few unix commands at the command-line, but it's still not something that anyone could do."

"I know, but I have a sysadmin lined-up to do it," lied 'King'. "He's on-side, and techy enough to do this."

"No," said York. "I appreciate your concern, but it would actually increase the risk. We'd need to somehow get them into the building, past Security, and don't forget that the RCS needs a fingerprint for the login. We could create another one, but that would mean getting them access to the building twice: once to swipe their finger for the login creation, and again on the night."

"I've thought of that," countered 'King'. "The person I have lined-up for this is a similar build and height to you. We can give him a sufficiently good disguise that he can use your pass. He'll go in late at night when there's just a bored night security guy on duty, the pass won't get more than a cursory glance.

And the fingerprint issue isn't hard: there are films that hold a good impression of a print, so he can run the film over the reader. The same technique was used to embarrass the German minister responsible for data security some years ago."

York considered the matter. He wasn't unduly concerned about being spotted at the RCS terminal: he was going to simply stay late and wait until the area was deserted. It would take about two minutes. And the idea of relying on someone else made him nervous.

"I don't know," he said. "It's simple enough if they know what they're doing, but a single mistake – especially forgetting to delete the fingerprint file afterwards – could be disastrous. And what if the security guard is on the ball, and the guy gets detained with my pass?"

"That's the beauty of your alibi. At the time the RCS is accessed, you're going to be at a police station reporting the theft of your wallet. If our tame sysadmin fails to report back that all is well, you'll turn up at work the next day and tell them that your pass was in your stolen wallet."

York thought about it. It seemed like a lot of work to negate a tiny risk, but King seemed to have thought it through, and he supposed an extra layer of protection did no harm.

"Ok, but I'll need to know he did everything to plan. I need to meet with him to make sure he knows exactly what he's doing, then meet again afterwards to confirm that everything has been done. In particular, I'll want a printout of a directory listing to ensure that the fingerprint file has been deleted."

"No problem," assured 'King'. "And we're going to have him do some practice runs on his own PC – you give him all the details of the relevant directories and files, and he'll do it enough times that it is second-nature on the night."

"Ok," said York. "He'll need the login details. The two software modules. The directory path for each. The directory path for the fingerprint file. And a diagram showing the location of the RCS server in the office."

"Sounds good. We'll need those at least a couple of days in advance, so he has time for the practice runs on his own PC. Can you email the files?"

"I'll need to encrypt them, and we'll both need to use disposable email addresses. I'll let you know the encryption key over the phone. That way there'll be no audit trail."

"I'll set up a gmail account as soon as we end the call."

"Ok, I'll get everything ready tomorrow, and email the files to you tomorrow evening."

"Until then."

* * *

Sarah Green was drinking her third cup of coffee of the morning as she studied flow-diagrams showing the steps that took place between a ticket agent logging a sale and the passenger obtaining their boarding-pass. When her phone rang, she was grateful for the interruption – any interruption.

"Green."

"Fisk here, Ma'am."

Green smiled. "Please, it's Sarah, remember: ma'am makes me feel old!"

"I certainly wouldn't wish to do that."

"You have some news?"

"Nothing major, just a little interest value, really. The Brits have solved the mystery of why Danny York became Daniel E. York – but as one mystery is solved, another unfolds."

"Oh yes?"

"The name change was apparently necessary because Danny York was a rather vocal critic of Airbus before Daniel E. York ended up working for them."

"Well, I guess he's not the first person in the world to post things on the net they've later had cause to regret, but he must have been rather forthright in his comments to have to go as far as changing his name! What on Earth did he say about them?"

"He criticised some of the fundamental principles of fly-by-wire systems."

Green was startled. "And yet he's now ..."

"Writing software for them, yes. Intriguing, huh?"

"Very."

"There's more. The reason for his criticisms. Remember that night crash at Schiphol, Amsterdam? An Airbus A320 skidded off the runway on landing?"

"I remember."

"One of the passengers killed on that flight was Stephanie York: Danny York's wife."

"My god."

Airline crashes were pretty rare events. Like most of those who had worked in the aviation industry at a reasonably senior level, Green tended to remember at least the basics of major crashes.

"But wasn't that one down to pilot error? Overshot the runway because the Captain failed to execute a go-around?"

"That was the primary finding, yes, but there were also some recommendations made in the area of the aircraft's software, and York – Danny York at the time – seemed to fixate on that. And what he posted wasn't just on a few Web forums. York wrote letters to newspapers, to the CAA, to his government representative ... He was very active about it."

"So a man whose wife died in a plane crash, and who wrote letters to the papers and to various government officials criticising the concept of fly-by-wire aircraft, is now writing software for them."

"Exactly."

"What do the Brits make of it?"

"They're still investigating. So far their best theory is that it's a kind of therapy for him. His lobbying efforts weren't successful, so maybe he decided to try to fix things from the inside."

Green considered this. Human beings were complex creatures, and the theory wasn't off the scale of possibilities. She couldn't imagine how it would feel to lose a spouse in such terrible circumstances, but if it had happened to her, could she really go and work for a company she held at least partly responsible for her husband's death? However noble her motives? She didn't think so.

"Do you buy that?" she asked Fitch.

"I do find it a little hard to get my head around the idea. But after 12 years in the job, nothing much surprises me any more."

"I guess not. But what if he's out for revenge against Airbus? Holds them responsible for his wife's death and wants to screw things up for them in some way?"

"That's possible, but I don't see him as any kind of threat. You lose your wife in a plane crash, the last thing in the world you want to do is put someone else through the same pain. I mean, yes, there are nut-jobs who totally lose it and go postal, but that's a sudden snapping. The guys who gun down people in shopping malls, it's not like in the movies, where they are sat at home for weeks carefully planning their attack. They use weapons they already own, and probably had no more idea than anyone else what they were going to do more than a day before they acted. You don't get taken on in this kind of role overnight, so it doesn't fit a threat profile to me."

"Well, you're the expert there. But I can't help thinking it's just too odd. If I were Airbus, I'd want to know about him. Are the Brits planning to tell them?"

"You know the Brits: if they can delay a decision, they will. I don't think they've quite figured out their official response to the Boston Tea Party."

Green smiled.

Fisk continued: "The official line is that enquiries are continuing and that a decision will be made once those are complete. But yes, my guess is that someone will have a quiet word with Airbus Security at some stage. But as I say, I don't see a threat here; I just thought you'd find it interesting."

"I do," replied Green, "and thanks for keeping me in the loop. I appreciate it."

"No problem, Ma'am."

Green laughed. "Now you're just doing that deliberately."

"Guilty as charged. I'll let you know if anything else turns up."

"Thanks, Dale."

* * *

York pressed send, and for the first time since he'd arrived there, felt he could finally relax a little. His role was almost over. The encrypted file was on it's way to King. All he had to do now was meet with King's sysadmin on the day, and check the printouts afterwards to ensure that everything had been done properly.

* * *

As York's tensions eased, Fox's had rarely been higher as he typed in the decryption password. What stood between him and the end of the airline industry was his ability to make sense of one of the two files he was about to open.

His googling strongly suggested that, while most of the code would be gobbledegook to him, he ought to be able, with enough care, to spot the only thing he needed to change: an airspeed check figure. He had searched for examples of the programming language C++, and it looked feasible.

He needed to find the piece of code that checked for a maximum airspeed of 25 knots. That piece of code would mean any aircraft in flight would be safe; he needed to change it to 750 knots, so every Airbus A340 in flight would be sent plunging to the ground.

But theory was one thing. It all rested now on his ability to identify that single line of code.

The code was two simple text files. It seemed almost absurd that something capable of changing the world could be opened in Notepad. He opened the first file.

Nothing happened! Notepad was just sitting there, stalled. This couldn't be happening! Not after all the carefu–

The file opened. He looked at the scrollbar, and immediately saw the reason for the delay in opening: the file was large. His relief turned to dismay as he started scrolling through page after page of unintelligible code.

* * *

Twenty-three miles away, in a cargo hangar at London Heathrow, a bored customs officer was scanning through the manifests of the pallets that had just been unloaded from a Fedex flight from Frankfurt International.

Customs officials around the world relied extensively on cooperation across borders. Within the EC particularly, they had a highly efficient intelligence network. If Customs officers at the point of origination had suspicions about a consignment, but couldn't find hard evidence of wrong-doing, they would flag the consignment so that it would show up in the manifests as an item of interest to Customs officials at the destination airport.

What happened next depended on a number of factors: the nature of the suspicions, any information held about the sender or recipient, and domestic priorities at the time.

But in addition to inspecting items flagged on the manifests, Customs officers also conducted purely random checks. A surprising number of Customs seizures were based on nothing more than the instincts of an officer on duty at the time. They referred to it as their 'nose'.

Even the most experienced and successful of officers – those with the best 'nose' – would struggle to tell you what it is they look for. There were established indicators, of course (kept a closely-guarded secret for obvious reasons), but often all the official could tell you was that 'something didn't seem quite right'.

But there were times, like tonight, when there was nothing flagged on the manifest, and nothing jumped out at you, so then it was back to Plan C: purely random inspections. These were the least likely to generate results, and the least interesting to conduct. On the night shift particularly, it could be hard to maintain concentration when all you were doing was having a poke around with little expectation of finding anything.

Senior Officer Jonathan Tibson found himself in exactly that situation as he skim-read through the manifest. But he was proud of his professionalism, and found little games to play to maintain his interest level when conducting random checks. Tonight, he was going to check the most sophisticated-sounding consignment, and the most mundane-sounding consignment.

The most sophisticated-sounding was a package described as 'Satellite Transceivers, Aviation (6)'. He finished his tea and went off in search of the relevant pallet.

* * *

'Keep it together,' Fox told himself. He'd expected the bulk of the code to be incomprehensible. All he had to do was find one line.

He knew from his conversation with York that the current threshold speed was 25 knots. All he had to do was search for the figure 25, and then look for a line that included that figure. His googling had suggested it would probably be along the lines of 'if something <25'. That was what he had to spot.

He tried searching for '<25' in the first file. No matches. He removed the chevron and searched just on the number 25.

There were three matches in the first file. None of them had IF clauses, and he couldn't make any sense at all of any of them. This wasn't looking good.

Steeling himself, he opened the second file and tried the same search for the number 25. The first match was close to the start of the file:

#define MINAIRSPEED 25

Yes! That was obviously what he was looking for, but there was no IF wording, just a whole succession of other #define lines.

He searched for the next example of 25. That one didn't look relevant. He jumped to the next. No. The next. No again. The next- but that was back to the beginning. There was only one relevant-looking line, and that was the #define MINAIRSPEED 25 one.

Fox was no programmer, but the meaning of the line seemed obvious: it was defining the value of the minimum air-speed. So the IF clause wouldn't use the value 25, it would use the label that line defined. He searched again, but this time for MINAIRSPEED. There was only one match:

if (sensor_airspeed < MINAIRSPEED) {

That was it! That was the air-speed check!

Fox could feel his heart thumping. If he understood this correctly, the first line, the #define MINAIRSPEED 25 one, told the code that it should treat the word MINAIRSPEED as equal to 25. So if he changed that line, changed that number 25 to 750, that should be it. Instead of checking that the aircraft was travelling at less than 25 knots, and thus on the ground, it would now check that it was doing less than 750 knots. Every airliner in the world would be flying at less than 750 knots (now Concorde was no longer flying, anyway). The fuel would be cut to all Airbus aircraft manufactured since 2002.

Fox was a cautious man. The code change seemed obvious, but he didn't want to jump to the wrong conclusion, miss something important and mess up the biggest thing he had ever done in his life by making a stupid mistake. He checked again. Both files. He searched again for every instance of the number 25. He even tried it as 'twenty-five' and 'twenty five' just in case. He repeated the search for MINAIRSPEED, again in both files. He tried the search as both upper-case and lower-case. He tried variants: MIN-AIR-SPEED, MIN_AIR_SPEED and MIN AIR SPEED.

For good measure, he repeated every search. He did it all one step at a time, with enormous care. He checked and double-checked every single character he typed. Every letter, every number. More than an hour later, he was finally satisfied. It really was that simple, that trivial: change the figure 25 to the figure 750.

He positioned the cursor at the end of the line:

#define MINAIRSPEED 25

He pressed backspace twice to delete the number 25. He paused. He saw himself as a down-to-earth man, not prone to excesses of ego, but as he readied himself to type the digits 7, 5 and 0, he couldn't help but feel a sense of occasion. One day, he told himself, schoolchildren would study this moment in class. There would be books written about it. Films made. He would be the man who saved the planet from the devastating destruction wreaked on it by the commercial aviation industry.

There would be criticisms, of course. He understood that. The scale of the death-toll made that inevitable. Not everyone would see the bigger picture: the billions of lives saved by acting to halt climate change. But most would, in time. Not immediately – he wouldn't be able to claim the credit for years, he guessed. It would be a big secret to keep.

He found himself searching for reasons to delay pressing the three characters. Somehow it seemed too trivial an action for such an incredible act. But finally he reached out and typed: 750. He pressed CTRL-S to save the changes.

That was it.

Fox was correct in his belief: it was that simple. He had indeed made the only change necessary to set the new minimum airspeed threshold to 750 knots. With this version of the software installed, the fuel would indeed be cut to all Airbus aircraft, including the ones in flight.

But Fox had overlooked one small but critical issue: in swapping a two-character number for a three-character one, the file size was now one byte larger. It would fail the file size check performed by the RCS, and alert the sysadmin that the wrong version of the file was being included in the update.

* * *

Tibson had completed his visual inspection of the consignments, and let Angus, the Labrador on drug-sniffing duties, have a good nose around. Neither had discovered anything of interest. The satellite radio kit appeared to be exactly what it was supposed to be. A quick google search on the model numbers checked out, and there was no sign of any tampering with any of the screws.

Tibson resealed the packages with tape, and affixed the HM Revenue & Customs Officially Opened sticker. He moved on to the most mundane-sounding consignment: 'Screws, Wood, 3cm (50,000)'.

* * *

16th October

York idly wondered about the total value of employee and contractor time spent reading routine emails on which they'd been pointlessly CC'd. Each day he spent 20-30 minutes skim-reading emails that had no real relevance to his work, but which one or more layer of management saw fit to CC to scores of people who would be equally bemused or bored by the content.

That morning, there was one particular email sent to the entire software development team that would normally have fallen into that category: ostensibly relevant to his role but of no practical concern.

To: A3xx series software development team

Subject: Quarterly update – 21st October – promotion to Category 2

An issue in the slats retraction warning system has been identified that can, under some flight configurations, cause a warning to be activated despite correct retraction of the slats. While this poses no risk to the aircraft, unnecessary cockpit warnings are a Category 2 issue.

A fix has been made, which will be included in the quarterly update on 21st October, promoting the update status to a Category 2. Customers will therefore be required to install the update within 10 days, ie. by 2359 hours GMT on 1st November.

Teams should thus anticipate that any support requests will arrive within this timeframe.

In this particular case, however, the email could not have been more relevant to York. It meant that, instead of having to wait two or three months to ensure that as many airlines as possible had installed the update, they could be confident that all airlines would have done so within ten days of the update going out. They could, in principle, trigger the system in less than a month's time.

While he still wanted to wait until he had quit Airbus, it was extremely good news. He would call King that evening to pass on the news.

* * *

22nd October

York again looked at the clock on the living room wall of his apartment, then again checked the time on his watch – just as he had done two minutes earlier, and at least a dozen times before that.

'King' was late. He and his sysadmin were supposed to have been at his apartment almost 40 minutes ago. He looked at the PAYG phone reserved for calls to 'King', but the agreement was that there would be no calls that evening except in dire emergency: the mobiles would be disposed of at the end of the evening, their SIMs shredded. While a 40-minute delay was making York extremely nervous, he couldn't justify classing it as an emergency. He would wait.

'King' had also made a few checks of his watch, but in a far more relaxed manner. He was parked up in his rental car one street away from Fox's apartment, and was simply allowing sufficient time to pass to provide a plausible explanation for the story he was going to present to York. He looked in the vanity mirror in the sun visor and messed his hair a little. He needed to arrive looking frazzled.

York jumped when the intercom system finally buzzed over an hour after the agreed meeting time.

"Hello?"

"It's me. Sorry I'm late."

York buzzed him in.

'King' was looking flustered.

"What's wrong?" asked York.

"I'm afraid we've got a bit of a problem. Tim – the sysadmin – hasn't shown up."

"Where was he supposed to meet you?"

"At the train station here. I took the lunchtime Eurostar to Paris, he had taken an earlier one. We were then due to catch the same train here, but in different carriages and then meet at the station. Only he wasn't there, and I can't reach his mobile. I waited for an hour, kept calling, but it went straight to voicemail each time."

"So what do we do now?" asked York. "The switch has to be done tonight, the update goes out tomorrow."

"I know. Let me try him again."

'King' hit the call button to redial the last call. What York couldn't know was that the number King had stored was the PAYG mobile being used to make the call, ensuring that it would go immediately to the generic Vodafone voicemail service.

"Voicemail again," said 'King', feigning frustration.

"Do we know whether he was on the train to Paris?"

"There's no way to know: the train arrived on time, I checked that, but Eurostar won't even confirm whether a passenger was booked on a train, let alone whether they travelled on it. It's all Data Protection these days."

"Ok, let's just give ourselves some breathing space here. The switch can be done anytime tonight, so there's no immediate cause for panic. Maybe he missed his train, caught a later one and you got his voicemail because he was in the Channel Tunnel or on a connecting train in the middle of nowhere with no signal."

"You could be right."

"And knowing your approach to security, you told him not to phone you except in emergency, right?"

'King' nodded.

"So he probably won't call until he gets to the station and you're not there. For now, we just wait."

Neither man said much as a further hour went by.

"Look," said 'King', finally, "I'll drive back to the station, make one last check there, make one more call to his mobile if he's not there, and then we'll need to decide what to do, ok?"

York nodded his agreement. He was trying to maintain a calm exterior, but felt scared: he hadn't seen a need to introduce anyone else in the first place, and now he didn't know what to think. Was this Tim a plant? Had the authorities somehow got wind of their plans? Were he and King about to get arrested? He didn't know what the charges might be, but conspiracy to cause chaos was bound to be some kind of offence. These days, who knows, it could even be under some kind of anti-terrorism legislation, even though they would be doing nothing more than causing inconvenience in order to expose a very real danger. Perhaps they might-

BZZZZ!

York was startled out of his reverie by the door buzzer. Was this it? Was it the police? He reluctantly pressed the Talk button.

"Hello?" His voice was dry.

"It's me, I'm back."

"Already?" It had only been a few minutes since King had left, he couldn't have made it to the station and back in that time.

"Let me in, Danny."

York had been so startled, he had forgotten to press the door release. He did so.

He opened the door to King: there was nobody with him.

'King' shook his head. "The bastard has let us down. I got a call from him just as I was walking to the car: he got cold feet when he arrived in Paris, waited around a bit and then took the next train back to London. Says he's sorry, but he couldn't go through with it."

York knew he should be annoyed, but his immediate reaction was relief: his fears about the authorities somehow being onto them were groundless. Or were they? Another fear immediately raised itself.

"Will he tell anyone?" asked York.

'King' shook his head. "No, he's a coward but not a traitor. He's still on our side, he just got scared about walking into Airbus HQ."

"Are you sure?" York persisted. "I mean, how well do you know him?"

"Well enough. Besides, he doesn't know the exact details."

"He has the files."

"No," replied 'King', reaching into his pocket to produce a USB key. "I told him to wipe the files from his own system once he'd done the dry-run, and I watched him do it. I have the files on the USB key. I was due to hand it to him tonight."

York reflected for a moment. "It still has to be done tonight."

"I know. I'll do it."

"You?" asked York. "No disrespect, but you're not a techy."

"I can follow instructions. I watched Tim do it, it didn't look difficult."

"It's not, not if you know the systems, but there are too many little ways things could go wrong given that you don't." York paused. "Anyway, it's no big deal: the original plan was for me to do it, you were just being over-cautious. Back to Plan A. I'll do it myself."

"Are you sure?" asked 'King', inwardly satisfied that York had made the decision he'd known he would.

"Totally. It has to be done tonight, or we'd have to wait another three months. I just want to get this done. There's really no risk." He took the key from 'King'. "With this, I don't even have to login to my own PC to get the files. I'll pretend the chip in my pass is playing up and get the security guard to let me past, so there'll be no record of me having even been there tonight."

'King' pretended to mull it over for a few seconds, before agreeing. "You've convinced me." He looked at his watch. "It's almost 10pm now. I guess as it's the night before an update, there might be people burning the midnight oil on last-minute revisions?"

York shook his head. "No, everything has to be tested and signed-off in advance, nobody will be revising anything now. Well, almost nobody."

'King' smiled.

"And I've done quite enough waiting around," continued York, "it's time to finish the job."

"How long will it take?"

"Literally two or three minutes. Copying two files, then deleting the fingerprint file from the system. I'll be there and back in half an hour tops."

"Mind if I wait here for you?" asked 'King', reaching into his bag and pulling out a bottle. "Balvenie, single malt. I thought we ought to have a drink to celebrate."

York smiled. "I guess we should, at that. I'll see you back here in half an hour."

York didn't share Fox's sense of the dramatic moment. There was no pause as he efficiently typed the codes to copy the two files. He was about to exit the directory when he suddenly stopped. Something was wrong. He stared at the directory listing. Yes, there it was: his file was one byte larger than the original!

How the hell had he managed that? He'd been ultra-careful, knowing that any discrepancy in the file size would be picked up by the automated RCS checks. The correct file size had been burned into his brain. He couldn't believe he'd been so careless as to make such a stupid mistake.

Nigel Fatherton, whose terminal York was using, was also cursing himself. He'd gone for drinks with a couple of guys from work, then when he'd got home found he didn't have his keys. He remembered taking them out of his pocket and putting them on his desk when searching for change, so he must have forgotten to put them back afterwards.

He didn't even know the names of his neighbours, let alone have the kind of relationship where you had keys to each others' apartments, so he'd had to make the 15-minute walk to work to fetch them.

He nodded to the security guard as he used his pass to open the electronic barrier and headed towards the elevators. The guard forgot him almost as soon as he passed out of sight; he was terminally bored already, and 6am was still a long way away.

York refreshed the directory listing. There was no doubt. He couldn't fathom how he could have made such a schoolboy error, but somehow he had. Thank god he'd spotted it. It was an easy thing to fix, all he had to do was reduce the length of one of the comments – text in the code that had no effect on the operation of the software but was there simply to tell other software developers what each part of the code did – by one byte.

He opened the file and quickly scanned the comment lines. There: that one would do.

/* Update log file */

He quickly removed the space between 'log' and 'file' so the revised line read:

/* Update logfile */

That was enough. He saved the file and did a new directory listing. The file size was now correct.

Fatherton exited the elevator and started walking towards his desk. As he passed the toilets, his bladder made its presence known. He wanted to just grab his keys and go, but the walk back home would be another 15 minutes, so he supposed he'd better visit the Gents before picking up his keys.

Still annoyed at himself for the mistake, York exited the directory and accessed the directory containing user logins. He found his own invented login and securely deleted the fingerprint file. Now there would be no way to tell who had used the login.

That was it. Done. He pulled the USB key from the slot, put it back in his pocket and walked across the floor. He passed the toilets and found an elevator waiting. He took the elevator to the ground floor, and waved to the guard. The guard used his pass to open the barrier, and York walked out of the main doors.

Walking back to his apartment, the file size thing started bugging him again. He was sure he'd checked it half a dozen times, knowing how critical it was. It didn't matter in the end – he'd caught it in time – but it wasn't like him. He decided to review the files back at his apartment.

Fox paced impatiently in York's apartment. The plan had gone perfectly: York had bought the whole thing, the reason for emailing the files, the cowardly sysadmin, the works. Now he didn't need York any more. Fox had the activation codes: he could take care of the rest from here.

York let himself back into his apartment, and found 'King' waiting for him, smiling.

"Is it done?"

"It's done," replied York, distractedly.

"What's wrong?"

"I just made a silly mistake, that's all. I fixed it, but I can't understand how I let it happen."

"What sort of mistake?"

"You remember I told you that the RCS doesn't do any detailed vetting of files, as only reviewed and tested files get that far, but it does do some basic validation to guard against someone copying the wrong file across?"

"I remember."

"It's a very basic check: filename and file size. My revised code had to be exactly the same size as the

267

original. Well, it wasn't. Somehow I messed-up and my file was one byte bigger than the original."

'King' tried to maintain a neutral expression as he feared the worst. Had York deleted the doctored file and over-written it with a copy from his own PC?

"What did you do?"

"I edited the file – just deleted one character from the comment. Trivial, but I'm furious with myself for making the mistake in the first place. Do you mind if we delay that drink for half an hour or so? I just want to review the file to see if I can understand how I did it."

'King' thought quickly: the whole scheme could fall over in the next few minutes unless he acted immediately. If York checked the file, he'd quickly spot the changed figure. He'd race straight back to Airbus to correct it, and the chance to end commercial aviation would be lost forever. More than that, he'd know immediately that there were only two people who could have done it: him or the (fictitious) Tim. Since what York was trying to do was essentially harmless, he might consider it worth confessing to that in order to report what he would doubtless consider an attempted atrocity.

Scratch that: there was no 'might' about it: York was in this because one person, his wife, was killed. An attempt to kill hundreds of thousands of people would be abhorrent to him. He wouldn't see the bigger picture, the billions who would be saved in the long-term, only the immediate deaths.

"I'm sorry," said 'King'.

"Sorry? Sorry for what?"

"It was me. When i copied the files to the USB key, I got curious about what computer code looked like – I've never seen any – so I opened the file. While I was having a quick look, I accidentally leant on the space-bar and added a whole load of spaces right at the end. I panicked a bit and closed the file, but in my haste I just hit carriage-return when it asked me whether I wanted to save the changes. I should have just told you, but, well, the truth was I was

embarrassed by my stupidity. I went back into the
file to delete the spaces. I was so careful not to delete
any of your code that I must have missed one of the
spaces. I'm sorry, I should have realised the
significance and told you about it, but at the time it
didn't occur to me that it could cause a problem."

'King' held his breath. If York didn't buy it, the
only solution was going to be messy. And while he
wasn't squeamish about giving the orders when
executive action was necessary, he wasn't keen on
hands-on action.

"You absolutely, 100% definitely didn't delete any
of the code?"

"100% certain. That's why I missed the space: I
was being so careful not to touch any of the code."

York laughed with relief. "Christ!" he exclaimed. "I
knew I couldn't have been so dumb! I just couldn't
figure it out. Thank god."

'King' laughed too, his relief just as genuine.
"Sorry again to have scared you like that!"

"Don't worry about it. But open that bottle: I sure
as hell need a large one now!"

* * *

30th October

Simon Russell, Head of Security at Airbus, was
staring at a letter from MI5 in London.

The letter was succinct but comprehensive. It
reported that an Airbus employee by the name of
Daniel E. York appeared to have taken steps to
conceal from Airbus a history which included his
wife being killed in the crash of Istan Air Flight
1951, and his subsequent public criticisms of fly-by-
wire systems. The report advised that York was not
considered a threat to the safety of aircraft, but it
was believed that he may have sought out the post
in order to in some way disrupt operations. It
recommended that Airbus carry out a review of all

code written by York, and any other code which he would have had the opportunity to modify.

Russell was a man accustomed to acting swiftly when circumstances demanded it. He picked up his phone to arrange an immediate emergency meeting between himself, the head of HR and the head of software development. The four of them convened in a meeting room on the 5th floor of the building just 24 minutes later. They were joined by an in-house lawyer the HR head had suggested join them.

Russell wasted no time on small-talk. As soon as his colleagues had read the memo, he launched straight in.

"Our secondary priority is to figure out how we missed this in the first place. But that can wait. The immediate questions facing us are: one, has York carried out any act of sabotage? Two, could he have done so in such a fashion as to endanger any of our aircraft? Gunther?"

Gunther Frison had been Head of Software Development at Airbus for four years, having previously headed up the avionics software division in Frankfurt. He'd also wasted no time, immediately calling in York's line manager to get full details of York's work.

"We'll know more very shortly, but right now the answers appear to be a tentative 'no' to the first, and a definite 'no' to the second. Dealing with the more important question first, the system York is working on concerns real-time monitoring of fuel performance by ground engineers. It's a read-only system. It does not, and cannot, have any effect on aircraft in-flight. The worst he could do is to somehow interfere with the fuel performance data reported to engineers such that they would make sub-optimal adjustments to the fuel-management sub-routines once the aircraft is back in the hangar."

"What if his code generated massive misreporting of the data? Could that fool the engineers into making adjustments that would burn fuel at a dangerously high rate? Result in aircraft being under-fuelled?"

Frison shook his head. "Definitely not. A huge amount of work goes into maximising the fuel-efficiency of our engines, so the fuel-management systems have a great deal of intelligence built into them already. The kind of parameter tweaks the airline engineers would make would fall within a very narrow range, and they would know that. If anything was grossly out, they'd spot it immediately. Even if they didn't, the update system wouldn't allow them to make changes that were out of range."

"Ok," persisted Russell, "that's the system York was meant to be working on; what other systems did he have access to?"

"Write access, nothing. Read access to the associated engineering update modules, but he wouldn't be able to modify any of those."

"So what's the absolute worst-case? What's the most damage he could have done?"

"That's what I've asked his line manager to ascertain. His initial view is that the worst-case would be his module failing to report any data at all, or reporting gibberish data, which would piss-off our customers but do no actual harm. He's going to call me once he's reviewed the test results from York's modules. Once that's done, he's going to hand-review York's code personally, but you know the drill: between peer-review and testing, the chances of any really bad code getting through are vanishingly small."

Russell nodded: it was an area the two of them had discussed at length on past occasions.

"As I understand it, the update that went out eight days ago includes York's code, and because one module was a Category 2, customers have ten days to install it – so most will have done so by now?"

"Yes, the vast majority. It's something you do at the earliest opportunity, not right at the deadline."

"Is there a way to rollback the update while we review York's code?"

"There is," replied Frison, "but we have to take a balanced view here. There just isn't any realistic way his module could in any way compromise the safety of aircraft, nor do we believe he'd want to. If we instruct customers to rollback the update, that does enormous harm to our reputation and raises a whole flood of questions. You know how these things work: the media gets the slightest whiff of a rogue coder at work and 12 hours later we have headline news questioning the safety of our aircraft."

"So we wait for the code review?"

"Yes. We're talking an hour or so before we know the bottom-line here. As I say, even if York's code does do something it shouldn't, it's hard to see how it could do anything more than cause minor inconvenience. That being the case, we can issue a replacement update with far fewer alarm-bells. Maybe even avoid them altogether by inventing a new Category 2 fix."

"You're sure it's safe to wait?"

"You know there are no absolutes, but for all practical purposes, yes: I'm sure."

Russell knew Frison would be a fool to make such a statement if he weren't certain of his ground. The safest thing for Frison would be to hedge. He wasn't doing so.

"Ok. What else needs to be done, once the test results and code review is complete?"

"We'll conduct a total audit of his account, from the day he walked through the door. As you know, our audit systems log all activity on all accounts. Every single command he has ever typed, every file he has ever accessed, will be in the logs. We will also do a bit-copy of his hard drive. Absolutely everything will be checked and double-checked."

Russell nodded again; he didn't believe in wasted words at the best of times. He would relax when, and only when, the audit was complete. He couldn't know, of course, that the audit was irrelevant, and that the activity they were looking for occurred in an RCS account they didn't even know existed.

Russell turned to the Head of HR, Camille Passerieu. "He can't continue to work here, even if everything comes up clean. He's too much of a wildcard, we could never trust him."

"I assumed you'd say as much," replied Passerieu, "that's why I brought Henri from legal along. Henri?"

"Like the majority of our software team, Monsieur York is a contractor, not an employee. He has a fixed-term contract of 12 months, at which point we have no further obligations toward him. With regard to terminating his contract prior to expiry, the position naturally depends on the outcome of the various investigations being undertaken."

"We're not waiting for those," said Russell, impatiently. "I want him escorted from the building by Security today."

"That's where things get potentially complex," said the lawyer. "His public criticisms of Airbus would definitely fall within the scope of 'behaviour likely to bring the company into disrepute' had they been made during the period of his contract, but of course his public pronouncements preceded his term here. Whether they could be used as grounds for early termination of his contract is unclear. A court might well take the view that-"

"I'm not making myself clear," interrupted Russell. "I don't care one jot about his contract. He can sue us, or we can just pay him off, I don't care. I just want him out of the building, today."

"I'm happy to terminate his contract and let him sue if he thinks he has a case," said Passerieu. "My guess is he won't. Whatever he was or wasn't up to, he knows he's misled us. I'm content to argue bad faith on his part. Worst case, we have to pay him and some modest legal costs."

"Sold," said Russell. He turned to Frison. "Gunther, can you lock him out of his account?"

"Already done. We sent someone to his area to say that we have some issues with the server his team uses, and that some accounts may not be able to login until the issue is resolved. We've locked out a couple of other people from his area so that it all looks credible. That should keep him from being suspicious for a while."

"Excellent work," said Russell. "Camille, do you need to issue him with any paperwork today, or can that be done later? I'd really like just to send someone from security to take his pass and escort him from the building right away."

"I'd prefer to issue a formal notice of termination, but that's just a boiler-plate one-pager. I can have that done within five minutes of getting back to my desk."

"Great. In which case, I'll have someone from Security waiting for you at your office. You do the termination notice, then call him and ask him to come and see you right away. You hand over the notice, we take his pass and escort him out."

York was drinking tea and chatting with two other colleagues who were also locked out of their accounts. With the update done, nobody was on a deadline, so the atmosphere was lighthearted. York did his best to play along with the mood. He did feel relieved that the job was done, but he'd become friends with a number of people there despite himself, and he couldn't help but feel disloyal. He wanted nothing more than to get out of there. He had no idea that he was about to get his wish.

"York," he said as he picked up his phone.

"Mr York, it's Camille Passerieu from HR. Would you mind popping up to my office right away? Room 5728 on the 5th floor. It will only take a few minutes."

"Um, sure. I'm just twiddling my thumbs at the moment anyway, problems with the server."

"Good, then I'll look forward to seeing you in a few minutes."

York's heart felt like it was trying to punch its way out of his chest. He'd been so careful, but had he made a mistake somewhere? Had they discovered what he'd done?

No, he decided. If they had, they wouldn't be inviting him up to HR for a chat, there would be a burly security guard at each elbow. He looked around. No sign of any uniformed thugs. All the same, 'right away' suggested something decidedly non-routine. He'd look up this Passerieu on the Intranet, except he couldn't login.

Couldn't login? And a call to see HR? That didn't seem like coincidence. But then he wasn't the only person locked out of his account: there were at least three of them. Did that mean Airbus was downsizing, and they were going to let some of them go? It made sense. There were three of them locked out, and they'd just completed an update. It would be the most logical time to let people go.

He almost laughed aloud at the absurdity of it: a situation that most would dread, a call to HR to be canned, and he was almost giddy with relief at the thought of it.

He glanced over at his colleagues. They were still joking around, so clearly they hadn't yet received a call. But then he was the most recent to join the team, so perhaps he was going to be first out the door and the others would follow.

His stomach still felt tight, and he could still feel his heartbeat, but this could be a good day. If they let him go, he'd be free of the need to keep up the act, they could go ahead with the day of chaos and finally the aviation world would have to face the fact that fly-by-wire aircraft were inherently unsafe. It wouldn't bring back Stephanie, nothing could, but it would make her death feel just a little less futile.

York was a little surprised to read the job title under Camille Passerieu's name on the door plate. Did the head of HR really fire people personally? He again felt his heart speeding-up, and hesitated before knocking. But there was no point standing there speculating: he knocked on the door.

"Enter."

York opened the door, and once more his heart lurched as he caught sight of the uniformed security guard standing against the wall. This looked serious. Or was this standard when you fired someone? He supposed some people might get violent when given the news.

"Daniel," Passierieu said as she gestured for him to take one of the two seats opposite her desk. He sat, waiting.

Passierieu didn't keep him waiting long. She handed him a sealed envelope with his name handwritten on the front.

"This is a notice of termination of your contract. It takes effect immediately. I will need your security pass, please." She held out her hand.

York's mind was whirling. He still didn't know what was going on. Had they discovered something, or was this a coincidence? Her manner seemed very brusque: shouldn't she be taking a gentler approach to a routine redundancy? Expressing appreciation for his work, explaining the difficulty of the circumstances in which the company found itself, expressing regret for the necessity of the action? He'd never been let go before, but that was how they did it in TV shows. Perhaps that was a myth, he thought.

Still trying to get a handle on what was happening, he lifted the pass chain from around his neck and handed it to her across the desk.

He didn't want to ask any questions. More than anything, he wanted to simply walk out of the door, out of the building, pack his bags and catch the first flight back to the UK. If he didn't ask, he couldn't hear anything he didn't want to.

But he had to know. He swallowed. He'd always thought that was something that only happened in the movies.

"May I ask the reason?" he asked.

Passierieu gave him a very direct look. "Your past comments on Airbus are incompatible with your working here."

York definitely didn't want to ask this next question, but again he had to know.

"That is the only reason?"

"It is a sufficient one. The officer will escort you to your desk where you may collect any personal belongings, then he will escort you from the building. You may collect personal effects, but no data media of any kind. If you have any personal data media in your work area – hard drives, USB keys, DVDs or the like – those will be returned to you after it has been determined that they don't contain any data belonging to Airbus. Every reasonable precaution will be taken to protect the confidentiality of any personal data present."

York nodded. He had been careful: he carried files back and forth where necessary on a single USB key that stayed in his pocket when not in use. There was nothing incriminating in or on his desk, nothing on his PC, nothing in his directory on the server.

The walk back to his desk, the silent security officer by his side, seemed to take hours. The officer was making no attempt at subtlety, it was obvious to everyone they passed that York was being escorted, and every pair of eyes followed him.

As he approached his desk, he could see that his two colleagues, the ones who had also been locked out of their accounts, were both using their PCs. Both looked up then quickly turned back to their screens. Had they known, and been asked to play along? He didn't think so, they'd seemed too relaxed while the three of them had been chatting. But clearly they knew something now, as they were both intently studying the code on their PCs and completely ignoring him. He wondered what they'd been told. Then again, whatever it was, when a soon-to-be-former co-worker is escorted by a security guard, you're not going to want to be seen talking to them.

There was no sign of his manager, and he felt grateful for the fact. York assumed she would know more, and he didn't want the embarrassment of even having to glance at her.

He didn't have much in the way of personal possessions at his desk. Partly a paranoia about his identity being discovered, partly a desire to detach himself from this place, not to see himself as in any way belonging here. He picked up the few things he had, and nodded to the guard. The two of them walked back towards the elevators.

York came to a sudden halt. The guard looked at him sharply, and he forced himself to walk on. But a sudden unpleasant realisation had hit him: if they knew about his statements about fly-by-wire, they must also know the reasons for them. Someone who has misgivings about something might set them aside when there's a juicy contract on offer. He'd known more than one contractor who could speak disparagingly about a company and then later take their pieces of silver from it when a contract opportunity arose. But if they knew about Stephanie, they had to know that he wasn't just here because he had a mild distaste he could set aside if the money was right. They had to know he had a reason to be here. And that meant that if they hadn't already learned the truth, it could only be a matter of time before they did.

Knowing his motivation had to be to in some way screw things up for Airbus, they would be going through his code line by line. Probably that was what his boss was doing right now.

He had covered his tracks reasonably well, he knew, but that was when he would have been just one of a number of suspects, and he could have bluffed it out. Now they would know it was him. They had his motive. They would be focusing all their efforts on linking him to the doctored code.

He felt sick as the elevator descended to the lobby. Was he going to find the police waiting there for him there? At his apartment? At the airport?

The doors opened and he and the guard walked to the electronic barriers. The guard gestured for York to go to the wide gate, the one used to let visitors with day passes in and out. The guard used his pass to open the gate and they walked through into the lobby. The guard turned to him.

"Please leave the building and the grounds. Do not attempt to return for any reason. If there's anything you've forgotten, it will be forwarded onto you. Do not contact any Airbus employees or contractors."

York felt like a criminal as he walked out of the main doors and into the bright sunlight. Well, he was fairly sure he was a criminal. He'd always been more realistic than King, and had known there was a fair likelihood that it would eventually be pinned on him. He'd been willing to face the consequences, but he'd wanted to know what those consequences might be, so he'd done some googling.

It had proved hard to find equivalent cases: mostly, when employees carried out an act of sabotage, it was on a much smaller scale. The scale here was much larger, and there was a great deal of premeditation. The disruption would be on a massive scale. A short jail sentence seemed likely. That had been ok by him; if that's what it took to bring this to the attention of the world, and to prevent other lives being lost, he'd have gone to jail knowing that it was a price worth paying.

But this, this was different. They were going to prevent it. Nothing would be achieved. He'd go to jail for nothing, and nothing would be different when he got out. Airbus would continue like nothing had happened. Airlines would continue to fly passengers on fly-by-wire aircraft. There would be other crashes, other Stephanies would be killed.

He needed to talk to someone, and there was only one person in the world he could talk to about this. He didn't have the PAYG phone he used to call King, but had his own mobile and King had made him memorise the number. King wouldn't like York using his own phone to call him, but the security precautions seemed pointless now. Whatever Airbus hadn't yet worked out, they soon would.

As he walked down the street on his way back to his apartment – his former apartment, he corrected himself, as he wasn't going to be doing anything there other than pack his things – he pulled out his phone and dialled King's number.

* * *

As soon as the call was connected, an application on a server in a building on the north bank of the Thames was triggered. The number called was logged, and a digital recording activated. Every word spoken on the call would be recorded in a 320kbit/s audio file logged against York's file number.

* * *

"It's York."

"What are you doing, calling me on your own phone, and using your surname?"

"It's over, they know everything."

"What do you mean?" The words were rushed, almost breathless, and his pitch high. York had never before heard King sound agitated: he had always been so calm and matter-of-fact about everything.

"I've just been fired. They found the things I wrote. They know that Danny York and Daniel E. York are the same person. I've just been escorted from the building by a security guard and told not to darken their doorstep again."

There was silence on the line for what seemed like an age before King replied, his voice sounding much more like his usual self.

"Ok, start at the beginning. Tell me everything that's happened."

York gave King a brief summary of events; there wasn't much to tell.

"So we don't know that they know anything about the code? All they know is that you've criticised them in the past."

"If they've found the letters to the papers, then they know about Stephanie. They know that one of their aircraft killed my wife. They'll know I didn't somehow decide that didn't matter and I was willing to work for them anyway. It'll be obvious I could only have been there to screw with them in some way, and they're going to go through every line of my code. They're going to find what I've done and recall the update. It only went out a few days ago, so the chances are that the update has been made to only a small proportion of aircraft so far. They'll ship corrected code and that will be that."

'King' was thinking fast. The previous game-plan had been to wait until after November 8th, to ensure that all airlines had carried out the update. If he could, he wanted to bring every last one of them down. But if York was right, he had to act immediately. It might mean only crashing a handful of planes, but that was better than nothing.

The problem was, he wasn't ready. He'd got the kit, but not the people in place. Realistically, he wasn't going to be able to act in the next 24 hours. Christ, this was a mess! Surely something so carefully planned and so close to fruition couldn't fall apart now?

"Listen, don't say or do anything precipitous. Maybe you're right, and they'll figure things out, but let's not assume anything right now. Give me some time to think things through."

"We don't have any time," protested York. "Someone, most likely several someones, will be going through my code right now. Don't forget, I deliberately wrote the revised code in a naive style in an attempt at plausible deniability. Once someone is looking for it, it isn't going to be hard to spot. My guess is they'll have the whole thing figured out within the hour. I'm going to be arrested this afternoon. And it's all going to have been for nothing."

"Are you at your apartment now?"

"I'll be there in a few minutes. There's no point in trying to hide, I'm not going to be heading to Rio. I'll go to my apartment, pack my things and wait for a knock at the door."

York didn't know the half of it, thought 'King': if Airbus really did find the code, there would be no knocking involved. There would be helicopters, SWAT teams, sub-machine guns and stun grenades.

'King' was still thinking. With the original plan, he would have arranged for York to cease to be a factor on the day of the mission, once everything was in place. But if York was arrested, that would put him out of reach. That was unfortunate, but 'King' was still confident he'd covered his own tracks. York had no idea of his real identity. The phone was an anonymous PAYG phone and he'd dispose of it that evening if York was arrested. There was nothing in the SOS offices to tie 'David King' to him.

There would be a photofit. He'd need to lay low for a while. He had friends dotted around the world in various places, one of them could be counted on to give him a place to hang out for a while. After that, well, he'd play it by ear. If it got masses of media attention, became a serious manhunt, well, then he'd need to make plans for a permanent change of identity. Plastic surgery and a life of obscurity somewhere. It wasn't a pleasant prospect, but it beat rotting in a jail cell somewhere.

But he didn't expect it to come to that. If the plot really was uncovered before anything happened, the police would crow about their success, it would be headline news for a day or two and then ... what? There was really no lasting story here. The police claimed that a major attack had been thwarted, and a sap had been taken in by some unknown guy, even assuming the authorities bought York's story. Nobody died. No dramatic footage to replay over and over again 9/11-style. No, the story wouldn't last long. There would be no worldwide manhunt, no Special Forces mission watched live from the White House Situation Room. He'd be able to slip quietly back into the country some way down the road.

It would, of course, be enormously frustrating. It was a brilliant plan, and a huge amount of work had gone into it. If all that ended up wasted ... Well, there was nothing he could do about it. Either York was right, or he wasn't. If he was, it seemed that they'd know it by the end of the day.

"Are you still there?" asked York.

"Sorry, yes. Thinking. Look, if you're right, then you're going to know it by the end of the day, right?" 'King' smiled despite himself at his own understatement.

"Very much sooner, I expect."

"Right. So do nothing for now. Go wait. If nothing has happened by the end of the working day, then nothing is going to happen. You'll be in the clear. So the safest course of action is to do nothing right now. If nobody has come looking for you by say 7pm, book a train home and we'll meet in London in a couple of days, ok?"

'King' was sure it wouldn't take longer than that to make the necessary arrangements for York to be found at home, an apparent suicide victim.

York didn't share King's apparent optimism, but he agreed with the logic. It didn't in any case change anything: his plan was to remain in his apartment for the rest of the day anyway.

"Ok," he said.

"And try not to worry: if the worst does happen, and you are charged with anything, I'm going to get you the best lawyer in the business. Remember, you're a sympathetic case. You lost your wife. You had only the most noble of motives. All you were trying to do is prevent future crashes and further needless deaths. The worst that would have happened had you succeeded was a few million businessmen had to postpone their meetings. It's not going to be a big problem, even if you're right about them finding the code."

York felt somewhat reassured. King's argument made sense. And in the worst case, if the authorities did try to throw the book at him, perhaps a court case could generate some publicity, draw attention to the issue and create pressure for the CAA and FAA to act.

"Thanks, that does make me feel a bit more optimistic."

"Try not to worry about it. Just pack your things and plan to catch a flight home tomorrow."

"I will," promised York.

* * *

MI5 had changed a great deal since the end of the Cold War. Originally a highly secretive organisation, it wasn't until 1989 that the government even admitted its existence – though it featured in many spy novels. Today, its headquarters on the north bank of the Thames were pointed out by tour guides on the tourist boats that plyed the river.

The days of shadowy figures making unaccountable decisions in total secrecy were, officially, over. Even when the authorities were dealing with investigations into serious crimes, phone-taps were viewed as an extraordinary measure, justified only when conventional means of investigation had proved inadequate. Each individual phone-tap had to be applied for by the police or security services, and each one had to be approved by the Home Secretary.

This was, however, 'a custom more honoured in the breach than the observance'. The 2,000 telephone intercept targets authorised by the Home Secretary each year were but a fraction of the total number in place at any one time. With MI5's target having shifted from foreign spies to suspected terrorists, the scope of its enquiries had been dramatically widened. Telephone taps were used routinely as part of a filtering process, designed to distinguish serious threats from the nutters who either issued threats or were engaged in supposed plots that were nothing more than bluster and fantasy to impress those who sympathised with their anti-establishment or anti-western democracy views.

As soon as the request had arrived from the FBI, York had been placed on a list of 'persons of interest' to MI5. When he failed the CTC, his status was officially raised to that of a 'potential terrorist threat' and his home and mobile phone numbers were added to the ECHELON database.

The popular conception of ECHELON was a giant computer system that intercepted hundreds of thousands of calls and listened out for keywords like 'bomb' and 'target'. The reality was much more complex. There was in fact no single system known as ECHELON, rather it encompassed the signals intelligence work carried out by the five signatories of the UK-USA Security Agreement: the USA, UK, Canada, Australia and New Zealand, collectively referred to as the Five Eyes.

While some of the analysis work carried out by the Five Eyes was indeed automated, this mostly related to identifying connections between targets. The contacts, not the content. If one 'person of interest' placed a phone call to a second 'person of interest', that recording would be automatically flagged for transcription and forwarded to the relevant agent for analysis.

The majority of the work performed by the Five Eyes network, however, was much more decidedly low-tech: lots of junior intelligence officers listening in to recordings and reporting suspicious content. What got listened to depended on both operational priorities and available resources. When resources were stretched, which was most of the time, low-priority material was not listened to in its entirety, but instead 'sampled', meaning that only a proportion of calls to or from a particular target were flagged for archiving.

York was a relatively low-priority target, so his sampling rate was set at 20%: one in five of his calls would be flagged for listening, the other four would be flagged for archiving. There was only a one-in-five chance that his call to 'King' would be listened to.

* * *

The hastily-assembled Airbus tiger team assigned to review York's code and activities was thorough.

York's code was being subjected to a line-by-line review by both York's line manager and two further hand-picked senior software developers. Each was tasked with not only ensuring that there was no malicious code present, but also that there was no code present whose effect wasn't completely clear.

Two IT security consultants were reviewing the audit logs that logged every single command York had ever typed, every directory he had ever accessed, every file he'd ever opened, every change he'd ever made to any file other than his own software modules.

A senior test engineer was reviewing the results of the automated tests carried out on York's code, looking for anything which might have been missed.

Yet another consultant was conducting a forensic analysis of the hard drive on York's PC.

Nothing was being left to chance, everything was being checked.

The team were all IT experts. They knew exactly what sort of thing to look for, and they knew exactly what York could and couldn't have done with the access privileges he'd held.

It was this that formed the crucial flaw in the investigation. Knowing what York's account did and didn't give him access to, they did the logical thing:

they checked the code in the quarantined directory of the project server, not the code on the RCS.

Like most serious mistakes, this wasn't really a conscious decision, it was a combination of habit, established practice and assumptions based on a detailed understanding of how things worked.

Habit, because the project server is where you would always go to examine project files.

Established practice, because it was written in stone that nobody but an RCS sysadmin accessed files on the RCS. It would no more have occurred to them to do so than it would have occurred to a train driver to drive through a red signal.

Assumptions based on understanding how things worked because the whole point of the quarantined directory on the project server was to hold the final, signed-off versions of the code that was then copied onto the RCS. The two versions would, they knew, be absolutely identical.

The team met at 7pm. All three code reviewers agreed that the code was flawless. There was nothing harmful in it, and nothing whose function wasn't clear. If anything, it was rather better commented than most code.

The audit team needed more time to complete a line-by-line review of the logs, but so far they'd found nothing untoward. Nor would they: York had done nothing suspicious under his own account. Even when emailing code to himself, he'd copied and pasted the code into the body of the email so that there would be no attachment.

Simon Russell was chairing the meeting and was unconvinced by what he'd heard.

"Ok, you guys are the experts, and you wouldn't be on the team unless you could be counted on to do a thorough job. But my job is to be suspicious and trust nothing. You're telling me his code is 100% clean, and that based on the audit so far he's done nothing even vaguely suspicious in his time here. I'm loathe to tell you you're wrong when it's your field not mine, but it just doesn't add up. York must hate Airbus. The only possible reason for him to be here is some kind of sabotage, yet he's been beavering away for months doing an apparently very good job for us. Something somewhere has to have been missed."

"Not necessarily." The comment came from Inge Bodden, York's line manager. "He didn't luck into this job overnight. He's gone to a great deal of trouble to take the necessary training to acquire the skillset needed for a role here. This is a man who does his research and thinks long-term. Agreed?"

"Medium-term, at least," conceded Russell.

"The project he was working on gave him no real opportunity for sabotage. It was a read-only system, with no possibility of interfering with aircraft operations. His research would have told him that nobody walks in the door here and gets immediately assigned to anything critical. He's a patient man. It seems clear that he was simply biding his time, waiting to get assigned to a project with the potential to cause real problems for us."

"How long would that have taken?"

"A couple of years, most likely," replied Bodden.

"Would he really have been willing to wait so long?"

"Coders are patient, methodical people. We have to be. And don't forget, he'd also have had to try to figure out some way around the myriad safeguards here. So he'd be doing two things at once: waiting to get access to a critical system, and learning the safeguards in the hope of finding a hole in them."

"Makes sense," said Russell. "Ok, continue the audit, and humour me with one further review of his code?"

"Sure," said Bodden.

"Ok," Russell told the meeting. "it appears we've dodged the bullet on this one, but that's down to luck as much as anything. We need to accelerate the CTC checks and tighten our recruitment procedures, and I'll be arranging individual meetings with each one of you to look at what further lessons we need to learn from this."

* * *

The algorithm on the MI5 server was designed to ensure that the predetermined proportion of low-priority calls were flagged for listening, but that the actual calls selected were random. So if 10 calls were made, two of them would be flagged for listening, but they wouldn't simply be the fifth and tenth calls intercepted, they might be call three and call seven, for example.

On the MI5 server, York's call to 'King' was randomly flagged as L: Listen.

* * *

Fox had wasted no time. As soon as he ended his call with York, he'd quickly packed a bag and made a reservation on a Eurostar to Paris. If things did all go to hell, it was going to be a matter of hours before his photofit was going to be at every UK port. The search would spread outward from there, but the initial focus would be on the UK. If he could get to Paris before that happened, he could grab a train and be anywhere in western Europe by the following day.

He'd bought a return ticket, returning the following morning. His plan was to rent a car, drive out of the city to a Formula 1 motel, selected because they were unstaffed: you made a reservation by card, something he'd do with an untraceable prepay debit card, then got a code which you used to unlock both the main entrance and your room door. He would wait for darkness and hopefully get into the room without being seen by anyone. After that, it was a question of just watching the news: there would either be nothing, or it would be the lead story – nothing in between.

* * *

Unlike Fox, York had no plan B: he was simply sat in his apartment waiting for the knock on the door.

King's assurances had calmed him. While he could see no way to avoid detection, King did seem to have the resources to make good on his promise to hire the best legal team. He clearly would make a sympathetic case, and since no harm would have been done beyond the minor hassle of issuing a replacement update, he didn't think the legal consequences would be too devastating.

His greater concern was almost the opposite: that a good legal team would downplay it to the point that the case would be viewed as too trivial. Unless it generated significant media attention, all the planning, all the work, would have been totally wasted.

That was the prospect he feared more than the personal consequences: that nobody would see the dangers, that aircraft would grow increasingly automated and that there would be further crashes, further deaths.

He couldn't let that happen. Regardless of the advice of his legal team, he was going to do everything he could to make the case headline news.

* * *

Fox had spent an uncomfortable evening with the motel TV channel tuned to i-Télé, the main French news channel, and his laptop browser constantly refreshing the BBC news website. There had been nothing on either.

He'd intended to stop checking at midnight. If the story hadn't broken by then, they had to be in the clear. But he'd found it impossible to sleep: there was simply too much hanging in the balance here. By 3am, he'd given up any hope of sleep, got out of bed and spent the next three hours flicking through the TV channels and browsing every news website he could find. Sky News. Every UK paper. Every French paper he could find online.

There was nothing in any of them. Not at 3am, not at 6am when his alarm went off. They were in the clear! The mission would go ahead. He showered, packed his bag and headed out to his rental car to drive back into town to take the Eurostar back to London.

* * *

York couldn't understand it. The code would have been glaring. The interaction between the two different modules meant that he hadn't necessarily expected them to figure out the whole thing at first glance, but the gist of what was going on should have been obvious, and at that point they should have pulled in a whole bunch of coders to dissect it. It shouldn't have taken longer than an hour before they had it figured out.

When 7pm had come and gone, he'd decided to stay the night and wait there until 10am. He was prepared to face the music, and really just wanted to get it done. 10am should surely have allowed them sufficient time to alert the authorities and come looking for him?

Yet 10am had also come and gone. No knock on the door. No phone call, even.

Had they decided to hush the whole thing up? Quietly issue an urgent instruction to airlines to rollback the update? Airlines had as much reason as aircraft manufacturers to keep quiet about aviation risks. Lost passenger confidence meant lost bookings and lost profits.

That had to be it. He knew his boss, he knew the team: they were all smart cookies. They couldn't have missed it. They were just keeping it under wraps.

It was a classic 'good news, bad news' scenario. Good news because his liberty and career would be safe; bad news because no court case meant no publicity.

Was there any way to rescue things? Make it known what they'd done? Show just how close they'd come to getting rogue code on board over a thousand airliners? His code was safe, but it mightn't have been.

York wasn't optimistic. He didn't consider himself in any way media-savvy – the failure of his earlier attempts to get the issue into the news had confirmed that – but he understood that 'something that would have inconvenienced lots of people nearly happened' wasn't news, and Airbus would take the line that the fact they'd caught it in time, albeit only just, showed that their safeguards worked.

He needed to talk things over with King. Using the correct PAYG phone this time, he placed the call.

'King' was zipping through the Kent countryside on board a Eurostar back to London when the call came in. Seeing 'Y' displayed on the caller display, he got up from his seat and walked quickly to the toilet at the end of the first-class carriage and closed the door behind him before answering.

"All clear?" he asked York.

"Yes. I think I've figured it out: they realise the damage it would do to their reputation if this became public knowledge, so they've decided to deal with it behind closed doors. My guess is they've asked airlines to rollback the update, citing a disk-duplication error or something. It's not like the airlines can examine the code: they just put the floppy into a slot on the flight-deck and press a button. They never see the code. Airbus then issues a replacement update and no-one is any the wiser."

'King' knew York had to be wrong. This was no innocuous code they could cover-up. But he had to play along.

"You're still assuming they figured things out," he said.

"It's inconceivable that they haven't, but ... Do you have the satellite comms kit?"

"It's on the way to me, why?"

"The test code I included to let us check how many aircraft had it installed. Let's assume Airbus takes the safest course of action. That means the rollback is done today, and they issue the replacement update without including even the clean version of my code. They can have that with airlines by tomorrow. The airlines then have seven days to install it, but at least some of them will do so sooner than that. We give it a few days, then transmit the test-code. If I'm right, we'll get nothing back. If we get any OK responses back at all, then I'm wrong and my code got installed."

"Sounds like a plan," replied 'King'. "Listen, I can't talk much now – are you back in London?"

"Not yet – I decided to wait until this morning. I'll get the next flight out, be back by early afternoon."

"Ok, I'll give you a call later on and we can arrange to meet up in the next few days.

* * *

1st November

"Morning, Ma'am."

Green laughed. "How's it going, Dale?"

"It's going," he joked. "Got an update for you on our friend Mr York."

"And there was me thinking you just wanted to hear the sound of my voice."

What the hell was she doing, wondered Green? Now she was flirting with him!

"That too, of course."

"Well, I guess you might as well fill me in on the update at the same time."

"I guess I might. As I suspected, the Brits took the 'quiet word with Airbus' approach. Well, 'quiet memo', actually. They checked out his code, and all was ok. They let him go anyway, unsurprisingly."

"How did York react?"

"He didn't, by all accounts. They terminated his contract without compensation, and York just faded away."

"No lawsuit?"

"Not so far."

"They've doubled-checked his code?"

"Every which way. Top-level meetings, complete IT audit, the works. Everything came out clean."

"It doesn't make any sense! He thinks the company killed his wife, yet he goes to work for them. He's there for months, does nothing wrong yet doesn't kick up the slightest fuss when they fire him. He had to have been up to something."

"Airbus agrees with you, but they reckon he was playing a long game. The stuff he was working on, he couldn't do any real damage. The thinking is that he was simply holding out until he got into a position where he could have a real impact. Likely would have taken him a couple of years. But even if he'd got that far, no-one thinks he had any intention of hurting anyone. Screw-up operations in some way, make a point, yes. Terrorism, no."

Green paused, then asked: "You know sometimes you just have a hunch?"

"Sure."

"And other times, you just had a theory, were proved wrong and can't let it go."

"Got that t-shirt, yep."

"How do you tell the difference?"

Fitch laughed. "Damned if I know."

"So what do you do when you can't tell?"

"You think Airbus has missed something?"

"They must have. The strain of working every day for a company you believe was responsible for your wife's death, that has to be enormous. Just walking in through the door each morning has to hurt. They think he could have done that for two years? Every fibre in me says no way could he do that."

"He did it for five months."

"Which brings me back to: I may be completely wrong. So what do you do when you can't tell whether or not a hunch is correct?"

"Well, ma'am ..."

Green smiled.

"It's pretty simple, really," Fitch continued. "The only real mistake is to stick with a hunch which is there only because you've failed to weigh-up the known facts. So if you were ignoring the fact that Airbus checked and found nothing ... if you were ignoring the fact that he's successfully walked through that door five days a week for five months ... then you'd be behaving foolishly. Also, if you run your hunch past other people and they say no, again you'd be foolish to ignore that. But if you've properly considered all the facts, listened carefully to opposing views and your hunch still says 'yes', then follow it. The worst thing that can happen is that you make a bit of a fool of yourself; the best thing that can happen is you solve a case or prevent a crime."

"I think I've considered the facts," replied Green.

"I think so too."

"I also think I listened carefully to our software development expert."

"You strike me as someone who listens to people."

"I hope so." Green thought for a moment. "But I should also listen to the FBI. What do you think?"

"I think Airbus is right. But I'm basing that on third-hand data. If my hunch were telling me otherwise, I'd want to speak to the man who made the call: the Head of Security at Airbus. Then I'd evaluate the validity of my hunch."

"You think that's what I should do?"

"It's one phone call. You've already demonstrated your ability to sweet-talk your way through any professional sensitivities an investigator might harbour."

Green could hear the smile in his voice.

"Do you have his details."

"Give me a second." Fitch opened the email and scanned it for the name. "Not in front of me, give me five minutes and I'll call you back."

Fitch was as good as his word. Green checked the time: 9:45am. Toulouse was five hours ahead, so 2.45pm there. No problem. She was ready to deploy her schoolgirl French to get past reception, but it wasn't necessary, her Parlez-vous Anglais was met with an immediate "Of course, Madame: how can I help?"

"Simon Russell, please. My name is Sarah Green from the Department of Homeland Security in Washington."

She still enjoyed the magical effect of that phrase. Receptionists and PAs rarely asked what her call was concerning, or told her that the person she was trying to reach was unavailable and could they take a message? A repetition of the magic phrase got her past his PA.

"Ms Green? How can I help?"

Green explained that she'd been liaising with the FBI in regard to the York case. She didn't mention that the liaison had been rather unofficial, and that her interest was driven more by personal curiosity than her actual professional duties. She did stress that it was on her recommendation that the CTC requirement was introduced.

"You know that we have dispensed with Mr York's services, I assume?"

"Yes, I was pleased to see that you dealt with the matter so quickly." She hesitated, unsure how much to level with Russell, before deciding simply to come clean. "Mr Russell, can I speak frankly?"

"Please do."

"I've read the report into the handling of the York case, and it's clear that you've taken swift and decisive action."

"But ... ?"

"I'm concerned that I'm going to offend you, so please understand where I'm coming from on this. This is my baby, so to speak. From everything I've been told, you have taken every precaution following the discovery of York's background."

"Ms Green, I don't think you asked if you could speak frankly in order to praise my work. Please, if you have any criticism or concern, I'd like to hear it."

Green felt relieved and grateful.

"That's just it," she said. "I don't have any criticism. All I have is a hunch that somewhere, somehow, we've missed something. It may be nothing. I might be completely wrong. I feel a little embarrassed calling you to discuss it, as I have no practical suggestion to make about anything further you could or should have done. I would just feel terrible if I ignored my hunch and later discovered there was something to it. Is there anything else any of us could have missed, do you think?"

There was silence on the line for several seconds before Russell replied.

"Right now, I can't think of a thing. But I can respect a hunch. As you say, none of us want to be kicking ourselves afterwards for failing to spot something. Let me give it some thought and get back to you. Where can I reach you?"

"Thank you, Mr Russell. I appreciate your attitude, I really do." She gave him her number and email address.

"I'll be back in touch soon, I promise."

Russell put down the phone and stared out of the window toward the airstrip. Had they missed anything? They'd checked his code, and everything he'd done on the project server. That ought to have covered everything relevant, but there was no harm in widening the net to include things that probably weren't relevant, but could conceivably be.

He picked up the phone again to call his deputy, Francois Duval, into his office. As soon as he arrived, Russell gave him a brief summary of the conversation.

"Do you think there's anything we could have missed?" asked Russell.

"Well, we checked everything relevant, but that's because we thought we knew what we were looking for. The CTC stuff, his code, the command audit – I'm confident those were done thoroughly. If there's anything we've missed, it'll be something we haven't checked because it didn't seem relevant."

"So now we check the stuff that didn't seem relevant."

Duval shrugged. "That's what's left."

"Ok, so we check everything that we can check that hasn't yet been checked. Everything we know about York. Every record we have."

The two of them set about making a list. York's attendance record: sicknesses, annual leave, any time off at all. His web history, both intranet and Internet. His schedule. His phone logs. His entry/exit logs. His email logs.

"How far back do we go?" asked Duval.

"Since we're working on the basis that we don't know what we don't know, we have to start from the day he arrived."

"Ok," said Duval, "so to summarise: we're looking at every database, every log, we have. We're starting from day one. And we don't know what it is we're looking for."

"That's about the size of it, yes," confirmed Russell.

To most people, it would have sounded like an impossibly vague brief, but both knew that sometimes that's the way it went in Security. Half the time you didn't know what you were looking for until you found it. They had good people who knew the score. If there was anything there to be found, they were confident they'd find it.

"Ok, so we're looking for absolutely anything unusual. Odd leave patterns. Working late more frequently than other members of his team. Lots of phone calls to the same number. Meetings or anything else in his schedule that doesn't seem obviously relevant to his work. Unusual websites he's visited. Email trails that can't be immediately explained. The works."

Russell nodded. He had an able deputy.

"It's one hell of a tall order. What's our deadline, and what resources can we apply to it?"

Russell thought about it for a moment. There wasn't a security professional alive who thought they had enough resources to do the job properly. They always wanted more personnel, more equipment, more intelligent software, more information. Every hour devoted to this would be an hour less covering another risk.

He did respect hunches. But at the same time he had to balance resources against risks. He couldn't go overboard on any one risk at the expense of others.

"Let's put a couple of people on it for a day, an initial top-line skim to see if anything immediate jumps out. After that, include it into the intelligence cycle."

Duval nodded. If they didn't find anything the first day, they would keep plugging away, a few man-hours a week.

* * *

2nd November

Fox had arranged for the satellite kit to be delivered to the SOS offices, using the tracking details to let him know when it had been delivered.

When the package finally arrived, he was horrified to see that each of the packages had been opened and re-taped, and that attached to each was a sticker proclaiming OFFICIALLY OPENED BY HM REVENUE & CUSTOMS.

He sat down slowly, staring at the packages on the floor.

If York was right that Airbus was onto the plan, then they must know how the attack was to be triggered. The satellite comms kit he had ordered was pretty specialist: there can't be too many orders per month, he thought, far less to customers other than airlines. Had the authorities contacted suppliers asking for details of recent orders, then intercepted them?

No. No, that didn't make any sense. If they already knew what the packages contained, and could see the delivery address, there would be no reason to open them.

Unless they wanted to place a tracking device into them? But again, no, that was absurd. If they'd wanted to covertly intercept the packages, they would hardly open them so obviously and plaster them with stickers telling him it had been done.

No, while this felt as scary as hell, this had to be coincidence. This had to be exactly what it purported to be: a routine inspection by Customs.

There were 12 boxes in all, six larger, six smaller. He started by unpacking one of the larger ones, containing one of the satellite transmitters. He was surprised by how unimpressive it looked. It looked initially like a rather old-fashioned suitcase, one of those 1970s black Samsonite ones. It unfolded in rather a clunky fashion into something that didn't look massively different to a standard satellite TV dish. A chunky cable led to a large battery-pack, the size of a car battery. There was then a mains lead and an RS232 cable, the kind that he hadn't seen on a computer since the 1990s.

He unpacked one of the smaller boxes to pull out a laptop that looked pure Steampunk. A Panasonic Toughbook. As he opened it, it revealed itself as a curious mix of old and new technology. The RS232 port and floppy drive made it look like a museum piece, while the touchscreen and stylus made it look like a ridiculously oversized tablet PC.

He connected the serial lead from satellite unit to laptop, but didn't switch any of it on. He sat there, mesmerised by it. It looked ugly, industrial, purposeful. But it also looked plasticky and old-fashioned. It didn't look like it was capable of killing half a million people. But it could, and, very soon, it would.

* * *

York and 'King' were stood on the roof of 'King's' apartment, one of the satellite comms systems set up in front of them. While the equipment might have looked crude, it was so far proving highly effective. As soon as it was connected, powered-up and York touched 'Acquire satellite' on the on-screen menu, the motorised dish set about a tracking routine designed to find and lock onto the ACARS satellite offering the strongest signal. It took only a few minutes to do so, reporting back a confirmed lock.

The software York had written to transmit the codes to the airliners couldn't have been simpler. There was a security module which demanded a 16-digit passcode to enable the software to run. After that, it was a single loop that started with the serial number of the first aircraft on the list, transmitted that serial number and the command code. It then listened for a OK response from the aircraft. If it received one, it added one to a counter and updated the display. It then incremented the aircraft serial number by one and looped back until it reached the serial number of the last aircraft.

There were 2497 serial numbers, each one of them representing one of the Airbus aircraft running York's software module. The transmissions were extremely brief, each one lasting only around 10 milliseconds. Waiting a response added another 5 milliseconds. Transmitting the code to all 2497 aircraft would take just three minutes or so.

At the end of that time, it would display the total number of OK responses received.

York ran his software. A prompt appeared on the screen:

Enter transmission code

together with an empty box.

York typed in the first 15 digits of the 16-digit password. He turned to 'King':

"The moment of truth. As soon as I type the final digit, it will begin transmissions and start counting the OK responses received. If my version of the code is installed, the counter will increase; if it isn't, it'll remain on zero."

"Any bets?" asked 'King'.

"A large one on zero, I'm afraid. There's no way they fired me without reviewing my code, and there's no way they reviewed my code and failed to spot the modification. Honestly, if you hadn't been so insistent, I wouldn't even have bothered to run the test."

"Well," said 'King', "no point debating the matter: let's see, shall we?"

York smiled. "Indeed. This was your concept, would you care to do the honours? The final digit is a zero."

'King' leaned over the keyboard. "So I just press the zero key and we're off?"

York nodded. 'King' pressed the zero key.

The display changed:

Code accepted

OK responses received: 0

Nothing happened. York nodded, a resigned expression on his face.

"It's not unexp-" he started, but stopped in mid-sentence as the display changed:

OK responses received: 1

York stared at the screen in astonishment.

"It can't be," he said.

"Well, it's only one plane so far."

York was about to explain that this was an all-or-nothing thing. Either they caught the code, in which case an immediate rollback message would have been sent, or they didn't, and even a single OK response meant that his code was live. But he didn't get the chance. The count was updating so quickly now that the numbers were almost blurred.

Both men watched in fascination as two digits changed to three and the numbers kept increasing. There were stutters as the code was transmitted to aircraft that were either shutdown or out of range of the single satellite they were using, but the count just kept increasing.

York had estimated that of the almost 2500 aircraft on the list, somewhere around 10-20% of them would be either in maintenance or otherwise shutdown. That left around two thousand or so able to receive the code. Their signal was reaching only one satellite rather than the six needed to achieve global coverage, so he was expecting the count to reach around 350-400 over the course of the three minutes, updating at about two per second.

But that had been just the abstract sums. In reality, he'd firmly expected the counter to remain on zero. He just couldn't understand how Airbus had managed to figure out enough to fire him on the spot without immediately reviewing his code. But it seemed that, somehow, they had.

'King' was openly laughing. "Danny, my friend, you are a genius! Have you ever seen such a beautiful sight?"

York was still stunned that it was working. He just shook his head in amazement, then smiled.

The smile hit 'King' in the gut a little. He regretted the need to remove York from the equation before the real transmissions. He'd like to share that moment with him, not just this test. It would be only right that the man who had done so much of the work share in the moment of triumph.

But he knew York would be incapable of understanding the need for the action they were taking. So this test would have to serve as their moment of shared pleasure in their success. It was a pity that York would have to die, but it was the nature of war, and he was under no illusion: this was war. It was a bigger and more just war than any in history. This was a fight for the future of the human race, and for the planet on which they lived.

Like any war, there would be casualties. There would be some innocents – those on the ground, and perhaps some of those in the air who flew reluctantly and occasionally when there was a pressing need and no realistic alternative – but the vast majority of the casualties would be those who put their own selfish desires above the future of the planet. Business travellers out to make a buck at the expense of the environment. Holiday-makers who thought that pumping CO_2 into the upper atmosphere was an acceptable price for their two weeks exploiting the locals in some far-flung holiday resort.

But it was the individuals you regretted most. Jen. Now Danny. Ordering their deaths wasn't an easy thing to do. But you had to think of the bigger picture.

The counter display halted. Both men looked at the screen in silence:

OK responses received: 362

Neither of them spoke for four or five seconds. York finally broke the silence:

"The number is spot-on for a single satellite. That gives us a little over 2000 worldwide."

"Then there's no reason we can't do this in the next few days?"

"We could do it tonight if we had the kit and people in place," confirmed York.

"That won't take long. I need to give the team a few days' notice, and make the flight and hotel bookings." 'King' broke off as a sudden realisation came to him: if they waited exactly one week, it would be 9th November, a date Americans write as 11/9 but the British write as 9/11! It was such a perfect thought that he almost commented aloud. He quickly collected himself. "Let's make it a week, to be safe. 9th November."

"The 9th it is," said York. "We need to test the remote activation system too – the server that will call the operators with the activation code. I suggest we do that in the next two or three days. But that'll just be a piece of software on your laptop with a wifi hotspot created by your phone, so you can do that test anywhere with a signal. Just to be safe, I recommend you do the test from wherever you plan to be when you activate it."

"I will," replied King. He paused, as if an idea had just struck him. "Oh, one other thing ..."

"What's that?" asked York.

"It would be good to have the system display a message to the operators in the other cities. A little thank-you from me. If I wrote a little text file, could you get your software to display it immediately after the transmissions are complete?"

"Trivially," said York. All I need to know is the filename, then you just copy it onto the desktop, where the software sits."

"Perfect, I'll just name it message dot text."

"I'll do it tonight, and you'll have the final version tomorrow."

'King' smiled. The final piece of the puzzle was in place.

* * *

3rd November

The 'thank you message' was in reality a friendly warning. Fox felt confident in the people he'd recruited, but he was a man who liked to cover all the bases. The message that would be displayed to the six agents was designed to guard against any who might turn out to be weaker than expected.

I must apologise for my failure to be completely frank with you about the nature of our enterprise. When you have finished reading this, you will appreciate the need for discretion.

You were told that your actions today would result in some casualties. What was not revealed to you was the scale of those casualties. I can now inform you that you and five others like you have just killed around half a million people.

The transmissions you just made cut the fuel supply to around two thousand Airbus airliners. Around 1300 of them were in flight at the time. 325,000 people on board those airliners will die. So too will around 175,000 others on the ground, in the towns and cities where many of those airliners will crash. Half a million people dead.

You will start seeing it on the news very soon.

I know that you will understand the necessity for the scale of the action we have taken today. Half a million deaths is a very sizeable number, but it pales into insignificance against the billions who will die if we continue to destroy the entire ecosystem of our planet. What we did today was to fight a just war. A messy one. A gruesome one. But a necessary one.

I know that all of you can be counted on to maintain absolute silence. I also wanted you to be reassured that the silence of your co-conspirators is certain. Even should one of them be tempted to go to the authorities, they would have no escape from the fact that they are, in the eyes of the authorities, a mass-murderer. No deal they could cut would result in anything less than life imprisonment without parole in a maximum security prison. It would be a brutal, miserable life.

It is of course absolutely vital that you maintain absolute secrecy yourself. You cannot even hint at your involvement in today's events, not even to your closest friend or lover.

Your hotel room was, as you know, booked in a false name. Wipe your fingerprints from the kit. Carefully. Do the same with the door handles and anything else in the room you have touched. Leave the kit where it is, and leave the hotel quietly. The funds you have been provided should be more than ample to get you safely home by sea or land. Should you need assistance, use the email address provided. Be discreet in your wording.

* * *

Russell read Duvall's email. The one good thing that could be said about negative reports was that they didn't take long to read.

He'd promised Green an update. He checked the time, and gave her a call.

"We've done a quick review of a whole range of databases. HR leave records. Web, phone and email logs and so on. Nothing jumped out as suspicious at first glance."

"At first glance? So you will look deeper?"

"We will. We have to balance resources, so we can't make this an intensive investigation given that we're already 99.9% certain there's nothing to find, but we're including him in the mix, so more checks will be made. If there does turn out to be anything else to find, we'll get there."

"Thanks, I appreciate your efforts on this."

"No problem, I'll let you know if anything comes to light."

* * *

Junior Data Processing Operator Melanie Farrow was having a boring morning. When she'd first applied to join MI5, she'd had visions of fascinating insights into secret operations. Her hopes had been given new life when she was assigned to the Telephone Surveillance department. What could be more interesting than finding out details of phone conversations between suspected terrorists and spies, she'd wondered?

She knew that as a junior recruit, she wouldn't be privy to top-secret information early in her career, but she hadn't appreciated just how uninteresting the work would prove to be.

The digital audio files on the server might contain all kinds of interesting discussions, but all she got to see was lists of filenames and a database that told her nothing about the contents of the recordings. Her task that morning was updating the status of a whole batch of file records.

MI5 was in many respects a hi-tech organisation with all sorts of sexy technology at its disposal. In other respects, however, it was profoundly old-fashioned, and a lot of its working processes dated back to the days when only typists used keyboards.

Someone somewhere a lot further up the hierarchy than her had made decisions about the status of various targets. They had done so on paper, and her job was merely to update the database to reflect those decisions.

She sighed as she picked up the next file. File number #57189002. York, Daniel E. Status change: Low-priority to Inactive.

Marking a file as Inactive meant that telephone surveillance would be cancelled with immediate effect. Existing files would not be deleted – MI5 was exempt from the Data Protection Act, and almost nothing was ever deleted – but would be archived.

Farrow noted that several of the recordings were marked as Unread, meaning that nobody had yet listened to them. The most recent of these was a call made from a French mobile number to a UK mobile number.

Unread files were not unusual in a low-priority case. Only a proportion of calls were listened to, and changing the status of a file to Inactive typically took a few days, so there were usually a few recordings made after those in charge of the investigations had decided the target was of no further interest.

Farrow selected Inactive from the drop-down menu and hit the Update button.

* * *

4th November

Julian Fox was taking no chances: he was carrying out the rehearsal precisely as it would be done on the day: sitting in his car in the queue to board a ferry to Calais. He would make the ferry passage, because there was no way not to without arousing suspicion. Nothing was being left to chance.

He knew this was just a rehearsal, that nothing would happen beyond six mobile phones ringing and a code being played to each, but somehow this felt real. It really did feel like half a million people were about to die.

He plugged the 3G dongle into his laptop and connected to the net. Fox typed from memory the IP address of an encrypted web-server hosted on a PC sitting alone in a serviced office they'd rented close to London's Heathrow Airport. When connected, the secure webpage prompted him with the single word: Authenticate. Beneath it were four input fields, all of them unlabelled, and a Submit button.

He clicked in the first and entered his username. Clicked in the second and entered a 20-character password: n&pz616$g^%99qxy21jg. It had taken him hours to memorise it, but the rule was that nothing was written down.

He clicked in the third box and typed today's date. Then he double-checked the time on his watch. Like the PC he was connected to, it was synchronised to an atomic clock signal in Frankfurt: both would have precisely the same time. It was 10:57 and 52 seconds. He waited for it to reach 10:58 then clicked in the fourth and final box and tapped in 8501. He clicked the Submit button.

The screen refreshed. The word Ready appeared, and below it a button: Activate. Fox sat and watched the seconds. 10:59:24. He waited. 10:59:31. He waited still. 10:59:44. Almost time. 10:59:53. He moved his finger onto the trackpad of the laptop. 10:59:57. He glided the pointer to the Activate button. 11:00:00. He clicked the trackpad button.

The screen display changed to Mission activated. The software on the PC in the Heathrow office was now using its built-in SIM card to make six automated telephone calls in sequence. On the day itself, the phones would be in London, New York, Tokyo, Jo'burg, Sao Paolo and Sydney. Today, three of them were with York, in London, three of them were in his car. He waited.

The first phone rang. He answered it and listened to the recorded message: 4 9 0 2 7 3 9 1 1 5 8 2 1 4 6 0. The display updated: London transmissions complete. The second phone rang. He answered it, and again listened to the code. The screen refreshed again: New York transmissions complete. The third phone rang. The code again. Tokyo transmissions complete.

His mind was not in his car in Dover. He was imagining each of the agents in turn entering those codes. Their laptops activating the transmissions. The planes plunging from the skies. He smiled. Not long now.

* * *

9th November

Duval was efficient but didn't often visibly hurry, so when he walked quickly into Russell's office and slapped a printout onto his desk, Russell knew he had to be onto something.

"What have you found?"

"A small thing. So trivial, it's not remotely surprising it wasn't spotted during the initial top-line review. In fact, I'm pretty surprised they caught it this time."

"What is it?"

"Here," said Duval, as he showed Russell the printout of the entry/exit logs. "22:18, the night before he's dismissed, York enters the building. It's a manual entry, transcribed from the paper logs kept by the security desk. So York didn't touch in at the barrier, but instead showed his pass to the guard. The guard recorded the reason for manual access as 'PC': Puce Défectueuse. Faulty chip. So York told the guard the chip in his pass wasn't working. He also exited manually, 14 minutes later. Yet here we are the following morning ..." – Duval pointed to another line in the access logs marked with a yellow highlighter – "and York enters the building normally, using the chip in his pass. We've just tested it, and it works fine."

Russell smiled. "Nice work. I'm assuming you've figured out what he was doing during those 14 minutes?"

"I've checked his account, and he didn't login that night. He logged-off as usual at 18:02 and exited the building using his pass at 18:09. After that, there is no further activity on his account until the following morning."

"So what was York doing here?"

"Well, usually when someone enters the building for a short time late at night, they've forgotten something. Door keys after a visit to the bar, usually. But claiming to have a faulty pass obviously means he wanted to cover up his visit – most people don't realise the guards log all the details of manual entries – so clearly he was up to something. The problem is, we don't know what."

Russell felt the tingle of sweat on his brow. "A covert visit the night before the software update? That cannot be coincidence."

Duvall nodded his agreement. "I agree. But as he didn't login, what could he possibly have done?"

"Used someone else's account?"

Duvall shrugged. "No matter how careful we tell people to be, there will always be those who are careless. But you know how carefully we firewall things: there would be only a handful of accounts who could access York's project code, and we already know his code is clean. My guess is he wanted to do something, got interrupted before he could login and abandoned the attempt."

Russell considered it. "It fits. But it still makes me nervous. Get onto Frison: tell him we want to know every account logged-in, every file accessed, every command run, during those 14 minutes." He paused. "In fact, I don't want to rely on that being York's only visit that night. Maybe he spotted the guard logging his entry or exit and found a way to sneak back later. Let's make it everything done anywhere on any of the PCs, any of the servers, anytime between 5.30pm that evening and 9am the following morning."

Duvall raised an eyebrow. "That's going to be a big job."

"I know. But I want it done. If Frison shows any reluctance, let me know and I'll give him a call myself."

* * *

Fox was conscious of the irony of having had to fly the transceiver operators to their respective cities. But sometimes you had to look at the balance of good versus ill, and in the scheme of things they were adding five passengers to the four million people who fly each day. And unlike the business travellers, destroying the environment to make rich shareholders richer, or tourists, happy to destroy the future of unborn millions for their own casual pleasure, those five passengers would be irrevocably changing the world for the better. In just 48 hours, the airline industry would quite simply cease to exist.

The role of the operators was simple, but a failure by any one of them would dramatically reduce the effectiveness of the attack, so each of them had been drilled repeatedly in both the setup of the kit and entry of the code into the software. By now, each of them could have done it in their sleep.

The attack would take place at 11am UK time. 6am in New York, 7am in Sao Paolo, 8am in Sydney, 12 noon in Jo'burg, 7pm in Tokyo. Each operator had arrived in their respective city at least 48 hours beforehand, ensuring that they would be rested before they carried out their mission. They were instructed to have the kit setup and ready a full hour before zero hour.

* * *

Russell needn't have worried: Frison showed no reluctance at all. While it was indeed a large task to examine all IT activity throughout the site in the course of 15-and-a-half hours, Frison hadn't reached his position without a keen sense of logic. While they would examine the logs of all servers and all PCs, and they would cover the whole night, it made sense to prioritise the 14 minutes York was known to have been in the building, and the servers with the greatest potential for harm.

There were a great many of those. There were separate servers for almost every aspect of construction, for example: changing the specs of just one of literally hundreds of thousands of individual components, from the thrust requirements of a complete engine down to the torque settings for an individual bolt, could easily have catastrophic consequences.

But York was a software engineer, and his unscheduled visit was the night before a software update, so Frison ordered the checks to start there: on all of the systems with any involvement in the recent software update.

Alain Bouvier was the IT engineer checking the RCS server. Only a handful of people had access, and there were extremely strict rules around the security of the system, so Bouvier considered it unlikely he was going to find anything, but it all had to be checked.

He opened the user log file for that day, and scrolled down, looking at the time-stamps. There was a login at 22:23. That in itself rang alarm bells. Aviation software was a methodical business. You didn't want last-minute dashes to the wire, so nobody should have been tinkering with anything in the final hours before the update went out. He looked at the name: Damian Evans.

Bringing up a browser, he logged onto the Intranet and clicked on PeopleNet, their online staff directory. He typed in the name and hit Search. No hits. Damian Evans did not exist.

This was bad. Very bad. Only senior sysadmins should have access to the RCS. The idea that someone who didn't even work there would have access was impossible: it had to be an alias. The alarm bells were deafening now.

Next he had to see what 'Damian Evans' had done. Ten seconds later, he had the answer: copied two files, both of them software modules.

Whenever a new version of a file was copied onto the RCS, the previous version was archived and quarantined. Bouvier typed in a command that asked the system to compare old and new versions and highlight the differences between them. It took only a few more seconds until he was looking at the revised code, neatly highlighted on the screen in front of him.

Jesus H! He couldn't believe what he was seeing. He had to remind himself that this was not something they'd caught, not something that might have been included in an update had they not spotted it, this was after the event. This update had gone out. It was installed in customer aircraft!

He picked up the phone to call Frison. Voicemail; Frison was on the phone. Bouvier copied the highlighted code and pasted it into an email to Frison. He didn't add any explanatory text, there wasn't time for that. He hit the Send button and started running at full pelt towards the elevators that would take him up to Frison's 5th floor office.

* * *

Dressed in smart casual clothing, the man looked much like anyone else on the flight as he picked up his laptop case and made his way down the jetway bridge from the plane into New York's JFK Terminal 7. No-one would have guessed that Neil Finton, one of Fox's closest confidants, had just flown for only the second time in his life.

Keenly aware of the need for the team to do nothing to draw attention to themselves, Fox had insisted that each of them study maps of their destination airport terminals, and watch YouTube videos showing them exactly what the terminals looked like and how the arrivals process worked. When you had a team of people vehemently opposed to aviation, making them blend in at an airport was not something you left to chance.

Finton stepped onto the travelator and was just one more face in the crowd as he made his way towards the baggage carousel. He glanced up at the screens to see that his luggage would arrive at Carousel 2. He started watching for a large backpack and a large, old-fashioned looking case with Fragile stickers on it.

Frison looked up, startled, as his door suddenly opened and Bouvier came bursting in.

"Open your email," said Bouvier without formalities.

Frison did so, and Bouvier came round to his side of his desk. You don't just take over someone's PC without asking their permission, far less so if that someone is your boss's boss's boss. The fact that Bouvier did so, clicking on the trackpad to open his email, spoke volumes.

"Look," he said, simply.

It was 23 lines of code, 15 of them in York's module, 8 of them in a separate module.

"I haven't worked it all through yet," said Bouvier, "but this bit" – he pointed to one section of the code – "tells the FADEC to cut the fuel flow to zero. I don't understand the airspeed reference, but this code apparently tells the FADEC to switch off fuel while the aircraft is in flight!"

Russell responded with a single-syllabelled expletive, then picked up the phone and dialled the direct extension for the CEO.

"It's Russell, Security. We have a major disaster on our hands. One of our former contractors has somehow managed to get rogue code into the most recent software update. That code will crash aircraft. Hundreds, maybe thousands, of them."

Bouvier admired the succinctness of Russell's report, but couldn't hear the other end of the conversation.

"We don't yet know exactly," said Russell, clearly a reply to the obvious question. "But we've got to let the authorities know immediately, right now, this minute. We've got to get all our aircraft on the ground before they end up there the hard way."

A pause, then: "Sir, you have to understand, this code is live in our aircraft right now. Whoever is behind this can crash them at will, right now. Not only can we ground every single Airbus airliner in the world, we have to do it. Yes, we can instruct them to rollback the code, but that can take 48 hours. We need to let the aviation authorities know about this and ask them to issue immediate emergency instructions to all airlines to land their Airbus aircraft with immediate effect. As in, get them on the ground at the nearest airport or airstrip big enough to land them no matter where that may be."

Another pause.

"Sir, if we don't do this, 9/11 is going to look like a picnic. We are talking hundreds or thousands of simultaneous plane crashes. Try that for PR disaster!"

Russell listened again, said a curt thanks and replaced the receiver.

"Is he going to do it?" asked Bouvier.

"He's convening an emergency meeting of the board. He doesn't seem to understand that there's no time for this. I'm going to call Green at Homeland Security. She's the one who first caught onto this, maybe she can bypass channels and go direct to the FAA. If the FAA acts, the rest of the world will probably follow."

* * *

There are established procedures for grounding aircraft when a risk is uncovered. Technically, grounding notices can be issued only by the aviation authorities: the FAA in the USA, CAA in the UK and so forth. This is done by notifying carriers that the aircraft's Certificate of Airworthiness has been withdrawn. Once airlines have been notified of this, it becomes illegal to operate that aircraft until the CoA is reinstated.

The public thus thinks of the aviation authorities as the all-powerful and impartial watchdogs who keep the aircraft manufacturers honest.

In practice, it is rare for aviation authorities to issue grounding notices on their own initiative; it is almost always the aircraft manufacturer who first notifies the authorities of an issue and requests the grounding.

Such requests are rare, and usually affect one particular variant of one aircraft model. Although discussions will take place regarding the request, approval is generally a mere formality.

But aviation authorities are not merely safety watchdogs, they are also charged with keeping civil aviation operations running smoothly. Very searching questions were asked when aviation authorities chose to completely ground all commercial aircraft over the first volcanic ash cloud scare, with many airlines arguing that the worldwide flight ban was a ridiculous over-reaction to a tiny risk. Test-flights and scientific analysis after the event suggested that the airlines were correct, and that the ban should have been imposed on a far more limited basis.

The total cost of the volcanic ash grounding ran into the billions of dollars, and the FAA was not keen to repeat what many within the agency admitted had been an error, albeit one that could not easily have been demonstrated to be one at the time.

Green had gone straight to Thomas Wilkinson, and Wilkinson called the FAA Director's, Howard Trock. To Green's frustration, Trock too insisted on convening an emergency meeting rather than issue instructions immediately, but the FAA building was a few blocks away and the meeting was arranged to take place within the hour. Green just prayed that would be fast enough.

* * *

As an environmentalist who normally never flew, jetlag was an unfamiliar sensation to Finton, especially when combined with the need to be out of bed at 5am. Activation time here was 6am.

Finton had practiced the kit setup over and over again, including a final dry-run the previous evening, and each time he'd completed the setup from start to code prompt in less than 15 minutes, but he was taking no chances. This time, it was for real.

He disapproved of the absurd luxury of the five-star hotel room. It had been chosen because its balconies overlooked Central Park and thus gave a clear view of the New York skies, a rarity in a city densely packed with skyscrapers.

He unsnapped the catches on the satellite dish case and opened the lid. It opened a full 180 degrees and then the hinges on the far side unlocked so the lid of the case could be completely removed. Finton did this, laying the lid on the bed.

He then lifted out the large battery-pack from the foam-padded slot on the right-hand side of the base of the case. The kit was designed to run on battery power for 10-12 hours at a time. The battery was fully-charged, but their instructions were to rely on it only if it was raining and the rain was reaching the balcony, otherwise mains power would be used with the battery pack there as backup. It was a dry day, so no chances were being taken: Finton connected up the mains cable and plugged it into a 2-way extension lead he'd run from the socket closest to the balcony door. He'd been warned that the nearest socket might not be very close, so they'd been supplied with four-metre extensions.

He then carried the battery-pack onto the balcony and placed it next to the desk he'd carried out there earlier.

The rest of the kit was a single unit that remained mounted in the base of the case. Finton picked it up, carried it to the balcony and placed it on top of the desk. He unfolded the arm of the satellite dish until it locked into place at a 45-degree angle. It was currently pointed at one end of the balcony, but the auto-lock software would take care of that shortly.

Finton plugged in the power cable then returned to the room to fetch the laptop case. He removed the power supply first, and plugged that into the other socket in the extension lead. The laptop battery was also fully-charged, and he likewise wouldn't be depending on that.

The final connection was the serial lead from the satellite unit to the laptop. The satellite end was already connected; the other end was a 9-pin connector that needed to be plugged into the port marked RS232 on the laptop. Fox had warned them all that the pins were delicate, and that the plug needed to be carefully aligned before it was pushed home. There was no click, it simply had to be pushed firmly into place and then the two blue thumbwheel screws guided into place and screwed tight.

Finton tightened the two thumbscrews then pressed the power button on the laptop. The laptop slowly booted up, then auto-ran the software to align the satellite dish. There was nothing for Frinton to do as the satellite dish began it's auto-seek pattern.

* * *

"Director Trock, you have to issue grounding instructions for all Airbus aircraft immediately, you have to!"

Green was not standing on ceremony: she'd made the statement the moment she walked through the door, ignoring Trock's outstretched hand as he stood up to greet his visitors.

Trock paused, somehow managing to convert the intended handshake into a gesture to take a seat opposite his desk.

"Sarah ..." began Wilkinson, afraid that Green's aggressive manner might make their task more difficult.

"Both of you, please, we are standing in the face of the greatest aviation disaster of all time. Hell, one of the greatest disasters of any kind. And it could happen within minutes. Every second counts."

Trock turned pointedly towards Wilkinson and away from Green.

"Mr Wilkinson, just how urgent is this, in your view."

Wilkinson nodded at Green. "Ms Green is right, Mr Trock. There's no way to tell what the timings might be, but everything is in place for this attack, so we have to assume the worst, that it will be enacted immediately."

"But grounding every Airbus airliner ... it will cost the airlines millions. Billions if it goes on more than a few days. How sure are you that this risk really exists?"

Green leant forward. "100% certain. I wish there were any doubt about it, I really do, but there isn't."

Trock continued to look at Wilkinson. Wilkinson nodded.

Trock stared out of the window. If he made the wrong decision here, his career was over. If the threat was baseless, and he grounded hundreds of aircraft unnecessarily, the financial and legal repercussions would be enormous. But if the threat was real, and he did nothing ...

He had no choice. He picked up the phone.

Green's relief was fighting with the knot in her stomach. She had persuaded Trock to ground the aircraft, but would it be in time?

* * *

The screen on Finton's laptop popped up a box: Satellite lock established.

He clicked the OK button, then minimised the satellite tracking app. Now that the lock was established, it would automatically make the tiny adjustments required to keep the dish pointed at the satellite.

On the desktop was an application simply called link.exe. He double-clicked this. A new window opened and a prompt appeared.

Enter code

Finton checked the signal on the mobile phone Fox had given him. It was strong. Now all he had to do was wait.

* * *

Rita Naden, ATC Shift Supervisor at New York's JFK airport, had never received such a bizarre phone call in her 18 years working in air traffic control. Had she not recognised the voice of the regional director, she would have taken it for a hoax, but she'd been assured that this was deadly serious. She set the frequency of her radio transmitter to 121.5Mhz.

121.5 MHz, also known as International Air Distress (IAD), was the civilian aviation frequency reserved for emergency transmissions. An aircraft in distress would use this frequency to make a Mayday call, and it was standard airline practice to leave their second radio set, Comm 2, set to this frequency. In this way, if they needed to make an emergency call, they could do so immediately, and they would also hear any distress call made by another aircraft in case they were able to offer any assistance.

Naden swallowed as she clicked her transmit button:

"This is an FAA emergency message. This is not a drill. I say again, this is not a drill. All Airbus airliners are to land at the nearest available facility with immediate effect. Civilian airport, military airfield, emergency airstrip – whichever you can reach fastest. We have reason to believe your fuel supply could cut out at any moment." Naden could visualise pilots listening to the message and staring at each other in disbelief. She added a bit that was not in the script. "People, we're not kidding here: if you are flying any Airbus airliner, get it onto the ground, now!"

She'd had no time to brief her controllers who were all staring at her.

"Ok, folks, you heard the message. There's no time to explain, and you won't have time to work aircraft individually. Just line them up in sequence and give them all discretion to make visual approaches and landings. We need those aircraft on the ground before they start falling out of the sky."

Similar messages were being broadcast from every ATC centre in the world. The big unknown was how long they had to get the planes on the ground.

* * *

Julian Fox remembered his dry-run, and smiled. This time it was the real thing: in a little over two minutes, around half a million people really would die, and the commercial aviation era would be over.

He was sitting in his car in the queue to board a ferry to Calais. From there, he had the same escape options as before should they prove necessary, but he didn't think they would be. York would also cease to be a concern at 11am.

As in the rehearsal, he entered the appropriate codes into the four fields on the webpage – then waited.

* * *

Air Traffic controllers had never worked so hard. It was impossible to actively control so many aircraft at once, so where visibility permitted they simply aligned aircraft into sequence based on distance from the runway, then instructed each to follow the one in front. Normal separation rules were ignored, this was 'Captain's discretion', and each captain was following the aircraft ahead as tightly as they dared. At busy airports like JFK and Heathrow, planes were landing in lines just 30 seconds apart. At airports with parallel runways, aircraft were landing two or more abreast.

Landing aircraft were turning off the runways onto taxiways, then doing high-speed taxis to make room for more aircraft behind them. Ones that made it to the apron were parking wherever they could – ATC had no time to assign gates.

There were aircraft everywhere.

* * *

Fox sat and watched the seconds on the laptop clock. 10:59:24. He waited. 10:59:31. He waited still. 10:59:44. Almost time. 10:59:53. He moved his finger onto the trackpad of the laptop. 10:59:57. He glided the pointer to the Activate button. 11:00:00. He clicked the trackpad button.

The screen display changed to Mission activated. The automated phone calls were now being made. Each of the agents in turn would be entering the codes. The laptops would be activating the transmissions. He watched the screen, which was auto-refreshing every few seconds.

* * *

When Fox had clicked that button, the software on the PC in the Heathrow hotel room used its built-in SIM card to make six automated telephone calls in sequence: London, New York, Tokyo, Jo'burg, Sao Paolo, Sydney.

In New York, at 06:00:24, Finton's phone rang. He listened to the sequence of numbers, tapping each of the 16 digits in turn into the laptop. He could feel the tingle of sweat in the small of his back. This was such a simple task: listen to a digit, type the digit.

Listen to the next one, type it. But a single error would mean the failure of his part of the mission.

He typed the final zero, and the display changed to a Code accepted – please read the important message below. The message puzzled him, as he'd been told only to expect a 'Code accepted' message.

The screen filled with text, and Finton began reading:

I must apologise for my failure to be completely frank with you about the nature of our enterprise. When you have finished reading this, you will appreciate the need for discretion ...

* * *

At Dover, Fox's display updated: New York transmissions complete. A few more seconds. Tokyo transmissions complete. Then in turn: Jo'burg transmissions complete. Sao Paolo transmissions complete. Sydney transmissions complete. Mission complete.

That was it. Killing half a million people was, with the right planning and preparation, that simple. The commercial aviation industry was now a thing future generations would know only through their history books.

* * *

Following the tragic death of his daughter, Skyways had told Richard Williams to take all the time he needed before returning to work. Williams had expected to take several weeks at least, but found that having so much free time was only resulting in him reliving the news over and over again. Both he and his wife were finding it claustrophobic being home the whole time, so he'd returned to work only a week later, given desk duties at first and then returned to the flight roster once cleared.

At the time the emergency message was broadcast by ATC centres around the world, Williams was in the left-hand seat of an A340-600 on a red-eye flight into New York's JFK airport. His first officer, Simon Cooper, was flying the aircraft, so Williams issued an immediate instruction:

"Apply maximum climb rate, and get as much altitude as you can beneath us before the power cuts out."

"Cimbing."

With Cooper looking after the aircraft, Williams turned his own attention to the flight computer. They were 17 miles out at an altitude of 5,200 feet. What Williams needed to calculate was whether, if their fuel was cut now, they could glide the remaining 17 miles before they fell into the Atlantic Ocean.

All aircraft can glide, some much better than others. A light aircraft like a 4-seated Cessna glides so well that a normal approach and landing is made with minimal power, and engine failure during an approach is generally not a huge drama. At the other extreme, a fighter jet, with its stubby wings, has very poor glide characteristics, and a glide landing is virtually impossible. An airliner like the A340 sits somewhere between the two extremes.

The glide performance is one of the parameters built into the flight computers, which also have live access to the aircraft's instrument data, so Williams was able to quickly do the sums. The answer appeared on the old-fashioned looking green LED display a few seconds before the FADEC cut the fuel flow to all four engines, and the engines flamed-out.

There was a feeling like being pushed forwards into a cushion of air as the engines ceased thrust. Primary electrical power was lost, with only battery backup available. Most electronic displays on the flight deck went blank – with only basic data displayed on the screens on the captain's side of the aircraft, plus the mechanical backup instruments.

When engine power is lost, this triggers the release of a latch towards the rear of the aircraft. The latch allows a Ram Air Turbine, effectively a miniature wind turbine, to fall under gravity and automatically lock into position. The blades of the turbine spin-up in the aircraft's slipstream and allow a small generator to produce just enough electrical power to activate backup instruments and a few key systems. It was these instruments Cooper now relied on to tell the altitude, airspeed and heading of the aircraft.

With the aircraft in a nose-up position, and zero thrust from the engines, a conventional airliner would have just seconds before it stalled: its speed reduced to the point where it could no longer fly. With fly-by-wire aircraft, the computer system prevented a stall, automatically pushing down the nose of the aircraft as required to maintain airspeed, but Cooper needed to do more than just prevent a stall, he had to get to the aircraft into its optimum glide configuration: nose-down sufficiently to maintain airspeed while minimising altitude loss. He quickly pushed the joystick forward and studied the airspeed readout in front of him.

The purser knocked on the flight-deck door then entered. All cabin power had been lost, and he looked suitably worried.

Williams wasted no words: "Prepare the cabin for an emergency landing. We have no power, so there will be no announcements. Judge our altitude through the window and get the pax into the brace position in plenty of time. That's all."

Passengers – pax in airline jargon – tend to think of cabin crew as little more than serving staff, but their primary function is safety, and they are well-trained in emergency procedures. The purser nodded, and withdrew.

In an emergency situation, it's common for the Captain of the aircraft to take the controls, but Williams was happy with Cooper's handling of the aircraft, so returned his attention to the numbers he'd seen on the flight computer just before the lights went out. Even with the few extra hundred feet Cooper had gained them with his climb, their maximum glide distance was 13.2 miles. Their remaining flight distance to the runway was 15.7 miles. They weren't going to make it.

* * *

9000 miles away, on an approach into London's Heathrow airport, an Asia Airways A380 lost all power at almost exactly the same time, but its captain had needed no calculations to reach exactly the same conclusion.

The A380 was the largest airliner in the world. Designed as a 747 Jumbo jet beater, it was a double-decker along its entire length and weighed 400 tonnes. This one had 525 people on board, and was at 2000 feet over east London. Captain Baker knew that they weren't going to get anywhere close to Heathrow.

Two thousand feet of altitude translated into just one mile of glide distance, while Heathrow was still 12 miles away. No flight computer was needed to tell the flight crew that a landing there was utterly impossible.

The runway of London City Airport was just off its right wing, but it was designed for far smaller aircraft and its runway was just 1080 metres long; the A380 needed almost three times the distance. Even if the lumbering bulk of the A380 could make the tight turn required, it would still be travelling at well over 100mph when it shot off the end of the runway into the surrounding water.

The pilots looked in vain for any open ground within range, but the aircraft was pointed directly towards the centre of the city. They could attempt a turn, but with just 60 seconds of gliding time, the turn would use up almost all of their remaining height, leaving them no hope of reaching the nearest greenbelt area.

Captain Williams grabbed the laminated card showing the standard approaches into JFK. While everything was programmed into the flight computers, aviation was a belt-and-braces business, and the checklists called for paper copies of key documents to be immediately to hand.

There were eight standard approaches into JFK, depending on prevailing winds and initial aircraft heading. The standard approach programmed into the auto-pilot and flight computers was a sweeping 180 degree turn to bring them in from the south. It was this path the flight computer had used to calculate the distance to run.

If they took a more direct approach, effectively cutting the corner and then doing a tight turn just prior to landing, Williams believed they could make it. With no flight computer available any longer, he couldn't confirm it, but visually he estimated that it would reduce their distance by more than the 2.5 miles they were short.

The problem was that the other aircraft all around the airport, each desperately trying to land, would not be expecting him to take the route he planned to take. It would put him into direct conflict with aircraft following the normal approach path. The meagre amount of emergency electrical power the RAT provided was not sufficient for radio transmissions, meaning that TCAS would no longer be operating, nor could they advise other aircraft of their intentions.

With no power available to any Airbus aircraft approaching the airport, the scope for avoidance manoeuvres was extremely limited. The chances of a collision on final approach was high.

* * *

Baker quickly concluded that their only hope was to glide down to a water landing on the Thames. It had been done once before by a much smaller jet on a much larger river: the Hudson in New York. The A380 was a huge aircraft, the Thames was far narrower and twistier, and it had far more bridges.

Paradoxically, despite its size and weight, the vast wing area of the A380 meant that its glide performance was better than most airliners. The river east of Tower Bridge was a series of snaking curves, with no chance of a water landing, but if they could clear the bridge there was a relatively wide and straight stretch before London Bridge.

The first officer configured the aircraft for minimum drag as the captain struggled desperately to stretch the glide. The north and south towers of the bridge were just 200 feet apart, while the A380's wingspan was 260 feet: they couldn't make it through the gap above the walkways, they would have to clear the towers if they were to make it.

All airline pilots regularly practice losing a single engine in the simulator (and two engines on four-engined aircraft), but the loss of all power is considered too unlikely a scenario to practice. Captain Baker had to judge things now by the seat of his pants.

He felt they had a good chance of clearing the bridge. As soon as they did, the first officer would use the speedbrakes to kill the lift and dump them into the river as soon as possible. A hard landing was a better option than a glide carrying them into the next bridge.

No, wait– the speedbrakes aren't on the emergency power system. Damn. He'd just have to drop the nose and flare at the last minute.

* * *

Williams didn't like the odds, but with no other airport within range, the only alternative was a water landing, and he liked that option even less.

Although he, like Baker, knew that water landings were possible, he also knew that success required near-perfect conditions and a great deal of luck. The famous Hudson example aside, most airline pilots felt that the phrase 'water landing' was a euphemism invented solely to reassure passengers during the pre-flight safety announcement.

While he'd been happy to let Cooper fly the aircraft so far, this was his job now. Succeed or fail, the responsibility would be his alone. Williams placed his hand on the joystick and his feet on the rudder pedals.

"My aircraft," he said briefly.

"Your aircraft," confirmed Cooper, acknowledging the hand-over of control.

* * *

Baker was struggling to hold the enormous bulk of the A380 on the delicate balancing point between a glideslope too steep to clear Tower Bridge, and a nose-higher attitude that would increase drag and reduce the gliding range. His task was made tougher by a lack of data. With full instrumentation, his first officer could provide him with information to help him judge the approach; with only basic instruments operating, all his co-pilot could do was call out height and speed.

This was seat-of-the-pants flying in an aircraft designed for anything but.

* * *

The approach Williams was taking was a diagonal cut across the usual 180-degree path. His plan was a tight 150-degree turn at around 1000 feet to bring them into line for runway 4 Right. He hoped that aircraft on the standard approach would realise his intentions sufficiently early to be able to make the relatively small jink necessary to land instead on the parallel runway 4 Left.

The closer they got to JFK, the closer their approach brought them into a near head-on collision path with aircraft on the usual approach. The one thing they had in their favour was the clear dawn skies providing excellent visibility. Both men were straining their eyes to get a clear view of the distant air traffic.

They were now five miles out. They could make out a long line of landing lights of aircraft approaching from the opposite direction, but they weren't yet close enough to tell the size of the gaps between them. They would need a sufficiently large gap to slot into early enough that a pilot approaching from their left could divert onto the parallel runway.

Four miles. The line of traffic looked incredible, like an unbroken chain of landing lights. The plan to somehow slot into this from the side was starting to look desperate.

Three miles. The line of lights had now resolved into two parallel lines of incoming aircraft. They could see that both runways 4L and 4R were being used, and that the aircraft landing on them were almost nose-to-tail. While Williams flew the aircraft, Cooper timed the gaps between landing aircraft.

"11 seconds. 13 seconds. There are just no gaps at all!" exclaimed Cooper. "It's the same on 4 Left – even if other aircraft realised our intentions, there is nowhere for them to go."

They were now down to 4000 feet. They needed to lose more altitude before beginning the turn. Two or three miles ahead of them, an American Airlines A320 clearly had the same idea and broke off for a right turn. Both men watched as the A320 executed a tight right-hand turn toward runway 4R. Neither of them could see a gap for the aircraft to slot into.

Both men held their breath as they watched the A320 bank like a stunt aircraft as it desperately attempted to slot into a gap that simply didn't exist.

They watched in horror as it and an A330
converged. For a moment, Williams thought the
A320 had made it ... before he was proven wrong by
a huge fireball as the aircraft collided a few hundred
feet above the ground.

"My god!"

"Jesus Christ!"

The two exclamations were simultaneous.

It was clear that their plan was doomed to failure.
They were out of options.

* * *

Baker could see it was going to be incredibly
close, but he believed they were going to just clear
the tops of the two towers on either side of Tower
Bridge. He was wrong.

The nose of the massive aircraft struck the first of
the two walkways connecting the towers. The flight
deck of the airliner was instantly crushed. Neither
of the pilots had time even to scream before their
bodies were pulverised by crushing impact with the
steel girders of the walkway. The impact broke first
one then the second walkway in two, shattered
glass, steel shards and the dismembered bodies of
the tourists in them spreading out in an arc from the
point of impact.

Less than half a second later, the leading edges of
the wings struck each of the two towers.

Each tower comprised four steel pillars, with
stonework connecting them. The steel pillars were
incredibly strong, designed to hold the weight of
both the walkways and the twin arms of the lifting
road beneath. But most of the fuel of an airliner is
stored in the wings, and the heat of the massive
explosions vapourised enough of the steel pillars
that both towers were devastated.

The south tower collapsed down onto the south
approach road, crushing the cars, buses and people
below. The north tower fell into the river. The

massive forces of the crash caused the twin halves of the lifting roadway to buckle, cars, buses and people thrown into the air to land in the river below.

The devastation was on an unimaginable scale. One of the most famous bridges in the world turned within seconds into a ruin; the fuselage of the aircraft and most of the wings all but gone; just the right wing-tip and tail sticking out of the water. Debris covered the surface of the river, ranging in size from handbags to cars. Many of the shapes in the water were bodies or body parts.

* * *

With his original plan left in tatters by the crash they'd just witnessed, Williams quickly decided on an even more desperate one.

"This may be crazy," he told Cooper, "but I'm taking us into Floyd Bennett Field!"

Cooper looked at him like he did indeed hold that opinion of the plan, but there was no time for debate.

"Ok."

JFK was not the first New York airport. The first one, opened in the 1930s and largely abandoned in 1971, was Floyd Bennett Field. Situated just across the water from JFK on Barren Island, it now served only as a museum and a heliport for the New York Police Department – but unlike most abandoned airports, its three runways remained intact. Williams knew this because he'd visited it a year or so ago: the place had some incredible aviation history, whose notable aviators included both Howard Hughes and Amelia Earhart.

He couldn't recall the runway lengths, but he did know they'd been used for some relatively large aircraft when engine thrust was very much lower than today and take-off rolls were longer. He also remembered walking the length of one of them, and it had seemed like a pretty long walk. None were likely to be technically long enough for the A340, especially with reverse thrust unavailable and relying entirely on brakes, but there were significant margins built into quoted figures, and an overshoot of a runway at relatively low speed had to give them greater survivability than attempting to set the aircraft down on water. The big question was whether their glideslope would extend far enough to reach the island.

Floyd Bennett Field was around three miles further than JFK, but the JFK approach required a tight turn into wind. By removing both the turn and the headwind from the equation, Williams reckoned they had a reasonable shot.

"We need maximum glide distance, so no flaps and leave the gear until the last possible moment."

On a normal approach, flaps were extended from the wings to enable a steeper and slower approach. But flaps, like the landing gear, created drag. By avoiding the use of flaps and dropping the landing gear as late as possible, they could minimise drag and thus extend their gliding distance. The downside would be a higher speed approach presenting even greater challenge stopping.

"Acknowledged," replied Cooper. "I'll see if we have a sheet for it."

Airliners carried full details of alternate airports in case a diversion was required. These included military airfields and abandoned airports whose runways were known to be in good order, but Floyd Bennett Field was unlikely to fall into that category: the condition of its runways was more happenstance than the result of any active care.

Cooper's check took only a few seconds.

"Nothing."

"No problem," said Williams, "it wasn't going to tell us much anyway. There's only one runway we can make, and that looks to be around 250 to 300 degrees. Call it runway 30." Runways were numbered according to their compass bearing, with the final digit omitted. "We're going to be landing with the wind, without flaps, and with no reverse thrust. Stopping is going to be interesting to say the least. But I'll take an overshoot any day over getting wet."

"With you there."

Williams eased the aircraft a few degrees to the left. All that would be required for the landing was a slight right turn just before touchdown.

"At least we won't have to worry about terrain warnings," observed Williams.

Normally, computer systems would be monitoring their altitude. As it wouldn't know that Floyd Bennett Field even existed – there would be nothing in its airport database – it would think they were in normal flight and warn them they were too low as they got closer. But with only emergency power, none of those systems were working now.

"True," replied Cooper. He thought for a moment. "You want the pre-landing checklist?"

He would never have asked the question in normal circumstances. No matter how many landings a crew had carried out on a particular aircraft, no matter how familiar they were with the procedures, checklists were used religiously. The idea of carrying out a landing without one would usually be unimaginable. But these circumstances were far from usual. Williams would have his hands full hand-flying the aircraft without power, and most of the checklist items would either be impossible without power or irrelevant.

"No point," replied Williams, echoing Cooper's thoughts. "Just give me continuous altitude and airspeed callouts all the way in."

Williams had been monitoring altitude against airspeed for some time and trying to estimate their glideslope against that earlier predicted by the flight computer. With no distance information available, he'd been using the airspeed and last known wind speed to come up with a rough-and-ready number. He estimated they were travelling 2.4 miles for every 1000 feet lost. It was going to be tight. Very tight.

"Got it," replied Cooper. "Altitude 1300, speed 160." 1300 feet, 160 knots airspeed. Williams eyed the runway threshold against a marker on the cockpit windscreen. Visually, it looked like they were going to fall short by 1-200 feet. They might or might not make it, but what was concerning him almost as much was the runway length: the closer they got, the shorter it looked.

Cooper kept up continuous call-outs, freeing Williams from the need to check his instruments and allowing him to have his full attention on the view through the windscreen.

"1200, 158."

"1100, 158."

"1000, 160."

Williams kept his eye on the windscreen marker. Lining up with a runway visually was in principle a simple activity: you kept a marker on the windscreen aligned with the runway threshold. If the marker fell short of the runway, you fed in more power; if it rose beyond the runway threshold, you reduced power. With no power available, however, all Williams could do was keep the nose angled for maximum glide distance. The marker became not something he could position at will, but merely a passive predictor of where they would touch down. So far, it still looked about 150 feet short of the runway threshold, pretty much at the waterline.

"900, 155." There was a note of warning in Cooper's tone at the airspeed reduction. Williams eased the nose down a touch in response.

"800, 159."

"700, 160. Let me know when you want gear."

Cooper was being the perfect first officer, ensuring that Williams had not forgotten without questioning his judgement.

"Will do."

Williams was still anticipating falling short of the runway, so wanted to leave things as late as possible. With power out, the landing gear would be lowered by gravity alone, hydraulics cushioning the drop of the gear, so the loss of power was not a concern from that perspective, but they had to allow time for it to drop and lock into place; judging the last possible moment would be a tough call.

"600, 163."

Williams was encouraged by the slight increase in airspeed, allowing him to ease the nose up a little. The marker moved beyond the waterline to the grass.

"Give me gear down at 400 feet," he instructed.

"Gear at 400," acknowledged Cooper, keeping his tone carefully neutral. He was not convinced that would give sufficient time for the gear to lower and lock, but this was not a time for debate.

"500, 160."

Williams pulled back the merest fraction on the joystick. The marker was still pointed at the grass, and they would lose some lift when the landing gear dropped into the slipstream, making the aircraft less aerodynamic.

"400, 160, gear down." Cooper pulled the large landing gear lever into the down position. They would usually expect to see three green lights once the gear locked into place, confirming that it was down and locked, but on emergency power they would have no confirmation beyond the sound of the gear latching.

There was a palpable feeling of deceleration as the gear dropped and Williams was forced to lower the nose to maintain airspeed. The windscreen marker dropped back to short of the waterline: the aircraft was going to land in the water. With the gear down, this was the worst of all outcomes, the outstretched gear would hit the water first, catapulting in the fuselage. Survival was unlikely.

"300, 155."

"I'm going to try to use ground-effect to give us a little more distance."

So far, Williams had been aiming to keep the aircraft at the angle of most efficient glide. Now, he pushed the nose down to increase airspeed at the expense of altitude. His gamble would be that the higher speed would allow an aerodynamic phenomenon known as 'ground effect' to extend the glide distance once they got closer to the ground.

Ground effect was when a cushion of air got 'squashed' beneath an aircraft, pushing back against the underside of the wings. This gave it increased lift, and would, Williams hoped, carry them to the runway threshold.

"200, 170."

The A340 was picking up speed as planned, but was now clearly pointed toward the dark water below.

"100, 180."

The secret to utilising ground effect was all in the timing: lifting the nose to flare the aircraft at just the right time. Too soon, and there would be no supporting air-cushion, and the increased drag of the nose-up attitude would mean the aircraft would hit the water even sooner. Too late, and there would be no time for the air-cushion to take effect.

"50, 190."

Williams waited. With power, the cockpit voice system would announce the final 50 feet in 10 feet intervals using the highly-accurate radio altimeter. Without power, the pressure-based altimeter wasn't sufficiently accurate to make such announcements worthwhile, so Cooper decided against trying to emulate it.

Just as impact with the water looked inevitable, Williams pulled back hard on the joystick to lift the aircraft into a high angle of attack, the nose pointed well into the air. The angle was so high Williams had to look partly to his left to see the water.

Time seemed to stand still. Both men waited for the terrible sound of the landing gear hitting the water, but nothing happened. The altimeter needle appeared frozen. Even the sound of the airstream rushing by seemed muted.

The shoreline flashed past, then grass.

BANG!

The sound of the main gear hitting the ground was enormous. Usually, you'd let speed bleed off and wait for the nose gear to fall before braking, but there was no time for such niceties now: they would run out of runway very rapidly indeed. Williams and Cooper acted in unison as they pressed their heels hard against the brake pedals.

BANG!

There was another, even louder noise as the nose-gear hit hard. Both men were pressing against the brakes for all their worth.

Two smaller bangs told them the front tyres had burst. Williams used right rudder to correct the slight weave to the left. Suddenly the rough concrete runway was rushing up towards the windscreen as the nose gear collapsed. There was a huge crunch accompanied by screams from the passenger cabin behind as the nose of the aircraft hit the concrete, sparks flying as the plane scraped along the runway at over 160mph.

With the nose gear collapsed, the pilots could do nothing to control either the direction or deceleration of the aircraft: they were every bit as much passengers as the people behind them.

The engines too were scraping the concrete, creating further masses of sparks. A fuel leak now would engulf the aircraft in flames in mere moments. The irony was the cut-off fuel supply that had led to the crash-landing was now saving them from fire. So long as the main gear held, the wing fuel-tanks would be protected.

The aircraft was now drifting towards the left-hand side of the runway. If the left main gear ran onto the grass, it would instantly dig in and either spin the aircraft around or rip off the gear causing the wing to hit the ground.

Williams and Cooper watched helplessly as the rough concrete surface sped past only feet away from the windscreen. Some of the concrete had partly broken-up, causing the fuselage to start tearing apart as it sank into missing patches then hit the far edge.

The drift to the left continued. Finally, the left-hand gear ran off the edge of the concrete and onto the muddy grass alongside the runway. The aircraft pivoted further to the left, but the speed was now low enough that the gear held. The nose ran off onto the grass with a massive whack, followed shortly afterwards by the right gear.

The aircraft slowed rapidly now it was entirely on the grass. The airfield had three runways arranged in a triangle, and the plane was now approaching the side of runway 15. It hit the concrete edge hard, the bottom of the fuselage now splitting like a tin can, the contents of the avionics bay beneath the flight-deck spilling out, smashed circuit boards and wiring scattered over the grass.

The left-hand engines hit next, twisting the pylons on which they were suspended, but the speed now was down to 40mph and the pylons held. The left gear hit and collapsed. This was the nightmare scenario of this crash: if the wing tore open, releasing the fuel, a fire was inevitable.

But the twin impacts had reduced the speed to almost nothing. The left wing remained intact as the aircraft came to a halt straddling the opposing runway.

The professionalism of the cabin crew was evident in the matter of just a few seconds before doors opened and slides deployed. Around 10 seconds passed before the first passengers came down the slides. The front slides were almost horizontal as the doors were now just a few feet above the ground. Two crew came out first to assist passengers off the slides as quickly as possible to clear the way for those behind them.

Within four minutes, everyone was off the aircraft. There were some injuries, but nothing major. The aircraft would never fly again, but both flight crew, all 15 cabin crew and all 426 passengers survived.

* * *

The scene at every major airport worldwide was the same: long lines of airliners gliding in, those already on the ground parked at crazy angles in every available spot.

Not every aircraft was fortunate. The crash into Tower Bridge was not the only one that day. It would be many hours yet before the full facts were clear, but they would be these:

Twenty-two aircraft had been just too far out of range of any landing strip, plunging into the ocean. Two went down over the Antarctic, one crashing, the other achieving a crash-landing on the ice that only delayed death for the survivors as they froze to death long before anyone could reach them. Four aircraft, including the two witnessed by Williams and Cooper, were lost in mid-air collisions. Seven fatally crash-landed at airports, three of them because the runway was blocked by aircraft that had come to a halt before managing to clear the runway.

Of the 1,336 Airbus airliners in the air when their fuel supply was cut, there were 31 fatal crashes or crash-landings. There were dozens of other non-fatal crash-landings. It was a very, very bad day – but not even close to as bad as it would have been without Green's persistence.

* * *

Fox closed the browser window, closed the lid of the laptop and switched on his radio, preset to Radio 4. He wondered how long it would take for the news to break, and how long before the world realised the true scale of what was taking place?

The news, when it broke just three minutes later, was not what he expected.

Aviation authorities around the world have declared an unprecedented emergency situation, with hundreds or thousands of airliners around the world being brought in for immediate emergency landings. The exact nature of the emergency is unclear.

Landing instructions were apparently issued some 25 minutes ago, and the scene here at London's Heathrow Airport is one the like of which even Heathrow veterans say has never been seen before. There are literally dozens of aircraft lined up what looks almost nose-to-tail on the approach to both runways, and the scene on the ground is even more chaotic, with airliners abandoned almost everywhere around the runways.

Nobody seems able to explain either the nature of the emergency or-

Sorry, we're just receiving reports of a major plane crash in central London! Unconfirmed reports say that the plane has collided with Tower Bridge, and there are reports-

Yes, that's confirmed, we're looking now at live coverage from the scene, and it is clear that a terrible accident has occurred. This is a truly staggering sight. The bridge lays in ruins, the wreckage of the aircraft ...

Fox was confused. Instructions issued 25 minutes ago? That was before the transmissions, yet if the authorities had figured this out in advance as York had suspected, they would have known about it a week ago. Why would they let things reach this stage?

It didn't make sense, but somehow they'd figured things out right at the last minute. The question was: how many aircraft had they managed to crash? Fox continued to listen to the radio and opened the

343

laptop. He launched the browser and quickly opened BBC, Reuters and CNN news sites in separate tabs.

Within minutes, it was clear that they had succeeded in crashing a significant number of planes, but also clear that many more had succeeded in landing. This was not the cataclysmic event he'd hoped for, but with ever more reports of crashes arriving at every moment, perhaps it was enough?

* * *

York watched the newsflash in absolute horror. He had no idea what could possibly have gone wrong. The airspeed check should have made this utterly impossible. This couldn't have happened and yet, somehow, it had. And he was responsible.

He reached for his phone, and dialled a familiar number.

"It's York. Have you seen the news? I don't understand it, I don't know how this could have happened."

'King' was at that moment in the queue for the Sea France crossing to Calais, and he knew precisely how it had happened. He looked at his watch: 11:13. York was due to tragically take his own life in exactly two minutes. The fifteen minute delay had been to allow time to cancel the instructions in the event that nothing happened and York's expertise was needed to correct matters. With the instructions firmly left in place, there was no harm in letting him know the truth now. Fox felt he owed York that much.

"My apologies, Mr York. I'm afraid it was necessary to make a minor adjustment to your code."

It hit York like a truck. The one-byte discrepancy! King had had access to the code for two days, and it was the file on King's USB key he'd installed. King-well, it was obvious now that was not his real identity – had modified the code to remove the airspeed check. 'King' had never wanted to save lives, he had wanted to kill people!

"Why?" he asked, finally. It seemed like such a stupidly inadequate question, but he had to ask it.

"There isn't time to explain, I'm afraid."

"Wh-" No sooner had York started to ask the question than the answer was blindingly obvious. He needed to get out of there, right now!

He hung up the phone and not even stopping to grab his keys, ran towards his front door.

* * *

Fox smiled in satisfaction as the line went dead. York's visitor had clearly arrived with perfect timing.

* * *

Fox was wrong: the visitor in question was running late. Only five minutes late, but the gentleman concerned was not happy with himself. He was all too well aware that in his line of work, even five-minute delays were not appreciated. Not good for business.

But so long as he got the job done, he thought, no-one need ever know.

* * *

York ran out into the street and looked left and right for a cab. There were several cabs in sight, but none with their orange light on. There was a stationary one a few cars back from the traffic lights, which were just turning green. He ran for it, pulled open the door and jumped in, just as it was about to pull away.

The passenger in the cab, a businessman in his 50s, was too startled to say anything at all, but London cabbies are rarely lost for words.

"Hey, pal, are you blind or something? This cab's taken."

"Please!" said York. "This is life and death! Get me to the nearest police station."

"It bloody well will be life and death if you don't get out of my cab right now."

"I'm serious," pleaded York, "you have to get me to a police station."

There was a blare of horns from the cars behind them as the cab failed to move off.

"Right," said the cabbie, "you want the police, you're going to get them. Apologies for this, Sir," he said to his passenger, "it won't take long."

The cabbie pressed a button on the data terminal on his dashboard. "That's an SOS button. It sends my exact location and a call for help to the control centre, and they immediately pass it to the police."

"Thank you."

"You won't be thanking me when you get arrested, mate."

The passenger decided he'd had enough, and thrust a £10 note through the window.

"Just let me out here, I'll get another cab."

The cabbie took the note. "I'm sorry about that, Sir."

"Don't worry about it," replied the passenger as he climbed out of the cab with a filthy look at York.

"Look," said York, "you're free now. Just take me to the nearest police station and I'll pay double the fare, triple. Whatever you like. Just get me to the police, please."

The cabbie eyed his new passenger in the mirror for a moment, then relented. He tapped a code into the data terminal to cancel the alarm.

"£30," he said. "That was a decent fare you cost me."

"No problem," said York, "but please hurry."

* * *

Fox relaxed into the comfortable seat in the first-class lounge of the Sea France ferry to Calais. It was done. Now all he needed to do was lay low for a few days until it was clear that nobody was looking for him.

A small glass of champagne was called for, he decided, as he watched the news footage on the TV screen above him.

* * *

Detective Inspector Catin had made York retell his story three times now, and he still didn't believe a word of it. Nobody walks casually into a south London police station to confess to having carried out what was looking like the world's biggest terrorist outrage, least of all the unlikely character in front of him. This was clearly an attention-seeking nut job, the type who 'confessed' to anything in the news to get their hour in the spotlight.

But DI Catin had got enough details out of York to carry out the basic checks. Details of the plane crash and his supposed wife's name. The name and phone number of his ostensible line manager at Airbus. And the presumed pseudonym and mobile phone number of the man he claimed had duped him into causing the crashes.

"Baxtor, check out the names of the passengers killed in the crash of Istan Air Flight 1951 at Amsterdam airport. See if there's a Stephanie York among them. If there is, find out the name of her next of kin."

DC Baxtor nodded and turned to his PC.

Catin turned to the other Detective Constable in the office, and handed him a piece of paper.

"Razaq, call this person at Airbus. Find out whether a Danny York worked for him on software development. If so, get a physical description of him and find out exactly what he did there."

Catin returned to his office to do a PNC check on York. The Police National Computer stored details of every convicted criminal, as well as 'persons of interest' to the police. It included details of persistent hoaxers. Catin tapped in York's name, address and date of birth.

The search took only a couple of seconds, and Catin could hardly believe what he was seeing: York was listed as wanted for questioning in connection with a suspected conspiracy to commit acts of terrorism! The contact given was at MI5. One short phone call later, and Catin's earlier skepticism was gone. York was the real deal!

MI5 had curtly informed him that his job now was merely to ensure that York was held securely, and that they would send a couple of their people over to carry out the interrogation.

Catin had been a detective for 18 years. This was the biggest case ever to land in his lap, and he wasn't going to let anyone tell him that his job here was merely that of a jailer. He reckoned he had 20 minutes to glean what he could before being pushed out of the picture altogether by MI5. He was going to use those 20 minutes well.

He poked his head into the open-plan office where the two junior detectives were on the phone.

"Razaq, Baxtor, forget all that, we have a live one. I need you with me, we don't have long.

He hurried back to the interview room where York was being held, the two other detectives stumbling to keep up with him.

"Tell me everything you know about this 'King' character," Catin said, without preamble. "In particular, we need to know where he is right now."

"I don't know," replied York. "I can give you the address of the SOS offices, which is the only address I have for him, and I can give you two mobile numbers: his normal one, and the special one he bought for me to contact him."

Catin pushed his notepad and pen across the table. York took out his own two mobiles, looked up each number in turn and carefully wrote them down.

Catin tore off the page and passed it to Razaq. "Get onto the networks, find out which those numbers are on and tell them we need an immediate location fix. Make sure they understand that by 'immediate', we mean right now this minute. We also need to know who pays the bills for each."

"I'm on it." Razaq left the room.

"And the address for SOS." Catin pushed the notepad back to York. York wrote down the address, Catin tore off that page also and handed it to Baxtor. "Contact the landlord for the building, find out who pays the bills and get whatever other details they hold."

"Done." He too left the room.

"Mr York, I need a detailed description of King. Triangulating his mobile signal gets us down to 100-200 metres at best. Officers are going to need to know exactly what he looks like. Height, weight, age, hair colour, distinguishing features, anything that will help spot him in a crowd."

* * *

Fox had been careful, but his plans had been based on York being the sole link to his King persona, and York was not supposed to have been in any position to tell anyone anything.

Cover for the David King identity was thus shallow. There was a bank account in that name, and payment for the SOS offices came from that account. But that was as far as the cover went. As soon as Baxtor had the account details from Regus, obtaining a copy of the bank statements – and thus details of how the account was funded – was simply a matter of faxing the appropriate legal paperwork to the bank.

Baxtor hurried back to the interview room. He knocked on the door and poked his head round the corner.

"Borrow you a moment, guv?"

Catin joined him outside, closing the door behind him. Razaq came rushing down the stairs at the same time.

"Ok, you first, Baxtor."

"David King has a bank account, but only one person has ever paid any money into that account, one Julian Fox. Mr Fox is known to police as the leader of Action On Aviation, the group behind the Heathrow protest where that girl died. He was questioned in connection with that death, but that was NFA'd."

NFA meant No Further Action, and Catin knew that could mean anything from police being satisfied all was well to being certain there was wrong-doing but being unable to prove it.

"Good work. Razaq?"

"One mobile is a unregistered Vodafone PAYG one, and that appears to be switched off. The other is a contract phone with O2. It's registered to ... Julian Fox."

"Have they got a fix on the location?"

"The last one they have is 15 minutes ago, several miles out to sea off the Kent coast. From the location, their guess is he's on board a Dover-Calais ferry. I've checked the timetables, and assuming he's leaving the country rather than arriving-"

"Seems like a safe assumption," said Catin dryly.

"-then there are two likely candidates, one P&O, one Sea France. Either way, we don't have long: both arrive at Calais in a little over 40 minutes. His passport records are being checked as we speak to try to determine which service he's on."

"Excellent work, both of you. With a following wind, we could have this whole thing wrapped up by the time MI5 gets here! I'll make the call to Special Branch."

* * *

Fox made the involuntary glance upwards everyone makes when a PA announcement is made, as if somehow looking toward the speakers could make the message clearer.

"Ladies and gentlemen, this is the Purser speaking. We are a short distance from Calais, but I regret to inform you that we have been asked by the port authorities to remain outside the harbour for a short time. We do not have any further details at this time, but we hope the delay to your journey will be a short one, and we will of course keep you informed as soon as we have any further information."

Fox could hear a few groans from the people around him, but on a day like today, most were counting their blessings, thankful they were on a ferry rather than a plane. For them, it would be a slight delay to their journey, for him, it could be rather more worrying. He thought he'd covered his tracks well, but he'd always known there was a risk of having to disappear, but he'd never imagined he could be caught on the day of the attack. He couldn't see any way they could have caught onto him, let alone tracked him down, this quickly.

Not unless York were somehow still alive.

He reached into his pocket for the PAYG mobile used for communicating with York before realising he'd thrown it overboard in the middle of the crossing.

He didn't want to risk using his own mobile: if York were found dead, the last thing he wanted was his number showing up on the Missed Calls list on York's phone. Did ferries still have payphones, he wondered? It seemed such an old-fashioned idea, but you did still see payphones dotted around, so presumably there were still people who used them.

He asked one of the lounge crew, explaining that he had left his mobile in his car.

"Yes, Sir, there is one close to the Information Desk on the deck below."

"Thank you."

The payphone was indeed there. It was a cellular one, with eye-watering call charges, and he had only a handful of change on him, but he only needed to know whether or not the call was answered.

He inserted a pound coin, got out his mobile, looked up York's number and dialled.

* * *

York and Catin both stared as the mobile started ringing. *Caller ID not available.* York reached for it but Catin stopped him.

"If it's King – not his real name, by the way – pretend to be still in your apartment and let's hear what he has to say for himself."

York picked up the handset and pressed the Accept button.

"York," he said.

The line instantly went dead.

* * *

Fox made his way out of the side door to the open deck area. He felt the ferry begin a slow turn to the left. He walked towards the front as the ferry circled back towards the port. He tried to see if he could see any signs of unusual activity on the dockside, but the harbour at Calais was a very long thin one, and he couldn't see anything.

"Ladies and gentlemen, this is your purser speaking again. I'm pleased to say that we have now been given clearance to enter the harbour. There will, however, be a short delay after docking before the doors to the car-decks are opened. You are requested to have your passports ready for inspection at the car-deck doors. If your passport is in your vehicle, you are requested to remain on the passenger decks until other passengers have disembarked."

Fox remained where he was, at the front of the ferry on the outside deck. He was staring ahead as the ferry made its way towards the docks.

As it got closer, Fox could make out a mass of blue flashing lights. He continued to stare. As the ferry got closer and began slowing, the lights resolved into literally dozens of police vehicles. Too many to count.

A major police operation to intercept his ferry on the day of the attack, and York still alive. It could mean only one thing. He started slowly, thoughtfully, making his way towards the back of the ferry.

* * *

"You had no right to question him, you were specifically told that we would be doing so."

The MI5 agent kept the volume of his voice normal, but his tone left no doubt as to the anger he felt when Catin brought him up to speed on developments.

"I had every right," replied Catin, calmly. "I had one terrorist suspect in custody, and a second one on the loose. It was likely that every minute counted, and that does indeed seem to be the case. Thanks to our fast action, the French police are waiting to arrest Fox the moment the ferry docks."

"Your amateurish intervention could easily have compromised the investigation."

"My entirely professional intervention has done nothing of the kind, but rather ensured that the most wanted man on the planet will very shortly be in custody."

Catin was wrong.

Fox knew he had little time to act. If caught, he knew he would spend the rest of his miserable life in a maximum-security prison. He knew there was no way he could handle it.

He looked down at the water far below. It was a hell of a drop. He had a vague memory of reading a news report of a suicide where someone had jumped from a bridge, and it was the impact of hitting the water that killed them, not drowning afterwards. He couldn't recall the height.

Well, he thought, it's not like there's an alternative. He'd have to chance it.

Amid the chaotic scenes on both the ferry and the dockside, the jump and splash might have gone entirely unnoticed were it not for a dockhand standing by the rear of the ferry smoking a cigarette.

* * *

Trock was the head of the FAA. Status reports from across the country would be pouring in, but he'd known that one of the most important sources of information would be from outside the organisation: he'd switched on the TV in his office and tuned in to CNN.

It had taken less than ten minutes before CNN reported the unprecedented number of landings taking place at airports all over the country and the world.

They'd been joined by other senior FAA staff arriving in Trock's office. It wasn't that there had been any particular reason for them to be there; once the grounding instruction had been issued, they'd been reduced to the status of helpless bystanders. But there was comfort in numbers. If the warning had been issued in time, they'd wanted to share in the relief and sense of achievement; if it hadn't, well, they'd at least wanted to be with their colleagues.

There had been spontaneous applause at the sight of the first live footage of plane after plane landing at JFK. Live footage followed from LAX, SFO and elsewhere. Green had felt like an enormous weight had been lifted.

Relief had turned to dismay as news broke of the first crash, then to horror as more and more crashes were reported – both on CNN and in phone calls to Trock. Conversation levels, initially excited, had dropped in both tone and volume.

CNN had a camera crew directly beneath the flightpath at JFK. They were filming the incredible sight of two unending queues of airliners descending through the skies at a far steeper angle than the usual gentle three-degree path. The camera operator had been alert enough to spot an airliner turn sharply to the right towards one of the two queues. Green and the others had the sickening experience of seeing the mid-air collision live.

There had been silence in the room.

"That's it, Sir," reported one of Trock's staff. "All Airbus aircraft are now accounted for, one way or another. 31 crashes or crash-landings. It will probably be several days before we have accurate casualty figures."

"Do we know how many were in the air? How many were saved?"

"We don't yet have worldwide numbers. Certainly well in excess of a thousand, so the number of aircraft saved is likely to be in four figures. Lives saved ... in the hundreds of thousands for sure."

Trock nodded.

Wilkinson looked across at Green. She looked utterly lost. He placed his hand on her arm.

"It's not the outcome we hoped for, Sarah, but you saved an enormous number of lives. A hell of a lot of people tonight still have husbands, wives, sons and daughters thanks to you."

Green said nothing. Wilkinson might be right, she thought, but those weren't the people she was thinking of right now. All she could think of was the people on board the 31 aircraft that hadn't made it. Their husbands. Their wives. Their children.

"It just feels so utterly unfair to have come this close. Half an hour earlier, maybe even ten minutes earlier, and we'd have prevented it. If I'd chosen that area to study sooner. If I'd been more persuasive with you-"

Wilkinson squeezed her arm.

"You have nothing to regret here, Sarah. It is me and ... others-" Wilkinson looked at Trock, who looked down at his desk- "who failed to listen to you. Left things too late. We're the ones with the responsibility for this, not you."

Green felt only frustration.

* * *

"Mr York, my name is Cartwright. I'm with MI5."

No first name or job title was given, noted York, nor was his colleague introduced. York merely nodded in response.

Cartwright turned to the two detectives and uniformed constable in the room. "Leave us, please."

"Now look here-" began Catin.

"Now, please," replied Cartwright.

Catin looked as if he was about to object further, then simply shrugged. The three of them walked out of the interview room. Cartwright's silent colleague closed the door behind them. Cartwright remained facing York.

"We know more of this affair than you might expect. MI5, the FBI and the Department of Homeland Security have all been taking an interest in you."

York thought that he ought to feel stunned by this revelation. Surprised, at least. But he actually felt nothing at all. He was numb.

Cartwright continued: "Unfortunately, the final pieces of the puzzle fell into place a little too late to prevent the tragedy which has occurred."

'The tragedy which has occurred,' echoed York, mentally. Such a neutral term. Cartwright made it sound like some unfortunate natural disaster, not something that he, York, had caused. A huge crime he had committed. No matter how unintentionally, he was a terrorist. He had caused the loss of thousands of lives. No; that too was too neutral: he had murdered thousands of people. Not deliberately, but they were no less dead for all that.

"I've told the police all I know, but I assume you'll want to hear the full story first-hand?"

Cartwright shook his head. "Between what we knew already, and what you have told the police officers here today, we believe that we have the full picture. The gentleman you knew as King was in fact a green extremist named Julian Fox. Thanks to the phone number you provided, we were able to locate him on board a ferry to Calais. A short time ago, a body was recovered from alongside that ferry. No formal identification has yet taken place, but there is no doubt in our minds that Fox is dead."

That got York's attention. York didn't know what he would have wanted to say to him, to ask Fox, but ... something. Now he would never have that chance.

"I don't know what else to say," said York.

"I don't think there's anything else to say, Mr York."

"Then why are you here?"

Cartwright turned to his colleague. "I think Mr York might appreciate a cup of tea. Would you mind?"

The colleague left the room.

Cartwright reached into his pocket, retrieved a small black capsule, and placed it on the table in front of York.

"Put it out of sight would you?"

York hesitated, then picked it up and studied it for a moment before putting into his right trouser pocket.

"The death of Mr Fox poses something of a difficulty, Mr York. We are satisfied that your role in the affair was a relatively innocent one. Your motives were pure, and certainly you did not intend anyone to be harmed. With Fox available to be tried for the crime, you would be very much of secondary interest. You could not expect to escape a jail term, of course. But the attention of the media, and thus of the public and their politicians, would be focused on Fox."

York listened, saying nothing.

"However, with Fox gone, the full weight of public disapprobation would fall upon your shoulders. Sympathy would be expressed for your tragic past, of course, but it is human nature in a situation like this for the baying hounds to demand that someone be made to pay. And you, Mr York, are now the only someone available."

"I understand," said York.

"You would be a figure of public hatred. The judiciary is entirely independent of the government, of course, but nonetheless, certain conversations would take place. The only possible sentence would be whole-life incarceration in a maximum security prison. For your own safety, you would spend that life sentence in solitary confinement."

York swallowed. He had been so lost in grieving for what he had done, he'd scarcely given any thought to legal consequences. He felt that anything thrown at him, he'd deserve. But he hadn't considered the reality of what that might mean in such stark terms as were being presented to him now.

"Mr York, the work I do predisposes one to a rather bleak and cynical view of the world. But I have not entirely lost my ability to feel compassion. The future you face is not one you deserve. But it is the only future you can now have. I felt that you should at least have an alternative. You should be aware that you will be taken to a cell at the conclusion of this interview. Before you are placed in the cell, you will be searched. Anything found in your pockets will be confiscated. Should you wish to avail yourself of the alternative, time is, I'm afraid, limited."

York stared at Cartright across the table. Cartright's face remained impassive.

The door opened and Cartwright's colleague arrived with two cups of tea, placing them on the table.

Cartwright picked up one of the cups and took a sip.

"Dreadful tea, I'm afraid," he said. He stood up. "Goodbye, Mr York. I imagine we shan't be meeting again."

"No," replied York, "I don't suppose we will."

THE END

This page intentionally left blank

Afterword

While the novel has been carefully researched, it has been said that a technothriller is the art of the plausible, not the possible, and 11/9 does take a few liberties with the facts. Two in particular are worth mentioning.

First, and most importantly, aircraft manufacturers are well aware of the risks that would be posed were it possible to control an airliner remotely, and take extensive precautions to ensure that this could not be done. ACARS is real, but there is in fact no link between ACARS equipment on board an aircraft and its flight control computers, and thus no way for it to be used to take control of an aircraft.

Second, the Amsterdam crash describes the aircraft automatically reducing reverse thrust after touchdown. In practice, this could never happen. The only circumstance where the aircraft can automatically reduce the throttle is during full autoland, and auto-throttle is disabled entirely after touchdown.

I fly regularly as a passenger on fly-by-wire aircraft manufactured by both Airbus and Boeing, and do so without any qualms.

This page intentionally left blank

The Billion Dollar Heist

A closed night-club in Brooklyn, New York. 10am Friday.

Jessica Sullivan reached into the attaché case next to her and pulled out a block of $50 bills. She dropped it onto the table in front of her. None of the seven others gathered in the backroom of the closed nightclub reacted in any way.

"You've all seen your share of those in your time. One hundred bills. A strap. In this case, it's fifty dollar bills, so that's $5000 there."

Sullivan looked round at the bored expressions. This wasn't news to any of them, she knew. She reached back into the box and pulled out nine more blocks, forming them into a neat row, end-to-end.

"Ten straps, that's a bundle. $50,000."

Nobody looked impressed: they'd all seen much more money in one place.

"I'll dispense with the visual aids now, I'm sure your imaginations can fill in the gaps. Package four of those bundles together, you've got a brick. $200,000."

Shrugs. There were eight of them in the room. $25k each was ok, but they were used to bigger things.

"Package four bricks together, and you've got a cash-pack. $800,000."

Sullivan could see a couple of them visualising that. She was starting to get their attention.

"Package 40 cash-packs together and you've got a pallet, or a skid. Thirty-two million dollars in a space just over one metre square."

Nobody was looking bored now.

"Three pallets per load. $96 million."

Every eye in the room was on her.

"Twelve loads. One billion, one hundred and fifty-two million dollars. But let's keep it simple and call it a billion in round numbers."

"And just where might this billion dollars be found?" The tone of voice was casual, the facial expression blank.

Sullivan smiled: "It's the amount of currency printed three times a week at the Bureau of Engraving and Printing at Fort Worth, Texas, in the weeks leading up to the introduction of a new bill design. A new design like, say, the new $50 bill being introduced two months from today. Which was what gave me the idea."

A thin Hispanic man in his 40s spoke up: "And you think we're going to steal some of this cash from the BEP?"

Sullivan shook her head. "No. No, that's not the plan at all."

"So what is this plan of yours?"

"We're going to steal all of it. We're going to steal a billion dollars."

Three seconds of silence. Longer than she'd expected; not much fazed this team.

"And your plan for this is ... ?" asked the same man.

"I haven't the faintest idea," smiled Sullivan.

"Ok, just so we have this straight, you want us to steal a billion dollars. You want us to steal it from probably the most secure facility in the world after Fort Knox. And you have no clue as to how we might do it?"

"Fun, isn't it?"

"You don't think we're perhaps over-stretching ourselves just a little this time?"

"I seem to recall a similar sentiment was suggested last time."

Perez tilted his head in amused agreement.

"So," said Sullivan, "we have some research to do. Are we all in for the fieldwork stage? Maybe a few weeks' work and say $50k for initial expenses."

They'd worked together on other operations. The previous one had been on a sufficient scale that $50k between them was a pretty small investment, so she was confident no further discussion would be needed. "Let's do the roll-call."

Sullivan turned to the man on her left. Sam Young was of indeterminate age. A con-man with a long and impressive history of successful frauds, his various disguises could have him look as convincing as a 30-year-old as he did as a 70-year-old. Despite having known him for many years, Sullivan was never entirely sure whether the face he showed to her and the rest of the team was his own or merely another disguise. Certainly he varied his appearance regularly; right now he looked like a 50-year-old accountant who enjoyed his food rather more than his gym.

Young had as many names as ages, and not even Sullivan knew his real one. She did, however, trust him implicitly: he was a confidence trickster, and would lie to a mark without a second thought, but he was completely loyal to those few people he considered friends.

It was Young who had introduced Sullivan to her current life. Formerly Head of Security for a major bank, she'd uncovered a highly sophisticated fraud. Her problem had been proving it. While she'd worked out how it had been done and by whom, she'd been far from confident that either the bank or the police could prove it. Without proof, it was doubtful whether the culprit could be convicted or the funds recovered.

The sum of money involved was significant, and frankly the bank cared more about recovery and discretion than it did about convictions. She'd managed to persuade Young – though that wasn't the alias he'd used then – that quietly returning the money would be best for all concerned. She'd expected a battle, but Young had been remarkably sanguine about it. She was sure this wasn't his first major fraud and that it wouldn't be his last, so perhaps he could afford a casual attitude to such things.

Unravelling the maze had been such a challenge, such fun. She'd felt more alive than she had in years. She hadn't wanted to admit it to herself at the time. Hadn't wanted to name the feeling. But finally she'd had to. Every time she'd solved a new part of the puzzle, figured out one more element of the intricately-planned fraud, she'd felt admiration at the sheer ingenuity of what the fraudster – the man she would later identify as Young – had pulled off.

It was when she found herself grinning at the sheer cleverness and gall of one particular aspect of the fraud that she'd realized that, much as she wanted to catch him, her motivation was no longer to exact justice, it was to win this enthralling game. And to meet the man who'd pulled it off. She wanted, she'd finally acknowledged, to congratulate him.

Crossing sides – joining forces with Young – had been a long and gradual process. And yet, looking back on it now, it had begun less than halfway through that investigation, before she'd even met the man responsible for it.

When Young finally issued the invitation, she'd been expecting it. She'd been ready to lay down the law. Her law. Nobody got hurt. No individuals lost out – not by more than pennies, anyway. But Young had beaten her to it. He'd said that if she chose to join him, she had to agree to the principles on which he operated. They were almost word-for-word what she'd been about to say.

She brought herself back to the present. Young winked at her. He too loved the hunt.

"Chung?"

Mike Chung had been the third person to join the team. Most operations of any scale these days required IT expertise, and in the early days it had been just the three of them. While Sullivan liked and respected each member of the team, she still thought of the three of them as the core team. Sullivan, Young, Chung.

Chung didn't generally take much persuasion. A slightly-built 35-year-old Hong Kong-born Chinese man who could pass for ten years younger, he was a freelance security consultant. While his website described him as a former hacker, the past tense was pure fiction.

Sullivan was convinced the money they'd made was almost an irrelevance to Chung. Each of them maintained legitimate businesses to provide an explanation for their evident income, but most of them did very little work in those. Chung was an exception, with a substantial client-base for whom he worked hard. He operated a very personal brand of ethics: while he happily used access to his client systems to add to his knowledge of different systems, he would never compromise any client network. On a previous project when one of his client systems would have provided the perfect solution to a difficulty they faced, he instead spent several days breaking into a competitor system to achieve what would have taken him 30 seconds on the system to which he already had legitimate access.

Chung generally said little — until you got him onto the topic of computer systems, then he could talk for hours.

Chung simply nodded.

"Lewis?"

Katrina Lewis was the only other woman in the team, though she couldn't have been a greater contrast to Jessica Sullivan. While Sullivan was feminine and elegant in her dress, Lewis was secretly contemptuous of women who played that game. Not that she didn't respect Sullivan – she had to, Sullivan had more than proven her intelligence and determination – she just didn't see why women dressed up in costumes and paint just because men

366

expected it of them, and was particularly disappointed when someone of Sullivan's intellect chose to do so. Lewis expected to be accepted for who she was, not her ability to match some male fantasy. Her short-cropped hair, absence of make-up and habitual uniform of baggy jeans and t-shirt was her way of making the point.

Part of it, she admitted, was a response to working in a traditionally male world. An electronics engineer who'd previously worked for the largest chip manufacturer in the world, she'd found it easier to fit in if she'd been seen as just one of the boys.

Lewis too loved her work. She boasted that there wasn't a circuit she couldn't design and build in her home electronics lab, and so far she'd lived up to that promise. She'd designed and built a sophisticated home automation system that managed everything from heat and light to running a bath.

Perhaps that was why they worked together so well as a team, mused Sullivan: they were all in it for the love as much as the money, and they all relished a challenge, no matter how much feigned grumbling they did at the outset.

"I'm in," said Lewis.

"Jackson?"

Scott Jackson was an ex-USAF pilot who'd flown everything from Apache helicopters to B52 bombers. He wasn't a soldier by instinct, but he had dreamed of flying since he was a five-year-old boy staring in wonderment at the turboprop aircraft that had over-flown his home when heading to or from a nearby airfield. It was not an unusual childhood fantasy, of course, but while other friends had moved on to dreams of being a firefighter or racing driver, he had never wavered from his vision of himself at the controls of one of those beautiful machines. One of four children in a not particularly well-to-do family, the military had offered the only route to fulfilling his dream, and he'd accepted the drudgery, discipline and disruption of military life as the price of the time he lived for: time spent in the air.

His flying career had been brought to a premature end in 1992 by the BRAC Commission. The Base Realignment and Closure Commission had been set up by the government to examine the USA's changing military requirements at the end of the Cold War. Jackson had for five years been a B-52 pilot. A key element of the nuclear deterrent strategy, they saw nuclear-armed service both as high-altitude bombers and as low-level infiltration bombers designed to fly beneath Russian radar. But with the fall of the Soviet Union, and the B-52 an elderly aircraft which had remained in production far longer than anyone had ever envisaged, Jackson found himself surplus to requirements. With just three years to retirement, he was one of hundreds of pilots retired to desk jobs. He'd deeply resented it, and when offered the opportunity for early retirement, he'd taken it without looking back.

Anything which provided an excuse to fly was fine with Jackson, and if there wasn't an obvious need for it now, he was sure he could find one.

"I'm in too."

"Perez?"

Raul Perez was the Hispanic man who'd expressed his skepticism. Ex-army OD (Ordnance Disposal), more colloquially known as bomb disposal, his service in Afghanistan had been the turning-point. It was, in his view, a clusterfuck. They called it a war while hampering them with rules of engagement more suited to a scout picnic than an armed conflict. They were allowed to shoot to kill only when in direct and immediate danger. The way that was defined meant that even if they were certain they could see insurgents placing a roadside improvised explosive device, they weren't allowed to shoot, they had to sit back and watch them complete it before moving in to disable it. The insurgents were well aware of this and frequently waited until the EOD team moved in before remotely detonating the device. There was only so much that could be done by robots, and Perez had watched too many of his friends die needlessly.

He was far from a coward. Cowards don't choose ordinance disposal as a career. He'd simply reached the point of not being able to sit back and watch more colleagues die without any meaning or purpose in a conflict which appeared to have no clear goal or exit strategy. He'd intended to wait the 18 months until his Service of Enlistment was up, but the death of a close friend attempting to defuse a car-bomb in a civilian area while they were as near-certain as they could be that the insurgents were just waiting for their approach to detonate it had been the final straw. A strenuous argument with the base commander had ended with a single blow to the commander's chin, a six-month stretch in Leavenworth and a Dishonourable Discharge.

There aren't many civilian careers open to you when all you know is bomb disposal, even fewer when you have a DD on your army papers. But to disarm explosive devices, you first have to be an expert in their design and construction. It had been fairly inevitable that he would find some unofficial means to put those skills to use.

He'd been friends with Jackson; it was not long before he was on the team.

He remained skeptical, but what else was he going to do? Besides, he couldn't really argue with Sullivan's point: all her ideas had sounded crazy when she first presented them.

"Pugh?"

Ryan Pugh, a rotund man in his late 60s with a beard which looked like he'd been growing it for most of those sixty years with scarcely a trim in sight, was a retired printer. Old-school, his career had been mostly spent in the days when type was set by hand and when it was not unusual to hand-cut print stencils for intricate work. He'd adapted well to first desktop publishing and then a graphic design world geared more toward the web than printed products, but missed the hands-on nature of his earlier work.

His retirement had not been entirely voluntary. When his wife had fallen ill with cancer, and their medical coverage reached its financial limits midway through her treatment, he'd needed a way to make a sizeable amount of money quickly. He'd received various approaches over the years for less-than-official document creation, and had always declined; Suzanne's illness changed that overnight. He'd got in touch with one of the men who'd contacted him six months earlier about some passports. Yes, he was told, there was always a demand for forged passports and driving licences, and if he could meet the exacting quality requirements of a forgery good enough to pass muster at banks, then he could be advanced the money he needed and work it off over a year or so.

His work had been good — extremely good — and he couldn't keep up with demand while also working in his day-job. He'd quietly started turning down his regular business, pleading pressure of work, and moved into his unofficial print business full-time.

Young had been his introduction to the team. A letter of credit had been required, good enough to remain undetected as a forgery for a week or two, and Pugh had been recommended as someone able to deliver the goods. His capabilities had been considerably extended by a partnership with Katrina Lewis for documents requiring an embedded RFID chip. Between the two of them, there wasn't much they couldn't create.

"Evans?"

Aaron Evans was an unlikely member of the team. A magician specialising in large-scale illusions, he'd had a successful career first on stage and later on TV, and had not been hurting financially. For someone in his position to take the risk of engaging in criminal activities would have seemed inexplicable to anyone who didn't know him. But to those who knew him well, it would have been far less surprising: Evans was enormously ambitious, and harboured the dream of being considered the greatest magician of all time. To have a series of big-time crimes pulled off thanks to his genius offered perhaps the most promising route to this, albeit one which could not be known until after his death. But that was ok with Evans: the knowledge of his future legacy was enough.

A billion dollars? To come up with an illusion to make that possible would surely guarantee his place in the history books!

"Definitely," he said.

Eight yesses, including her own.

Sullivan nodded: "Then we have some research to do. I've done a little googling, and the good news is that the vault opens at least three times a week. Bank notes wear out, and need to be replaced, so three times a week new bills leave the vault and are transported to the twelve Federal Reserve Banks scattered around the USA. All of the commercial banks get their cash from the Federal Reserve. The exact amounts presumably vary with the denominations involved, but the BEP website says that the total amount transported averages over $700 million a day, alternating between the BEP facilities in Washington DC and Fort Worth. But in the weeks leading up to a new bill design, the daily amount hits over a billion."

"How is the cash transported?" asked Evans. "I assume they don't just stick it in a few Brinks Mat armoured trucks and schlep it halfway across the USA?"

"No," replied Sullivan. "Army convoy to Carswell Air Force Base, then it's transferred to Galaxies and flown to air force bases local to the Federal

Reserves. From there, another army convoy. I flew out there for a few days for a little recce work, observing the convoys as they leave."

"And what did you learn?" asked Perez.

"They would not make an easy target."

Perez gave Sullivan a quizzical look. "That's it? That's what you learned? I think we could have guessed that much!"

Sullivan grinned. "There are three separate convoys, each with twelve semis and a whole bunch of army vehicles, all of which look decidedly unfriendly. Six helicopter gunships overhead, following at low-level: they don't look terribly friendly either. The three convoys take separate routes, which appear to vary every day, with no obvious pattern. Whether the money is split between them, or there are two real convoys and one dummy, or one real convoy and two dummies, I don't know."

"Seems there's quite a lot we don't know," observed Jackson.

"That's what fieldwork is for," replied Sullivan, calmly. "I've only been able to witness the convoy departures. I was in a building high enough to get an overview, but it was too far away to see any great detail. What we need now are some more detailed observations at ground level. The convoys are Mondays, Wednesdays and Fridays. We need to get ourselves out there, and we have a few preparations to make, so I suggest we view the one on Wednesday."

To continue reading The Billion Dollar Heist, please visit:

www.airbookpublishing.com/bdh/

Printed in Great Britain
by Amazon

83579108R00214